Amish Sweethearts

Center Point
Large Print

Also by Leslie Gould and available from Center Point Large Print:

The Courtships of Lancaster County
Minding Molly
Becoming Bea

Neighbors of Lancaster County
Amish Promises

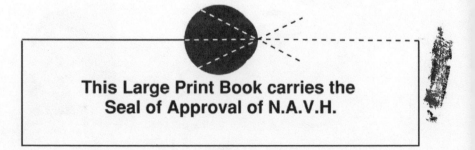

NEIGHBORS OF LANCASTER COUNTY
• BOOK TWO •

AMISH
SWEETHEARTS

Leslie
Gould

CENTER POINT LARGE PRINT
THORNDIKE, MAINE

This Center Point Large Print edition is published in the year 2016 by arrangement with Bethany House Publishers, a division of Baker Publishing Group.

Scripture quotations are from the King James Version of the Bible.

This is a work of fiction. Names, characters, incidents, and dialogues are products of the author's imagination and are not to be construed as real. Any resemblance to actual events or persons, living or dead, is entirely coincidental.

The text of this Large Print edition is unabridged. In other aspects, this book may vary from the original edition. Printed in the United States of America on permanent paper. Set in 16-point Times New Roman type.

ISBN: 978-1-62899-897-9

Library of Congress Cataloging-in-Publication Data

Names: Clark, Mindy Starns author.
Title: Amish sweethearts / Leslie Gould.
Description: Center Point Large Print edition. | Thorndike, Maine : Center Point Large Print, 2016 | ©2016 | Series: Neighbors of Lancaster
Identifiers: LCCN 2015048738 | ISBN 9781628998979 (hardcover : alk. paper)
Subjects: LCSH: Amish—Fiction. | Large type books. | GSAFD: Love stories. | Christian fiction.
Classification: LCC PS3603.L366 A875 2016 | DDC 813/.6—dc23
LC record available at http://lccn.loc.gov/2015048738

For our friends
Col. John J. McGraw, retired,
and Ann McGraw,
two extraordinary people
who serve so many,
including me and mine.

PROLOGUE

MAY 2010

Lila Lehman yanked the chickweed from between the rows of beans as her thoughts drifted to Zane Beck, once again. Against her will. If only she thought about Reuben Byler half as much as she did Zane. Tossing the weeds into the pile on the grass, she tucked her dress around her knees and sank down into the furrowed soil.

Reuben was going to pick her up in an hour to go for a drive in his new courting buggy. Why was she thinking about Zane?

Her *Dat*, her grandparents, and Reuben's father—who just happened to be the bishop—all thought she and Reuben were a good match. And they were right.

Reuben was kind and helpful, with a caring heart. He'd be good to her and any children they might have. She couldn't make her family any happier—especially her father—than by marrying Reuben.

But instead of thinking about him, she couldn't keep her thoughts from Zane. Or from all they'd shared over the last nearly six years. She thought of the books they'd read together. The world events he'd talked about. The poetry they'd memorized.

He'd won her heart with his enthusiasm. He embraced her Amish community, even when he didn't truly belong. He questioned everything and never stopped talking—about what interested him, about Lila and her family, about his parents and brother, about his studies, his teachers, the universe. He'd made her world so much bigger.

What would she have thought about if she'd never known him? The latest gossip? Recipes? Housework? Certainly not global concerns, history, and literature. Her life would be so empty.

The first time she'd seen Zane, standing at the field gate, she'd found him fascinating. The way he stood—as if he belonged when he obviously didn't. The way he flicked his bangs away from his face. The way he carried himself—like a grown-up even though he was still a boy.

She had no idea, all those years ago, how much it would hurt to watch him grow into a man. To see him change in such appealing ways. To have him share with her and want to hear her opinions. To value what she had to say, even though she only had an eighth-grade education. Sure, Zane could be intense, and there were times when he acted too sure of himself. He'd say he was decisive—but she sensed he was often confused and unsure. That was where Reuben was much more dependable—but then again, he was also four years older than Zane. True, Reuben had gone through an awkward phase, but he'd always been sure of what he wanted.

The warmth of the soil radiated up from the ground. She gazed toward the sun, shielding her eyes with her hand and began to quote Wordsworth.

"What though the radiance which was once so
  bright
Be now for ever taken from my sight. . . ."

A rustling stopped her. Probably her younger brother, Simon, sneaking up on her again. Or maybe her twin, Daniel. Mortified, she stumbled to her feet, brushed her hands against her apron, and straightened her *Kapp*. No one was in front of her. She spun around.

Zane stood at the gate, his honey-blond hair pushed back on his forehead. He wore jeans and a white T-shirt, the sleeves tight against his biceps. Lila kept her expression blank, trying not to let on how much she'd missed him. Or how her heart raced.

He grinned and started quoting the poem from where she'd stopped.

"Though nothing can bring back the hour
Of splendour in the grass, of glory in the
  flower. . . ."

The words hung between them, in the stillness of the warm spring day. The breeze stirred up the earthy scent of the soil. A honeybee buzzed among the squash blossoms.

For a moment Lila considered leaving the garden, taking Zane's hand, and leading him to their childhood fort. Beside the creek, in the shade of the poplar trees, they could step back in time. She could almost feel the mud between her toes.

She exhaled. Meeting together at the fort was no longer a possibility. Everything had changed in the last year. She and Zane hadn't talked at all since February, since her sister Trudy's sixth birthday party. He'd gone on and on about his college plans—someplace in Michigan. At first Lila didn't understand. For the longest time he hadn't wanted to talk about the future at all. He'd said he never wanted things to change. He wanted to keep living on Juneberry Lane forever. So she was annoyed with Zane for talking about college at all and then bragging about going, but as he continued she was devastated by the fact that he really would leave. Her best friend would soon be gone—forever.

Zane opened the gate and grinned again. "I have great news."

She tilted her head.

"I wanted to tell you first. I found out I got a scholarship, nearly a full ride. It was announced at our debate today."

He really was leaving. Lila struggled to speak and finally asked, "What did you debate?"

"The Iraq War."

"For or against?"

"For," he answered.

She couldn't even force herself to smile. "But you're a pacifist." At least that's what he'd been saying for the last four years, much to his father's chagrin.

His expression hardened. "Maybe I'm not." What had changed in him in the last few months? He used to think it took courage to be a pacifist, to take a stand against war. Had he flip-flopped on his principles?

At least he was going to college—and not into the military right out of high school, as his father had. At least he was committing to something.

Zane stepped closer. "I've been thinking about a lot of things. . . . I think I was too quick to judge before. Especially about the Army."

Lila gasped. "It would kill your mother if you signed up."

He shook his head. "Who said anything about signing up?" He frowned. "But I'm not a coward."

"Really?" Her heart ached. What had happened to her friend?

Zane crossed his arms. He knew Lila wasn't implying he was a coward if he didn't join the Army. He knew, in fact, she'd think him a coward

11

if he did. But he also knew she believed he lacked courage because he'd stopped being her friend, without saying a word to her. After Trudy's party, when he'd been a jerk by going on and on about college in front of her and her whole family, he'd stopped sharing his lessons with her. He stopped wandering over to say hello. He stopped going down to their fort.

Zane had boasted about college that day because it had hurt to see her with Reuben. It made his heart ache to watch her serving him cake and coffee and then clearing his plate and cup. It had physically pained him to witness the way Reuben looked at her.

So Zane had started talking—and then couldn't seem to stop. He wasn't even looking forward to going to college, but he wanted to have something in his future to focus on. He was so embarrassed by his drivel that he'd avoided her after that though, thinking the time apart might help him feel more settled. Until today. He'd worked up enough courage to share his good news—and his new idea.

All he wanted was for her to listen. To understand.

"I need to go," Lila said.

"Wait." Zane swallowed. "Please."

He'd had an argument with his dad the night before. Maybe it would devastate his mom if he joined the Army, but it certainly wouldn't hurt his father. He'd challenged Zane, telling him he shouldn't go to college if he didn't know why he was going. *"You need to commit to something,"* he'd said. *"Something you can make a living at. I knew at eighteen the military was right for me. Don't go to college unless you're sure."*

When Zane joked that maybe he'd sign up, his dad told him not to bother, that he wasn't soldier material. His dad would know. He'd been in the Army full-time, and then once he was medically retired he'd started working for the Veterans Affairs in Lancaster. He knew soldiers and was right in saying Zane wouldn't make a good one.

But his words left Zane unsure about everything. About going to Michigan. About what to study. About what he wanted to do to make a living. He couldn't seem to come to a decision and stick with it. He thought the scholarship would make a difference, but now standing in front of Lila, faced with losing her, it didn't. Not at all.

Lila turned to the sound of a buggy coming up the driveway. "He's early."

"Who's early?"

"Reuben."

Zane's heart fell. He'd been foolish to try and talk with her.

Lila turned back toward him, started to say something, stopped, and then said, "Just a minute."

She stepped to the driveway and called out a

13

hello to Reuben. He pulled the horse and buggy up beside her and then waved. "What do you need?" he shouted to Zane.

"I was hoping to talk with Lila."

"Go on inside," Lila said to him. "There's a pie on the counter for you—banana cream."

Zane called out, "It'll only take a minute."

Lila turned toward him and shook her head. "Nothing with you only takes a minute."

Zane swallowed. He hated it when Lila was snippy. But he deserved it. "It really won't take long," he said. "I promise."

Without responding, Lila turned back to Reuben. Zane looked away, not wanting to witness an intimate glance between them. Or a mutual one of annoyance—with him.

But then Reuben called out to Zane again, saying, "All right."

Zane waved and Reuben urged his horse on toward the hitching post as Lila stepped toward the gate.

Zane held it open for her and motioned down the field toward their old fort.

She shook her head. "Let's talk here." She pulled the gate shut, staying on her side.

Zane leaned over the top rail, toward her. He tried to keep the hurt from his voice. "So are you and Reuben officially courting?"

Lila rammed her fists into the pockets of her apron. "We're going to go for a ride."

Zane stood up straight. "Who else would you court, right? Everyone's always wanted the two of you to get together."

Lila didn't respond, but he knew he was right. "Would you at least walk with me?" His muscles tightened as he spoke.

She met his eyes. "Just tell me what you want."

He exhaled. "I'd thought taking some time apart would be good—so we both could see how we felt. But I missed you a lot. Even more than I thought I . . ."

She pursed her lips.

"I had this idea that maybe you could come to Michigan too." He rubbed the back of his neck. "There are Amish communities there," he quickly added. "I thought maybe you could get a job at a shop or something."

"Why?"

His face grew warm. "So we'd be closer."

Lila shifted her weight, leaning away from him. "And then what?"

He shrugged. "I thought we could figure it out . . ."

"Figure it out?" Her voice escalated. "What is there to figure out?"

"I thought . . ." Zane swallowed. "I thought maybe we could . . ."

She stepped back and crossed her arms.

He swung the gate open again. "Please walk with me. I don't want your whole family to hear us." Most importantly, he didn't want Reuben to hear.

She hesitated a moment but then passed through, just as she had countless times before.

As they walked, Zane said, "Are you and Reuben planning to marry soon?" She was only seventeen—young even for an Amish girl. But she could easily marry in a year or two.

"Does it matter?" she asked, her eyes focused on the poplar trees ahead of them.

Zane cleared his throat and then said, "I've been thinking." She'd often teased him about his *thoughts,* but she'd always been willing to listen to them. "About my future. About you. About us . . ."

When they reached the trail to the fort, he gestured for her to go first, but she shook her head. He reached for her right hand.

"Lila," he said as his other hand fell to the small of her back. He pulled her close. She didn't pull away.

Time stopped. This was where they belonged. Through the gate, between their homes. Just as it had been all these years.

His heart raced. "Come to Michigan with me."

She pulled away. "That's impossible."

Why had he bothered to try? He didn't have a chance with Lila. Whatever they'd had was over. He couldn't stand the thought of her marrying. He had to get away from Juneberry Lane, the sooner the better. He couldn't stay and watch her court Reuben—not even for the summer.

Lila rubbed her palms together. It had felt so good to have her hand in Zane's again—for a split second. But she'd come to her senses. She couldn't court Reuben with Zane around. He needed to go to Michigan, without her. The sooner the better. Her only hope to get him out of her heart was to get him out of her life.

She tipped her head away from him. She'd never felt so *ferhoodled*. And Zane had frustrated her plenty of times before.

Lila's mother hadn't left the Amish, not even when she became pregnant by an *Englisch* man. Not even after she had Lila and Daniel. Lila would never leave either. She couldn't disappoint her father like that, not the man who had raised her even after her mother died. She would never do that to her Dat, not after everything he'd done for her. She'd never do it to her mother's memory either. Both her parents would want her to join the church.

She must be strong, like her mother, and let Zane go.

He bent toward her. "Do you still think about *uns*?"

Her eyes began to swim. He'd used the Pennsylvania Dutch word for *us*. She'd taught him that word, along with every other word she could think of until he was fluent in her language. How dare he use it now?

Anger overcame her sadness. She blinked her tears away. "There is no *us*. Don't you get it?" The force behind her words surprised her. "We weren't meant for anything more than childhood friends. We're grown now. It's over."

Zane stepped back from her outburst.

Without meeting his eyes, she said through clenched teeth, "Go away. To Michigan. Or somewhere else. The farther the better."

He balled his hands into fists. "Maybe I *will* join the Army."

"Right," she answered, unable to hide the sarcasm in her voice. He'd never do that, regardless of his earlier bravado. It was just more of his talk, of his inability to commit. He was so unlike Reuben.

His biceps flexed under the sleeves of his T-shirt. "I'll go much farther than Michigan."

"Good," she said. She didn't care where he went. As long as it wasn't in Lancaster County.

He turned abruptly and marched away from her. She waited, half hoping for a moment that he'd return. She'd apologize. They'd go down to their fort together. She'd say she didn't mean what she'd said.

But he disappeared behind the hedge at the end of the field.

Both relief and sadness rushed through her as

18

she swiped her fingers under her eyes. How could she be so frustrated with Zane and so heart-broken at the same time?

"Lila!" Reuben stood at the gate waiting for her, his thumbs looped in his suspenders. Under the brim of his black hat, she imagined his eyes were still kind—although probably a little impatient too.

"Coming," she called out.

As she made her way to the gate, she whispered the next line of the Wordsworth poem.

"We will grieve not, rather find
Strength in what remains behind . . ."

She wasn't sure what remained. But hopefully she would find her strength in Reuben.

1

DECEMBER 2012

Zane pulled his truck into the gas station, figuring he might as well fill up and delay arriving at his parents' house for a little while longer. He jumped down, inhaled the icy air, and rubbed his bare hands together. He'd been away from Pennsylvania for the last two and a half years—for basic in Oklahoma and then more training in Texas—and had missed the winters. He had ten days to enjoy the cold.

The man in front of him returned the nozzle to the pump. "Zane?" The guy squinted into the low afternoon sun, shielding his eyes. "It's me. Daniel."

Zane wouldn't have recognized his friend. He wore jeans, a down jacket, work boots, and a stocking cap. There was nothing Amish about him. But the blue eyes and smile definitely belonged to Daniel.

"Hey," Zane said, extending his hand. "I didn't recognize you."

Daniel laughed and swept Zane into a hug, slapping his back. "Long time no see."

It was hard for Zane to explain why he hadn't returned home until now. His parents and little brother had traveled to see him several times at Fort Hood, and that had worked out just fine.

He glanced over Daniel's shoulder. Against his will, he was looking to see if Lila was with her twin. There was someone in the cab of his truck. A woman. Zane's heart raced.

Daniel released him and stepped back. "What brings you home?"

Zane shrugged. "Mom's been bugging me to visit." It was only two weeks until Christmas, but he wasn't going to stay that long. He had his reasons for getting back to Texas. Duty and all of that.

Daniel nodded toward Zane's truck. "Nice rig."

"Thanks," Zane replied. "Yours too." They both laughed. Daniel's was a beater that looked as if it had gone three hundred thousand miles at least.

"Do you remember Jenny?" Daniel asked.

"Of course." She was Reuben's stepsister.

Daniel nodded toward his cab. "Come say hello."

Relief, mostly, filled him that it was Jenny and not Lila. Zane elbowed Daniel as they walked. "I always thought you two would get together."

"*Jah*, well, nothing's for sure—yet. I need to figure out how to support a family first." Daniel opened the driver's door. "Look who's here."

Jenny wore a long coat and a black bonnet on her head. She was still Amish, although she wore a little color on her lips and on her cheeks too. Maybe she hadn't joined the church yet—but she looked as if she might soon. She said hello and Zane said how nice it was to see her. Then he stepped back and put the freezing cold gas nozzle into his truck. Daniel told Jenny he'd be just a minute and closed the cab door.

"What have you been up to?" Zane asked.

"Working construction. Building houses mostly. Rooming with a group of guys."

Zane nodded. Daniel was obviously on his *Rumschpringe*. He wondered what Tim thought of him running around. "How's everyone else?"

"*Gut*. Simon's working the farm." He grinned. "And hating every minute of it. Rose is helping around the house. Trudy is a third grader. Dat's the same as ever."

Zane nodded as he held on to the nozzle. If Daniel didn't say anything about Lila, he wasn't going to ask.

Daniel grinned again—this time in a teasing way. "Lila's working at that restaurant out on the highway. The one all the tourists go to. She just got the job a couple of weeks ago. She also does Dat's books and pretty much everything else around the house and yard."

Zane concentrated on the nozzle.

"She's taking her sweet time with Reuben. He'd like to be married by now, but she says she's too young." Daniel puffed out his chest and looked toward the cab of his truck. "We're turning twenty in a month though."

Zane nodded. He'd turn twenty-one in two months. The twins were less than a year behind him.

Daniel shoved his hands into the pockets of his jacket. "I imagine Reuben will be bringing up marriage again soon." He waited for a moment, as if he expected Zane to say something.

Zane would have liked to have come up with something, preferably witty, but the lump in his throat kept him from speaking at all. The nozzle jerked, and he let go of the handle.

"Well, I'd better get going," Daniel said. "Maybe we can hang out while you're home."

"I'd like that," Zane said, putting the nozzle back in the holder and pulling out his phone.

Daniel took out his—an old flip phone—and they exchanged numbers.

"Tell everyone hello," Zane said.

"Ditto," Daniel said. "It's been a while since I've seen your folks." He shrugged. "And Adam. How old is he now?"

"He'll turn eight next month," Zane said.

Daniel shook his head. "That's hard to believe."

They both smiled. Zane slapped Daniel on the shoulder. "We're getting old, buddy."

Zane took his time leaving the gas station. In fact it wasn't until the car behind him honked that he eased forward. Daniel had turned right onto the highway, but Zane turned left. He'd take the long way home.

The night Adam had been born there had been a horrible ice storm, and Lila and her Aenti Eve, her Dat's sister, came over to help. When he thought of that night he didn't think about putting his mother's van in the ditch. Or how badly his dad was still torn up by the war. Or the house catching on fire. Or the ambulance coming.

No.

He gripped his steering wheel more tightly. What he thought about was how calm Lila had been through the entire ordeal.

He'd thought a lot over the last two and a half years about how graceful Lila was—and what a spaz he was. He'd been stupid the night Adam was born, but he hadn't been at his worst. Joining the Army the day after his and Lila's argument was by far the most idiotic thing he'd ever done.

One day he was thinking about becoming a pacifist and slowly easing—maybe—into the Amish way of living, although he hadn't had the chance to tell Lila he was willing to consider it. He'd handled it all wrong. And then she'd told him the farther he went the better, and there he was the next day signing his name on a form committing himself to the exact opposite of the Amish ideal.

Lila had told him more than once that being both impulsive and stubborn was a really bad combination. And his dad had told him he wasn't military material, but that he needed to commit to *something*. Later, after Zane had joined, his dad apologized and told him he hadn't meant for Zane to join the Army. But both Lila and his father had been right—he needed to do *something*, far away from Lancaster County.

He'd hoped the Army would be the answer, and it had been in some ways. But it hadn't provided the connections he'd longed for.

He slowed behind an Amish buggy, the orange caution sign bright, warning of possible harm. Zane passed when he could, glancing at the driver, but it was too dark to tell who it might be. A few minutes later he made the turn onto

24

Juneberry Lane. The Army had calmed him down and made him more centered—out of sheer frustration. There wasn't much he could control anymore. He'd finally had to stop fighting the system and submit to it.

Out of habit, even though it had been over two years since he'd been home, he glanced down the Lehman driveway. White sheets hung on the line, blowing in the icy wind, but that was all he could see. For all he knew Lila was behind them.

No wonder he hadn't come home in all this time. She haunted him.

The branches of the cedar tree ahead swayed, and he got a whiff of the Lehmans' dairy. The odor never bothered him. It smelled like home.

He tightened his grip on the steering wheel even more. No one could have had a better childhood than he'd had. All those hours playing with the Lehman kids in the field, along the creek, in the fort, and back and forth between the two houses. He thought it was normal at the time. He didn't realize it was the next best thing to heaven. In fact, when he thought of heaven, that's what he imagined. Playing with the Lehman kids. Thinking he had a future with Lila. Spending all their extra time outside, together.

He steered around the curve. Ahead was his parents' house, built by his great-great-grandfather over a hundred years ago. A Christmas tree twinkled in the front window, and brightly colored bulbs framed the roofline all the way over to the brick kitchen. He hoped Dad hadn't put up the lights. He hated the thought of his father on a ladder.

He stopped his truck next to his mom's van and sat with the engine running for a moment until Adam stepped into view and pressed his nose to the glass.

Zane turned off his truck as Adam came flying out the front door. Zane jumped down, his arms wide open. "Bub!" he called out, using the nickname he'd given his brother as a baby, and swept him up into a hug.

Adam had gone to bed and Zane and his parents sat at the kitchen table drinking decaf. Zane could have handled the real stuff, but his parents claimed it messed with their sleep. They seemed a little older than when he'd seen them last spring.

"Why can't you stay for Christmas?" Mom asked.

He pushed back in his chair. "I need to leave by the twenty-second."

Mom clutched her mug with both hands. "But your grandfather is flying in that night."

"I know," Zane said. "But I just saw him and I told him my plan. He understands." His grandfather had flown to Texas and taken Zane out to dinner on Thanksgiving Day. He was that kind of guy. Zane had told him he wouldn't see him at

Christmas, and he hadn't set him up for a guilt trip the way Mom was trying to do.

His dad cleared his throat. "Son, what's going on?"

Zane shrugged. "I need to get back to Texas is all." He couldn't bear to be on Juneberry Lane on Christmas Eve. From the time he was thirteen, he and Lila used to meet at their fort after their families had all gone to bed and exchange gifts. Usually a book or a blank journal. Once he gave her a bookmark with beads on it that he'd bought at a shop in Strasburg. She said it was the prettiest thing anyone had ever given her.

His father gave his mother a questioning look, but Zane couldn't see her response.

"Anything you need to tell us?" Dad asked and then grinned. "Did you meet someone? And you want to spend Christmas with her."

Zane shook his head. "Nothing like that." He'd dated a few times in the last couple of years, but he hadn't found anyone who intrigued him. No one who challenged him. No one he cared about even a sliver as much as he'd cared for Lila.

His dad looked disappointed. "You have plenty of leave."

Zane hesitated and then said, "We're being mobilized. I have a lot to do to get ready." He paused a moment, waiting for Mom to respond. When she didn't say anything, Zane added, "We'll deploy toward the middle of January."

Mom stood and dumped her coffee in the sink.

"Afghanistan?" his dad finally asked.

Zane nodded. Troops were coming home from Iraq—not being sent. "I'm going with our civil affairs unit." He'd scored high on the language section of his test when he enlisted and had been studying Pashto since he got out of basic. Then he'd completed advanced individual training and been assigned to a civil affairs unit. He'd heard one of his officers describe the unit as being like the Peace Corps, but with rifles. He liked that idea. He was excited to use the language and to help the Afghan people with infrastructure, medical needs, and educational structures, but not so thrilled at the thought of having to fire his gun. He prayed he wouldn't have to.

His dad's eyes watered a little, but then he put his arm around Zane's shoulders. "We're proud of you."

Zane shrugged. "You shouldn't be. I haven't done anything."

"You've been studying hard," his dad said. "You're doing what you need to."

Mom stood with her back toward him, staring out the window into the darkness.

"Mom?" he said.

"Yeah," she answered. "I'm here."

"And?"

She shook her head and finally turned toward him. "I don't want to go through this again."

Zane sighed. He knew what she was thinking. Why had he joined the Army? Why hadn't he gone to college like he was supposed to? Would he return from Afghanistan injured and broken like his father? A rocket-propelled grenade in Iraq had hit his dad's Humvee, and one of his soldiers had been killed. Dad's leg—and his soul—had been pretty torn up. It took quite a while for him to recover as much as he had. He'd always walk with a cane.

"I'm sorry," Zane said to his mom as he stood. Stepping to her he thought of the line from Milton's Sonnet Nineteen. He recited, " 'They also serve who only stand and wait.' " Perhaps he'd taken the line out of context, but it seemed apropos. "It will be harder on you than me," he added.

She shook her head. "It will be harder on you—I'll just worry more."

His phone buzzed in his pocket. "Sorry," he said again, stepping to the doorway. It was Daniel. Who had he expected? But then his heart began to race. Maybe Lila was calling on her brother's phone.

"Hello?"

"Hey, I know this is crazy"—it was Daniel—"but my crew boss is looking for someone to help out until the weekend, and I was thinking about how much you liked construction back when we were building our fort." He chuckled. "Would you like a job for a couple days? Just cleanup and stuff like that."

"Maybe," Zane replied, thinking fast. He glanced at Mom. Adam had school the rest of the week, and she was working at the hospital.

"You'd need steel-toed boots and leather gloves. And warm clothes." Daniel paused for a moment. "What do you think?"

"Sure. Where should I meet you?"

Instead of frowning, Mom's face lit up. He guessed she thought he was getting together with a friend.

Daniel gave Zane the address and told him to arrive by seven sharp the next morning. "See you then," Zane said. The work would keep him from sitting around the house thinking about Lila.

Zane hung up and turned to his dad. "Do you have a pair of boots and gloves I can borrow? I'm going to work with Daniel for a couple of days."

His dad shot Mom a look, but she just nodded. His folks were like that. Maybe they didn't always approve of his choices, but they didn't interfere. He appreciated it—although he wished they'd stepped in when he rushed to join the Army. Then again he hadn't given them a chance to talk him out of it before he signed on the dotted line. It had all happened so fast.

"Hey," Zane said, turning back toward Mom. "Don't tell anyone about Afghanistan yet, all right? Wait until I go back."

Mom's eyes grew teary. "Not even Eve and Charlie?"

Zane nodded. Especially not Eve and Charlie. They were Lila's aunt and uncle, besides being his parents' best friends. He didn't want Lila coming around just because she was worried about him. That would be worse than not seeing her at all.

The next morning he met Daniel at the work site, just outside of Lancaster. The project was a three-story office building. As he shook hands with the supervisor, the man thanked him for helping out.

Daniel worked with the others to hang drywall while Zane picked up scraps of lumber, swept up sawdust and nails, and refilled the supervisor's coffee mug from the trailer several times. By the end of the day he stepped in to help with the drywall, thankful he'd been lifting weights for the last two years. It was hard work, but he enjoyed it. He hardly thought of Lila at all.

At quitting time, the supervisor slapped him on the back. "Are you willing to come back tomorrow?"

"Sure," Zane answered. That would be Friday. Then he'd spend the rest of his leave with his family.

"I appreciate you helping out. Daniel said you're in the Army, but if you ever need a job, let me know."

"Thank you," he replied.

The next day was pretty much the same—lots of cleanup and then helping with the drywall. But at quitting time, as they were walking to their trucks in the dark, Daniel said, "I stopped by the house last night. Lila said she didn't know you were home."

"I haven't had time to visit," Zane responded, hoping his voice sounded casual.

"She said to tell you hello." Daniel opened the door to his beater truck. "You should stop by the Plain Buffet. That's where she's working. She waits tables on Thursday and Saturday nights."

Zane's heart skipped a beat.

"It's really good to see you," Daniel said, shaking his hand. "It hasn't been the same since you left."

When Zane arrived home, Adam ran out to greet him, just as he had the day before and the day he arrived. "Simon's here," Adam said.

"Shouldn't he be doing chores?"

Adam smiled. "He finished already. I helped him."

"That's cool." Zane had loved helping milk the Lehmans' dairy herd when he'd been a boy.

Adam beamed. He was smaller than Zane had been at that age, and more bookish. Zane said a silent prayer that the kid would never join the military.

Adam grabbed Zane's hand. "How come you

don't have chickens anymore? Or a few sheep?" Zane asked.

Adam shrugged. "Mom keeps saying we'll get more."

"Would you like more?"

"Not really." The boy pulled Zane up the steps. "Being around Trudy's chickens is enough for me."

Zane chuckled. "Are they Trudy's now?"

Adam nodded. "Rose hates chickens."

"What about Lila?" Her name caught in Zane's throat.

"She has too much other stuff to do."

Zane could imagine. The laundry. The cooking. The preserving. The shopping. And she worked too. He hoped Rose was a good helper, but unless she'd changed in the past two years she probably wasn't.

He sighed. People did grow up.

He followed Adam into the house and hung his coat by the Christmas tree. It all seemed a little garish to Zane. His choice would have been just ornaments—no lights.

Through the doorway to the kitchen, he could see his dad and Simon at the table, but as soon as Simon saw Zane he was on his feet and hurrying into the living room. "I can't believe you've been home for two days and haven't stopped by. I had to track you down." He gave Zane a hug. "What does Daniel think he's doing? Hauling you off to work with him. You should be home relaxing. With your feet up."

Zane chuckled. "It's good to see you too."

Simon had grown. He was taller than Zane, and he'd filled out. He'd never be as big as his Dat, but he definitely took after that side of the family. His hair curled a little on his forehead and although he wore Amish clothes—the barn pants, the shirt, and suspenders—his hair was no longer in a bowl cut. Zane imagined that Simon would take full advantage of his Rumschpringe.

"So how's the Army?" Simon asked.

"Oh, well, you know. It's there."

"So, are you finally all that you can be?" Simon grinned.

Zane laughed. "Jah. Pretty much." He hesitated. It felt weird not to tell Simon about shipping out to Afghanistan. Simon had always idealized the Army and had grilled Zane's dad through the years about his experiences in Iraq.

"You have a birthday coming up, right?" Zane said to Simon.

"Yep. I'll be eighteen, next week. Adulthood here I come!"

Zane chuckled. "So you have big plans, I take it."

Simon beamed. "Boy, do I." He sighed and said, "I'd love to stick around but I'd better get going—against my better judgment. Rose is cooking tonight."

"Say it ain't so," Zane joked.

Simon stood and then grinned. "Some things have changed since you left, but not everything. If anything Rose is feistier than ever—and not any better of a cook."

"It's good to see you," Zane said, wrapping one arm around Simon.

"You should come down and see everyone."

Zane shrugged.

"We've missed you," Simon added, his voice skipping just a little. "All of us."

Zane slapped his friend's shoulder, hoping he wouldn't say any more. The last thing he wanted was to show his emotions. "I'll definitely see you again before I go."

As Simon headed to the door, Zane walked with him and then waited on the porch. Simon turned around and pointed to the lights on the roofline. "Nice, huh?"

Zane cocked his head. "Did you put those up?"

Simon grinned. "Jah."

"*Denki*," Zane said, truly meaning it, erasing the image of his father on a ladder from his mind. Simon had always connected with Dad. Zane had been the odd one out.

He watched as Simon disappeared into the field. It was completely dark and overcast. No moon, not even a star shone through. Zane was sure Simon knew the way by heart though.

Zane was pretty sure he did too, but he wouldn't

go that way. He didn't want to walk through the field or get that close to the old fort or go eat at the Plain Buffet on a Thursday or Saturday night. It was hard enough to fight his memories as it was.

He pulled the two nickel-size pieces of green jasper from his pocket. He'd found the stones, smoothed by time and water, down by the creek before he left for basic training. He'd kept them with him ever since. He'd take them to Afghanistan with him too. They were as close as he wanted to get to the past.

The next week, Zane hung out with Adam. They cleaned out the barn and the old chicken coop. Got chocolate cones at the creamery in Strasburg. Rode the train. On the day before Zane planned to leave, they went into Lancaster and had lunch with their dad while their mom was Christmas shopping. After Dad introduced Zane around the office, Zane couldn't help but notice the photo on his father's desk. It was of the two of them, taken after boot camp graduation. While his father had been proud of him, Zane was simply thankful he'd survived in one piece.

That afternoon, when they returned home, Rose brought Trudy down to play. Rose *had* grown up. "I'm sixteen now," she said with a flirty smile. Her hair had darkened, and her brown eyes shone. She was pretty in a different way than Lila, in a way similar to what people in the Englisch world seemed to value. She was also gregarious in a way Lila had never been, standing close to him and touching his arm to make sure he was paying attention to her.

Zane was relieved when she left.

Trudy and Adam sat at the table and played a trivia game for kids. *What's the molten rock called when it's inside the earth? Magma! What scent is most linked to memory? Smell!* Zane couldn't help but smile. They were geeks—just like he and Lila used to be.

Zane played with them until Trudy won, and then they bundled up and went outside. He followed. They didn't head toward the creek as he expected. Instead they marched to the far side of the chicken coop, where a piece of plywood was flat on the ground. A branch bordered one side of the wood and a bucket sat on the other side.

It looked as if they were playing house. Zane headed to the edge of the field, just to have a look. He shoved his hands in the pockets of his jacket, thinking about Daniel saying that Reuben wanted to be married by now. Why hadn't Lila agreed? It would make everything easier. He felt as if he was holding his breath.

Someone started up the field toward him. Probably Simon. By the time the figure reached the halfway point Zane realized it was Tim. Lila's father was still as big as a house. Some things grew smaller as Zane grew older, but not Tim. He wore a gray work coat, a straw hat, and work gloves. And he lumbered along, just like always.

Zane groaned. He both loathed and loved the guy. He'd spent much of his childhood dodging Tim, and yet he absolutely respected the man. Zane wouldn't do anything against Tim's wishes. Which meant his relationship with Lila stayed platonic, even though that wouldn't have been his first choice. As it was, it was the right choice. Anything more would have made losing her all the harder. At least that's what he thought. It certainly wasn't what he felt.

Tim was more authentic than anyone he'd ever met. You never had to guess with the man. He pretty much never wanted anyone but his own kids around, except for Reuben. As helpful as Zane used to try to be with chores and fieldwork, Tim never appreciated it. Zane had never felt like anything more than a bother. Worse, he'd felt like a threat. But now that Lila was seriously courting Reuben and Daniel and Jenny looked like a sure thing too, Tim didn't need to be worried about Zane's influence on his children anymore. Maybe he'd be nicer.

"Zane," Tim said as he approached, extending his hand. "Simon said you were home. I kept expecting you to stop by, and when you didn't I figured I'd better come down."

Tim shook Zane's hand hard, and when he finally let go, he clapped him on the back. "I bet it's good to be home," he said.

"Yes, sir." Zane cringed, realizing that he felt the same way toward Tim as he had his boot camp sergeant. Nevertheless it was good to see him.

Tim asked how Zane liked Texas.

"It's fine," Zane responded, "but it doesn't compare to here."

Tim nodded as if he'd expected Zane's answer. "Well, I'm glad you miss us. And I'm glad your *Mamm* and *Dat* will have you home for Christmas."

Zane shook his head. "I'm leaving tomorrow."

Tim stepped back and focused on Zane's face. "Why so soon?"

Zane shrugged. "I need to go back, is all."

"Is that true?"

Zane's face grew warm. "Yes, sir, I need to report back to duty."

"Well, it's good to see you," Tim said. "You've been missed by both households on Juneberry Lane."

Zane nodded in response, trying to ignore the lump that had lodged in his throat.

"Rose asked me to collect Trudy," Tim said, pointing toward the chicken coop. "Are they playing house?"

Zane nodded, a little jealous that Tim didn't

seem to mind that Adam and Trudy played alone. Then again they were still young. Tim called out to Trudy, and she quickly responded. In no time she was skipping off with her father, pausing for a moment to turn and wave both of her mitten-covered hands at Adam.

Trudy was three years younger than Lila had been when the Becks moved to Juneberry Lane, and had the same fairy look, blond hair, and blue eyes. It all took him back to that first day, standing at the gate, watching the Amish girl with her siblings.

By the time Zane and Adam reached the house, their dad had arrived. Both parents were in the kitchen, and Mom called out, "We're going out to dinner tonight."

Adam grinned.

Zane would rather have soup and sandwiches and stay home, but he didn't want to disappoint his brother.

"We thought we'd go to the buffet," his dad said once he turned on the highway. It wasn't until they pulled into the parking lot that Zane realized it was the Plain Buffet. Thankfully it was a Friday and Lila wouldn't be working.

"Let's go, Bub," he said to Adam. "And see who can eat the most."

"We order our drinks and then go fill our plates," Mom explained as she took off her coat and chose a booth. Zane's mouth watered at the

40

smell of the place. Ham. Roast. Mashed potatoes. Gravy. Stuffing. It smelled like an Amish kitchen.

A couple of minutes later, Zane spotted Lila coming out of the back with a tray of drinks. He began to panic, but Adam was sitting on the outside of the bench. It wasn't like he could slip away without making a scene.

If she saw him, she did a good job appearing as if she hadn't. By the time she made it to their table, Zane decided she was either the world's best actress or else she no longer cared for him at all, not one iota. When she stopped by their table, she gushed, "Shani, Joel. Adam, Zane. It's so good to see all of you." She made eye contact with everyone but Zane.

Her eyes were bluer than he'd remembered. Her hair had darkened a little, probably because it was winter, but the part he could see that wasn't covered by her Kapp was still blond.

"Daniel said you work on Thursday and Saturday nights," Zane said. His mother glared at him, but he didn't care. Lila had told him to leave her alone, and he didn't want her to think he was stalking her.

"I picked up an extra shift." She turned her gaze toward him. "What would you like to drink?"

"Water," he answered.

"Okay," she said. "I'll be right back. Go help yourselves."

She seemed so poised. But not in a good way.

In a plastic way. He'd always loved her honesty—now she seemed fake.

Adam waved his hand. "I want a Coke!"

"Oh, of course," she said. "I'm sorry. What else can I bring for drinks?"

Joel ordered decaf for him and Mom.

As Lila started to leave, Adam announced, "Zane's going back to Texas tomorrow."

She turned back toward the table, her eyes a little watery, and finally focused on Zane. "So soon?"

He shrugged.

"He's going to—"

Zane put his hand on Adam's leg, but he was too late.

"—Afghanistan," Adam blurted out.

Lila's face turned pale. "When?"

Zane swallowed and managed to sputter, "Next month."

"Oh," she said again and turned without saying anything more.

Zane must have made a face because Adam frowned and then said, "You're leaving tomorrow. I thought it would be all right to say something to her."

Zane moved his hand to Adam's shoulder. "It's fine."

"Mom says that Trudy and I are a lot like you and Lila when you were kids."

"That's true, Bub, but we grew up."

Adam wiggled away from Zane's hand. "Trudy and I will always be friends."

Mom slid out of the booth, a sympathetic expression on her face. "Let's go get our food."

Zane tousled his little brother's hair. "Show me how much you can eat."

2

Lila placed the Becks' drinks on their table while they were filling their plates and then kept busy with her other tables, feeling sicker by the minute. She knew she was avoiding them—but she couldn't help herself. She couldn't bear to be that close to Zane. With his broad shoulders and square chiseled face, he no longer looked like the boy she'd grown up with. His hair was a lot lighter than it had been, probably from the Texas sun. And considering he was in the Army, he looked as if he needed a haircut. She mourned the long bangs he used to brush away from his forehead when they were kids. For the last two and a half years she'd still been thinking of him as a teenager, but he was a man now.

After ten minutes she didn't feel any better and told her manager she wasn't feeling well. She felt as if she'd been kicked in the stomach by one of the cows, although she didn't say that. He told her to take a break.

She breathed into a paper bag in the break room, trying not to hyperventilate, until her Mennonite friend Mandy came in. Lila put the bag down. "Hiccups," she said, hoping Mandy wouldn't notice that her hands were shaking.

Mandy wore a cape dress and Kapp, but she drove a car. Since her family wasn't Old Order Mennonite, her parents had let her buy a smart phone with her tip money.

She seemed to know all the *Youngie* in Lancaster County, both Mennonite and Amish. She'd also taken a liking to Lila's brothers, Simon in particular, even though he was a couple of years younger. Mandy deemed him "cool" the week before. She wasn't wild, at least Lila didn't think so, but she did seem to find her way to a fair number of parties. Apparently Simon did too, according to what he kept telling Lila. He told her other disturbing things too—like that he wanted to join the Army. But she was pretty sure he was just trying to annoy her.

"Do you mind checking to see if anyone in my section needs a drink refill?" Lila asked.

"Sure," Mandy said as she sashayed out the door.

By the time Lila returned to the floor, the Becks were headed toward the exit. When they reached the parking lot, Zane scooped up Adam and flung him over his shoulder. The little boy raised his head in laughter.

Mandy elbowed Lila as she went by. "Whatcha lookin' at?"

"Nothing." Lila began collecting the plates and then pocketed the ten-dollar bill on the table. Shani and Joel had overtipped when they came in after she first started too. This time she hadn't deserved a tip at all.

"Well, I'd say he's worth looking at." Mandy stared after Zane.

"I knew him when we were kids—that's all. I'm courting Reuben, remember?"

"Right." Mandy gave Lila a wry smile and headed on toward her section.

Tears stung Lila's eyes. Was that what all those years had come to? Zane being classified as someone she "used to know"? And now he was headed to Afghanistan. She brushed at her eyes. How many times had she prayed the U.S. would get out of there before it was his turn to go?

At closing time she called Daniel to ask him for a ride. Snowflakes were starting to fly, and she still felt shaken up by what Adam had disclosed. Reuben had volunteered to get her earlier in the day but it was a long ride in a buggy from his place.

"Sweet dreams," Mandy said as she left, waving on her way out the door.

A minute later Daniel pulled up and honked. "See you tomorrow," Lila called out to her supervisor as she hurried out the door and into the falling snow.

Relief flooded over Lila as she hurried around to the passenger door. Jenny wasn't in the cab with Daniel. As much as she loved her friend, she wanted to talk to her twin in private.

"Denki," she said. "I really appreciate the ride."

"No problem," Daniel answered. "I don't like it when you walk home."

She fastened her seat belt. "The Becks came in tonight."

Daniel grinned. "I knew you couldn't avoid him entirely."

"I wasn't avoiding him."

Daniel rolled his eyes.

"Why didn't you tell me he was leaving tomorrow?"

"I didn't know." Daniel turned onto the highway. "I figured he'd be staying until after Christmas. Why is he going so soon?"

"Maybe because he's shipping out to Afghanistan."

"What?" Daniel swerved over the center line.

She put her hand on the dashboard. "Watch the road."

Daniel pulled back. Thankfully no one was coming.

"Adam's the one who told me, and Zane didn't seem happy that he did." That hurt too. Why wouldn't Zane want all of them to know?

Her brother let out a big sigh and said, "He

didn't say a word about going to Afghanistan. To Simon either."

"Did he seem the same?" she asked Daniel. "When he was working with you."

"Kind of," Daniel answered. "He still seemed pretty intense, but he laughed too." He shrugged. "I don't know. We've all grown up, right?"

Lila nodded. Despite his bad driving, Daniel had turned into a responsible man. True, he was on his Rumschpringe, but Lila was sure he'd join the church and marry Jenny as soon as he had enough money saved and a plan for the future. The truth was he worked too hard for much running around.

Dat wasn't happy with Daniel having a truck and a cell phone, and the conflict between them had led Daniel to move out of the house. Lila tried not to feel in the middle, between the two, but she couldn't help it. She suspected it would soon be even worse with Simon. But then again he'd always been Dat's favorite, so maybe there wouldn't be as much tension.

"You should try to talk to Zane," Daniel said, gripping the wheel. The snow was thicker now.

"When?"

"Tonight."

"I should just go knock on Joel and Shani's door at ten thirty and ask them to wake up Zane so I can say hello?"

"Who says he'll be asleep?"

"He's probably leaving early in the morning so he can get a full day of driving in."

Daniel slowed for a buggy. "It's just really weird that he came all this way and you two haven't talked."

"We said hello in the restaurant."

"That doesn't count. You were such good friends." Daniel steered around the buggy. "By the time he's home from Afghanistan you and Reuben will be married."

Lila sank against the back of the seat.

"What's wrong?" Daniel asked.

"Nothing," she answered.

Daniel shook his head, as if clearing it. "I know you'll always care about him. All the time we were growing up, it seemed like the two of you belonged together. But I didn't really get things back then—"

She interrupted him. "Stop." Her temples began to throb.

"Maybe Dat was right," Daniel said, ignoring her, "about no good coming from having Englisch neighbors. Do you remember that? That was when he tried to forbid us from hanging out with Zane. But then he softened . . ."

Lila closed her eyes.

"Sis," Daniel said. He hadn't called her that in years. "Maybe I was wrong. Maybe it's better you didn't have a chance to really see Zane. You'll marry Reuben soon. Zane will just be a memory.

Your childhood friend. Just like he was my childhood friend."

Even though she knew Daniel was right she hated to hear him say it.

After her mother had died, Lila had felt a horrible loneliness—until Zane moved next door. Her friendship with him had brought a wholeness to her life. But then that disintegrated too.

It wasn't that she felt overcome by her losses. Many people she knew had lost a parent or had some sort of tragedy. But Lila did feel as if something was missing from her life.

"Do you ever think about our biological father?" she asked her twin.

Daniel made a face and shook his head. "No. Why would I?"

"Because we have his DNA."

Daniel shrugged. "What does that matter?"

They'd never met their father. They knew nothing about him. Not even his name. It wasn't that Lila necessarily wanted to find the man or meet him. But she'd like to have the option. Perhaps that would help fill in the gap in her heart.

Daniel turned onto Juneberry Lane and then down the driveway. "Will you come in?" Lila asked.

He shook his head.

"Dat's asleep."

Daniel yawned. "I have to be up early."

She thanked him, jumped down, and closed the door, but instead of going to the house, she turned toward the field. The snow was beginning to stick, making the whole world lighter. She could see all the way to the poplar trees.

What if Zane was waiting for her at their fort? She'd gone down to the creek a couple of months ago when she couldn't stop thinking about him. Either Trudy and Adam hadn't found the fort or else they hadn't claimed it because it was just the way it had been those last nights she'd gone alone after Zane had joined the Army, hoping he would meet her there before he left.

She trudged through the field and at the halfway point turned toward the trees. When she reached the creek bank, she whispered, "Zane?"

No one replied. She said his name again, but louder. It was darker under the trees and the mud hadn't frozen yet, making the ground slippery. There was no light in the fort. Christmas Eve was fast approaching. It used to be her favorite day of the year. Not anymore.

She watched the snowflakes disappear into the darkness of the creek for a moment and then said his name one more time. Again, no one answered. Feeling foolish she headed back home. By the time she reached the back steps, she was thankful he hadn't been there. What would she have said if he had been?

Lila was up by five the next morning, trudging through the now-deep snow to feed the chickens

50

and gather the eggs. Dat hadn't had a chance to shovel the path before milking. Later he would, and plow the lane with his tractor too. He'd bought a used one a couple of years ago. It had metal wheels, like all of the tractors owned by Plain families in Lancaster County, but it had decreased his workload by quite a bit—and provided Simon with the only farm chore he actually enjoyed. As she headed back to the house, she turned toward the lane, wondering when Zane would pass by. Perhaps he had put chains on and was already gone. She hoped he'd drive carefully in the snow. Maybe he'd wait at least until the roads were plowed.

She woke Rose and Trudy and fixed hotcakes for breakfast, her gaze wandering to the window. They all ate after Dat and Simon came in from the milking. Once the dishes were washed Lila told Rose she was going to their grandmother's quilt shop. "I need to pick up some things to finish gifts," she said. "I'll be back after a while."

Trudy asked to go too. Lila almost said no, but she changed her mind. She hadn't seen her little sister much in the last few days. Lila told Trudy to dress warmly, while she hitched up the horse to the buggy. By the time they reached the highway, the plow had cleared it.

Trudy chattered away about Adam and then about school. Her teacher wouldn't be back after Christmas vacation because she was moving to

Florida. "Our new teacher is coming from Maryland," Trudy said.

Lila had lost track of what was going on at school. Dat had been taking Trudy when he went into the lumberyard. Lila and Rose split the other days, but Lila didn't go into the school much anymore. She supposed she should.

"She's older." Trudy snuggled under the wool blanket.

"Oh?"

"Jah, we've been told to be extra good. She's had years of experience teaching and won't put up with any bad behavior."

Lila stopped herself from laughing. There was no worry that Trudy would misbehave. That was the main reason Lila didn't go into the school much anymore. She didn't have any concerns. If Simon were younger and still in school it would be another story.

She urged the horse on as she half listened. Their grandmother had moved her quilt shop into Strasburg a couple of years ago. Her business had been booming, so much so that their grandfather had shut down his small engine repair shop and did the books and also often manned the counter at the quilt shop so Mammi could concentrate on her handwork, talking with customers, and teaching the classes she offered several times a week. Two women also helped out in the store part time.

Even though she grew up just a few miles away, Lila still found the village of Strasburg enchanting with its brick buildings, hand-hewn log cabins, and centuries of history. Traffic wasn't bad, probably because of the storm, and Lila found a place to park not far from the quilt shop.

"Can we stop at the creamery?" Trudy asked as she jumped down. "Zane took Adam there a few days ago."

Lila's heart contracted at the thought of Zane there. One time when they were all still kids, Shani had piled them all into her van and taken them to Strasburg for ice cream. That particular time the creamery was packed with tourists, so instead of sitting at a table they all strolled down Main Street with their cones.

They had stopped at the cemetery, and Lila and Zane read the inscriptions on the gravestones, finding veterans who fought in the Revolutionary War or Civil War. A small flag marked all of those headstones. It sent a chill up her spine. Later, when Zane shared his American history book with her, she thought of those people and when they lived, some of them way back when Strasburg was on the old Conestoga Road, which connected Philadelphia to the West, as far back as the early 1700s.

She thought of her ancestors, who'd come to Pennsylvania around the same time, although they did their best to avoid fighting in any of the wars or getting involved in the politics of the day. Their history was solely about family.

Had Zane given her a thought when he'd taken Adam to the creamery? Had he remembered their time in the cemetery together?

"We won't have time to get ice cream today," Lila said to Trudy. She didn't have the money either, but she didn't need to say that. After she hitched the horse, she took her sister's hand and headed toward Thread by Thread, the clever name Mammi had given her shop years ago. "Did you see Zane while he was home?"

Trudy nodded. "Yesterday. Rose took me over. Zane played that trivia game with me and Adam." She grinned. "But he let me win."

Everyone in her family had had a chance to spend time with Zane—except for her.

Trudy pulled away from Lila and skipped ahead. As she rounded the corner she saw their grandfather, wearing his heavy coat and black hat. Trudy ran toward him. Dawdi lifted her and carried her into the quilt shop.

Mamm's parents had left the Amish church back when Lila and Daniel were little. Mammi and Dawdi had become Mennonite, the kind who drove cars and even watched TV. Dat had been upset with them for years for leaving the Amish church, and after Mamm died, there was a short time he didn't allow any of the Lehman children to see their grandparents. But then, thankfully, Aenti Eve stepped in and took them to visit anyway. Lila couldn't imagine her life without Mammi and Dawdi. Dat's parents had died years ago, and she barely remembered them.

By the time Lila reached the front door, Trudy was already in the shop, wrapped in her grandmother's arms. As a Mennonite, Mammi still wore a cape dress, although made from printed fabric, not solids, and a rounded Kapp instead of the heart-shaped Amish style. As soon as she looked up, Mammi said, "Lila! It's so good to see you." Her eyes were bright and full of love and her smile wide, both as cheery as the shop. The front window let in the natural light, Christmas quilts and bolts of fabric covered the walls, and the scent of cinnamon from the basket of dipped pinecones in the corner filled the space.

Trudy wouldn't let her grandmother go, so Lila stepped into the hug, all of them giggling as they clung to one another. Finally, Mammi sat down in a chair, scooped Trudy onto her lap, and said, "Eve's on her way. Hopefully she'll get here before you leave." Aenti Eve sometimes quilted with Mammi on Saturdays.

Mammi was her usual warm self, but her face was pale. Most likely she was tired from the Christmas rush. "Are you feeling all right?" Lila asked her grandmother.

"A little weary, perhaps. We've been extra busy." Mammi looked up at Lila. "What brings you in today?"

"I need some binding to finish my Christmas gifts," Lila answered. She was making placemats for Eve, Rose, and Jenny. And an apron for Trudy as well as for Adam and Shani, for their baking days.

Mammi pointed to the hard candy jar on the counter and told Trudy to go help herself while she helped Lila.

"I've been wanting to talk with you," Mammi said. "The new woman I hired is quitting in two weeks. Moving to Ohio." She put her arm around Lila as they stood in front of the binding. "Would you consider working for me?"

Lila didn't respond, sure Dat wouldn't be happy with her working so far from home.

"You can think about it," Mammi added. "Talk with your father. See if it would work for all of you."

It was a bit of a drive—definitely farther than the restaurant.

Lila nodded and picked out a package of red binding. "When do you need to know?"

"By next week would be good. If you don't want the job I'll need to advertise."

Trudy bounced back toward them just as the door swung open and Eve came through. She wore jeans, a cloth coat, and boots. Trudy spun

56

around and rushed toward their aunt, her arms wide open.

Eve and Charlie went to Mammi and Dawdi's church, but Eve didn't wear a Kapp.

However, she and Charlie did live a simple lifestyle. They drove a black sedan. Lived on an acreage with chickens, a few steers, a couple of horses, and a big garden. And Charlie rode a bicycle to work most of the time.

Eve had graduated from college a year before and taught kindergarten at a public school. They all hoped she'd have a baby soon, but of course no one talked about it. Maybe Eve and Shani did, but Lila wasn't privy to any of that information.

Once Trudy released their aunt, Eve gave Lila a hug. "I haven't seen you for so long. How are you?"

"*Gut*," Lila said. "Busy with work and everything."

"Have you seen Zane?" Eve asked.

"Last night. At the restaurant," Lila answered, hoping her voice didn't sound as shaky to everyone else as it did to her. "He left this morning."

Eve shook her head. "Shani called. He's staying another day at least. The weather is worse south of here, and they were worried about the roads."

Lila couldn't think of anything to say.

"Which is lucky for us. If Charlie gets off in time, we'll go over tonight."

Lila nodded, aware that her grandmother was watching her.

Eve took off her coat. Lila tried not to look too closely, but Eve appeared to be as thin as ever. She couldn't imagine that her aunt and Charlie were purposefully not starting a family. Perhaps Lila wasn't the only one with problems.

But Zane's staying an extra day put him one more day closer to Christmas Eve. She wished he was on his way. The sooner the better, as far as she was concerned.

3

Shani pulled the sugar cookies from the oven, her face flushed from the heat. The sweet smell from baking combined with the fresh pot of coffee brewing, making the entire kitchen smell heavenly.

She half listened as Simon and Zane kidded each other at the table. Apparently, Eve had told Lila that Zane was staying another day. She told Rose, who told Simon, who came over before having to start the milking and relayed the transformation of information. "The Amish grapevine is better than a cell phone," he said.

If only all the Lehman kids were crowded into her house like the old days.

Joel and Adam had gone into town on an

"errand," which she knew was code for Christmas shopping. She hoped Adam would help her frost the cookies later in the evening.

"I'm thinking about signing up," Simon said.

Zane pushed back his chair. "Signing up for what?"

"You know."

Shani turned toward the table.

Zane shook his head. "I have no idea what you're talking about."

"The Army. Like you did."

Shani's eyes began to burn. "Don't joke like that," she said to Simon.

He grinned at her, wrapping his hands around a mug. "Who said I'm kidding?"

"You can't join the Army," she said.

"Why not?"

"You're Amish. Anabaptist. Nonresistant."

"I haven't joined the church yet." He grinned again.

"Dude," Zane said. "Mom's right. Stop joking." Zane stood and refilled his coffee cup.

"You're not old enough to—" Shani stopped.

"Eighteen," Simon said. "Tomorrow."

Zane groaned, and Shani went back to sliding the cookies onto the rack. Simon couldn't be serious.

Simon stood and snatched a cookie.

"It's hot," Shani warned.

He juggled it up and down. "I can handle it." He

took a bite. "Delicious," he said and then shoved all of it into his mouth.

Simon was a crack shot. He was the one who always got the first deer when Tim and his boys went hunting. Tim wasn't one to brag, but he had commented on Simon's skills a few times.

Zane sat back down with his coffee. "Promise me you're joking," he moaned.

"You're off to Afghanistan," Simon answered. "I should at least be able to join."

"And then you'd be off to Afghanistan too."

"Nah," Simon answered. "We'll be out of there soon. Don't you think?"

"I doubt it," Zane answered. "And even if we are, something else will come up."

Shani shivered, despite the heat from the stove. Who would have thought back in 2001 that the U.S. would still be in Afghanistan eleven years later. Technically it was now longer than the Vietnam War had been. Afghanistan was the longest war the U.S. had ever been in. And Zane was about to become a part of the conflict.

She swallowed hard. Being a military mom was as challenging as she'd thought it would be. She was proud of Zane and his service, and she absolutely supported him, but at the same time, after Joel's deployment in Iraq and now Zane's upcoming deployment, she was weary of war. And as much as she tried, she couldn't help but worry about him.

At least he'd agreed to stay another day. She didn't have to say good-bye to him yet. She glanced at the clock. Four p.m. It was time for her to get supper going. Eve and Charlie would be over soon. She needed to make the spare bed up for her father too. He was flying into Philly later in the evening and driving down in a rental car—one with four-wheel drive. She felt a wave of gratitude again that Zane was staying another night. He'd see his grandfather and go to church. Maybe she could talk him into staying until Christmas morn. He seemed a little more relaxed. She couldn't help but think that seeing Lila had been good for him.

If Shani could have chosen any girl in the world for Zane it would have been Lila, but she knew it wasn't a possibility. There were some things in life that a mother had to just let go. And she thought she had, until last night in the restaurant. It was evident that Zane and Lila cared for each other. But Lila would never leave the Amish, and she couldn't imagine Zane becoming Plain. He loved the community and support of the Amish, but he valued education too much.

"Come help me with the milking," Simon said to Zane, grabbing another cookie.

Zane hesitated.

"For old time's sake." Simon had that grin on his face again. "Rose was making snicker-doodles. She might give you one, although

61

they're not as good as Lila's—who didn't have time to bake today before work." He grabbed a third cookie, and Shani swatted at his hand. "Rose's aren't as good as these either." He grinned at Shani one more time and turned back to Zane. "You can wear Dat's boots. He won't be home from the lumberyard until late—I'll tell him then about my big plan." Simon winked at Shani as he stepped out of the kitchen. He had to be kidding about joining the Army. There was no way he'd do something so foolish.

The boys—they were still boys to her—clamored out the front door, and Shani scooted the cookies to the back of the counter and cleaned up the baking things.

She had chicken marinating, but she needed to get the potatoes baking and make a salad. She wasn't a great cook, but she'd definitely improved since they'd moved to Juneberry Lane. Mostly thanks to Eve. So many things in her life were in thanks to Eve—and the rest of the Lehmans too.

Two hours later, Joel and Adam were home, Zane had returned from helping with the milking, and Charlie and Eve had just arrived.

Shani took in the scene of the men and Adam standing around the Christmas tree as Eve finished setting the table. Her heart contracted in gratitude. She wouldn't think about Zane going off to Afghanistan, not tonight.

After they all gathered around the table, Joel said a short prayer of thanks, including that Zane was still with them. As they passed the food around, Eve said she'd quilted with Leona that morning at her shop. "Lila and Trudy stopped by," she said.

"Yeah," Zane answered, "Simon said you'd told Lila I wasn't leaving yet. So he came over and hung out."

"How's he doing?" Eve asked. "I haven't seen him for a while."

Zane shrugged. "As impish as ever. He says he wants to join the Army."

Eve shot Charlie a concerned look.

"What?" Zane asked. "You don't think he's joking?"

"We hope he is," Charlie answered.

"He said something to us early in the fall—that he was considering it when he turned eighteen." Eve frowned. "It's hard to tell with Simon."

Shani shook her head and then changed the subject. "How's Leona?"

"Good. Her business is booming. And, of course, she was thrilled to see Trudy and Lila today."

"I thought Lila had to work," Shani said.

"She went in this afternoon."

Zane shifted in his chair and asked Charlie how things were at the fire station.

"Crazy," he replied. "We had one of our worst

accidents in years when that semi sideswiped the buggy on the highway."

Shani nodded. They'd all been horrified.

"The mom is out of the hospital," Charlie said. "But she'll be in a body cast for a few months. The two boys have come out of it all right, but they'll all be grieving for a long time for the little girl."

Shani hated those accidents—it seemed as if they were happening more and more. Or maybe she was just more aware of them. She knew the Amish family would be well supported, but nothing could make up for the loss of a child.

After a silent pause, Eve turned toward Zane. "So how's the Army?"

"Good," he answered. "Did Lila tell you I'm headed to Afghanistan?"

Eve's hand went to her throat. "No."

"Yeah, Adam spilled the beans last night." Zane tousled his brother's hair in an affectionate manner, but Adam still turned red.

Charlie cleared his throat. "When do you deploy?"

"Next month."

The men started talking about the Army. Charlie had left the Reserve a year after he and Eve married, and Joel had been discharged after his injury prevented him from staying in, but Shani knew both of the men still felt the Army values deeply.

"How do you like the other soldiers in your unit?" Charlie asked.

"Some are great. Others are entitled whiners," Zane answered. "I'm not sure what made them join."

Shani suppressed a frown. They'd probably joined for better reasons than Zane, who, at least it seemed to her, joined to prove his dad wrong and escape his pain over losing Lila.

"Keep your head up," Charlie said. "And know we'll all be praying for you."

"Thanks," Zane said. "I am excited about speaking Pashto. The classroom is one thing, but I'll soon know how well I can do though in the field." Shani was sure he'd do fine. He'd always been good with languages. He could speak both Spanish and German. And, with Lila's help, he could speak Pennsylvania Dutch too. Although Pennsylvania Dutch was strictly an oral language, which made it difficult for outsiders to learn, Shani knew that Pashto, with its forty-four-letter Arabic alphabet, was Zane's biggest challenge so far.

The topic turned to the weather, sports, and then Shani's dad flying in from Seattle.

"Why don't we ever go out to Washington State?" Adam asked.

"We used to sometimes, back when your dad was stationed out west."

"Before I was born?"

Shani nodded.

"Everything happened before I was born." He crossed his arms.

"Not everything," Zane said. "Living here have been the best years, honestly."

"It's easier for Grandpa to come here than for all of us to fly out there," Shani said to Adam as she reached for his plate.

Charlie turned to Zane. "When will you be home again?"

"I'm not sure," Zane answered.

"Are they still doing furloughs?" Charlie asked.

"Yeah, although our dates are tentative as far as how long we're staying. It depends on how our mission goes."

That was the most he'd said about his assignment. Shani hoped he'd say more but he didn't.

The next morning, Shani's dad was up early making pancakes for all of them when Shani shuffled in to the kitchen. He already had the coffee started. "It's four thirty in the morning West Coast time," she said. "Why are you up so soon?" He hadn't gotten in last night until after ten.

"I wanted to make pancakes for Zane," he answered. "Before he goes off to war."

Shani teared up as she poured her coffee. Her dad had fought in Vietnam when he was Zane's age.

He put his arm around her. "You've got to trust God with him. Otherwise you'll drive yourself crazy."

She nodded, too choked up to speak. He was right. She just wasn't sure how she was going to do it.

Zane came in the back door, bundled in his coat and his father's boots.

"Where have you been?" Shani asked.

"Out for a walk."

"Did you go down to the old fort?"

He shook his head. "I walked down the lane and back."

After breakfast Zane said he thought he'd skip church. Shani started to say something, but her father pursed his lips and she stopped. By the time they left, Zane was in his room and didn't come down to tell them good-bye.

"He probably needs some time alone," her dad whispered as he followed her out to the van. Joel sat in the driver's seat, warming the engine. She knew he'd tell her the same thing.

She had a hard time concentrating on the sermon until the end, when their pastor, in closing, said, "For unto us a child is born, the healer of humanity and of all creation, the prince of peace. This is indeed good news and great joy for all people."

She bowed her head as the pastor prayed, asking to feel the peace of Christ and the joy of

67

Christmas. *Lord,* she prayed, *I need your peace. I need to trust you with Zane.* She didn't want to feel half crazy the whole time he was gone.

She honestly felt it was easier to have a husband go off to war than a son. Why was that? She sighed. Because Joel talked with her—he Skyped, he e-mailed, he wrote letters.

There was no guarantee Zane would contact them regularly. She felt hollow inside. Who would he confide in if not his parents? She hoped someone.

He'd been close to Daniel, and Simon too, through his growing-up years, but Shani knew it was Lila that Zane used to talk with the most. He hung out with the boys, but in a walk through the field or during a language lesson or a few minutes in their fort, she knew he and Lila shared their feelings more than he ever did with her brothers.

Looking back, Shani realized she should have discouraged it. She was more aware of what was going on than Tim or Joel. Men, generally, didn't see that sort of thing as much, although she knew Tim feared it at the beginning. Considering how things had turned out, maybe she should have listened to him more carefully then. His fear hadn't come to fruition. His children hadn't been impacted that much by Zane after all. Daniel would marry Jenny. Lila would marry Reuben. They'd stay in their church and raise their families. All would be well.

But her child had been hurt—and was still hurting. And now he was going off to war.

The piano began the first few notes of "Joy to the World," and the congregation stood. Shani resolved to be more understanding of Zane for however long he stayed. She wouldn't pressure him.

When they arrived home, he was chopping wood. He'd left his phone on the kitchen table and it buzzed a couple of times while Shani fixed lunch.

When Zane came in he checked it and then said, "Charlie asked if he could stop by and give me one last bit of advice."

Shani couldn't imagine what Charlie wanted to tell Zane, but she was thankful for his concern.

Zane sighed. "I guess I'll stay until morning. I'll get on the road after breakfast."

Shani nodded in response, just so he knew she'd heard him, and stared straight ahead. Maybe he wouldn't stay until Christmas—but she was grateful he'd stay until Christmas Eve morning.

It was midafternoon by the time Charlie came by on his way home from work. He rode his bike since Eve had kept the car to go to church.

Zane told Charlie to throw his bike in the back of his truck, and they could talk while Zane gave him a ride home. Shani stood at the window and watched as they loaded the bike and climbed in the cab, and then as Zane backed his truck around and headed up the lane.

"Come sit," Joel said from the couch. "You've been twirling around here for the last week." Her dad had gone to take a nap, and Adam was playing with Legos on the other side of the tree.

Shani sat beside her husband. Joel reached for her hand and said, "I'm getting a glimpse of what it was like for you when I was gone. I think maybe it's harder staying behind."

She shook her head. "It's really not. But the waiting is—endless." Her heart began to ache, and she leaned her head against Joel's shoulder, remembering the line Zane had quoted. *"They also serve who only stand and wait."*

Joel put his arm around her and pulled her even closer. "It'll be all right," he said.

She knew he couldn't know—not for sure—but still the words brought comfort.

4

Zane turned onto the highway, fumbling for his sunglasses in the console and then putting them on. The afternoon sun reflected off the snow-covered fields as he turned west. "So what did you want to talk to me about?" Zane asked.

Charlie smiled. "No small talk first?"

Zane shook his head. "I figured it was important."

"Honestly, I'm not sure if it is or not," Charlie answered. "But I feel compelled to say it."

"Sounds serious."

Charlie sighed. "It might not be. Or I might be totally misreading the situation."

Zane tensed but didn't say anything.

"It's about Lila."

Zane figured. He stayed quiet.

"I don't know what happened between the two of you, but I do know she used to be your friend."

Zane still didn't respond.

"And now you both seem to be attempting to pretend as if the other doesn't exist."

Zane shrugged.

Charlie hesitated but then said, "I just don't want to see you throwing away a friendship that lasted so many years because of a misunderstanding."

Zane swallowed hard. There wasn't a misunderstanding. He understood things all too well.

"I'm just guessing, but I'm thinking maybe you wanted more from your relationship with Lila."

Zane tightened his grip on the steering wheel. It didn't matter what he wanted.

"I faced that with Eve when she was courting Gideon, and I was ready to walk away until I realized that I'd rather have just her friendship than not have a relationship with her at all."

Zane stared straight ahead.

Charlie stayed quiet.

Finally Zane said, "So how do you think that would have worked out if she and Bishop Berg had married? Do you think you and Eve would still be friends today?"

"Probably not," Charlie answered. "But it would have come to a natural end."

"Yeah, well, that's what happened with Li—" He choked a little trying to say her name. "With us. It came to a natural end. One with Reuben attached."

"I'm just saying that you can treat her with kindness. You both seem out of sorts."

"What makes you think Lila is out of sorts? She seems to be doing fine to me." She was cool as the icicles hanging from the telephone lines when he saw her at the restaurant.

"She doesn't mention you to Eve. She never asks about you. She never brings up a memory about you. It's not normal, considering you were friends for so long."

"Sure it's normal," Zane said. "For someone who doesn't care."

Charlie shook his head. "You're proving my point."

"Your point is flawed," Zane said. "You got the girl. She chose you." Zane swallowed hard, trying to get rid of the bitterness in his voice.

"You're right," Charlie said. "But at one point I didn't know if she would, and I chose to be her friend."

"Yeah, well, how old were you? Thirty?" Zane turned off the highway.

"Twenty-eight."

"Close enough." Zane stopped at an intersection and waited for a buggy to go by. "And Eve was a grown woman—right? Not seventeen." True, Lila was almost twenty now, but she'd only been seventeen when he left. "And you two were making your own decisions—right? Isn't that how it was?"

Charlie sighed. "Yeah, you're right. I'm just asking you to be polite to Lila. Kind, if you can. This has been hard on her too."

Zane swallowed again and turned his truck down Charlie and Eve's driveway. Their two-story white house sat back on their acreage in the middle of a grove of pine trees. The whole setting was like a dream—a snow-covered dream right now, but by spring they'd have calves frolicking in the pasture. And their big vegetable garden would be brimming with plants that would soon be heavy with more produce than they could use. And someday—probably soon—they'd have children.

"Thanks for the ride," Charlie said as Zane pulled up behind their black sedan.

"Sure thing." Zane was glad he had his sunglasses on as he tried to shake away the jealousy he felt. He climbed down from the pickup and dropped the tailgate so it was easier for Charlie to drag his bike out. Once it was out of the truck bed, Zane slammed the tailgate shut.

Eve stepped out on the porch, wrapping a shawl around her shoulders. She waved and then started toward the men.

Charlie wrapped an arm around Zane. "You know I'd do anything for you, right?"

Zane nodded, hugging Charlie back. Sadness replaced the bitterness he'd felt a few minutes ago. Charlie had been a good friend to him for years. He'd filled in when his dad was injured and out of sorts. Charlie had always encouraged him, along with setting a good example of what it meant to be a man. "Thank you for everything," Zane said as he stepped away. "I appreciate it."

Eve hugged him too, and then stepped to Charlie's side.

"I'll write," Charlie said.

"Thanks." Zane stepped toward his truck. "I'd better get going."

They both nodded. "Godspeed," Charlie said as he continued to hold on to the bike with one hand and his wife with the other.

As Zane drove away he pushed his sunglasses up farther on the bridge of his nose and tried to pray. It seemed as if he couldn't manage to put a whole thought together anymore, let alone a sentence. Just mismatched feelings. *Kind to Lila* was as much as he could manage after she'd broken his heart so badly.

Christmas Eve morning, after a late breakfast, Zane hugged his grandfather good-bye first and then his dad. Next was Adam and last his mom.

She squeezed him close and said, "Be safe, baby."

He used to hate it when she called him that, but this time it brought comfort. "I will," he said. "Nothing's going to happen."

"I know," she answered. "Just be careful. Driving too. And thank you for staying for longer than you intended."

He nodded, feeling a stab of guilt for not staying longer. It would be his third Christmas away from home. Lila used to call him stubborn. He guessed he'd proven her right.

"If you want, we can fly down to Texas before you go and drive your truck back," Dad said.

Zane nodded. "I'll think about it." It would save him from having to store his truck for a year.

He climbed into his cab, waved again, and then backed around. As he drove off, the four of them stood on the porch, all waving. When he glanced into his rearview mirror for the last time, Adam was running down the lane. But then he stopped and put his hand up to his brow. Zane honked and kept on going.

Zane wished he were a better son and brother. A better grandson. They were all more than he deserved. He'd been in a funk the last two and a half years, and he needed to get out of it. He should have gone to church with them the day before. It would have meant a lot to Mom. The truth was he'd been in a funk with God the last few years too, probably because he hadn't gotten his own way.

He sighed. It was time for him to grow up. He was going to need God now more than ever, and Charlie was right, he needed to stop sulking around the whole Lila ordeal.

He slowed as he came to the Lehmans' driveway, out of habit, and glanced down it. Someone, either Rose or Lila, was hanging wash on the line. Maybe he could just say hello—and then good-bye. He turned and proceeded slowly. It was Rose at the clothesline. She smiled and waved. He couldn't very well turn around without saying hello, so he parked his truck and climbed down. Then he remembered the book he'd been reading, a collection of essays by pacifists. He'd leave it for Simon. He stepped around to the passenger side and fished the book out of his duffel bag.

Rose grinned at him as he turned around to greet her, and then she said, "It's good to see you."

Zane ignored her comment and asked if Lila was around.

"She's in the kitchen," Rose answered.

Maybe Lila was by herself. Or even if Trudy was with her that would be all right. He hurried up the back steps and knocked on the door. Trudy answered it and grinned.

"Who is it?" Lila called out.

Trudy motioned for him to come in, her eyes dancing. He stepped into the kitchen as the little girl said, "Look, Lila, it's your Christmas surprise!"

Lila stood at the sink, wearing a blue dress that made her eyes extra bright. When she saw him her mouth opened and then closed and opened again. He feared she might be angry, but it didn't seem she was. In fact, if anything, she seemed shy.

Finally she said, "You're here."

"I'm leaving," he said. "But I wanted to give this book to Simon." He held it up.

Lila read the title. "He won't read it."

Zane's face grew warm. "Would you?"

An expression of pain quickly passed over her face. "Why? I know what I believe."

"Touché," Zane said, tucking the book under his arm. He exhaled and then said, "I also wanted to say merry Christmas, to you."

"Denki," she said. "To you too."

"And . . ." He glanced at Trudy. "I hoped we could talk for just a moment. . . ."

Lila turned toward Trudy. "Run down to the pantry and get me a jar of peaches."

She put her hand on her hip.

"Go along," Lila urged.

Trudy complied.

Zane took a deep breath. "I wanted to apologize. I haven't been very kind to you since I've been home."

"Well, you haven't been mean," she said.

He nodded. "But I've avoided you. I'm sorry."

She faced him. "Denki," she said. Her voice was steady, but she looked uncomfortable. She opened her mouth as if to say something more, but the sound of a car door slamming interrupted her.

"It's probably Daniel," she said. "And Simon."

She stepped to the window, the ties of her Kapp bouncing against her collarbone. "They've been in town. Simon wouldn't say why."

Zane felt awkward, as if he were a boy again. He shouldn't have come into the house. He should have found Tim first.

"Is your Dat around?" he asked.

"Jah," Lila said. "In the barn. I'll walk you out." She grabbed her coat as Trudy came marching up the basement stairs.

Someone yelled outside. Lila opened the door and Zane followed her down the steps. Trudy came after him.

Simon stood by Daniel's beater pickup with his hands cupped around his mouth and shouted, "I said I joined up."

Zane stopped at the bottom step. Surely he'd

misheard. But as he followed Simon's path of sight, Zane realized he was yelling at Tim. The man stood in the doorway to the barn, his hand to his ear. Simon had to be joking.

When they were children Simon's favorite song had been "I'm in the Lord's Army." He'd clomp around the field singing it at the top of his lungs, marching and saluting and moving his arms to ride a horse and then fly like a plane. That was Simon. He was just as animated now.

He yelled, "I joined up!" a third time.

"Go talk to him," Lila hissed at her brother. "Don't stand here and yell."

Simon grinned, waved at Zane, and then lumbered toward the barn, calling back over his shoulder. "You didn't think I'd do it, did you?"

"No," Zane muttered under his breath. Louder he said, "And I don't think you did. Why would the recruiting station be open today?"

"It was," Daniel answered. "It's not a federal holiday."

Zane shook his head. "You're kidding."

"Nope. They're only closed tomorrow."

Zane couldn't think of a way an Amish kid could legally hurt his father more. For all the years Tim favored Simon over the twins, look what it had gotten him.

Tim and Simon spoke for a moment, and then Tim hit his hand against the frame of the barn door.

"I'd better go . . ." Zane said, but he was too late. Tim was heading toward him, followed by Simon and then Reuben. Zane glanced at Lila, but she stood frozen in place.

"You did this!" Tim shouted at Zane as he marched toward him.

"No," Zane said, stepping back, the book still tucked under his arm. "I didn't."

"You influenced him."

Zane shook his head. "If I did, I didn't intend to."

"He tried to talk me out of it." Simon hurried to catch up with Tim. "So did Joel, so don't blame the Becks." Simon grinned. "Blame me." Out of all of the Lehman kids he seemed to be the only one who didn't care what his father thought. The only one who wasn't afraid of him.

Rose came over from the clothesline, the empty basket in her hands. Daniel stepped to her side. As Tim approached, he called out to Daniel. "What were you thinking? Taking him to the recruiter."

Daniel squared his shoulders, but his voice wavered. "He said he wanted to go shopping."

Bile rose in Zane's throat. "Get out of it," he said to Simon. "You don't want to do this." True, Tim had been a tough father, but it wouldn't be anything like basic training with a sergeant shouting obscenities and all the other stuff that went on. Simon had no idea just how innocent he really was.

Simon crossed his arms. "It's what I want."

Reuben joined the rest of the group and stepped next to Lila. Zane moved away, marveling at how he'd managed to put himself in the middle of the latest Lehman family drama.

"Get in the house," Tim said to Simon. "You too," he barked at Daniel. "We'll get to the bottom of this." He turned to Reuben. "Go back and finish in the milk room. Lila, go with him. The driver will be here any minute."

Tim glanced at Zane, but he didn't say a word.

Simon reached out and shook Zane's hand. "Don't worry about this. I would have joined whether you'd been home or not."

"You're crazy," Zane answered, shaking his head.

Simon broke into another stupid grin. "*Doppick*," he said.

Zane nodded. "Yeah, this was really dumb." He added, "You're going to need a lot of prayer."

Daniel bumped against Zane's shoulder as he walked by. "Keep your head down," he muttered. "And take care."

"You too," Zane quipped.

Reuben raised his hand in a half wave. Zane gave a nod in return.

"Bye," Lila murmured, not looking Zane in the eye, and then followed Reuben toward the barn.

Trudy gave Zane a hug and hurried up the steps after her father. Rose swayed slightly, the basket

on her hip. She smiled as if oblivious to everything that had just happened. "We'll all miss you,
Zane."

He waved good-bye to her and continued on to
his truck, dropping the book on the passenger seat
after he climbed in.

As he backed out of the driveway, he looked in
the rearview mirror. Reuben reached the barn
door and went on inside. Lila stopped and turned
toward him, waving slightly. Halfway down the
Lehmans' driveway, he had to pull over and wait
for the milk truck to go by. Then he shifted into
first, accelerated, and headed for the highway.

Finally he was on his way, wishing he'd left at
the crack of dawn instead.

5

Lila and Reuben stood side by side outside the
barn as the driver transferred the milk into
the tank of the truck. "Have things been this crazy
around here for long?" Reuben took his hat off
and ran his hand through his dark brown hair.

Lila wanted to laugh. Reuben wanted order and
predictability. Something that was hard to come
by in the Lehman household. "It's just this stuff
with Simon," she answered.

Reuben cleared his throat. "Did Zane come
over much while he was home?"

Lila shook her head. "Not once, until this morning. He wanted to drop off a book for Simon—on his way out." Perhaps she'd never know, besides his apology, what he'd wanted to say to her.

Dat came down the back steps of the house and waved toward the barn. "Go clean out the milk vat," he yelled.

"Come on." Lila tugged on Reuben's arm. They worked on rinsing the vat and then washing it in silence. Sometimes, especially when they were in the buggy, Lila didn't mind that Reuben was quiet. But there were other times when she longed for conversation. He only read *The Budget*, no books, and didn't keep up on world events. Sometimes he talked about what he was building. A bench. Or table. Or cabinet. Every once in a while he'd mention some bit of information he'd heard at the lumberyard, about someone who was ill or had to put their horse down or had lost a crop. He never said it in a gossipy way. He was always sympathetic.

Lila appreciated that—but she still longed to talk about ideas. To learn new things from him. To have him challenge her thinking. Right now, she wanted to talk to someone about losing her best friend, how it still hurt two and a half years later. How it hurt worse today than ever. She wanted to talk about her brother enlisting in the Army too.

Instead they continued to work in silence, and by the time they were done, the milk truck was long gone and Dat was up in the field on the tractor. Lila and Reuben headed to the house.

She hung up her coat in the mud porch and stepped into the kitchen, with Reuben following her. Simon sat at the table, a silly grin still on his face. Daniel sat slumped in his chair, looking forlorn. It appeared they'd been waiting for her.

Simon hopped up when he saw Lila and wrapped his arm around her shoulder. "I told you I'd do it."

"Don't bring me into this," she said, twisting away from him.

"You should tell her to lighten up," Simon said to Reuben. "Live a little. Stop doing everything that's expected of her."

Reuben crossed his arms.

Lila shook her head. Simon knew Reuben was as responsible as she was. If not more so.

"I should get going," Daniel said. "Before Dat tears into me again."

"What did he say?" Lila asked.

"He blamed me for setting a bad example for Simon. Apparently it's my running around that forced him to join the Army."

"Well, and you driving him there," Lila added.

Daniel threw up his hands. "He lied to me—said he wanted to shop."

"This early in the morning?"

84

Daniel glanced at Simon. "Yeah . . ."

"I didn't lie," Simon said. "I was shopping for a new life."

Lila shook her head in disgust. "Dat's not blaming Zane, then?"

"Oh, no. He is," Daniel said. He deepened his voice and in a mocking tone said, " 'I knew nothing good would come from that boy. I've known it for the last ten years.' "

Lila grimaced. "It's only been eight."

"Well, it probably feels like ten to him."

Lila shook her head again. Their father had been perfectly fine with the Beck family all these years, after working through things at first. True, if she and Zane had become any closer he wouldn't have been. But they didn't. Their father appreciated Shani and Joel. He was fine with Trudy playing with Adam.

The Becks had been good neighbors. She hated the thought of Dat revising their history together now, just to blame Simon's foolishness on others.

"Where's Trudy?" she asked.

"Back in your room with Rose. Finishing up some Christmas stuff."

That was what she needed to do too. The day was slipping away, and she still had a lot to do.

"See you tomorrow," Daniel said. "If Dat allows it."

"You're not coming tonight?" Lila asked her twin.

He shook his head. "I'm going to Jenny's."

She didn't blame him. Monika and Bishop Byler were having both of their families over. One big happy blended family. Lila actually wished she could go with Reuben, but she couldn't leave her other siblings and Dat alone. They'd be miserable.

Lila patted her twin's shoulder as he passed by. "See you tomorrow."

Daniel nodded but didn't say any more.

"I should get going too," Reuben said. He'd only stopped by to bring her a plate of goodies from his sister, Sarah, and had then offered to help Dat. Reuben was probably happy to escape too.

He nodded toward the door.

"We'll see you Wednesday," Lila said. Their family would visit Reuben's and then their grandparents on the day after Christmas. She had until then to finish all of those gifts at least.

When Reuben didn't leave, Simon laughed. "Lila, you're so dense. Reuben wants to talk with you. In private."

She glanced up at Reuben. He nodded again. She followed him out the door, grabbing her coat again. More snow had started to fall. She prayed Zane would beat the worst of the storm.

Reuben headed toward the barn, and she followed, hoping he wouldn't want to talk for long. She'd never get her gifts finished and Christmas Eve dinner on the table if she didn't get to work soon.

After he retrieved his horse, they walked back to his buggy. For over two years now they'd been going to singings. Two times he'd brought up marriage, but she'd said she was too young.

"I heard Daniel and Jenny are thinking of marrying soon," Reuben said as he hitched his horse.

"Daniel needs to find a better job. And they'll both need to join the church," Lila replied.

Reuben turned toward her. "When do you plan to join?"

Reuben was five years older than she was and had joined several years ago. "I'll take the class this spring," she said.

A pleased expression passed over his face. "Do you believe we have control over whom we fall in love with?" he asked.

"Of course," she answered. "Love is a commitment, right? We have to choose it."

He narrowed his eyes. "Do you love me, Lila?"

Her breath caught. "Of course." Why did he need to bring this up now?

"Can you tell me?"

"Now?" she blurted.

He nodded. "I need to know if my continuing to wait for you is the right thing to do. I don't want us to court and court and court only to have

87

you change your mind. . . ." His voice trailed off.

He was asking about her love, but he'd never told her that *he* loved *her.* Was he waiting for affirmation from her first?

Anxiety swept through her and she crossed her arms. "Could we wait to talk about this?" she asked. "When we have more time? When I'm not feeling overwhelmed?" She still needed to get the dinner rolls started. And finish her sewing. And get the gifts wrapped.

His face fell. "Of course. I'm sorry."

"Denki," she said.

He sighed. "See you Wednesday," he said as he led the horse and buggy to the driveway.

She nodded and said, "Merry Christmas," and then headed toward the house.

The tears started before she reached the halfway point. She kept her head down as she waved at Reuben rolling by in his buggy, and then ran up the steps, hoping Simon wasn't still in the kitchen.

Of course he was, along with Rose and Trudy.

She hurried on through with her coat still on, hoping they wouldn't notice her face.

"What's the matter?" Rose asked, rising to her feet and following Lila. "Reuben didn't break up with you, did he?"

Lila shook her head and dashed to the bathroom, closing the door and locking it before Rose could follow.

"Let me in," Rose said as she pounded on the door.

"I'm fine," Lila said. "I just need to wash my face." She sat down on the toilet lid and grabbed the hand towel, burying her face in it, trying to keep from sobbing. But it was impossible.

"Lila?"

She didn't answer. She'd hated Christmas since her mother had died. Dat was always in a bad mood. The younger children had expectations she couldn't meet. She did her best to cook the foods Mamm had and keep the traditions, but she always failed.

Having Zane stop by had made her think of all the Christmas Eves the two of them snuck out of their houses and met down at their fort. That had always been the highlight of Christmas for her. She still had the gifts Zane had given her, all tucked away in a box beneath her bed. The bookmark was still her favorite. If he'd stayed another night, would he have visited the fort? Perhaps that was why he left.

If he'd stayed another night, would she have ventured down there, hoping to meet him? She cried harder.

Once she married she wondered if Rose would take over trying to put Christmas together. That made her cry too. Daniel had already left. Simon would be off in the Army. Lila would marry Reuben sooner or later. Everything was changing.

She'd imagined all of her siblings staying close by, all of them having families. That wouldn't happen now. Daniel would become closer to Jenny's family. Simon would be gone. She'd go off with Reuben to his house.

Another sob wracked her.

"Lila!" Rose knocked again.

"Give me a minute," she answered, standing and washing her face. Christmas wasn't the only reason she was missing Mamm. What advice would she have for her about Reuben?

Lila sighed. She knew. All she had to do was look at the choice Mamm made. Instead of marrying Lila's father, she'd picked Dat.

Lila dried her face and finally opened the door, to find Rose still standing in the doorway.

"What is it?" her sister asked in an unusually sympathetic voice.

Lila shook her head.

"If it's not Reuben, then is it Zane?"

Lila started toward the kitchen. "It's nothing," she said. It was everything. Missing Mamm. Christmas. Simon. Reuben asking her if she loved him.

Jah, and Zane.

Lila stayed up late into the night on Christmas Eve, running the treadle sewing machine until Dat stumbled into the living room and told her to go to sleep. She'd finished her gifts for Rose and Trudy, and her fingers were nearly numb from the cold anyway. She'd have to finish the others after Christmas dinner.

"You should have planned your time better," Dat said as he stepped toward the hall.

"Jah . . ." Lila muttered. She hadn't planned for the extra shifts she'd worked in the last week or the drama around Simon joining the Army or how drained she felt after seeing Zane again.

The Christmas Eve dinner had seemed like drudgery. Every year she tried to make things festive for the others, but this year she couldn't seem to manage to drum up any Christmas spirit. Hopefully by tomorrow she'd be able to enjoy their day together.

Before she went to bed she put candy in the dishes Trudy, Rose, and Simon had left on the table. She knew Zane's family filled stockings for Christmas morning, but her family followed a simpler tradition. If only she could simplify her relationships like that too.

Once she was in her room, she shivered in the cold as she pulled her flannel nightgown over her head and then slipped between the sheets of her icy bed, pulling the quilts her Mamm had made up to her chin. Rose stirred in the double bed that she shared with Trudy. Dat believed children should share a room. The bedroom Aenti Eve used to have had been the guest room since she left—except they never had any guests. Sometimes when Lila felt desperate to be alone she would read or do handwork in Eve's old room, but Dat wouldn't have been happy if she made a habit of it.

She rolled toward the wall, her teeth chattering. A tear seeped out of her eye. Rose stirred again, and then Trudy called out in her sleep.

Lila held her breath for a moment, but then Trudy called out again and stumbled from her bed and made her way to the single bed.

Lila threw back the quilts, and Trudy crawled in beside her. Lila curled around her little sister, who immediately fell back to sleep. It had been a couple of years since Trudy had crawled into bed with Lila. Perhaps the conflict between Dat and Daniel and Simon had upset her more than she'd let on. Lila drew closer to the warmth of her sister, whispering, "Merry Christmas," as she drifted off to sleep.

Christmas morning she went through the motions, bleary eyed and yawning, as she made breakfast and then served it. Trudy had already eaten the candy in her dish by the time Daniel arrived midmorning. He ate a leftover slice of ham as Dat called everyone into the living room.

Only Trudy was excited. The rest of them seemed to just be going through the motions. As they all sat down Lila couldn't help but notice there weren't many presents on the table by the door. Although some Amish families had a tree, her family never did. Not even when Mamm was alive.

Lila hadn't talked to Dat about what he planned to buy for everyone. She hoped he'd planned something—not for her, but at least for Trudy, Rose, Simon, and Daniel. Although now Dat probably didn't think Simon deserved anything.

Dat read the Christmas story, and then they all bowed their heads in a silent prayer. Lila tried to concentrate on Jesus coming to earth as a baby, but she kept thinking about Zane. She figured it would take him two days to get to Texas. Did he have a special friend waiting for him when he arrived? Maybe that was why he'd avoided her when he was home. Her face grew warm. She'd been foolish for not thinking of that sooner, but that would be for the best. For both of them. Zane deserved an Englisch girl who could share his life. She'd never begrudge him that.

Finally Dat stirred, ending the prayer, and the rest of them raised their heads.

Trudy rubbed her hands together. "Time for presents!"

Dat frowned. "We give as a reminder of what God gave us," he said. "The focus is not on what we receive."

"I know," Trudy said, scooting back on the couch. "I want to give my presents too."

Dat cleared his throat. "I didn't get gifts for

you three older kids this year," he said. "You're adults now." His eyes landed on Simon for a brief moment.

Lila nodded. That was fine.

Trudy frowned, until Lila asked her to pass the gifts around. All of the children had gotten Trudy a gift, and Dat had bought her a set of mixing bowls and cookie cutters. She was ecstatic. She was thrilled with the apron Lila had made her too.

Rose seemed oblivious that the others didn't have gifts and made a big deal over the set of serving platters Dat had bought her for her hope chest. She was gracious about the place mats and napkins that Lila had made for her also.

Thankfully Lila had bought the boys gifts— T-shirts, socks, and cans of shaving cream.

Trudy had bagged a stack of cookies that she'd made with Shani for everyone.

Simon ate his cookies, marveling at how delicious they were. Trudy giggled and told him she'd make him more with her new mixing bowls. Lila suggested the others play a game while she headed into the kitchen to make the stuffing. Except for Trudy's cookies, no one had given her a present.

After a few minutes, Daniel joined her. "It was a lot of fun at Jenny's last night. We opened gifts and then all sang carols together. Reuben said he wished you could've come along."

Lila shook her head.

"He did," Daniel insisted.

"I'm not questioning that," Lila said. "But who would have made dinner here? Or put Trudy to bed? Or made the gifts for Rose and Trudy?"

"You have a point." Daniel shrugged and then yawned.

"Looks as if you stayed too late last night."

He grinned. "Maybe."

Rose didn't come to help until Lila asked. By then Dat had fallen asleep in his chair and Simon and Daniel had gone outside. By the time dinner was ready, Lila felt frazzled.

Someone needed to find the boys, so she did it herself, thinking a walk in the cold might help her feel more settled. She flung her coat over her shoulder and headed out the back door. The sun remained hidden by the clouds. Even the snow appeared gray, as if the world had lost its color. As she approached the barn, she yelled, "Daniel! Simon!"

The sound of a gun startled her and then filled her with anger. Why were they target practicing on Christmas?

She stepped around the back of the barn. At the edge of the woods, Simon aimed at the target. Another shot. He hit the red center.

"Simon!" she yelled.

He turned, his eyes beady. Daniel stood behind him but started shuffling toward Lila. Simon stayed put.

She shivered. Shooting at a target was one thing. Even a deer. How could he possibly think he could shoot at a person?

"Dinner!" she shouted, and marched back toward the house, thinking of Zane on the road on Christmas Day. She had never felt so lonely in her entire life.

The next morning Dat cornered Bishop Byler in Monika's kitchen as other members of the two families gathered in the living room. Simon had stayed home. Lila stared at the bookcase Reuben had made for her Christmas present. He didn't read—but he'd made a home for the few books she'd managed to collect over the years. She'd given him a runner for his table.

Dat's voice rose. Lila hadn't expected him to talk with the bishop about Simon, but she was guessing that was the topic. It wasn't like her father to talk about family problems, especially not with the bishop. Dat was a private person, but it seemed he was willing to swallow his pride if it meant finding help to prevent Simon from going. At least Simon hadn't joined the church yet, so it wasn't an issue of him being shunned.

Reuben sat beside Lila and inched closer. Monika smiled. For as much as everyone else had pressured Lila to marry Reuben, Monika hadn't. She said she learned her lesson with Eve. It was one of life's ironies, Monika had said, that she

ended up marrying the man she'd tried to force on Eve.

Monika hadn't pressured Daniel and Jenny either. She simply said they needed to rely on God's timing.

"Have another piece of candy," Monika said as she passed the plate of divinity to Lila. She passed it on to Reuben. When Lila was still in school, after Aenti Eve left to marry Charlie, Monika would come over and take care of Trudy and then be around after school for all of the children. Even after she married the bishop she continued to care for all of them, until Lila finished her last year of school. At fourteen, Lila wasn't fully equipped to run a household but she figured it out. By then Trudy was three. She'd always been a compliant child. Rose, on the other hand, at nine, had been more of a handful than Trudy.

Dat's voice grew louder. "You talk to him, then. I've probably said too much already."

Lila turned her head toward the kitchen, surprised at her father's admission. Dat had done his best to portray their family as stable all these years. Thanks to Monika, Shani, and Aenti Eve— when she was allowed to help—the family had survived. But Lila longed for them to be doing well. Especially for Trudy's sake. Lila feared her little sister had no idea what a normal family was like.

97

"What's going on?" Monika asked Lila.

Jenny shot Daniel a look. He'd obviously told her. Lila was surprised neither of them had told Monika.

"Simon," Lila said, as if that explained everything.

It wasn't until Monika asked Lila if she'd like more coffee that she realized she'd drained her cup. She nodded, and Monika was immediately on her feet and headed to the kitchen.

"How about another cup?" Lila heard her ask the men. Then she said, "Come join us. We all want to spend time with the two of you."

Gideon and Dat followed Monika back into the living room. Monika's relationship with her first husband had been especially sweet for an old Amish couple, at least from what Lila remembered. They hugged in public, and Monika was always saying corny things about him. But then he died from a heart attack and a year later she married Gideon.

Even as a twelve-year-old, Lila couldn't imagine that Monika's second marriage would be as good as her first, but it seemed to be. She and Gideon definitely respected each other and though they weren't as affectionate, at least in public, they seemed to deeply care for each other. She was a good support as a bishop's wife, treating people in the district with empathy and concern. Perhaps Monika made such a good wife

to Gideon because of the deep love from her first marriage. Or maybe that was just what kind of woman she was.

Lila doubted that Monika questioned her love for either of her husbands. Most likely she'd simply committed herself to loving them. It gave Lila hope she could do the same with Reuben.

After a while Dat said he'd head on back to the house while the children went to their grandparents' place. "You can go in Daniel's truck," Dat said.

Rose frowned, most likely opposed to being squished in the back seat of Daniel's small cab.

"Will Simon meet us there?" Lila asked.

Dat shrugged. "Perhaps not," he said, giving the bishop a look.

"What about going to Eve and Charlie's?" Lila asked. They always went the day after Christmas. It was the only time all year Dat visited their house.

"I talked to Eve last night. They're going to meet you at your grandparents'."

Lila furrowed her brow, thinking about Dat arranging everything. It wasn't like him.

Jenny stayed at her house—there wasn't room for her in the pickup. Everyone, even Trudy, stayed quiet as Daniel drove south. Their grandparents had moved into a cottage on the outskirts of Strasburg the year before, leaving behind the acreage and old farmhouse. Now they had a big lot, a chicken coop, and a large garden. That was it.

After they'd filed into their grandparents' home, and gotten hugs from each, and then from Charlie and Eve too, Mammi asked where Simon was.

When none of the children answered, Mammi asked, "Is something wrong?"

Trudy wringed her hands. "He's joined the Army."

Mammi gasped. "Has he left already?"

"No," Lila answered, holding on to her coat. The comforting scent of Mammi's lavender talcum powder seemed incongruous with the pain in Lila's heart. "He's at home."

"Dat and the bishop are talking with him," Trudy said.

Lila shook her head. "We don't know that."

Rose elbowed her. "Don't be stupid. Of course that's what they're doing."

Lila ignored her sister and looked past her grandmother. Dawdi, Eve, and Charlie all had worried expressions on their faces.

"Come on and get warm," Mammi said, reaching for Lila's coat. "You must be freezing."

"We rode in Daniel's pickup," Trudy said. It was still a thrill for her to ride in a vehicle.

"Oh," Mammi said. She wouldn't say it, but Lila was sure she felt surprised Dat allowed it—

not for Lila and Rose but for Trudy. He did his best to try to keep her from being influenced by the older kids, but of course it couldn't be helped.

They filed into the cozy living room. A small Christmas tree, decorated with quilted ornaments and bright lights, sat in the corner, and several red candles were lit around the room. The scent of evergreen filled the air.

While the others visited, Lila helped her grandmother put together a light meal of leftover ham, potatoes, rolls, and broccoli and cauliflower salad. Lila's hand shook as she dumped the rolls in a basket. "Sweetie," Mammi said, "is it Simon you're worried about?"

Lila started to nod but stopped herself. "Everything feels upside down."

Mammi placed the last piece of ham on the platter and turned toward her. A strand of gray hair hung from her bun. She looked a little weathered, more so even than a few days earlier. Lila hoped her grandmother could get some extra rest now that the holiday shopping season was over.

"What else is going on?"

Lila pursed her lips. She shouldn't have said anything. "Maybe it's just that I'm tired."

"Maybe you need a rest. Have you thought about the job offer?"

Lila nodded.

"You could live here, with us. In the upstairs room."

Lila hadn't talked to Dat about Mammi's offer. Everything had been too chaotic. But the job was tempting. So was living with her grandparents. After sharing a bedroom all these years, the cottage loft would be an escape. But she couldn't leave her sisters.

"You've been taking care of others all these years." Mammi's kind blue eyes met Lila's and watered just a little. "I would love to take care of you for a while, before you marry."

Lila swallowed the growing lump in her throat.

Mammi turned to the sink to wash her hands. "Do you have an answer for me, then?"

"Jah."

"And?"

Lila swallowed hard, again. "I can't. It wouldn't be fair to Rose. Or Trudy."

Mammi met her eyes again. "It might be good for Rose to be in charge and learn to care for a home."

Lila nodded. That was true. "But it wouldn't be good for Trudy." Or Dat. She didn't want to upset him any more than he already was.

"What will they do when you marry?"

Lila shrugged, her eyes filling with tears.

"Sweetie," Mammi said, clasping Lila's hand. "Does this have to do with Simon planning to leave?"

Lila's gazed drifted away from Mammi and toward the others in the living room. "Jah." But it was more than that. The Army had taken Zane and now Simon. She was terrified that she might lose both of them.

6

Two days after Christmas, Adam played beside the tree with his new Legos as Shani dug her cell phone from her jacket pocket. She checked it again to see if she'd missed a call. Zane had texted when he reached Texas, but she hadn't talked to him since he left.

She headed down the hall to her room as she unlocked her phone and pressed Zane's number. It rang several times before he answered. She sat down on her bed, her gaze falling on the wooded area outside the window.

"Hey, Mom," Zane finally said. "I have you on speaker phone."

"Where are you?"

"On my way to lunch."

"Driving?"

"Yeah . . ." His voice sounded stilted.

"How's Texas?"

"Good."

Back when Zane used to talk nonstop, Shani never thought she'd miss it. But she did.

A woman's voice came over the line, saying, "Turn here."

Zane wasn't alone. Shani smiled.

"Should I call later?" she asked.

"Hold on a second," Zane said.

"It looks like a dive," the woman said. "But the food is great."

The phone clicked, and Shani realized Zane had put her on mute. She stood and stepped to the window. Snow hung on the branches of the evergreen trees and even though it was only mid-afternoon, the wooded area was gray and dark.

The phone clicked again, and Zane said, "I'm back."

"Is it warm down there?" Shani asked.

"Yeah, in the high seventies."

That sounded like a dream.

"What are you having for lunch?"

"Indian food."

Shani smiled again. It had never been his first choice in the past. "Who's the girl?"

"One of the soldiers in my unit."

"Does she have a name?"

"Come on, Mom." His voice sounded light. "Don't get your hopes up."

Shani didn't reply.

"Her name is Casey," Zane finally said. "But she's just a friend. And she went on ahead into the restaurant, just in case you're wondering if she's listening."

"Where's she from?"

"All over. She's a Navy brat."

"And she joined the Army?"

Zane chuckled. "Yeah. Go figure." He cleared his throat and then said, "Listen . . ."

Shani interrupted. "You need to go."

"How'd you know?" he asked, and then laughed a third time. Shani smiled at the thought of him actually being happy. "But first, if you guys really want to come down before I ship out, I'd like to have you take my truck back home."

"Of course," Shani answered. "We'll be there. Text me the dates, and we'll get tickets tonight."

"Thanks," Zane said.

"Tell Casey hello," Shani added, keeping her voice light.

"It's not like that," Zane replied. "Really."

It was Shani's turn to laugh. "I can hope, can't I?"

Zane didn't respond to her question, but instead asked if Simon had been over since Christmas Eve.

"No. Why?"

"Just wondering," Zane said. He quickly added, "I'll call in a couple of days."

"Okay, I'll e-mail you the flight info tonight."

"Bye," he said and hung up before she could tell him she loved him.

As she headed back to the living room,

wondering what was up with Simon, Adam called out, "Eve's here."

Shani quickened her step. That was exactly what she needed to take her mind off Zane. By the time she reached the front door, Eve was walking up the steps, but then she turned. Shani stepped out on the porch and saw Tim marching toward them.

He waved, first at Eve and then at Shani. He wore his long work coat and straw hat. His beard seemed to have more gray in it than the last time Shani had seen him.

Shani waved back to him. "Come on in for a cup of coffee."

"Denki," he replied, quickening his step even more. Shani held the door open for Eve and then for Tim. "Is your father still here? I wanted to speak with him before he leaves."

"He's out back, looking at the apple trees. He should be coming in soon."

"I'll go find him," Tim said.

Adam came from around the Christmas tree. "Can I go out too?" he asked Shani.

"Of course." She turned back to Tim. "Come back for a cup of coffee when you're done. Tell Dad to also."

He nodded and without waiting for Adam went back out the front door.

"Bundle up," Shani said to her son as she led the way to the kitchen. He nodded. He always

106

did. He didn't love the cold the way Zane had when he was a boy. He was so much less daring than Zane was, and she was grateful for that.

As Shani measured the coffee she asked her friend, "How was yesterday? At Leona and Eli's?"

"It was all right, but Tim didn't come over."

"Oh?"

Eve nodded. "Simon didn't come either. He's done something crazy—"

Shani's eyes met Eve's pained expression. "He didn't," Shani said, remembering his jokes about joining the Army.

Eve nodded. "He did."

Shani filled the carafe and then poured the water into the machine. "When did he do it?"

"Christmas Eve morning."

Zane knew. That's why he'd asked if she'd spoken to Simon.

She pushed the Start button. "Why would he do that?"

"You're not playing your role of Army wife very well."

"Ex-Army wife." She grabbed two mugs from the cupboard. "My role now is Army mom. And neighbor. How could Simon do that?"

Eve shrugged. "We haven't talked with him about it—not since he joined."

"Is Tim furious with us?"

"Why would he be?"

"Don't be kind." Shani leaned against the

counter. "Why wouldn't he be? Simon grew up on Joel's stories. It had to have influenced him."

"Joel only answered Simon's questions. Charlie answered his questions too. It's life. No one can protect their children from the world, not even Tim."

"That doesn't mean he won't blame us." Then again, Tim had seemed fine in the way he'd just interacted with her. "When does Simon leave?" Shani asked.

"I don't know. The girls didn't say."

Shani pulled out the carafe and slipped one of the mugs under the stream of coffee, just as Tim and her father came into the house. Her dad was lighthearted. Tim must not have told him about Simon.

She put the coffee on the table for the men and then finished filling mugs for Eve and herself. Shani debated saying something to Tim, but then Adam came in and she made him a cup of hot chocolate.

Tim drained his cup, thanked her father for his input, and then said he had to get back to work.

After Eve left, Shani asked her father what Tim had asked him.

"We settled the lease for another year." Her dad shrugged. "But then he asked if, as a parent, you'd ever done anything I didn't approve of."

"And what did you tell him?"

"Well, that I didn't approve, at all, of you getting married at nineteen. But you were technically an adult."

Shani frowned. "And what was your advice?"

"That I made sure you knew I loved you. That I supported you, no matter what happened. That was my advice to him—to show his love to his kids."

Shani turned toward her father. "He didn't tell you that Simon enlisted?"

Her father's face paled. "No."

Shani couldn't imagine how Tim would incorporate her father's advice into Simon's situation. It would be more like Tim to use shame, not love, to try to win the boy back. And Shani was certain that would never work with Simon.

The next morning, after her father left for the airport, Shani with Adam at her side knocked on the Lehmans' back door, a plate of peanut brittle in her hands. Lila answered, an uncomfortable look on her face.

"We're a few days late," Shani said, "but merry Christmas."

"Denki," Lila said. "I have something for you too." She glanced over her shoulder as a chair scraped on the kitchen floor.

Then Simon said, "I thought you'd already told me what you wanted to say when Gideon was over."

"I've thought of a few more things," Tim said.

Lila's face reddened.

Shani whispered, "Now's not a good time, is it?"

Lila grimaced. "How about if I bring my gifts over in a few minutes? I should get Trudy out of the house anyway."

Shani handed her the plate. "We'll see you whenever you can make it."

When they reached the driveway, the door slammed and Simon pounded down the back stairs. Shani kept walking, not wanting to interfere.

"Wait!" he called out.

She turned.

"Is Joel home?"

She shook her head. "He went in to work today."

"When will he be home?"

"Probably midafternoon." It was the Friday after Christmas. He hoped to come home early.

"I'll be over then," Simon said and then headed toward the barn, or more likely his shooting range behind the barn. Shani had heard him target practicing earlier in the day. She doubted Tim was happy about that either.

Lila and Trudy didn't come over until long after lunch. "Sorry we're late," Lila said, stamping the snow from her boots on the mat inside the door. "Dat needed me to update his books. And we can't stay. I need to get ready for work." She thrust a package wrapped in brown paper and tied with red yarn toward Adam and then the second one toward Shani.

Trudy grinned at Adam. "Lila gave me one too." He pulled a forest green apron, made from the same fabric as Tim's shirts, from the paper.

He smiled back at Trudy and then thanked Lila. She gave him a quick hug and then nodded to Shani's package.

Shani opened it quickly and pulled out a baby blue apron.

"It matches mine." Trudy clapped her mittens together.

"Thank you so much," Shani said.

"They're for when we make cookies," Trudy said.

Shani nodded. "We're going to be baking in style."

Trudy clapped her mittens together again. "Dat gave me bowls and a baking set for Christmas."

Adam's eyes lit up, and then he pulled her around the tree. "Come see my new Legos."

"Could she stay for the afternoon?" Shani asked Lila. "I'll walk her home later."

Lila frowned. "Are you sure?"

Shani nodded. She loved having Trudy visit.

"Denki. I'll tell Rose." Her voice dropped to a whisper. "Things have been—tense around the house. Trudy doesn't seem to notice, but I keep thinking it has to be hard on her."

"Because of Simon?" Shani asked.

"Do you know?"

Shani nodded.

"Jah. Simon and Dat." The girl sighed. "I'm sick of both of them."

After Lila asked Trudy if she wanted to stay—of course she did—she said good-bye and headed back down the steps.

Shani grabbed her coat, buttoning it up as she followed Lila outside. "Is there anything I can do to help?"

Lila turned toward her and her blue eyes watered—maybe from the cold. Maybe not. She shook her head. "Pray, I guess. I'm afraid the conflict between the two of them is only going to get worse before Simon leaves." She sighed and then said, "Dat's always been so fond of Simon. I don't think he ever saw this coming."

"But you did?"

"Well, not this. But something. Simon's the only one of us who doesn't care what other people think." One snowflake fell and then another.

"I've never thought of you caring much about what others think," Shani said.

Lila shook her head and smiled, just slightly. "How could I help but care? I'm Plain. We all care. We're expected to conform and we do. Except for Simon." She turned toward the lane and then called back over her shoulder, "Thank you for having Trudy."

"Thank you for letting her stay. I hope your shift goes well."

Lila nodded, waved, and quickened her step. For the first time Shani wondered what Lila might do with her life without the expectations from her father and community. She would make a great teacher or nurse or accountant. And one day, she'd definitely make a great mom.

When Shani reached the porch, Joel's pickup came around the curve in the lane. She waved and waited. "You're home early," she called out as he climbed out of his cab.

He nodded. "I brought some work home." He grabbed his briefcase and then his cane. "Simon called me."

"I knew he wanted to talk with you. But I didn't think it was an emergency."

"I don't think it is. He just wanted to know when I'd be home. He said he had something to ask me."

"Trudy's over," Shani said, stepping toward the door.

"Simon and I can talk in the kitchen."

She nodded. A moment later, just after Joel had stepped inside, the sound of footsteps bounded across the porch.

"That was fast," Joel said, opening the door to Simon. Shani stepped to Joel's side.

At the bottom of the steps stood Tim, his arms crossed. "Talk him out of it," he said. "I'd do the same for you, if it were your son."

113

"I can't change his mind." Joel glanced from the door to Tim. "I never encouraged this."

"The question is," Tim said, rocking back on his heels, "can you discourage it? Tell him how to get out of it."

Simon faced his father. "I'm not getting out of it. And for one last time, neither Zane nor Joel ever encouraged me to do this. It's what I want. That's it." He stepped around Joel and Shani, into the house.

"I'm sorry," Joel said. "He'd joked about it, but I had no idea he was serious."

"Can he get out of it?"

"Maybe, if he talks with his recruiter. But he'd have to want to do it. He's eighteen . . ."

"Jah, and never more of a boy," Tim said.

"It's cold," Shani said. "Everyone come inside."

Tim shook his head.

"I'll see what I can do," Joel said.

Tim nodded and then turned toward the field. Joel gave Shani a helpless look. She felt the same way. There wasn't anything anyone could say to Simon to change his mind.

7

After Lila's shift at the Plain Buffet ended, she picked up the phone in the back room to call Daniel for a ride.

"I can take you home," Mandy said from the hallway. "I have the car tonight. My dad's tired of picking me up."

The two women bundled up in their coats and rushed out through the empty parking lot to Mandy's car. After Mandy started the engine, she took out her phone. "I just got a Facebook account," she said. "Don't tell anyone." She flashed a smile.

"What's your boyfriend's name?" She held the phone so the screen came on.

"Reuben?"

Mandy laughed. "No, your Englisch boy-friend."

"I don't have—"

"Zane, right?"

"He's not—"

"Is he friends with Simon?"

Lila rubbed her hands together to warm them. "Jah, since we were all little."

Mandy rolled her eyes. "No. On Facebook."

"Simon doesn't have a—"

"There he is. Zane Beck." She held the phone

closer to her face. "He needs to update his privacy settings."

Lila craned her neck.

Mandy turned the phone toward her. There was a large photo of the poplar trees along the creek between the two houses and then a small photograph of Zane. Just a head shot. But below that was a picture of Zane, wearing a gray T-shirt that fit tightly across his chest with *ARMY* across the front, and beside him stood a petite woman. She had on an *ARMY* T-shirt too. Her dark hair was pulled back in a ponytail, and she had a big smile on her face.

"Don't worry," Mandy said. "The girl just posted the photo. Today."

"What?"

"She posted it to Zane's wall. It's not like he put it up there." Mandy turned the phone back toward herself and touched the screen with her finger. "Here's another photo of him and the girl. Casey. From a couple of months ago. She seems to be the only one who posts on his wall." She held the phone up for Lila to see. The photo was taken in front of a brick building. Both wore Army uniforms.

Casey. Lila had been right about Zane having a girlfriend—or at least a friend. Her chest tightened. She focused on keeping her voice even as she changed the subject. "So Simon has one of these accounts?"

Mandy nodded. "I helped him create it last night, on my phone." She touched the screen again. "Oh, look. He stole Zane's cover photo. The little sneak."

Simon's big photo was the same as Zane's—the poplars and the creek. Instead of a headshot, he had a photo of a deer's head—probably the one he shot last fall. Mandy scrolled down. There was a photo of Simon at his shooting range and another one of him by Daniel's truck. Dat would explode again if he knew Simon had let someone take an image of him.

"How did he take the photos?"

Mandy smiled. "On my old phone."

Maybe Mandy and Simon had been hanging out more often than Lila realized. "Is Daniel on Facebook?" Lila asked.

Mandy shook her head. "Not that I know of. If he is, he's not friends with anyone I know." She dragged her finger along the phone again. "You're prettier than she is."

"Than who?" Lila asked.

Mandy squinted. "Casey Johnson. Zane's Englisch girlfriend."

Lila sank back against the seat.

Mandy put her phone into her pocket, and then shifted the car into reverse. "Daniel's having a party tonight. Want to stop by?"

Lila shook her head. Good thing she hadn't depended on him for a ride.

"Just for a minute?"

"No thank you," Lila said.

Mandy laughed. "You're nothing like your brothers."

Lila smiled, just a little. "I'll take that as a compliment."

Mandy turned left instead of right.

"Where are you going?"

"Just a little detour."

Daniel only lived a mile away. Lila shook her head. "I won't go in."

"You can wait in the car," Mandy said. "I'll be fast. Simon has something he wants to give me."

Daniel lived down a side road in a run-down house with three guys on his construction crew. Lila had never been in the house and had no desire to.

Mandy parked alongside another car and left the motor running while she ran inside. Lila could only imagine how Mandy's father would react if he knew where his car was. Lila had met Mandy's parents at the restaurant. Her father wasn't quite as imposing as Dat, but he was definitely cut from the same cloth.

A couple of people stepped out on the porch. Lila squinted through the exhaust smoke that swirled around the car. When the two started down the front stairs she realized one was

Mandy. The other figure, a guy, was leaning against her.

Lila groaned. It was Simon, and he'd obviously had too much to drink. He stumbled a little coming down off the last step, but Mandy supported him. Lila stared straight ahead. The last thing she wanted to do was get out of the car and help. If she didn't make eye contact, they wouldn't expect her to.

Finally the back door opened and Simon slurred, "Hi, sis."

Lila didn't respond.

Mandy opened her door and slid onto her seat. "Guess it's a good thing we stopped by," she said.

"Or not," Lila responded.

"*Ach*, don't be mad." Simon leaned toward Lila, his breath foul.

She plugged her nose. "Fasten your seat belt."

Mandy shifted the car into drive, Simon clicked his seat belt, and Lila kept her hand over her nose.

If he couldn't manage to get out of bed in the morning, she could expect another row between Simon and Dat—that was for sure.

Simon leaned back and said, again, "Don't be mad."

Lila tucked her shoulder up to her face. The moonlight on the snow lit up the fields. Silently she recited a short poem she'd found a couple of years ago in a book of Zane's.

The sun's gone dim, and
The moon's turned black;
For I loved him, and
He didn't love back.

It was by Dorothy Parker, if she remembered correctly. Perhaps Zane had loved her once, but the words were true tonight. They were true every night.

"Do you have any tomato juice at home?" Mandy asked. "That's good for a hangover."

They did, but Lila didn't answer. She wasn't going to involve herself. She kept her eyes on the dark landscape. A dog slunk under a fence. A barn owl swooped down over a field.

Simon didn't say anything more. Maybe he'd fallen asleep.

"Do you work tomorrow?" Mandy asked, turning off the highway and down Juneberry Lane.

"Jah," Lila answered. "The lunch shift."

"I'll see you at the shift change, then," she said.

"I think I'm going to be sick." Simon leaned against the window.

"Hold on," Mandy said.

As she steered the car to the edge of the lane, Simon swung open the door, letting in the icy air. He unbuckled his seat belt and slid out of the car in one move. Thankfully he closed the door behind himself.

Lila looked the other way, into the woods behind her father's house, back where Simon had his shooting range.

As a child, she'd never wanted to grow up, especially not after her mother died. She'd wanted to stay thirteen, the golden year before she was done with school, back when she and her siblings played with Zane every day. When she could run as fast and far as the boys and swing across the creek on the rope. When their whole lives were ahead of them and yet there was no thought past the next day and what they would play.

Simon fell against the door and then opened it and slid back onto the seat. "I feel better," he said.

"You might as well drink toilet bowl cleaner," Lila said. "You're poisoning yourself just the same."

He wagged his finger at her but didn't say anything.

Mandy pulled back onto the lane, and a minute later down the driveway to the house. "Thank you," Simon said to her, "for everything." Lila wondered what else he meant, besides the ride.

Lila thanked Mandy and climbed out quickly, hurrying toward the back steps and then into the house. She made her way through the pitch-black kitchen to the table and felt around until she found the matches and the lamp. After she lit it, she looked around. Rose had mostly cleaned up, but there was still a dirty frying pan on the stove. Lila lifted it and sniffed. Cabbage and onions. She'd rather clean it now than in the morning.

By the time she was drying it, Simon finally came in.

"I feel much better," he said again, much too loudly.

"Hush."

"You hush," he said, grabbing the side of the table. Once he'd steadied himself, he blurted out, "Don't you get tired of always doing the right thing?"

"No," Lila answered. "I don't." She snapped the dish towel toward him and then hung it over the back of a chair to dry. Turning toward the lamp, she said, "Good night."

"I know you still love him," Simon said.

She froze, her hand in midair.

"Jah." His voice rose again. "You're courting Reuben, but you love Zane. How do you live with yourself?"

She spun around and blew out the lamp. He was drunk. He didn't know what he was talking about.

"I know you," Simon said as she started toward the hall. "You've always loved him."

"Stop it," she hissed, turning back toward him even though she couldn't see him in the dark.

"You want to know if he loves you back, don't you?" Simon's breath reeked.

"No." She stepped away. "I don't."

"Sure you do." She guessed he smiled but couldn't tell. "But I wouldn't tell you, even if you asked." Something lit up the room—a flashlight? Too flat. She realized it was a phone. Like Mandy's.

"He has a girlfriend," Lila said, nodding toward the phone but turning her head from his rancid breath. "Mandy showed me the photos on Facebook." The stab of pain in her chest, again, surprised her.

"I doubt it's true," Simon said, stepping toward her. "He didn't say anything about her when he was home. You can't use that as an excuse not to live your own life."

He started for the hall, bumping into her as he passed, the light of the phone bobbing along. "Zane's been much more faithful than you have."

"You don't know what you're talking about," she said.

If he heard, he ignored her. He turned down the hall, bumped against the wall, and then made his way to the bathroom. Lila stayed in the dark kitchen, hoping he wouldn't come back. He didn't. He bumped against the hall wall again and then finally fumbled his way into his bedroom and shut the door.

Instead of going to bed, Lila stepped into the living room and sat in Dat's chair. The moonlight made its way through the window. Trying to distract herself from what Simon had said, she curled up and looked at her hands. In the dim light they reminded her of her Mamm's. Young and worn at the same time. Lila didn't mind the worn look—it meant she worked hard, taking care of her father and her siblings, helping to provide for the family.

She knew her mother had loved Dat, but Lila also knew the relationship wasn't easy for her Mamm. Her mother didn't want to leave the church and marry Daniel and Lila's biological father. "I was a foolish girl to get myself into that position, but always remember God worked good from it," her mother had once said, the only time she talked about it. "And always remember that your Dat truly is your father. He's the one who cares for you."

And he had, in his own way.

All fathers had their struggles, Lila was sure. She knew things weren't perfect between Zane and Joel. She knew there were times when Joel was distant and other times when he didn't try to see things from Zane's point of view—but he was never harsh.

She didn't expect marriage to be easy, but she didn't expect it to be hard with Reuben either. They would be respectful and kind and caring. In the long run, it wouldn't matter that she didn't love him now. She was committed to Reuben. That was what would last.

"How do you live with yourself?"

She was doing the right thing in agreeing to marry Reuben, wasn't she? She didn't really love Zane. She'd had a crush on him when they were young, that was all. Monika had once said that was often what first love was. An infatuation. That's what it was with Zane. Lila was sure of it. Simon didn't know what he was talking about.

The wood stove gave off a little heat but not much. She sank deeper into the chair, clasping her hands around her knees and drawing them to her chest, wishing she had a phone like Mandy's. Not to send Zane a photo but to look at the ones of him from time to time. For a moment tonight, looking at his picture, he hadn't felt as far away. And seeing him with Casey made her face reality.

She sighed and climbed out of the chair. No, it was a good thing she didn't have a phone. She had no business looking at photos of Zane Beck—not even ones of him with another girl.

Lila awoke at five a.m. to Dat yelling at Simon to get out of bed. She rolled onto her stomach and pulled her pillow over her head. A few minutes later, Dat yelled again. Rose groaned and Trudy stirred.

Lila stumbled from the bed. As her feet hit the floor, the icy cold shot up her legs. She fished her slippers out from under the bed, grabbed her robe, and stumbled out into the hall.

She could see Dat by the dim light coming from the lamp in the kitchen, standing in the door-way to the hall, ready to yell again.

"I'll get him up," Lila said. "Go on out. He'll be right behind you."

Dat hesitated but then followed her instructions.

Lila bumped against the wall, rubbed her eyes, stepped to Simon's door, and knocked gently. He didn't respond.

She cracked it open. "Simon."

He still didn't respond, but his bed creaked as he flopped toward the wall.

Lila stepped into the room. It had that boy smell—dirty laundry and crusty socks mixed with sweat, even in the dead of winter. She stopped at his bed and shook his shoulder.

"Go away," he muttered.

"Time to milk," she said.

"Can't you do it?"

"Jah, right. And you'll cook breakfast? I don't think so." She shook him harder. "Get up now."

He groaned.

"It's not going to be any easier in the Army."

"I won't be as dumb then."

"Don't count on it." She shook him again. "Get going. I told Dat you'd be right out."

He slid one leg out from the covers. He still had his clothes on from the night before. "Brush your teeth," she said. "Or the smell of you will frighten the cows."

Once he had his second leg out of bed, she headed back to her room and dressed and then continued on to the kitchen to start the coffee. Simon looked at the pot longingly as he shuffled by.

"You can have some when you're done," she said.

He grabbed his coat but missed his sleeve. Lila stepped to his side and held it out for him. "What made you so sure about joining the Army?" she asked.

He shrugged. "I've always wanted to."

She couldn't even make the simple decision to go work for Mammi. How could he decide so easily to change the course of his entire life?

She pointed to the door. "Get going." He frowned at her but did as she said.

He'd always be her baby brother. She'd felt maternal toward him from when he was little, even though she was less than two years older than he was. She still felt that way—mixed in with feeling infuriated with him too.

An hour and a half later, Simon came in for breakfast and collapsed in a chair at the table. "Give me coffee," he moaned.

"Get it yourself," Lila responded. She might love her brother, but she wasn't his servant.

He grumbled and shuffled toward the counter

as Lila flipped the hotcakes. Simon left his coffee black and staggered back to the table as if he were ninety.

"Where's your cane?" Lila asked.

"Jah, I could use one today." He took a sip of coffee.

"What did Dat say?"

"Who cares?" He took another sip and stared out the window. Lila put the platter of hotcakes in the oven and went to wake the girls.

"I forgot to tell you," Simon said when she returned. "Mammi left a message on the barn phone—she wants you to stop by. She said it's important."

Lila couldn't go to Strasburg today, not with working the lunch shift. She'd have to wait until tomorrow after church.

She turned toward Simon. "When do you leave?"

He shrugged. "The recruiter is supposed to tell me this week."

She and Rose would have to share his milking responsibilities. It was impossible for her to take Mammi's job. She already felt half buried. And it was only going to get worse.

Sunday afternoon, after they'd all returned from church, Lila took the buggy over to her grand-parents'. Trudy had wanted to come, but Lila told her to stay home and rest. The girl had a cold, and Lila didn't want her to get worse.

The day was overcast, but the temperature had warmed up some and the road was slushy, causing droplets of ice to fly against the windshield of the buggy as cars sped by. Lila pulled the horse to the right, onto a side road to take the back way, hoping to save him from being pelted. By the time she reached her grandparents' house shadows were already falling.

She unhitched the horse, put the blanket over him, and then knocked on her grandparents' front door. Finally Dawdi opened it. He wore slippers and a rumpled sweater and seemed a little out of sorts, as if she'd woken him.

"Were you napping?" she asked as she gave him a hug.

"No." He tugged on his gray beard. "Just resting."

"Simon said Mammi left a message."

"Jah," he answered. "She did. Friday afternoon." He turned toward their bedroom. "I'll wake her."

Lila had never known her grandmother to nap. "Is she all right?"

Her grandfather kept walking. "I'll let her explain," he said over his shoulder. "Make yourself comfortable."

Lila sat down in the rocking chair. A cold cup of tea sat on the coffee table next to her grandmother's Bible and a box of tissues. Perhaps her grandmother had a cold too.

Her grandfather left the bedroom and stepped into the kitchen. The water ran for a moment, followed by the hiss of the gas and the burst of the flame, just as her grandmother stepped out of the bedroom. She wore a housedress and her gray hair was in a single long braid, nearly to her waist. Lila had never seen it down.

Her grandmother's hand went to her throat.

Lila stood, alarmed, and hurried across the room. "Mammi? What's wrong?"

When she reached her, Mammi leaned against Lila. "Oh my. You looked like your mother for a moment, rocking in my chair."

Lila's heart pounded as she stood and led her grandmother to the sofa and sat down beside her. She sensed her grandfather watching, but he didn't join them.

"Simon had just been born when she was the age you are now." Mammi's eyes filled with tears. "You've always looked like her, but never more than just now."

Sadness spread through Lila. She knew she resembled her mother. Rose looked like Dat's side of the family while Trudy favored their mother too. Mamm had never told Lila what her biological father looked like. Eve had known him, but she never talked about him either.

"Simon said you called." Lila was eager to change the subject.

"I did." Mammi took a deep breath and then

exhaled slowly. "I had some tests done, before Christmas. I got the last of them back on Friday."

"Tests?"

"Medical tests."

Lila's heart raced. "What kind?"

"A biopsy." Mammi paused. Lila wanted to put her hands over her ears. Her grandmother sighed. "I have breast cancer. I wanted to tell you first, before the other children."

That's what their mother had died from. "What stage?" Lila managed to squeak.

"Four."

Lila wrapped her hands around her grandmother's bicep and clung to her.

"It's not a death sentence," Mammi said. "I'm older than your mother, which in this case is actually a good thing." Lila quickly did the math. Her grandmother had been twenty when Lila's mother had been born. Her mother would now be thirty-eight if she hadn't died. Mammi was fifty-eight.

"Breast cancer usually grows faster in younger women," Mammi said. "And remember your mother didn't start chemo until after Trudy was born." Mammi patted Lila's hands. "Our insurance is good, so we don't have that concern." The Amish didn't buy insurance, at least not most of them. They relied on mutual aid—helping one another out in times of medical emergencies, but as Mennonites her grandparents could buy insurance.

"Your Dawdi will go talk with your father tomorrow and explain. And talk with him about telling Trudy. Rose too."

"Simon's leaving soon."

Mammi nodded. "I'll tell him and Daniel. The three of you are grown now, I feel all right talking with you. But I wanted your father to know before we tell the younger ones."

"All right," Lila said.

Mammi took Lila's hand. "I also wanted to let you know that I shouldn't have pressured you about the job. Before I knew I was ill, I thought having you here would be good. I thought I could spoil you some before you marry and have a family. But I'm glad you declined. I don't want this to be your burden."

A sob rose up in Lila's throat. "Oh, Mammi," she said. "What about the shop?"

"We'll hire another girl. We'll manage. I'll have chemo after the surgery."

"When is the surgery scheduled?"

"It's not yet—first they need to make sure my heart is strong enough for surgery."

Lila leaned closer, breathing in Mammi's lavender scent, still clinging to her arm. "Do you have heart problems too?"

Mammi shook her head. "A heart murmur is all. It's a standard procedure to run some tests."

A rustling from the kitchen stopped the conversation. Dawdi came toward them with mugs on a tray.

As they drank their tea Mammi said, "I asked the doctor, and he said my having cancer doesn't mean it's hereditary. It's a different kind than your mother's."

Lila nodded. She hadn't even thought of that.

Mammi took her hand. "No matter what happens, I want you to know I've had a good life. Losing your mother broke my heart, but you children have brought me so much joy. And I'm grateful to have had this life with your grandfather. I've had the privilege of loving him for forty years." Mammi squeezed Lila's hand. "I pray for that for you and Reuben, for a marriage of love and respect. For years of happiness too."

"Thank you," Lila managed to say, fighting back her tears. She thought about talking with her grandmother about Zane for a split second but decided not to. That would only burden Mammi, and that was the last thing she needed right now. "You've had a good life, Mammi, and you have decades more of it to go."

Mammi squeezed her hand. "I hope so."

Lila left after she finished her tea, and as she drove home she forced herself not to think about what her grandmother had said about loving Dawdi, that it was a privilege. Instead she thought about her grandmother not wanting her to move in with them now—not wanting Lila to care for her.

But that was exactly what Lila wanted to do. She felt more herself with her grandmother. More connected to her mother. More the woman she thought she might have grown into if her mother hadn't died. More confident. Less worried about what others thought.

Mostly though she wanted to take care of her grandmother. She *needed* to care for her. Simon was right. It was time for her to do something *she* wanted.

The day after New Year's, Trudy was well enough to go to school. Lila drove her, lost in her thoughts about Mammi again, trying to figure out how to approach her Dat. It had been three days since she'd spoken with her grandmother, but she still hadn't come up with a plan. She had a goal though—by the time Mammi had her surgery, she wanted to be living in the cottage with her grandparents. She wanted to care for Mammi. It was up to her to make it happen.

Trudy prattled away. "I wonder if the new teacher will really be as strict as everyone says," she said once the school was in sight.

"That's right," Lila said. "I'd forgotten she was starting today."

"Will you come in and meet her?"

Lila squinted into the morning sun. "Sure," she answered and smiled at her little sister.

The new teacher was middle-aged, probably around forty. Her hair was streaked with gray, and she was a little plump. As Trudy turned shy and half hid behind Lila, the woman's hazel eyes brimmed with kindness and dimples flashed as she smiled. "Whom do we have here?" she asked.

Lila took her little sister's hand and pulled her forward. "Tell her your name."

"Trudy Lehman," she answered.

"I'm pleased to meet you," the woman said. "I'm Elizabeth Yoder. But please call me Beth."

Trudy nodded.

"We've been looking forward to meeting you," Lila said. "I'm Trudy's sister. Her other sister, Rose, sometimes brings her and picks her up. And our Dat too."

"Excellent," Beth said. "I look forward to meeting the whole family."

"I have two brothers too," Trudy said. For a moment Lila feared she was going to tell Beth that Simon had joined the Army, but Trudy stopped.

A flash of concern passed through Beth's eyes, as if she just realized that Trudy didn't have a mother. "I have two brothers also," Beth said. "But I bet mine are quite a bit older than yours."

That made Trudy smile.

Beth met Lila's gaze. "Come in anytime you want. Before school, after school, the middle of the day. You're always welcome."

"Denki," Lila responded and then bent down and kissed Trudy's cheek. "See you after school." She headed out the door and then hurried down the steps. She liked Beth. A lot. It would be good for Trudy to have an older teacher—to have someone around the age Mamm would have been if she'd lived.

8

Zane stopped on the sidewalk outside one of the gyms, dreading going in. The Texas sun warmed his face. He turned toward it. It was the middle of January and the forecast was for a high of seventy.

Fort Hood stretched out in front of him. He'd never get used to how flat and brown the landscape was. Like the dry back of a Texas rattlesnake. True, way off in the distance along the horizon were some hills, but they were just as brown. He slipped his cap from his head, shoving it into the side pocket of his uniform as he pushed through the doors into the cavern-like warehouse. Zane's unit and scores of others had to update their paperwork, make sure their vaccines were current, and that all their legal documents

136

were in order before deploying. Squinting, he scanned the signs around the room, found the one for vaccinations, and stopped at the end of the line.

A half hour later, he stepped out of line to try to gauge how much time he had until he reached the front. He'd hardly made any progress. At this rate, it would take all day to check on his shots.

"Hurry up and wait, huh?" Casey said as she bumped into him.

"Yeah," he answered.

She'd pulled her dark hair into a bun at the nape of her neck, the exact same way Lila wore hers—minus the white Kapp. Casey's camouflage cap was neatly folded and slipped into the side pocket of her pants. Just like his. And her neat-as-a-pin jacket was buttoned over her brown Army T-shirt. Camouflage looked good on her. Better than it did on him. She embraced the Army more wholly than anyone he knew.

His first day back from home, she'd said how much she missed him and hinted at an interest in a closer relationship. He'd quickly said that he was very thankful for her *friendship,* emphasizing the word. He'd been relieved she'd only hinted and then dropped it. He didn't want to lose her as a friend.

"How many shots do you have to get?" she asked.

"I think I'm all caught up." He grimaced. "I hope." But he needed to have his paperwork rechecked and approved.

"What are you up to tonight? Reading?" She teased him a lot about how much he read.

He shrugged.

"Want to come out with us? We only have another week until we'll all be forced to become teetotalers." It was another thing she liked to tease him about. That he didn't drink.

He shrugged a second time.

"Seriously, Zane. You should work on shedding your holier-than-thou rep before we deploy." She *was* serious. "You're not endearing yourself to the other guys."

He met her eyes. "Thanks for your concern. I get it. But I'm not going to go to a strip club with them in the name of bonding."

She rolled her eyes. "We're not going to a strip place—I promise. Just one of the local dives. We'll play some pool. It will be fun."

"One problem," he said. "I'm not twenty-one."

She shook her head. "Right. And you're probably the only twenty-year-old on base without a fake ID."

"Was the Army supposed to issue me one?" He smiled. "Because if they were, someone dropped the ball."

"Stop it," she said. Casey had just turned twenty-one, but he was pretty sure she'd had a fake ID before that. "Maybe we could all meet at someone's house. Would you come then?"

"Probably." He saw her point about bonding. He did get a weird vibe that some of his team had a problem with him.

His phone buzzed in his jacket pocket, but he ignored it.

"Go ahead," Casey teased. "I don't mind. I'd do the same to you."

It was a photo from Simon, showing a close-up of his shooting range target—his bull's-eye was practically a black hole. Zane frowned. Simon had been texting him constantly since he got his new phone. Another buzz and a photo of an evergreen tree covered with snow came through.

A pang of homesickness shot through Zane.

"Gonna share?" Casey teased.

He turned the phone toward her, to show her the tree, just as the phone buzzed again.

"Ooh-la-la. This could explain a lot." She laughed.

"A tree?" He turned the phone back toward himself. A profile of Lila was on the screen. She was hanging sheets and clearly didn't know Simon had taken a photo. She had on her heavy coat and a stocking cap on her head. A long blond strand of hair hung down around her face. She wore gloves with the fingers cut out and was pinning a sheet.

"Who is that?" Casey asked.

He clicked his phone off.

"Zane," she teased, "who's the girl?"

"No one," he answered, stepping out of line again. He'd learned not to react to others in the Army. To play it cool. But he didn't want to share anything about Lila with Casey—or anyone else in the Army.

At least Lila wasn't visibly Amish in the photo, thanks to her stocking cap. He couldn't imagine Casey's teasing otherwise. Still, it was obvious there was something different about her. She was hanging wash on the line in January for one thing.

His phone buzzed again.

Casey stared for a moment and then grinned at him.

He sighed.

Another photo. But this time Lila knew Simon was taking her photo, and she was mad. Her blue eyes were wide and so was her mouth. His heart contracted, against his will.

"Gonna share?" Casey stepped to his side.

He clicked the phone off and slipped the phone into his pocket. "Not this one." He sent a silent thanks to Simon. The guy was crazy. Shame on him for taking Lila's picture, but still Zane was grateful for an image of her he could take with him.

Zane changed the subject. "So what else do you still have to do?"

"Write my what-if-I'm-killed letter," she said with a groan.

Zane needed to do that too. Some units waited until they were in-country, but they were required to do it before they left. He wouldn't write much, just how much he loved his parents and Adam. In his opinion, it was a macabre task they were forced to do. No one wanted to think about dying before they'd even left the States.

"So are your parents coming for our send-off?" she asked.

"Yep," Zane said. "How about yours?"

"Nah," she answered. "They're on Maui for a month, looking for a house to buy. I told them not to bother."

Zane frowned. "And they listened to you?"

She shrugged. "It's not like anything's going to happen." Her gaze drifted away, and then she waved.

Another soldier from their unit, Grant, approached, holding his file, along with his sidekick, Wade.

Grant would be in charge of communications while they were in the field and was a solid, handsome guy with an alpha attitude. Wade, on the other hand, was a born follower. As far as looks he could be Grant's brother—both had dark hair, buff physiques from working out every day, and movie-star smiles—but Wade trailed Grant around like a puppy dog. Ironically, he was one of the intelligence specialists in the unit. He'd be tracking relationships between villagers and looking for informants.

"Are we on for tonight?" Grant asked Casey. Zane knew Grant had a wife and kid. He couldn't imagine wanting to leave them for an evening when they were so close to deploying.

She nodded and then said, "Could we all meet at your place?"

He wrinkled his nose. "Probably . . . I'll send you a text."

"Great," Casey said. Then she added, "Zane's gonna come."

"You're kidding?" Grant slapped Zane on the back. "I thought you were too good for us."

Wade nodded in agreement.

Zane laughed and shook his head. "Just too young."

"Seems he didn't get his government-issued fake ID when he joined the Army," Casey joked.

"It's not too late," Grant said. "I have connections, . . ."

"Thanks," Zane said and then muttered under his breath, "but no thanks."

The sun was setting as Zane stopped his truck in front of the house and double-checked the numbers. The place was small but tidy. The lawn, green and mowed. Red, white, and purple petunias bloomed in pots on either side of the door. It was hard to imagine Grant taking the time to do the yard work.

He pulled out his phone and looked at the

photos of Lila one more time. He couldn't help but laugh at the one of her mad. He'd definitely seen that look before; the last time was the night before he joined the Army.

Casey pulled behind him in her Jeep. It was the right house. He grabbed his water bottle—hoping no one would expect him to drink if he had something in his hand—and jumped down, stuffing his phone into the back pocket of his jeans. It wasn't that he was against drinking, theoretically. But he didn't want to, not when he was underage. Plus he'd heard too many stupid stories about soldiers drinking together.

He'd make an appearance to try to connect with others on the team. That was all.

"Howdy," he said to Casey as she climbed out of her car.

She smiled. "Glad you came. Grant bet me fifty bucks you wouldn't show up." Her hair hung halfway down her back, and she wore a tank top, shorts, and flip-flops. Her pink toenails sparkled. "How about some help?" She nodded to the back of her rig.

He followed. She lifted the hatchback and nodded at the case of beer. Next to it was a jumbo bag of tortilla chips and a rectangular container.

"I didn't bring anything," Zane said.

"Don't worry about it. You're with me." She smiled again. She smelled good, like lilacs or something, maybe. He'd bought Lila some lilac

143

hand lotion one Christmas. He grabbed the beer and followed Casey into the house.

Grant's wife was named Donna. She seemed pleasant enough but not exactly happy to see all of them. She had a toddler on her hip, and it looked as if maybe she was expecting another baby. Zane didn't say anything though. He'd hate to be wrong.

He held the case of beer under his arm and his water bottle in his hand and reached out his other hand to shake hers. When he tousled the baby's hair, both the little boy and his mother smiled.

"Can't believe you came," Grant said to Zane and then frowned. Zane hoped Casey wouldn't make him pay. He motioned toward the beer. "Put that in the kitchen."

A couple of the other guys from his unit, including Wade, and one of the gals had already arrived and were playing Grant's Xbox. They barely glanced up as Zane followed Casey into the kitchen. The floor plan of the house was open, with a straight view from the living room into the kitchen.

Zane opened the fridge. There was another case of beer in it but not much food. A plastic gallon of milk with a couple of inches left, three jars of baby food, some grapes, and a bunch of condiments.

Casey took the lid off her container. It was one

of those layered dips, like his mom made sometimes. He'd eaten before he came, expecting there wouldn't be much food, but the dip looked good.

He took a sip from his water bottle. "I see you brought your own," Grant said.

Zane held up the water bottle. "I guess you could say that."

Grant's wife came into the kitchen, put the baby in the high chair, and took one of the jars of baby food from the fridge.

Casey stepped to the woman's side as she sat down in front of the baby and started feeding him.

"Will you stay on base while we're gone?" Casey asked.

Donna nodded. "My family's back in Michigan. But there's no place for us to stay there. My mom has a little apartment and my dad's living up by the border, out in the woods."

Grant drifted into the living room, a beer in his hand, and collapsed onto the couch.

"How old is your little one?" Zane asked Donna.

"Fourteen months. He's about done with baby food. I just give it to him at night now—helps him sleep better."

"Hey, babe," Grant yelled from the other room. "Could you bring us those chips? And dip?"

She shook her head but stood and handed Casey the jar. As Donna grabbed the chips and dip from the counter, Casey gave Zane a look of panic. Once Donna was out of the kitchen, she turned to Zane. "What am I supposed to do with this?"

"Hold it," he said with a laugh, but the baby started to cry.

"Here," he said, taking the jar from Casey and sitting down in the chair. He used to love feeding Adam when he was a baby. He dipped the spoon in the jar—definitely squash—and flew it around for a moment. The little boy stopped fussing and followed the spoon with his eyes. "Here it comes," Zane announced.

The baby opened his mouth, took the bite, and smiled.

"Where'd you learn that?" Casey asked.

Zane shrugged and loaded the spoon.

"You have all sorts of secrets, Zane Beck." She stood behind him. He wished she hadn't worn the lilac fragrance.

Before he knew what was going on, Casey had slipped his phone from his pocket.

"Hey," he said, keeping his cool. The phone was locked. She couldn't see anything. He kept on feeding the baby.

"Don't you lock your phone?"

Had he not locked it before he shoved it into his pocket? Still he didn't react. But he did say, "Don't you mind your own business?"

"There's the photo I was looking for," she said. "I've been thinking about it all day." She

146

paused a moment and then laughed. "There's another one."

Zane winced, feeling as if he'd just betrayed Lila.

Casey stepped to his side. "Who is she?"

He didn't make eye contact as he slid another spoonful of food into the baby's mouth. "A neighbor, from back home."

"It's from a 'Simon.' "

Zane shook his head. "That's her brother. He was obviously tormenting her." Casey just didn't know how badly, since Lila probably had never had her photo taken before.

Zane ignored the footsteps coming into the kitchen. "Look, he's good with kids too," Grant said in a sarcastic voice.

Zane kept feeding the baby.

"What do you have?" Grant asked Casey. "Zane's phone?" Excitement filled his voice. "Did you find something incriminating?"

Casey shook her head. "Of course not."

"Let me see." As Grant snatched the phone from her hand, Casey gave Zane a panicked look.

He shrugged and kept feeding the baby. There was nothing to be done. Grant zipped through the photos. Zane didn't have many on his phone. A few of Adam. One of his parents with his grandfather. One of the old fort down by the creek, from when he was in high school.

"Get a life, Beck," Grant said as his wife came back into the kitchen.

Grant must have backtracked to the photos of Lila because his wife said, "She's Amish, isn't she?"

"Amish?" Casey met his gaze. "But she doesn't have a bonnet on."

"It's cold out," Grant's wife said. "That's why she has a stocking cap on. But who else would hang sheets on a line in the snow?"

Casey stepped closer to the phone and looked again. "Is she?"

"Yep," Zane said, scooping out the rest of the baby food. "All my neighbors back home are Amish. Could I have my phone back, please?"

Casey took the phone and slipped it back into his back pocket, pushing a little too hard.

"Wow, no wonder you're so weird," Grant said. "You have an Amish girlfriend."

His wife punched his arm as she said, "Knock it off."

"Hey, guys . . ." Grant called out as he headed back into the living room.

"Sorry." Casey seemed genuinely regretful. "*Is* she your girlfriend?"

Zane kept his voice even. "No. They're pacifists." Nonresistant, the correct term, wasn't a word most people understood. Pacifists didn't believe war was justified. Nonresistant meant not fighting back or resisting authority at all—

not even if it was justified. "And I'm in the U.S. Army, right?"

Casey nodded, but she had a puzzled look on her face.

"She was never my girlfriend." Not technically anyway. "We were friends."

"But not anymore?" Casey asked.

"Yeah."

"What happened?"

Zane shrugged. "We grew up."

"I lived close to an Amish settlement back home," Donna said. "They kept to themselves, but they were good people."

"Yep, they are." Zane stood and put the jar and spoon on the counter by the sink. "Your baby is a lot of fun."

"Thanks. He'll become a big brother while you're all over there." She wiped the baby's mouth with his bib, lifted him from the high chair, and patted her belly. "I'm due in July."

She wasn't as far along as he'd expected. "Congratulations," Zane said.

"Yeah, well . . ."

Zane hoped Grant would be able to get back for the birth, but he didn't want to say anything. It wasn't his business.

Casey headed into the living room.

"The Amish girl is really pretty," the woman said. "She looks like she has a lot of spunk."

Zane nodded but didn't say any more. Donna

seemed nice, but he didn't want to talk about Lila with her. Or with anyone. He followed Casey into the living room and ate some chips and dip. He watched a round of Mortal Kombat that Grant and Wade were playing and tried to stifle a yawn. Next he stood beside Casey while she chatted with another one of the women in the unit. Finally he said he had some paperwork he needed to do for the next day and slipped out the front door.

He didn't allow himself to look at the photos of Lila until he reached his room. He knew he should delete them. He had no business having her image on his phone. She wouldn't want that, not at all. But he couldn't do it. Instead he texted Simon back and thanked him for sending the pictures.

A week later, as Zane leaned against a wall inside the base Burger King, waiting for his lunch, he pulled up a new, blank e-mail on his phone and typed in Lila's old e-mail address. When he was a junior in high school they'd managed to meet at the Strasburg public library and Zane had made an e-mail account for her and then sent her a message. He talked her through the steps to pull it up, answer it, and resend.

A couple of times, before they stopped talking, he'd sent her messages. The first one she had answered in five weeks—the next time she'd gone to the library. The second one she hadn't answered at all.

If he sent her one now would she answer it? He could wish her a happy birthday before he left.

He closed his e-mail account. That was a stupid idea.

His parents and Adam were on their way, and Zane needed to leave to pick them up at the airport. He'd just stopped to grab a burger. As his number was called from the counter, Casey stepped through the door.

"Hey!" She waved. "I thought you were on your way to the airport."

"I am," he said. "I'm grabbing something to eat first."

"I hope I'll get to meet your family," she said.

He stepped up to the counter. "You will," he answered over his shoulder. He'd just have to make sure Mom understood that he and Casey really weren't dating.

"What are you doing here?" He turned toward her, his bag and drink in his hands. She didn't eat fast food. He'd heard that from her a hundred times in the last year.

She nodded toward the parking lot. "I saw your truck."

"Oh." He followed her to the door. "Did you need something?"

She shook her head. "I just wanted to say

151

hello." She waved and started to her Jeep. "See you soon."

"Yeah," he said. He liked Casey, a lot. It felt as if she was the only one in their unit he could count on to have his back.

After he finished his burger, Zane popped one of his Pashto CDs into his stereo and responded to the questions as he drove. "Where is your leader? How many weapons do you have? Where do the Taliban live? Do they cross the border into Pakistan?"

It wasn't a tourist's list of phrases—that was for sure. No asking about the bathroom or a cafe on this CD.

As he neared the airport his phone buzzed.

He clicked on Speaker and said hello.

"It's me," Adam said. "We just landed."

"I'm almost there, Bub," Zane answered. "See you in a few minutes." His heart raced as he turned toward the airport. To think he originally hadn't wanted them to come. He slowed his truck, grateful his parents had persisted.

Once they had the luggage stored in the back, Zane's father climbed up front with him. Mom and Adam sat in the back seat of the cab. Adam hadn't had the privilege of all the road trips Zane had as a kid, crisscrossing the U.S. as the Army transferred the family around. Adam had flown out to Oklahoma when Zane graduated from basic training, but besides that he hadn't seen much of the country. Driving from Texas to Pennsylvania would be a lot of fun for him.

"Zane?"

"Sorry, Mom. What did you say?"

"I asked if we'd get to meet Casey."

He groaned. "Only if you promise to behave. There's not anything between us, honest. I don't want you getting ideas." He didn't want Casey getting any either.

Before they reached the security checkpoint at the base, Zane's phone buzzed. He ignored it.

"Do you remember being here before Dad deployed?" Mom asked.

He nodded. He, his dad, and Charlie had thrown a football around. It was the last time he'd played catch with his father. He'd played a few times with Charlie after they moved to Pennsylvania, but it wasn't the same. Dad had wanted him to play football in high school, but Zane didn't have any interest in it. Instead he ran cross-country.

Zane handed his ID, and his parents' too, to the MP as his phone buzzed again. It was Simon, sending more photos of his shooting target. Once Zane had his ID back, he shoved his wallet back into his pocket and continued on.

"What's the word on Simon?" he asked.

"He's leaving for basic next month," Dad said.

"How's everything going . . . with that?"

Dad sighed. "Well, Tim's not happy, of course. And it's going to mean more work for the girls."

Zane nodded. He'd thought of that.

Adam chimed in, "And their grandma's sick."

Zane caught Mom's eyes through the rearview mirror. "What's wrong?"

"Cancer," Mom said.

Zane's stomach flipped. "What kind?"

"Breast."

"Oh, no." Before he could stop himself he asked, "How's Lila?"

"Worried," Mom answered. "She hopes to move in with Leona and Eli and help, if she can figure out her other responsibilities. It's too much for someone who's not even twenty."

She was almost twenty. Another week.

"You were a mom by the time you were her age," Dad said over his shoulder.

"That's right," Mom responded. "And Lila's mother had three babies at that age. But I'd bet Lila still has more responsibility than either one of us did. She waitresses. She does Tim's books. She's the primary caregiver for Trudy. She oversees everything in the home—meals, laundry, gardening, sewing . . ."

Zane shivered involuntarily. "Rose helps."

"Sure," Mom said. "But Lila's the one who's responsible."

"Maybe if she moved in with Leona and Eli she'd get a break," Zane said.

Mom didn't answer for a long moment, but she finally said, "If caring for someone with cancer would be a break, then something is not right for that girl."

Zane didn't respond. He turned left, past the Burger King.

"I'm hungry," Adam said.

"We'll get some food soon," Zane said.

Because Dad was retired Army, he was able to get a room reservation at the on-base hotel. Once they were checked in, Zane helped carry their luggage to their room, and then they headed back out to the parking lot. His parents wanted to go to a sit-down restaurant, not a fast-food place.

"Sounds good," Zane said. He didn't mind eating again. As he pulled around toward the street, Casey turned into the parking lot. She pulled up to his pickup and rolled down her window. "Hi," she said. "I was just at the PX, picking up a few last-minute things." She smiled past him.

"These are my folks," Zane said. "My dad, Joel. My mom, Shani. And my little brother, Adam."

"Hi," Casey said, waving her hand and smiling again. "Pleased to meet you."

"We were just going to go eat," Mom said from the back seat. "Want to join us?"

Casey looked at Zane. "Sure," he said.

"All right. I'll follow you."

"Want me to drive so you can ride with her?" Dad asked, thankfully in a low voice.

"No. This is fine," Zane answered, pulling

155

forward. Once Casey had turned around, he glanced in the rearview mirror at his mom. "But remember, Casey and I are just friends."

She nodded, but he doubted she believed him.

9

Shani liked Zane's friend. Before they ate lunch, Casey bowed her head respectfully as they prayed and even added an "Amen." Then as they enjoyed their salads and sandwiches, Casey asked how their flight was, asked Adam about school, and disclosed that she was a little nervous about their deployment but happy to be able to apply all she'd learned.

As she finished the last of her salad, she leaned toward Shani. "Zane said you have Amish neighbors."

"That's right," Shani said. "We've lived next to the Lehmans for eight years now."

"Trudy's my best friend," Adam said.

"Oh?" Casey responded. "How old is she?"

"I just turned eight," he said. "And she'll turn nine next month."

"Cool," Casey answered. "So she's not the one I saw the photo of." She elbowed Zane.

Shani tensed. "They don't do photos . . ."

"Simon sent it," Zane said. "He was being a smart aleck—like usual."

"Of who?" Shani asked.

"A really beautiful young woman," Casey said. "Blond hair. Blue—"

"Must be Lila," Adam said. "She's Trudy's big sister."

Casey grinned and elbowed Zane again.

He grimaced, and Shani wondered what was wrong.

Joel cleared his throat and said, "Do you know what route you'll take? Through Ireland and on to Kazakhstan?"

Zane shook his head. "Do you think they tell us stuff like that? It's not like it matters."

"Well," Joel said. "It's always good to know what to expect."

"Dad hurt his leg in Iraq," Adam said to Casey.

Her dark eyes filled with concern. "Really?"

Adam nodded.

"What happened?" Casey asked.

"An RPG hit our Humvee, back in 2004," Joel said. For years he didn't offer up information about the attack, but the longer he worked with veterans, the easier it became for him to talk about it.

Casey didn't elbow Zane this time. Instead she turned toward him. "Why didn't you tell me?"

He shrugged. "It never came up."

She wrinkled her nose and turned back to Joel. "My dad flew missions over Iraq way back in Desert Storm. He was Navy. He retired before Operation Enduring Freedom started though."

"I worked with some Navy guys over there. In fact," Joel said, "I used to tease Zane when he was little that if he was going to join the military he should join the Navy. Or the Air Force. But he didn't listen to me."

Casey smiled. "Well, I hate the water. There's no way I was going to join the Navy. The thought of being on a ship for six months was more than I could stand."

The conversation continued about the military and the upcoming deployment. "I'm excited," Casey said. "I'll be part of an FET—a female engagement team. There will be four of us who will work with the women in the village on safety, hygiene, and hopefully education. There will be a team in the other group too."

Shani felt good about the work they'd be doing soon. The endeavor, including Zane's part as a translator and Casey's work with Afghan women, made her feel more positive about the deployment.

After a while Casey said she should get going and pulled a twenty from her wallet.

"No," Joel said. "Our treat."

"Oh, thank you," she said. "It's been so fun for me to spend time with a family. I'm the youngest of three, and we don't get together much anymore." She slid out of the booth. "See you soon," she said, smiling at Zane.

He slid out too and stood. "Thank you for joining us."

She brushed his shoulder with her hand and thanked Joel again and told all of them how nice it was to meet them. "I'll see you soon," she added.

After she left the waitress brought the bill and Joel went up to the counter to pay, with Adam tagging along.

"She's nice," Shani said. "I really like her."

Zane nodded.

"Does she go to church? Or the chapel on base?"

"Some," Zane said. "It sounds like her family went to church while she was growing up."

"Well I think she's delightful."

Zane shook his head.

"What?" Shani asked.

"We're just friends," he said. "Army buddies. Nothing more."

"Is there someone else?"

"Mom, I'm going off to war. And I'm not even twenty-one. I still have plenty of time to find a girlfriend."

She nodded. "I just feel . . ." She wasn't sure how much more to say.

"What?"

"Like you had your heart broken . . ."

He shook his head again. "I'm fine."

"And I worry about you, going off to Afghanistan. I want you to have someone to talk with."

If only he could talk with Lila when he was

overseas. She would be able to help him process what he was feeling.

He shifted his gaze toward the front of the restaurant.

"I mean, I hope you'll tell Dad and me what you're going through. But you haven't much, not for the last couple of years, and . . ." Shani's voice trailed off.

He pursed his lips.

Had she said too much?

She sighed. "How often do you think you'll be able to communicate with us?"

"I don't know," he said. "I should be able to e-mail when I'm on base. And I should be able to use my phone while I'm over there—just to make calls. I set up my plan that way."

Shani said, "Don't worry about what time it is for us. Call whenever you can."

He nodded.

He turned toward her again. "I know this isn't easy for you," he said. "Especially after what we—you—went through with Dad. But I'll be all right. Please don't worry."

She couldn't explain to him that it felt harder to let him go. That was why she wished he had someone special to confide in. She hoped he and Casey at least had a friendship that would offer support for Zane. And Casey too.

But along with everyone else in his life, Zane seemed to hold Casey at arm's length. He had

been polite and cordial during lunch, but that was all.

"When are Casey's folks coming?" Shani asked.

"They're not," he said. Then he quickly added, "She's fine with it."

"Isn't she close to them?"

"Close enough, I think. Her older brother and sister are in the service too. I don't think it's that big of a deal in her family anymore." He shrugged. "Besides, she plans to make a career of this so they'll have another chance."

It was hard for Shani to imagine that it wasn't a big deal to Casey's folks, but Zane was her firstborn. Maybe that was the difference.

The next morning the weather turned cold, so instead of holding the deployment ceremony outside, it was moved to a gym, where the friends and family sat on bleachers. There were around thirty in Zane's unit. They marched in, wearing their fatigues, and then stood in formation.

Joel took her hand as Shani's heart swelled at the sight of Zane. He stood with his arms close to his sides, straight and tall. He'd gotten a haircut the evening before—it was as short as she'd ever seen it. Casey was two rows ahead of him, perfectly poised too.

Their commander approached the microphone and said, "At ease." He was a captain and look

161

much too young to be in charge. Or maybe she was getting old. The soldiers put their hands behind their backs and relaxed a little. He spoke for a few minutes about their mission. They'd be providing infrastructure, health care, and domestic support to the Afghan people, hoping to win their hearts and minds away from the Taliban. Zane's language skills would definitely be needed.

A woman sitting below their family bounced a baby, probably around one, on her lap. After a few minutes, she held him up to her shoulder. He raised his head up and grinned at Adam, who began playing peek-a-boo with the little one. The woman turned to see who was there and then smiled in relief. "Thank you," she mouthed to Adam. Shani patted him on the leg.

After a short speech the band played the "Army Song."

Shani sang the words in her head:

"March along, sing our song, with the Army of the free.
Count the brave, count the true, who have fought to victory . . .

. . . For wher'er we go,
You will always know
That the Army goes rolling along."

Zane used to sing the song when he was little. He'd heard it a dozen times from the ceremonies he'd been to before Joel was injured. She couldn't help but get a little teary eyed thinking of him as a little guy singing words that meant nothing to him at the time. Now he was all grown up and one of the brave.

Once the music was done, the group was dismissed. Shani told the woman how cute her baby was and then asked who her soldier was.

"Specialist Turner. Grant is his first name." She nodded toward the middle of the gym. "He's the one coming toward us." A solid-looking guy who looked to be a few years older than Zane was headed their way.

"Who is your soldier?" the young woman asked.

"Zane Beck," Shani said as Joel stood, leaning against his cane.

"Oh, I know him," the woman answered. "He came over to our house." She stood and shifted the baby to her hip. "You're the ones with the Amish neighbors."

Shani nodded, thinking of Casey's comment. Funny what people remembered.

"Zane's a great guy."

Shani smiled as the woman's husband approached.

"These are Zane's parents," she said.

Joel stuck out his hand to the soldier. "Joel and

Shani Beck—and Zane's little brother, Adam."

"Grant and Donna Turner," the soldier said. "And Alex."

"Pleased to meet all of you," Shani said.

Joel and Grant started talking, Adam tickled the baby's foot, and Shani asked Donna if Grant had been deployed before.

She shook her head. "This is his first time."

"Do you have support here?"

"Some." She patted her belly. "I have another baby on the way—due in July—so we'll see how that goes."

As they chatted, Shani told her a little about Joel's deployment to Iraq and how much Skyping helped.

"Was he injured there?" Donna asked.

Shani nodded as Casey approached them, saying hello to Donna and then Shani and Adam.

Zane approached but stood back a little, until Shani said, "Come here."

He complied, and she gave him a hug, which he endured. "What now?" Shani asked.

"How about if we all go get something to eat?" Casey said. "Our last meal, so to speak. We could go to that barbecue place off base."

Shani nodded in agreement. Zane had joined the men's conversation. Another soldier joined the group too, positioning himself next to Grant.

Shani touched Joel's shoulder and said, "Sorry to interrupt, but would you all like to join us

164

women and Adam for some Texas barbecue?"

"Sounds good," Grant answered, and Joel smiled and nodded.

Zane introduced the other soldier to her as Wade. He seemed like a nice guy too. He shook her hand warmly as he smiled and said, "I'm very pleased to meet you, ma'am."

Zane didn't say anything as they walked to the parking lot, not even when Adam caught up with him and grabbed his hand. Once they reached the pickup Zane said, "I hope you don't have the idea that my unit is one big happy family, because it's not."

"Casey sure seems nice."

"She is . . ."

"And Grant and Wade seem likeable."

Zane shook his head. "They're not."

As she climbed into the back seat Shani said, "Well, Grant's wife is lovely."

"Yeah," Zane said. He didn't say it, but Shani was pretty sure his tone implied he couldn't figure out why she married Grant.

The next morning they told Zane good-bye in front of his barracks. Adam hugged him long and hard. When he finally pulled away, Zane tousled his brother's hair and said, "Send me e-mails, Bub. And hopefully we can Skype."

Shani hugged him next, followed by Joel. After he was done, Joel stepped back. "I know we haven't always seen eye to eye, son, but I hope you know how proud I am of you."

"Thank you." Zane said. "I signed up for all the wrong reasons, but I'm excited about this assignment. I hope I can make a difference."

Joel nodded. "God has a plan for sending you. We'll hold on to that when we're worried."

Zane put his hand up. "I'm not worried, and I don't want any of you to worry either." He wrapped his arm around Adam. "Especially not you, Bub."

He pulled a large manila envelope from his backpack and handed it to Joel. "Would you keep this for me? The title to my truck is in there—and other stuff."

Joel nodded. "I'll give it back when you get home."

Zane grabbed his duffel bag and headed toward the bus where the others were congregating. Donna, with Alex in his stroller, stepped to Shani's side as both Grant and Wade followed Zane.

Shani asked Donna how she was doing.

"Not so good," the young woman said. One of her hands clutched the handle of the stroller and the other was cupped around her stomach.

Shani put her arm around Donna and squeezed her shoulder.

"Thanks," Donna whispered.

The soldiers fell into formation. A few minutes

later, they marched toward the bus. Besides Zane, Shani kept her eye on Casey and Grant. None of the soldiers turned to wave as they boarded. Shani tried to swallow the lump in her throat.

Shani, Joel, and Adam stood, alongside Donna and Alex, until the bus rolled away. Once the bus was out of view, they all said subdued good-byes and then Shani watched Donna push Alex to her car.

Finally Joel asked, "Shall we go?"

Shani nodded, knowing if she spoke she'd cry, which she didn't want to do. Once Joel was injured and then retired, she never dreamt she'd go through sending off someone else she loved to war. Even when Zane joined the Army, she hoped both wars would wind down and he wouldn't have to go anywhere.

Adam ran ahead.

"What's in the packet?" Shani asked Joel.

"You know."

"No . . ."

Joel's eyes watered. "His will. A copy of his orders. Insurance stuff. And, like he said, the title to his truck."

"Oh," Shani said. She remembered now.

After stopping by the hotel, loading their luggage, and checking out, they headed east.

"It's so flat," Adam said, his nose pressed to the window. "And brown."

"Not all of Texas is like this," Shani said.

"I miss home," he said.

Shani nodded. She did too.

By the time they turned north, onto the interstate, Adam had fallen asleep.

"I hope I didn't pester him too much," Shani said.

"Zane?" Joel asked.

She nodded.

He didn't respond.

She leaned toward him, brushing against his shoulder. "Did I?"

He smiled. "Maybe a little."

She sighed. She was so used to coordinating everything at home. It was hard to stop.

"Zane's always needed his space, right? He's never wanted our opinions or our ideas." Joel shook his head. "When he began criticizing the wars, I should have just listened instead of challenging him."

Shani patted his forearm.

"I felt bad—as if my injury was for nothing. Even worse, I started dwelling on Samuel's death again." Joel grasped the gear stick, as if throwing it into reverse might change what had happened. Samuel had died in the same attack that injured Joel. "Zane really knew how to push my buttons," Joel said. "Instead of realizing that and working through things with him, I told him he wasn't soldier material, which I'm sure contributed to him joining." Joel shook his head. "Isn't that ironic? I didn't intend that at all."

She knew he didn't. "You apologized to him. Remember?"

He nodded. "But the thing is . . ." Joel said, "he turned out to be a fine soldier."

"He takes after you in that," Shani said.

Joel frowned. "I'm sorry." He let go of the gear stick and reached for her hand.

"Don't be," she said. "It's life."

Joel sighed and then said, "When Zane was born I always imagined him playing football, but he didn't. And I doubt Adam will either."

Shani nodded. "Does that bother you?" Joel had been a football hero in his small Wisconsin town, growing up.

"No, not at all. I'm just saying what I imagined, you know—way back when." He let go of her hand, passed a semi, and then pulled back into the right lane. "I never imagined Zane joining the Army, I never even wanted that for him. It didn't fit his personality at all—even though he's become a good soldier. Now here he is, going off to war."

Shani waited for him to explain further, but when he didn't, she asked, "What are you saying, honey?"

"Just that it's not about us, is it? It's about them. Who God created them to be. I just wish I hadn't interfered."

"But God is using Zane being in the Army,"

169

Shani said. She hoped Zane appreciated who God had made him to be.

Joel ran his hand over his mouth. "I just can't bear the thought of anything happening to him."

Fear clenched her heart again. "Unfortunately that's one thing that neither of us can control."

10

Lila sat beside Jenny in the shed on her friend's farm during the Youngie singing. It was chilly, and Jenny's Mamm and Gideon had put propane heaters around the benches.

Reuben sat across the aisle from her. They hadn't finished the conversation from Christmas Eve yet, but she expected they might tonight. She'd been twenty now for almost a week. But before she thought seriously about marriage, she needed to take care of her grandmother. The doctors finally determined Mammi was strong enough for surgery, and it was scheduled for a week from Friday. Lila had a plan to go take care of her grandmother, but so far could find no way to implement it. She could see to Dat's books at her grandparents' house, and she'd wanted to suggest that he hire someone to help with the milking after Simon left, but she knew they couldn't afford it. Especially if she took time off from her restaurant job. Simon was complicating her life far more than she could have imagined a few weeks ago.

On the men's side of the room, directly across the aisle, Reuben sat between Daniel and Simon. A couple of times, Lila caught Daniel stealing a look at Jenny and once Reuben turned his head and smiled at her, his eyes kind.

Simon, on the other hand, had his eyes on a group of girls who were a year younger than he was. Lila wasn't sure why he'd come at all. He was leaving for basic training in two weeks. It wasn't as if he'd court a girl between then and now, and besides it seemed as if he were going out with Mandy. Not courting, that was for sure. Lila was sure he had no intention of marrying her—at least not in the next four years. But maybe they were dating, in a casual way. Lila didn't understand Simon, not at all. Both his upcoming exit from their home and his current presence at the singing only added more drama to their family and the community, something they could all do without.

As the group sang the final words of "How Great Thou Art" Jenny elbowed Lila and said, "Want to help with the food?"

"Sure," she answered, relieved the singing was over. She'd been attending them for almost three years. At first it had been fun to see the other Youngie and spend time together, but she felt as

171

if she were outgrowing them now. She followed her friend to the back of the room.

Monika had a big pot of hot chocolate ready to serve. "Go on into the house and get the popcorn balls," she said to Jenny. Lila followed her friend out the shed door and into the crisp cold. They walked briskly, their breath hanging in vapors, to the kitchen door. Bishop Byler came out with a tray of peanut-butter spread and crackers.

"Come on in," he said, holding the door with his foot for the girls. Lila gave him a smile as she entered the house. When she thought of marrying Reuben, one of the things that appealed to her, along with having Monika as a grandmother to her children, was having Bishop Byler as a father-in-law. He was kind and gentle and always made her feel valued.

The kitchen was warm from the roaring fire in the wood stove. Lila held her hands out to it for a moment. The area was large and even with just a lamp lit, the yellow walls brightened the room. She'd always been a little jealous of Jenny's house—even though she knew it was wrong to covet what her friend had.

The girls had each lost a parent—Lila, her mother and Jenny, her father—within six months of each other. They had that in common. But within a year Jenny's mother had married Bishop Byler. Lila knew that didn't make up for Jenny losing her own Dat, but Jenny's life returned to a new normal at least. Lila felt as if her life still teetered on the edge of chaos.

She grabbed the second tray of popcorn balls and followed Jenny out to the shed.

As the boys gathered around, Reuben stood at her side. Monika dipped hot chocolate from the pot into cups and encouraged everyone to "Eat yourself full."

She wagged her finger at Simon. "I don't want any leftovers," she said. "They'll ruin my girlish figure." He laughed with her as she patted her middle.

Once everyone was served, Monika sought Lila out. "I heard about your Mammi's diagnosis," she said. "How is she doing?"

"All right. Her surgery is scheduled for next Friday."

Monika made a *tsk-tsk* sound. "Does she have enough help? Is their new church treating them right?"

They'd been going to their "new" Mennonite church for nearly twenty years.

"Jah," Lila said.

"I heard you might be working with your Mammi—helping her out."

Lila shook her head. "I'd like to but . . ."

"What's holding you back?"

Lila's face grew warm, even in the cold shed.

"She needs to help Dat with the milking."

Simon had come up behind her. "Since I'm leaving."

"Oh, goodness," Monika said. "That's right. Look at the position you've put your family in."

Simon put his arm around Lila. "I didn't know about Mammi when I signed up."

Monika put her hand on her wide hip. "Can't you get out of it?"

Simon shook his head and then pulled Lila close. "Sorry, sis."

She wiggled away from him. He wasn't helping her feel better, not at all. She'd have been miffed about having to help with the milking no matter what, but to not be able to go help Mammi when she was ill was maddening.

Monika must have sensed Lila's pain because she said, "Don't worry. Something will work out. God will provide for your grandmother."

Thankfully Reuben didn't mind leaving early, and soon they were on the road, bundled under layers of wool blankets. Lila sat next to him, closer than usual. It was the coldest night of the year so far.

"Do you want to go help take care of your Mammi?" Reuben asked.

"Jah," Lila said. "Of course."

"I could help your Dat with the milking, in the mornings."

"No, that would be too much for you."

"I'd be back in time to open the lumberyard. It wouldn't be forever, right? Just until your grandmother is back on her feet."

"That's right," Lila said.

"Were you and Rose going to split the work?"

"That was my plan," Lila said. She could imagine Rose trying to get out of her half of the milking, but no one would eat breakfast if Rose didn't cook it.

"Then I could do it in the morning—for you—and Rose can take her turn in the afternoon," Reuben said. "I could talk to your father about it."

"Denki," Lila said. "I can't tell you how much I appreciate it, but I doubt Dat would agree to it."

"I could ask him," Reuben said. "Tonight."

She paused for a minute and then said, "I'll bring it up with him. Not tonight, but tomorrow."

They rode in silence, as they often did. True, he didn't make her heart race the way Zane did, and there were times she longed for a more meaningful conversation with him. But nonetheless he was comfortable to be around, and no one was kinder to her. He turned onto Juneberry Lane and then down her family's driveway.

As they reached the house, Daniel's pickup roared up behind them. Simon jumped out, waved, and then ran up the back steps. Daniel swung his vehicle around and then took off back down the driveway to the lane.

Lila groaned. "Want to come in anyway?"

"Sure," Reuben said. They unhitched his horse and put her in the barn, out of the cold. As they hurried on to the house, Lila clapped her gloved hands together, trying to warm up her hands.

By the time they got in the house, Simon had the fire in the stove roaring. Dat was on his way to bed but stopped when he saw Reuben. "Good to see you," he said. The two had worked at the lumberyard together for years, and Dat got along as well with Reuben as anyone, probably better.

"See you tomorrow," Dat said to Reuben, and then he nodded his head at Lila before lumbering to the hall and off to bed.

Lila cut the cherry cobbler and first served Reuben and then Simon. Rose poked her head into the kitchen. "I thought I heard Reuben's voice," she said.

Simon stepped behind her and mocked her words.

Lila smiled but Reuben didn't respond. Rose joined them at the table.

"Can I have some of that cobbler too?" Rose pointed toward Reuben's plate.

Lila sighed as she cut one more piece. How was Rose going to handle the milking every day when she expected others to serve her?

Reuben asked Simon where he'd do his basic training.

"Fort Benning," Simon answered. "In Georgia."

As Lila slipped Rose the plate of cobbler, she couldn't help but be a little jealous of Simon. She'd always wanted to travel and see the places across the country that Zane had told her about. She wasn't jealous as far as how hard Simon's training would be though. Or what he'd be doing. Or that he'd be living permanently so far outside his community, both spiritually and physically.

"How do you think basic will be?" Reuben asked.

Simon laughed. "I've survived Dat all these years. I'll be fine. I doubt any Army sergeant could be worse."

Lila was sure he didn't have any idea what he was talking about. Her brother was committing himself to a philosophy that was the opposite of how he'd been raised.

"I have no doubt you'll survive the physical part just fine," Lila said. "But I worry about the impact such a harsh environment will have on you."

"Ach," he responded. "I'll be okay."

Lila shook her head. Rose had a smirk on her face as she turned to Simon. "Dat said he wished you were more like Reuben."

"Rose," Lila said. "Dat didn't say that." Their father hardly spoke at all, and he never said anything negative about one child to another. At least Lila had never heard him say anything like that.

"No, he did," Rose said. "When I had to help finish up with the milking tonight because Simon ran out on him again." Rose smiled at Reuben, nearly batting her eyes. Lila suppressed a smile when Reuben's face turned pink. Rose had a presence about her that Lila lacked. She never doubted her little sister was attractive, but in the last year she'd become quite the flirt too. At sixteen she should be going to singings. Lila hoped Dat would allow it soon, even though he'd probably worry about Rose. It would save them all a headache—and perhaps heartache—if her sister married young.

Simon shrugged. "Dat can say what he wants. I know I've disappointed him." He shoved a bite of cobbler into his mouth. "But he'll get over it."

Lila doubted he would.

Simon shoved another bite into his mouth and then reached over and slapped Reuben on the back. "You're the man, Reu."

Lila wanted to roll her eyes. Simon sounded so ridiculous. She served herself a portion of cobbler and then sat down. But Simon was right. Reuben was the man. Maybe Dat *would* let him help with the milking.

Simon kicked her under the table. "Whatcha thinking about?"

She kicked him back. "What a pain you are."

Simon laughed and reached across the table for the cobbler pan, dragging it toward himself.

"You'll be bored when I'm gone—just wait and see."

She hoped, if all went as planned, that she wouldn't be around once he was gone. She wouldn't stay at Mammi's long though. Just to get her through her surgery and recovery. She remembered how much Mammi helped all of them when their mother was ill. If their mother hadn't died she'd take care of Mammi now. It was the least Lila could do. Surely Dat would see that.

The next morning, after Dat finished breakfast, he asked Lila to get started on the taxes.

"I'll do it," she said, "after I take Trudy to school." She worked at the restaurant in the afternoon and the laundry needed to be done. Rose would have to see to it.

"I'll ride with you to take Trudy." Dat pushed back his plate.

"You could just take her," Lila replied.

"I'd rather ride along," he answered and headed down the hall to his room.

Lila told Rose, who was reading the *Budget Newspaper* in the living room, to get started on the laundry and then told Trudy to meet her outside after she'd grabbed her lunch and books.

Lila slipped into her boots and coat and headed out to hitch the horse to the buggy. By the time she swung around to the house, Dat and

Trudy were both waiting for her, all bundled up.

Trudy climbed into the back, and Lila handed the reins to Dat after he climbed into the front.

A light snow had fallen during the night, and the horse laid out fresh tracks as she sped along. Trudy asked Lila and Dat if they'd come in to say hello to her teacher.

"I expect so," Dat answered.

After that, Lila and Trudy played I Spy until Lila said, "I spy a little white building."

It was the school, of course. One of the saddest times in Lila's life was her last day as a scholar. She'd been jealous of Zane that he got to continue, but at least he shared his lessons with her. She loved school so much that she'd considered becoming a teacher, but waitressing paid better. The money she made helped keep the family out of the red.

It was hard to make a living as a farmer. A few in their district had recently gotten rid of their dairy herds. One family had opened up a tourist shop instead and was doing quite well.

Dat would never agree to that sort of a business arrangement though. He'd hate having Englisch people traipsing all over the farm. And Lila couldn't blame him.

Beth stood at the door of the school. She didn't have a coat on, just a shawl wrapped around her lavender dress as she welcomed the children inside, smiling warmly at each scholar. The more

Lila saw of the woman the more she liked her.

"Some of the kids have invited our teacher home for supper," Trudy said as Lila stopped the horse. "Could we do that?"

Lila nearly shuddered. She couldn't think of anything more uncomfortable. Dat wouldn't talk. Rose would talk too much.

"I'd like that," Dat said.

Lila nearly fell out of the buggy. What was her father thinking?

Trudy clapped her hands together. "When should we ask her?"

"Anytime you'd like to," Dat answered. He never would have allowed any of the older kids to ask a teacher home. Of course their teachers had been in their early twenties. That wouldn't have been of any interest to Dat.

By the time Lila and Trudy reached the steps, Dat was already at the top, shaking Beth's hand. When Dat let go, Trudy reached for her teacher's hand. "Can you come to supper at our house tomorrow?"

"I'd be delighted to," Beth replied, and then directed Trudy into the classroom.

Lila turned to go as Beth told Dat that she looked forward to seeing him the next evening.

"Five thirty, if that works for you," Lila said over her shoulder.

Beth said it did.

As Lila and Dat walked back to the buggy she

realized he hadn't said a word to Beth. Why had he come?

"It will be good to have Beth to supper, jah?" she finally said, breaking the silence.

Dat nodded his head but didn't reply.

Lila took a deep breath. He seemed to be in a good mood. Not very talkative, sure, but certainly not in a bad mood.

"I was thinking I'd like to go help Mammi after her surgery."

They climbed into the buggy, and Dat gripped the reins.

"I wasn't going to bring it up because I knew you'd need me to help with the milking with Simon gone."

"That's right," he replied.

"If someone else could help what do you think of me going?"

"We can't afford to pay anyone."

"I know, but Reuben volunteered. He said he'd come over every morning."

Dat's mouth turned up a little and then he said, "He did?"

"Jah. I didn't ask him."

They rode in silence again, and then Dat finally said, "That would be a lot for him."

Lila nodded.

"When do you want to go to Strasburg? Not before supper tomorrow, right?"

Lila almost laughed. "Of course not." Then she

realized he wanted to make sure she'd be around to cook for the teacher. "Not until next Thursday. Mammi's surgery is a week from Friday."

"What about your job?"

"I could get some time off." Business was so slow that she wasn't getting many hours anyway. "And I'd help at the shop while I'm over there. Mammi said she'd pay me."

Dat tugged on his beard with his free hand. "Let me think about it," he said.

Lila spent the morning organizing Dat's expenses for the business. When she returned to the house to see how Rose was getting along with the laundry and dinner, she found her sister sitting in the living room reading again.

"You need to help more," Lila said.

"I am," Rose said, her eyes still on the page. "I'm just taking a little break."

"Dat and Simon will be in to eat in fifteen minutes."

Rose jumped to her feet. "I didn't realize it was so late. Can you help me get something on the table?"

"No," Lila said. "I have to get ready for work. You're on your own." It would be good for Rose to be in charge for a while—although maybe not so good for Dat and Trudy.

The next afternoon, as Lila peeled the potatoes for supper and Trudy drew a picture for Beth, Dat opened the back door and poked his head in. "I just wanted you to know," he said to Lila, "that I thought about your request, and I don't think it's a good idea."

She turned toward him from the sink, her heart sinking. "Why?"

"We need you here."

"I'm not going to stay forever."

"Of course not. When you marry you can leave, but you need to remain here until then. Eve can help your grandmother." Dat remained in denial that Eve had a teaching job. Besides, it shouldn't be her responsibility. Lila didn't respond, and Dat left, most likely to go finish the milking.

"Where did you want to go?" Trudy asked in a quiet voice.

Lila turned toward her little sister. For a moment she'd forgotten she was there. "To take care of Mammi, because of her surgery." Dat had finally told Trudy and Rose about Mammi's cancer the week before.

"That sounds like it would be a good idea."

Lila nodded, tears stinging her eyes. She turned quickly back toward the sink, dragging her forearm across her face. Trudy didn't say any more and neither did she.

A half hour later, Dat opened the back door again, this time for Beth. She brushed snow off her coat onto the mudroom floor and then stepped out of her boots and onto the kitchen linoleum.

Trudy had just finished setting the table and hurried to greet her teacher. Rose had a pitcher of water in her hand, ready to put it on the table.

"Add more wood to the fire, would you?" Lila whispered to Rose as Trudy hugged Beth.

Rose rolled her eyes. Lila was tired of her sister's I'm-so-overworked phase. Simon came in from the barn a couple of minutes later, and once he and Dat had washed up Lila directed everyone to the table, seating Beth between Dat and Trudy.

Lila had made meatballs, mashed potatoes, roasted Brussels sprouts, baked bread, and was serving applesauce also. For dessert, she'd made a chocolate cake.

Simon cracked a joke about the Brussels sprouts being his favorite. Even Beth could tell they weren't.

"I didn't cook them with you in mind," Lila said.

He grinned.

"Are you the brother who joined the Army recently?" Beth asked as she passed the mashed potatoes to Trudy.

The little girl blushed. Probably because she knew Dat wouldn't want her sharing family information.

Simon grinned again. "Jah, that's me. You're getting a close-up of the prodigal son—before he leaves." He turned toward Dat. "Isn't that right?"

Dat ignored him.

Simon speared a Brussels sprout with his fork and then shoved it in his mouth.

Lila wondered if Dat wished Trudy would have waited to invite Beth to dinner until after Simon left.

"Trudy also said her grandmother is ill," Beth said.

This time Trudy didn't blush—but she didn't say anything either. When no one else spoke up, Lila said, "Jah, she's been diagnosed with cancer."

"I'm sorry," Beth said, turning her gaze from Trudy to Lila. "My grandmother had cancer when I was about your age." She spoke directly to Lila.

Trudy pushed her potatoes to the middle of her plate. "Lila wants to go take care of Mammi, but Dat won't let her."

Lila gasped and then managed to say, "Trudy." Then she looked at Dat. He kept his attention on his plate.

Simon and Rose both stared at their father too, waiting for his reaction.

Beth didn't notice—or ignored—the tension in the room. "I was able to care for my grandmother when she was ill. She and my grandfather lived in the *Dawdi Haus* behind my parents' home, and I wasn't teaching yet." She took a bite of bread. "Delicious," she said, but her focus shifted to Dat. "It was a really good experience for me. For one, it convinced me that I would make a better teacher than caregiver. And my grand-mother passed a lot of her wisdom on to me." She smiled. "I actually listened. Plus"—her attention was fixed on Dat—"it sets a good example for children and grandchildren to care for the elderly. That's part of our values, right?"

Lila expected Dat to tell Beth that she didn't understand their situation. Or didn't know what she was talking about. Or that Mammi had left the church and had no wisdom to share. Instead Dat smiled back, just a little, and said, "Perhaps I was too hasty." He met Lila's gaze but didn't say anything more.

All Lila could do was nod to let him know she'd heard him.

After everyone had enjoyed the chocolate cake, Simon, Dat, Trudy, and Beth went into the living room.

Lila and Rose started to clean up, but then Dat came back into the kitchen and asked, "Do you plan to join the church soon?"

"Jah," she answered. "I'll take the class in the spring."

"If you're serious about joining the church and getting on with your life, then I think it would be all right for you to help your Mammi for a short time," he said. "Ask if she still needs you. Between Reuben's help and Rose's we should do all right." Dat sauntered back into the living room.

Lila grabbed her coat and started out the door, but Rose called out, "Wait!"

"What?" Lila spun around.

"You can't be serious about going away."

"Of course I can."

Rose's lip turned down in a pout, but Lila ignored it and hurried out the door to the barn.

Thankfully, Mammi answered the phone. Out of breath, Lila told her she could come and help.

"No," Mammi answered. "It's too much for you."

"I want to. I need to," Lila blurted out. "And Dat will allow it."

Mammi paused and then finally said, "Oh, sweetie, if you're sure. . . ."

Lila leaned back against the desk in the corner of the room. "He just wanted to make sure you didn't have anyone else helping you. Like Eve—"

"Of course she said she could help when she can, but she can't take time off from teaching."

"That's what I thought," Lila said. "I'll stay with you and work in the shop too."

"*Wunderbar*," Mammi said. "But what about the milking . . . now that Simon is going to be leaving?"

"Reuben said he'd help with it."

"Oh my," Mammi said. "He's a good man, isn't he."

Lila agreed, her heart swelling a little at the thought of his sacrifice for her. "I'll call you back tomorrow. If all goes well, I'll have Simon bring me over the day before surgery. He wants to tell you good-bye."

"I'd like that," Mammi said.

Lila assured her grandmother she'd be in touch soon and then hurried back to the house to help Rose finish the dishes. Her sister just had the table cleared. The food wasn't even put away. Lila began running the dishwater and scrubbing the glasses.

Laughter erupted in the other room. "They're playing Yahtzee," Rose said, her voice filled with disappointment.

"Go join them," Lila said. She knew how much her sister enjoyed playing games. If Reuben could serve her so generously, the least she could do was do the same for Rose, even if just for an evening.

11

The second evening in Bagram, after a day of training that included a simulated exercise of going house to house against insurgents, Zane headed with Casey to the Subway on base. The base was the size of a small city and accommodated ten thousand soldiers, contract workers, and Afghan police and military personnel. There was a dual runway, an air tower, hangars, and

189

warehouses close to the busy airfield. Barracks, mess halls, office buildings, a hospital, stores, a theater, restaurants, and training facilities lined Disney, the main street that ran a big circle around the whole base.

The place was at almost five thousand feet and cold. As they picked their way down the muddy street, Zane wished he'd put another layer on underneath his uniform.

The other three women in Casey's FET unit were quite a bit older than she was—late twenties and early thirties—and didn't include Casey much. She didn't seem to mind. She seemed to prefer hanging out with Zane. He wasn't sure what others in the unit thought. It didn't matter, as long as she, their sergeant, and their commander didn't have any misconceptions.

Grant and Wade started to follow them. "Care if we join you?" Grant called out. "Or would we be interrupting?"

Wade laughed.

"Come on," Zane called back to them as he motioned them forward. "The more the merrier."

Casey rolled her eyes.

"What?" Zane asked quietly.

"They're getting on my nerves."

Zane understood, but he wasn't going to say anything. Not even to Casey. Jet lag, too much time together, and the stress of being so far from home were all building. Zane wondered if he was up to the task ahead of him, and he was sure everyone else felt that way too. But none of them were talking about their fears.

Grant had been a smart aleck all day, until the sergeant called him out. Then both he and Wade had snickered behind Sarge's back. Zane was tired of their attitudes too, but he knew not to make things worse. Grant already thought of him as a Goody-Two-Shoes.

"What I wouldn't give for a beer," Grant said as he and Wade caught up with them. "You too, Beck?" Grant laughed. "Oh, I forgot, you're too good to drink with your brothers."

"Find a beer and I'll drink with you," Zane countered, grateful they were on a dry base. He'd be twenty-one in less than a month, but he wasn't going to let anybody know. Not that it would matter over here anyway.

"Yeah, well, about that," Grant said, lowering his voice. "This dude in the mess hall said it's really not that difficult to come by. Maybe not beer, but the hard stuff."

"Drop it," Casey barked as she reached the door first and pushed it open. Zane grabbed the handle, holding it for her.

Casey turned toward Grant. "I mean it. If it's not one thing it's another with you. Can't you just be normal for a change?" She shifted her gaze to Wade. "You too."

Wade backed off, but Grant put his hands up

in mock surprise. "Must be someone's time—"

"Knock it off," Zane said, letting go of the door, leaving Casey inside, and taking a step toward Grant, who was still on the outside, standing next to Wade. He crossed his arms. "Everybody's tired. Give it a rest."

Before Grant could answer, Zane swung the door open again and Wade stepped in, followed by Grant. Casey let both of them go before her and fell back by Zane. "Thanks," she said.

Zane gave a quick nod. It was going to be a long deployment—that was for sure. He felt sorry for Wade. The guy needed to stop being a follower—especially of Grant.

As they waited in line, Casey said to Zane, "Your beard is looking good."

He smiled. "Yeah, well, it's my first attempt."

"Really?"

He nodded. He'd been in the Army since he was eighteen. It wasn't like he could have grown one before then. As a civil affairs team, they were encouraged to grow beards to be more accepted by the Afghans.

"What's with the mustache—or lack of?" Casey teased.

"It's not doing so well." He grinned. He'd shaved it in some weird symbol of solidarity with the Amish men he knew. The truth was, way back in Europe the Amish men didn't grow mustaches because soldiers did. It was his small

gesture, as a soldier, of honoring those who believed in peace and who had given up their homeland centuries ago to find it. He knew the symbol was also ironic, considering he *was* a soldier. But the small secret act of solidarity made him smile—on the inside, at least.

After they finished eating, he walked Casey back to her barracks in the rain and then pulled out his phone and looked at the photo of Lila again. He hadn't brought a laptop or iPad. He didn't want to pack one around. He had his cell and he'd buy a card for it, but only the calling would work—not the Internet or texting. He'd have to rely on the base computers to send an e-mail home—but at least he still had his photos.

He jogged to the service center and entered as a soldier stepped away from one of the desktops. Zane quickly sat down, pulled up his account, and drafted an e-mail to his parents, saying he'd arrived and everything was going well. He said it was cold, wet, and muddy, and that they'd go into the field in a few days. He hit Send, leaned back in the chair, and then decided he'd send an e-mail to Simon too. He pretty much said the same thing, but asked Simon to let him know when basic was done and how it went.

Again he considered sending Lila an e-mail. He clicked on a new message and typed in her address. Then he stared at the blank e-mail. What did he want to tell her? That he missed her? That

he thought about her all the time? That he'd been crazy to join the Army but he felt good about the work ahead of him? That he wondered how long it would be until she and Reuben married?

It was time to put his wounded pride behind him. Perhaps they could be just friends.

He typed:

Dear Lila,

It is cold and muddy here. Lots of rain. We can see the snow on the mountains from where we are. We will soon be going into alpine valleys past those mountains to start our work.

I think about your family and wonder how your grandmother is doing. How it will be for all of you when Simon leaves. I remember all of our afternoons playing down at our fort as the happiest in my life.

He stopped. He hadn't written anything about her at all. Not even a birthday greeting. He pressed his hand against his thigh. And he wouldn't. She'd be more apt to reply if he kept things general.

Please e-mail me back when you can.

Zane

He clicked Send, logged off his account, and pulled his phone from his pocket, flipping through his photos to the ones of Lila once again.

The civil affairs team flew over the mountains during the night to avoid detection, landing at their forward-operating base camp just before dawn. The place was much smaller than Bagram, with a single airstrip, a handful of concrete buildings, tents, a mess hall, a clinic, and a small commissary. There was also a market where Afghans sold colorful scarves, linens, skullcaps, and baskets.

By the time they smelled bacon cooking in the mess hall, the sun was rising. Zane stopped at the entrance and turned east, toward Pakistan. He shielded his eyes. They had been warned they could expect rocket attacks—and firefights—but hopefully only around the fenced perimeter. He was definitely in a war zone.

After breakfast, two MRAPs—Mine-Resistant Ambush Protected Vehicles—arrived for their trip to a village up in the mountains. When their Afghan guide appeared, Zane greeted him in Pashto, but the man didn't respond in the extended Afghani greeting Zane had been taught to expect. Instead he responded in English with a gruff "Good morning." He didn't seem to have an accent, and he'd obviously spent a lot of time around Americans.

Grant elbowed Zane and laughed. The guide rode up front with the driver, and the rest of them, including the other three women from Casey's female engagement team, strapped into their seats. Sarge sat next to Zane and leaned his head toward him. "We should meet the Afghan translator by this afternoon. He's a respected elder in the area. We'll give you some time to get acquainted and figure out how much you can understand. As we work I need you to listen in on his conversation with other leaders and see if you think they're trustworthy."

Zane nodded.

The sergeant turned his head, but then added, "I've worked out furloughs. You're going home the middle of May."

Zane had hoped to go home much later than that. He didn't mean to grimace, but he must have.

"I know," Sarge said. "We'd all rather go home during the last half of the deployment, but Grant needs to go in July because of the baby, and I promised my wife I'd be home by the middle of August, when school starts for our kids."

Zane glanced at Casey.

"She's going home the end of May. You could see if she'll trade with you."

Zane shook his head. "It's fine."

Sarge nodded. "Thanks."

All the windows in the MRAP were tinted green and bulletproof. Through the years the Army had progressively added more armor to the Humvees, and those improvements more effectively protected soldiers from being injured or killed, but the MRAPs did an even better job. The side windows were narrow and high, and Zane was lucky enough to have one next to him. He was tall enough to see out of it onto the hills, which were brown and dry—more like Texas than Lancaster County. Dust billowed up and into the adjacent fields and some seeped into the vehicle, drying his throat.

The villages they passed were small, with walls made from mud and stone around them. The homes were made from mud too. As they gained altitude, juniper and yew trees appeared. He knew in the spring, from his studies, that honeysuckle, currants, and rhododendron would bloom. The landscape grew greener and more rugged as the vehicle continued to climb.

Zane thought back to the tough job Sarge had of scheduling everyone's furloughs. It wasn't that he wanted his leave to be during the second half of his deployment to make the deployment go faster. He just didn't want to go home so soon. He didn't want to have to avoid Lila again. He didn't want to worry about Simon and wonder how Adam was really doing and see the worry in his parents' faces. If he'd left his truck in Texas, he could go there instead, but that would hurt his family. He could go see his grandfather in Seattle, but that would offend his parents too.

He'd met a soldier in Bagram who'd gone to Australia for his furlough. He said the last thing he wanted to do was go home to the U.S. during his leave—it would only make him more home-sick. Zane wished he would have thought of that, but again, it would hurt his parents. The guy he'd talked with was in his midthirties and single. His parents probably weren't as engaged in his life as Zane's tried to be in his. He sighed and leaned back against the seat, shifting his thoughts to the translator he'd soon be meeting.

He hoped his Pashto was good enough to understand him in the field as he spoke with other Afghans. His thoughts drifted to what he'd learned about Afghanistan during their preparation. It wasn't the uncivilized place some people thought. It had a rich history, shaped by trade routes and the Silk Road. Advanced civilizations had been established very early in the country and then decimated again and again by invaders. Through the centuries elders had to decide whom they would form alliances with, and their decisions were usually based on which side would most likely protect their families.

A couple of hours into the trip, the driver of the second vehicle, the one with the commander's team in it, radioed that the women in the other FET group needed to stop.

Grant rolled his eyes. "I knew this would happen. Traveling with women is as bad as traveling with kids."

"Keep it up, Turner, and you'll be hitchhiking back to base," Sarge said.

The women in Casey's FET group rolled their eyes, but Casey didn't respond, and neither did Zane. All four women pulled their scarves over their heads, though, clearly ready to get out. A few minutes later the driver pulled over next to a group of conifer trees. The women darted behind them first, and then most of the men took a turn. The guide stood beside the vehicle and smoked a cigarette. Zane thought about his dad when he returned from Iraq and how he'd smoked for a while. War had all sorts of consequences. He couldn't help but wonder how it would affect him.

"When is that mustache going to grow in?" Grant teased Zane.

"What do you mean?" Wade asked. "I saw him shave it the other day."

"You're kidding." Grant shook his head. "You get weirder every day."

Zane smiled and walked back to the MRAP. After they crawled back in, most everyone dozed until the MRAP came to an abrupt stop at a village. Sarge got out with the guide. Zane craned his neck to see out the window. A man wearing a turban and *perahan tunban*, the traditional men's tunic and loose pants, came to the gate in the wall. The scrubby trees along the wall dipped in the wind. The ground wasn't covered with snow, but piles of it were pushed along the stones. Sarge zipped his coat and pulled the collar up to his ears.

Zane dug his stocking cap and gloves from his bag. They were on an alpine plateau, and it was clearly going to be cold.

A few minutes later the sergeant returned. "We'll all stay in this village tonight. In the morning the other team will go on to the next village."

Zane's team disembarked, except the driver, who drove the MRAP around to the back of the village, outside the wall.

Sarge pointed to an empty house made of mud bricks and directed the team to get settled, but then he motioned for Zane to follow him and the guide. Zane heaved his pack onto his back and quickened his step. If he'd been sane—instead of blinded by both love and rejection—almost three years ago when Lila told him to go away, the farther the better, he never would have found himself in Afghanistan. But he was glad he had. It was unlike any culture he'd ever seen or even imagined back then, and he never would have studied Pashto otherwise.

A barefoot boy darted out in front of them. A goat, tied to a post, bleated loudly. Ahead a woman stood in the doorway, holding her scarf in front of her face.

A sense of purpose welled up in Zane. He was connected to these people. They were created in God's image. It was a village of families, not unlike the Amish—except these people's lives were constantly threatened, while the Amish lived in peace. He said a silent prayer, asking God to bless their mission.

The village consisted of about fifteen homes. Zane knew the families were all related in some way, connected by blood and culture and religion. Not unlike the Amish. Except, again, for the violence around them. And, of course, the difference in religion. The woman he saw tending to two children wore a hijab, a veil, and not the enveloping burqa. He'd been told their dress would probably vary from village to village.

The guide pushed open a door to a house and entered. Sarge followed, and then Zane. Two men sat on mats on the floor, around a teapot, and they held cups in their hands. The guide motioned for Sarge and Zane to join them. "*As-salaamu' alaykum*," the older man said, as the guide sat down.

"*Wradz mo pa kheyr*," Zane answered.

"What did you say?" Sarge asked.

"It's an afternoon greeting."

The older man smiled. He wore a skullcap and the traditional clothes.

"*Zama num Zane Beck de*," Zane said.

"Your name?" Sarge asked.

Zane nodded.

"I am Jaalal," the old man said with a bit of an accent. "And we can speak in English. I studied it as a young person and have been using it regularly for . . . the last eleven years." Obviously other Americans had been working in the area before them.

"Jaalal is a respected elder here," the guide explained.

"Peace to you," the old man said, bowing a little to Sarge and then to Zane. "How are you? Are your souls healthy? Are you well? Are your families well? Long life to you!"

"Thank you," Zane answered, remembering his training. "We are fine and our families are well." Though he wasn't certain about the health of all their souls. He found the long greeting charming. He'd been taught that the Afghans were polite and respectful. It seemed to be true.

The older man poured tea into little cups and added sugar and powdered milk. He passed cups to Sarge, then Zane, and then the guide.

Zane sipped his tea, knowing serving it was as ancient a tradition as the greeting and served as an excuse to stop, visit, and enjoy the moment. The tea was sweet and good. As he put the cup down, the curtain in the doorway rustled, but Zane couldn't see who was behind it.

The guide explained that Sarge's group would be doing community building—focusing on safety issues, hygiene, and education but also assessing the infrastructure of local roads and services. He didn't add that one of the goals was to win support away from the Taliban or that they hoped to gain intelligence to help stabilize the country. The guide spoke about the women in the group and that they wanted to get to know the women in the village. The older man nodded.

"They also want to take back space from the enemy," the guide said, "to make sure this area is stable before the Americans leave."

The older man nodded again.

Zane marveled at the word choices—*space* and *stable* in particular. It sounded as if the guide had been reading Army manuals. They hoped the villagers would trust the Americans instead of the warlords. But that trust had to be won—it couldn't just be expected.

The group discussed strategies, compensation, and a game plan. They would start by visiting the eight villages in the area. The visits would take a couple of weeks at least. They'd use this first village as home base.

"Could one of the women in our group meet with your wife?" Sarge asked Jaalal.

"In the morning. She will have time then," he answered. Then glancing at Zane, he said, "I will help the young man translate."

Zane said, "*Manana*."

"You are welcome," Jaalal responded, a twinkle in his eyes.

Zane looked forward to working with him.

Sarge appointed Casey as the spokesperson for the FET, and the next morning Zane sat with her and the guide back in Jaalal's house. This time his wife sat beside him. She was thin and weathered and hunched over a little as she held her purple scarf tight against her chin, but she had a sparkle in her eyes too.

After the customary greeting from Jaalal, Zane introduced himself and then Casey. The woman nodded. Zane was so relieved she understood him that he hardly noticed when she said, in English, "My name is Aliah." She smiled, and Zane began to laugh.

Her husband explained that she'd picked up some English, but not a lot, through the years. Aliah motioned to the plate of fried bread sprinkled with sugar. Zane took one and bit into it. He took another bite, chewed, swallowed, and then smiled. It was delicious.

"It's called *gosh-e fil*," Aliah said.

"Manana," Zane replied.

Aliah motioned to Casey, and she took one too. When Zane finished his, Aliah insisted he take another.

A few minutes later, as they began discussing

what Casey and her team had planned, the curtain over the doorway moved, just as it had the evening before.

Jaalal said something so quickly in Pashto that Zane couldn't understand him. A young man pulled the curtain to the side and stepped through. He was small and appeared to be a young man, but his face had a weathered appearance, one of time spent in the outdoors and maybe of suffering great tragedy too.

"This is our grandson Benham," Jaalal said. "He lives with us."

Zane stood and shook the man's hand, greeting him in Pashto. Benham appeared shy and didn't respond. Zane introduced Casey, but Benham simply nodded and didn't look her way. Zane was pretty sure the young man hadn't spent time with Americans the way his grandparents had. He slipped back through the curtain.

In a soft voice Jaalal said, "Our son and his wife, Benham's parents, were both killed at the beginning of the war when he was six."

"Taliban?" Zane asked.

Jaalal shook his head and without another word on the topic directed the conversation back to Casey's plan. Zane did the math. Despite his weathered appearance, Benham looked to be about seventeen. If the Taliban didn't kill his parents, then most likely the Americans or perhaps the Afghan army killed them, perhaps accidentally. Either way, it would have been a tragedy.

Two hours later, full of tea and sweet pastries, Casey and Zane left Jaalal and Aliah's home. Zane was pleased with the progress they'd made, and by the look on Casey's face, she was too.

"It's about time," Grant called out to them. "We're running late because of the two of you." Wade stood beside him, his arms crossed.

"Give me just a minute," Casey said.

Zane didn't respond but followed her toward the house where they were billeted. As he turned toward the door, he saw Benham standing at the far end of the compound, smoking a cigarette. Zane waved, but the young man turned his head away, toward a woman sweeping an earthen stoop. She wore the more traditional burqa, but by the way she carried herself Zane guessed she was older. Benham gazed past her, beyond the wall and toward the mountainside.

Excitement, apprehension, and confusion rushed through Zane as he entered the house. He liked Jaalal and Aliah. If he could help Casey and her team make life better for the women and children in the villages, that would be a worthy task. If he could make a difference in the lives of Jaalal and his village, including Benham, Zane would count it a privilege. His heart swelled with gratitude. God really did have a plan for him.

12

L ila talked with her supervisor and made arrangements to take a month off work. "Call me in a few weeks," the woman said, "and let me know how things are going."

Mammi wouldn't have started chemo by then, but she should be nearly recovered from her surgery.

On Wednesday morning Reuben came over to do the milking, and Lila worked alongside him, showing him what to do. He slowly picked up on the tasks involved. He definitely was more gifted in working with wood than animals. Simon came out late, which annoyed Dat, but he didn't say anything. Lila was sure Dat would enjoy working with Reuben more than with anyone else.

When Lila told Reuben good-bye and thanked him again, he smiled and then said, "I'd do anything for you, Lila. You know that."

She believed him.

That afternoon Lila contemplated walking down the lane to see if Shani was home, thinking she should ask her if she'd invite Trudy over more often while Lila was gone. But then Lila would have to decide whether to ask about Zane or not. She knew he'd left for Afghanistan. Shani, Joel, and Adam had gone to Texas to tell him good-bye and then had returned with his truck.

Lila put on her coat and boots and walked down the back steps. An icy wind howled through the tops of the trees. Dat was working at the lumber-yard but would get off in time to pick up Trudy, so Lila didn't need to go out. She looked out over the field toward the poplars and wondered what the weather was like in Afghanistan. She imagined it was hot, but she actually knew nothing about the country. Perhaps she'd pick up a book at the library.

A sense of dread overtook her. Zane was off to war. She knew he was a translator, but she also knew he carried a gun. Would he have to kill? She shuddered. He wouldn't come home the same if he did—she was sure of it. She'd never forget the sorrow and anger in Joel Beck's eyes after his time in Iraq. But she'd never know what happened to Zane, not more than what Shani or Eve told her. Tears stung her eyes, and she blinked quickly, turning back toward the house. She wouldn't go over to Shani's—not now. She'd call once she was at her grandparents' house. Maybe she'd be able to leave a message, a quick one, and not have to ask about Zane at all.

On Thursday she packed her things in the back of the buggy and then she and Simon took Trudy to school.

"I really love Beth," Trudy said as they turned onto the highway.

"I thought she was supposed to be mean," Simon teased.

"Strict," Trudy corrected. "And she is, but she's still really nice. She reminds me of you, Lila."

Simon snorted.

Lila rolled her eyes. "Strict is good," she said.

"No, you're not strict," Simon joked. "You're definitely mean."

Lila gave Trudy another hug after they climbed down from the buggy, and then Lila walked in with her and told Beth that she was going to help her grandmother after all.

"I'm so glad," Beth said.

"Thank you for encouraging Dat to allow it," Lila said in a soft voice.

Beth nodded, a glimmer in her eyes.

Trudy hung her coat in the entry, but Lila lowered her voice anyway. "I'm worried about Trudy. I've never been away from her."

"I'll show her extra care and kindness," Beth said, patting Lila's arm. "Don't worry. I'm fond of all my students, but Trudy already has a special place in my heart."

"Denki." Lila sensed Beth was genuine. And she suspected that her love for Trudy had something to do with her being motherless. The woman had a good heart.

Lila hugged Trudy one last time. "When will I see you?" Trudy asked.

"Soon," Lila answered. "I'll let Rose know when she can bring you for a visit. Could you make Mammi a card?"

Trudy nodded, her lower lip quivering.

Lila hugged her again and hurried out the door as Beth wrapped her arm around Trudy. Once she was back in the buggy, Lila asked Simon if they could stop by the library on the way into Strasburg. "I want to get some books for Mammi," she said.

"Doesn't Mammi have her own books?" Simon joked, turning the horse back onto the road.

Lila ignored him. She planned to look for a few quilting books and some historical biographies. Mammi liked that sort of thing. And it might be just what she would need to pass the time. Lila pulled the wool blanket up to her shoulders and stared at the white landscape as her brother drove down the Strasburg Pike. A strip of fog had settled across a field, hiding the bases of three silos on the far side. Their tops appeared as if they were suspended from the sky. Ahead, a willow tree hung heavy with ice. A border collie ran along the fence line, barking. Lila closed her eyes, trying to imagine what it would be like with Simon gone. She was almost glad she wouldn't be at home. As much as he annoyed her, life would be so much duller without Simon around.

The library was new and built on the edge of town, surrounded by fields. When Simon pulled into the parking lot, Lila asked if he was coming in. He held up his phone and grinned. "But it's so cold out," she said.

"How long do you plan to be?"

She shrugged. "Not long."

"I'll come in if it gets too cold."

She opened the buggy door and jumped out, wrapping her scarf around her neck as she hurried into the library. Heaps of snow had been plowed around the edges of the parking lot, and the sidewalk had been shoveled so many times that there was nearly a tunnel leading to the entrance. The library had just opened for the morning, and not many patrons were inside. She hurried to the section where the geography books were kept. She'd get the book on Afghanistan first, in case Simon did come in. She didn't want him asking questions about her interest in the country, or more accurately teasing her about it. It took her a few minutes, but she finally found one.

She then hurried on to the biography section, pulling a book on Dolley Madison, one on Eleanor Roosevelt, and another on Helen Keller. Then she headed to the shelves that held quilting books. After picking out three, she glanced at the computers and contemplated checking her e-mail. She could send Zane a short message. But she decided against it and turned toward the check-out desk as Simon came through the front door, rubbing his bare hands together.

"What's that?" he asked as the librarian slid the book on Afghanistan across the scanner, picking it up before Lila could slip it into her bag. Her face grew warm.

He flipped it over and smiled at Lila, but not his regular grin. It was more of a sympathetic expression. "Who are you thinking about in Afghanistan?"

She ignored him, thanked the librarian, and slipped the other books into her bag.

"Lila," her brother said.

She walked toward the exit, sensing him behind her as she pushed through the door, continued on through the snow, and then toward the buggy. Just as she reached it, something hit her in the back of the head. She swung around. Simon had a second snowball in his hand and the book tucked between his other arm and side.

"Don't you dare," Lila hissed and started to cry.

Simon tossed the snowball into the air and caught it. Lila stared at him, tears rolling down her cheeks. He dropped the snow. Lila climbed into the buggy.

When Simon was settled on the seat he handed her the book but didn't say anything. Once they were back on the highway, he reached over and patted her shoulder.

The gesture made her cry more.

"You can't tell me you don't love him," Simon finally said.

She wasn't going to tell Simon anything.

He glanced at her and said, "You can't marry someone you don't love."

"Reuben is a hard worker and kind." She paused. "And he's Amish."

"Zane is a hard worker and kind too. And he loves you."

"What do you know about love?" Lila asked.

"More than you think," Simon answered, turning his attention back to the road. "And obviously more than you."

Mammi hugged Simon one last time. "Call us any time. Day or night."

"I won't be able to call during boot camp," Simon said. "But I'll call as soon as I'm done."

"Write then," Mammi said.

"Ach, you know I'm not much for that."

"Do you have envelopes and stamps?"

Simon shook his head.

"I'll be right back." Mammi headed over to her desk in the corner.

Simon turned to Lila and spoke softly. "I know you're worried about Zane, and me too. But don't be. He's going to be all right. I will too. But you *should* worry about yourself." It was quite the speech for Simon.

Lila hugged her brother. "I'll be fine." As she

pulled away, she added, "You'd better write me too. Even if it's a few lines to let me know everything's okay."

He nodded. "I'll be praying for you, sis," he said.

Tears threatened Lila again. Simon had never mentioned prayer before. "Denki. I'll be praying for you too."

Mammi returned with addressed, stamped envelopes.

Simon thanked her. Dawdi opened the front door and then walked out with Simon. She'd try not to worry about him. She didn't think he had any idea what he was getting into, but out of all the young Amish men she knew, she thought Simon would be best able to handle the Army.

Lila put her things away in her room, and then Dawdi drove Mammi and her over to Thread by Thread. An older woman who went to the same church as Mammi and Dawdi was working. There was one customer in the shop, an Englisch woman.

Lila had spent enough time in the quilt shop to know where everything was, but Mammi gave her a quick tour anyway and then took her into the back room that doubled as an office and storage. Mammi showed her the safe, the filing cabinet, and the overstock. "Dawdi will handle all of the deposits," Mammi said.

A bolt of green fabric caught Lila's attention. For a moment she thought it was a camouflage pattern, but on closer inspection it was a pattern of leaves.

"Would you want to help me with a project?" Mammi asked. "While you're here."

"Of course," Lila said, although she couldn't imagine that Mammi would have much energy for projects after her surgery.

"I'm making a quilt for Simon," Mammi said. "And I already asked if Eve and Shani would like to make one for Zane at the same time. Single quilts so they won't take long. I think it would be nice for our soldiers to have some love from home to keep them warm."

Lila nodded. She couldn't think of anything better for Zane and Simon. But she wasn't so sure she wanted to spend time with Shani and Eve as they made something for Zane.

She couldn't stop herself from thinking about Zane, no matter how hard she tried. Although she did want to learn about Afghanistan, the less she actually heard about Zane the better. But she couldn't tell Mammi any of that.

"I'd be happy to help make the quilt for Simon." She didn't imagine Mammi would be able to handle much handwork while she recovered. "In fact if you do the planning, I'll do the work."

"Good," Mammi said. "Actually the squares are all cut and ready to be pieced. I'll show you when you get back home."

Lila stayed at the quilt shop and worked with the older woman until late afternoon, and then she walked back to Mammi and Dawdi's house, along Main Street and the stately brick houses that she so admired. The sun was setting, and she was thankful for the sidewalk. It was much safer than the roads around home. As she walked, bundled in her heavy coat, scarf, and mittens, she prayed for Mammi and then for Simon, Trudy, and Rose. She prayed for Daniel and Jenny and then Dat. As she neared Mammi and Dawdi's cottage, she whispered a quick prayer for Zane too.

That evening, after a dinner of beef stew, she began piecing the squares for Simon's quilt. Mammi had used the green fabric Lila had seen in the storage room, along with browns and purples. At bedtime, she packed the cut pieces to work on the next day at the hospital.

She awoke early, and as she dressed, in relative warmth compared to home, she thought of Reuben doing the milking for her and whispered a prayer of thanks, realizing she hadn't prayed for him the evening before. Then her mind wandered to Zane. She remembered the book about Afghanistan and opened it and started reading. It started out describing the geography of the country, some of the most varied in the world. The highest mountain was over twenty-four thousand feet. Rivers cut through many of the valleys, creating rugged landscapes. She kept reading.

"Lila!" Dawdi called up the stairs. "Breakfast is ready."

She shut the book quickly. She'd intended to fix it, but she'd gotten lost in the geography of Afghanistan. She slid the book under her pillow and hurried to the stairs, chastising herself for acting like Rose.

Five hours later Lila and Dawdi were sitting in the waiting room of Lancaster General Hospital when Shani appeared in the doorway. "Eve told me Leona's surgery was today," she said as she started toward them. "Any word yet?"

Lila shook her head. "She's been in surgery for three hours."

Shani sat down beside Lila. "The surgeon should be out soon."

Dawdi leaned forward and asked Shani how Zane was doing.

"Good. We had an e-mail several days ago. They'd finished their orientation and were headed to the field."

"Where is he?" Lila asked.

"The eastern part of the country, but that's as much as he said."

Close to Pakistan, then. Lila exhaled. "Will he be able to communicate much with you?"

"He has his phone, so I'm hoping he can call."

Shani shrugged and then smiled. "If not, I'm sure he'll e-mail when he's back at base."

Lila nodded, and Dawdi asked how the weather was there.

"Sounds as if it's cold where he was going. They'll be in the mountains."

Zane would likely be traveling around in rugged terrain with people shooting at him, perhaps. Not wanting to dwell on that, Lila asked, "How's Adam doing?"

"Fine. He'd love to see Trudy sometime."

"Did Eve tell you I'll be staying with Mammi and Dawdi for a month?"

"No," Shani said. "I didn't know that worked out."

Lila nodded. "It happened rather quickly. I'll be helping in Mammi's shop too."

Shani's face lit up. "So you'll be part of our quilting group, then?"

"Mammi just told me about it yesterday." Lila bent down and pulled the square she'd been working on out of her bag. "Mammi did the cutting, and I've started the piecing."

"For Simon?" Shani asked.

Lila nodded.

"He hasn't been by since we got home from Texas. When does he leave?"

"Next Wednesday." Lila wondered if Shani and Joel would go down to the house and seek Simon out to say good-bye, chancing an awkward encounter with Dat. They probably would. They weren't as intimidated by Dat as Lila was. Shani's eyes drifted past Lila, a serious expression on her face.

Lila turned. The surgeon walked toward them, still in his scrubs. "She's in recovery," he said. "The lump was bigger than we thought, but I think we got it all. You can go on down and see her."

Lila and her grandfather must have both appeared a little shocked, because Shani asked, "Would you like me to go with you?"

Dawdi nodded.

"Follow me," Shani said.

A few minutes later they were all standing at the end of Mammi's bed. Shani stepped to the side of the bed and took her hand. "Leona, Eli and Lila are here."

Mammi turned her head to the side and opened one eye. Shani stepped back and Dawdi stepped forward. He took Mammi's hand from Shani, and then leaned down to kiss Mammi's cheek. Tears filled Lila's eyes as Shani stepped to her side and wrapped an arm around her, pulling her close. "I can only imagine what you're feeling."

Lila nodded, guessing Shani assumed she was thinking about her mother. For a long moment she hadn't thought of Zane at all. At least Shani wasn't guessing about that.

"By tomorrow she'll be doing much better," Shani said.

"I hope I'm able to take good care of her," Lila said.

"You will," Shani answered. "And if you have any questions, call me. I'll help."

"Denki," Lila said, meaning it with her whole heart. She knew she could count on Shani.

13

On the third Saturday of February, Shani, Joel, and Adam sat around their kitchen table. The smell of bacon hung in the air as they stared at the screen of their laptop, waiting to hear the tone of Zane's Skype call.

"Maybe they were delayed," Joel said.

Shani swallowed hard, trying to rid herself of the anxiety creeping up her throat. Zane had sent an e-mail the night before saying they were back at base for a couple of days, and he'd try to Skype. *Try,* she reminded herself. She shouldn't have gotten her hopes up.

"What time does your quilting start?" Joel asked.

"In a half hour, but that doesn't matter. I'd rather wait." It was already a half hour past the time he'd hoped to call.

"I'm going to go get my book," Adam said.

"Good idea," Shani responded as he left the kitchen. A moment later she heard him running up the stairs.

"It's nine p.m. there," Joel said.

Shani nodded, wondering if Zane's team had gone off base for the day or if they had a day of rest. She knew the MRAPs they traveled in weathered IEDs and grenade rockets better than the Humvee Joel had been riding in, back in 2004, but nothing was completely safe.

She jumped at the jingly tone of the Skype call, but then relief washed through her and she quickly pushed the Accept button, silently saying a prayer that she wouldn't overwhelm Zane with her concern. She needed to stay calm.

At first the photo was pixilated. Then it was fuzzy. Finally Zane's face appeared. He wasn't the clean-cut soldier she'd last seen. He wore a beard, at least as much of one as she'd ever seen on him. Joel pushed the microphone button twice and said, "Can you hear us?"

Zane waved, and then his voice came through, "Hello."

"How are you?" Shani asked.

Adam returned to the room, his book in hand, and positioned himself behind Shani.

"What are you reading, Bub?"

"*The Lion, the Witch, and the Wardrobe.*"

"Ahh, I love that one," Zane said, and just like that they were all talking as if he wasn't in Afghanistan at all.

"Did you have a good birthday?" Shani asked. He'd been out in the field.

He held up a cookie. "Starting yesterday, yes. Thank you for the package."

She smiled. She'd sent him a box of twenty-one snickerdoodles, his favorite, vacuum-sealed.

Shani asked him about Grant and Wade. He said they were fine but didn't elaborate. "Casey is the same as always," he added with a grin.

Shani laughed. "How'd you know what I was going to ask next?"

Zane shrugged and grinned again.

Toward the end of the call, Joel asked about their mission.

"I can't give particulars," Zane answered.

"Of course," Joel responded.

"But lots of good things are happening. I really like the Afghan people I'm working with. Would you pray for protection for them?"

"Yes," Shani said.

"We have one translator in particular that I've connected with. We're doing good work. I feel the best I have about—what I committed to do."

"Great," Joel said. "You've always been so good at building relationships."

Shani just nodded because she had a lump in her throat that she couldn't speak around. Plus she didn't want to get mushy on him.

Joel leaned closer. "How is the language part going?"

"Good. The learning curve is pretty steep, but I'm improving."

Shani had a feeling he was being modest.

"I should be back down in the valley in another couple of weeks. I'll let you know and hopefully we can Skype then again. And then in April too. But then in May I'll be home for furlough."

Shani found her voice again. "That's fantastic!"

"Why so soon?" Joel asked.

"It's just how the schedule worked out," he said. "Mid-May. I'll get you the exact dates next month."

"What do you want to do when you're home?" Joel asked.

"Hang out. Eat. Sleep," Zane replied. "Spend time with all of you. The usual."

Adam stepped closer to the screen.

"We'll talk in a couple of weeks—okay, Bub?"

Adam nodded.

"See you all then," Zane said. "I love you."

"We love you too," Shani said, her heart full. Zane waved and then the signing-off tone bleeped, and he was gone.

They all stood stunned for a moment until Adam said, "He seems good."

"Yeah." Shani put her arm around Adam, pulling him close, and reached for Joel's hand and squeezed it. He squeezed hers back. Finally she felt a measure of peace about Zane. He was growing. He was learning. He'd asked for prayer. God was working in his life.

By the time Shani reached the back room of Thread by Thread, the other women had settled in around the quilt frame. The green, brown, and purple squares of Simon's quilt that Lila had pieced together stretched across it. "Sorry I'm late," she said as she dropped her bag on the chair closest to the door. "We were able to Skype with Zane this morning."

"How is he?" Eve asked.

"Good. Better than he's sounded since . . . well, since he joined the Army," Shani answered. When Lila stirred a little on the other side of the frame, Shani wondered if she'd said too much. She hurried to explain. "It sounds as if his translating work is going well, and he's making good connections with the Afghans he's working with."

"What a blessing," Leona said, looking up from where she sat in her rocking chair. She was obviously supervising. She wasn't up to stitching yet.

"He asked for us to pray for protection for the Afghan people he's getting to know," Shani said.

Lila looked up but then quickly dropped her head again. Leona clucked her tongue. "I'll pray too," she said. "It would be a privilege."

"How are you feeling?" Shani asked, stepping around the frame to give the older woman a hug.

"Much better. I finally seem to be healing."

Shani squeezed the woman's shoulder, but gently. Lila had called her two weeks before to check Leona's wound. It had been fine, but understandably unsettling for a nonmedical person.

Next Shani hugged Lila. "How are you, sweetie?"

"Good," Lila answered. "Everything has been fine this week. Right, Mammi?"

Leona nodded. "I'm afraid I'm doing so well that Lila will get bored and want to go home."

"Ach," Lila said. "Don't count on that. Peaceful is not the same as boring."

"And how are you?" Shani asked Eve, giving her a hug next.

"Good," Eve responded, looking up into Shani's eyes as she released her. Shani knew she wasn't. Eve had been hoping to get pregnant since her wedding day, and a few weeks ago she'd thought she was. But she'd been disappointed again.

"Zane's coming home sooner on furlough than we expected," Shani said as she sat back down. "Around the middle of May."

"That is soon," Leona said.

Lila kept her head down, and Shani couldn't see her reaction. Eve looked up from the quilt, her eyes bright. "That's wonderful."

Shani nodded. Her anxiety rose again, fearing what could happen between now and then. *Help me to trust,* she prayed. It had been easier after seeing him on the computer screen, having him ask for prayer. Now it felt a little harder again. She knew seeing his face didn't make him any safer, not in reality, but still it had felt that way. When he'd first shipped out, she'd sought out some military moms support groups online but after just a few days she realized the chatter was making her more anxious, not less. She knew the sites worked for lots of moms—just not for her. Quilting on Saturdays was much more beneficial to her.

The shop door buzzed, and Lila pulled her needle through the fabric and said, "I'll get it."

Eve and Leona were both silent for a moment, but then Leona said, "Reuben has come by a few times."

Shani smiled. "He seems like such a nice man."

"He is," Leona said. "He adores Lila. He's helping Tim with the milking every morning so Lila can be here with me."

Shani hadn't realized that. She thought Rose was milking two times a day. "That's awfully kind of him," she said.

Leona nodded. "When he's here, he dotes on her. I think he'd do anything for her."

If anyone deserved to be waited on, it was Lila. Shani wouldn't be surprised if she and Reuben married next November, just before Zane would be getting home from Afghanistan. That made her both happy and incredibly sad, all at the same time.

The voices in the shop grew louder, and then Trudy poked her head into the sewing room. She ran to Shani first, giving her a hug, and then Eve, and finally she stopped at her grandmother's chair. Leona put her arm around the little girl. "I'm so glad you came to see me. Where's Rose?"

"She and Lila are talking. Rose wants her to come home."

"I bet she does." Leona drew the little girl closer. "How about you?"

A tear rolled down Trudy's cheek. "Oh, dear." Leona kissed the top of her head. "Go tell her to come on in, and you can sit on her lap. She and I will talk. She'll go home soon."

Trudy obeyed her grandmother and returned, pulling Lila along. As soon as Lila sat, she pulled Trudy onto her lap. Rose followed, a disgruntled look on her face, but she brightened a little as she hugged her grandmother.

"How are you?" Leona asked.

"Tired," Rose answered. "The milking. All the chores. Taking Trudy to school and picking her up." She sighed. "It's exhausting."

Shani glanced down at the quilt, even though she didn't even have a needle in her hand yet, so her expression wouldn't give her away. Every woman in the room—except for herself—did or had worked harder than Rose. But still Shani felt sorry for the girl. She was only sixteen, and housework didn't seem to come naturally to her, the way it did some women. She wasn't getting the chance to explore life and spend time with other people her age, which a girl with her personality would understandably crave.

"It takes some time to get used to," Eve said.

"Rose is tired of taking me to school," Trudy said, snuggling against Lila.

"Ach, I didn't mean what I said," Rose countered. "Just yesterday morning when I was so tired I kept falling asleep while I was trying to drive the buggy."

Trudy turned her face up toward Lila's. "Can you come home? You've been gone a long time."

"Soon," Lila said, squeezing her youngest sister.

"That's what you said last time," Trudy said. "Hasn't it been *soon* yet?"

Lila smiled. "How about if you help with Simon's quilt? You can use my needle and I'll get another."

Shani listened as she pulled a square for Zane's quilt from her bag.

Trudy said, "My stitches are too big."

"No. They're perfect. He'll know you did them, and he'll feel your love."

Trudy smiled a little and then said to Lila, "I miss Simon. And you."

Lila nodded. "I really will be home soon, and Simon will visit in May."

Shani focused on her piecing again. *May.* Hopefully at the same time Zane was home.

"How's Dat doing?" Lila asked.

"Fine," Trudy answered.

"Beth has come by a few times," Rose said, sitting down by Eve.

"Who's that?" Eve asked.

"Trudy's teacher," Rose answered. "She has the hots for Dat."

"Rose!" Lila's face grew red.

"It's true," Rose said. "I can't imagine why."

A smile passed over Eve's lips. Shani couldn't help but smile too. Maybe it wasn't too late for Tim Lehman to find love.

"Do *you* like her?" Shani asked Rose, as if she were conspiring with her.

"If she can make breakfast and milk cows, I adore her." Rose stood, stepped over to Lila's sewing basket, pawed around for a moment, and then retrieved a needle. "Dat really does want you to come home," Rose said to Lila. "He said Mammi should be doing all right by now."

Mammi nodded. "I am." She rocked forward in her chair and leaned toward Lila. "I appreciate what you've done, but it sounds as if your family needs you."

Lila nodded but didn't say anything.

Shani wondered what would happen to the family when Lila and Reuben married. Perhaps instead of living in the house by the lumberyard they'd live in Tim's house. Shani shuddered a little. She couldn't imagine how hard that would be on the young couple. But that was from her Englisch perspective. Lots of young Amish couples lived with relatives and seemed to do fine.

14

The first Saturday of March, Lila stood in her upstairs room in her grandparents' cottage and put Simon's quilt into the box. She'd completed the stitching yesterday at the shop. There was no reason to stay any longer. Mammi would start chemo the next week, but Dawdi would take her to her treatments. Their church members would bring in meals, and with Lila taking two shifts a week at Thread by Thread, they would get by. She'd call her manager at the Plain Buffet and start picking up shifts there too. Tourist season would soon be gearing up, with weekend travelers and then a constant flow of visitors.

She stepped to the window, looking over the chicken coop, garden, and large yard that belonged to Mammi and Dawdi. It was all so peaceful. No cows mooing to be milked. No siblings complaining. No father grumping around. Even though she'd been helping Mammi, it had been a restful time for her. Dawdi's voice came up the stairs. "Lila! Reuben's here."

She closed up the box and headed for the stairs. By the time she was halfway down, she could see Reuben at the bottom, smiling up at her. She was pleased to see him, but he still didn't make her heart race.

"Need any help?" he asked.

"Everything else is by the door," she said. "I just need to drop this by the shop for the UPS driver to pick up for Simon."

Mammi stood behind Reuben. "Dawdi and I will take it." She held an envelope in one hand and a large plastic bag in the other. "A letter came for you from Simon."

Dawdi took the box from Lila, who took the envelope from her grandmother.

"And I put a bunch of scraps together for you in this bag." She lowered her voice. "You're doing such a good job with your quilting that I thought you might want to do something more creative. Like a crazy quilt."

A customer who took classes from Mammi was making a crazy quilt, using velvets and other fancy fabrics and textured stitches, and Lila had commented on how nice it must be to work so creatively. "Thank you," she said to her grandmother, taking the fabric from her and peeking into the bag. There were remnants of blue fabric from Zane's quilt and the green and purple from Simon's. There were more prints included too.

All of it was fancier fabric than what she had at home.

She wasn't sure if she'd have time to work on the project, but she'd give it a try.

She was ready to go, but then Mammi asked Reuben if he had time to stay for a cup of tea.

"I'd like that," he answered, as Dawdi put the kettle on.

Lila put the bag down by the front door and sat at the kitchen table to read the letter. Simon only wrote two paragraphs, saying basic training was a "blast," that he was "doing fine," and that the Army was more than he hoped it would be.

He asked how Mammi was doing and said that he hadn't had time to get homesick, but he thought about everyone in the fifteen seconds it took before he fell asleep at night.

"How's he doing?" Reuben asked.

"He sounds good," Lila replied.

"Jah," Mammi said. "I received a letter too. I'd say he's enjoying himself."

After they had their tea, Reuben carried Lila's things out to his buggy as she told her grandparents good-bye, hugging them and thanking them.

"No, thank *you*," Mammi said.

Lila shook her head. It was hard for her to explain, but staying with them had filled her up even though she was serving them. They loved her unconditionally, no matter how little or how hard she worked, something she didn't often feel at home.

Mammi hugged her again and then whispered in her ear, "I think Reuben is a fine young man. He'll make a good husband."

Lila nodded, clutching the bag of fabric to her chest, as Reuben returned for her. She was certain her mother would agree.

It was the first warm day of spring. Forsythia and daffodils were blooming, and tulips were beginning to poke up through the ground. Soon the countryside would be full of blossoms. She'd start the church membership class tomorrow, just like she'd told Dat she would. In another couple of months she'd be able to join. Sometime after that, she'd marry Reuben.

She asked Reuben about his Dat and siblings. He said everyone was fine. She asked how the milking had been the last week.

"*Gut*," he said.

He'd done so much for her. She thanked him again. Then they rode on in silence. She needed to talk, but perhaps that was what other women were for. She sighed.

"Everything all right?" Reuben asked.

She nodded. "I just sometimes wish——"

He glanced at her.

"——that we talked more."

"What do you want to talk about?"

"What our dreams are. How we feel about things."

"I'm feeling good," Reuben said, turning his attention back to the road.

She sighed again and then asked, "Could we stop by the library?" She had the Afghanistan book in the bottom of her bag to return—she'd renewed it once but wanted to return it before going home.

"Sure," he answered. When they reached the parking lot of the library, an Amish man a couple of years older than Reuben called out to him.

"Go on in," Reuben said.

Lila quickly put the Afghanistan book in with the returns and then wondered if she had time to send an e-mail. She could send one final message to Zane before she married Reuben, thanking him for his kind words on Christmas Eve. It would be her last correspondence ever with him.

A computer was available, and she sat down and logged on. Her heart raced. She had an e-mail.

Of course it was from Zane.

She inhaled as she clicked on it. It was dated February 1, over four weeks ago.

Dear Lila,

It is cold and muddy here. Lots of rain. We can see the snow on the mountains from where we are. We will soon be going into valleys past those mountains to start our work.

I think about your family and wonder how your grandmother is doing. How it will be for all of you when Simon leaves. I remember all of our afternoons playing down at our fort as the happiest in my life.

Please e-mail me back when you can.

Zane

"Lila?" Reuben stood across the table from her. She closed her account without looking up. "Are you all right?"

"Jah," she answered. "I was just checking on something."

He gave her a puzzled look but then said, "I'm going to go look at the carpentry books."

"I'll just be another minute," she said, feeling guilty but quickly clicking back onto her e-mail account and Zane's message anyway. She hit Print, logged off, grabbed the paper from the printer, and paid the librarian for the copy. As she strode toward the recipe books, she tucked his e-mail into the bottom of her bag.

Reuben found her ten minutes later, skimming a book of chicken recipes.

"Ready?" he asked.

She nodded and held up three books. "I just need to check these out." She hoped the recipe books would inspire her to get back into cooking.

She'd mostly made soups and stews at Mammi and Dawdi's, along with muffins and scones and salads. Dat would never survive on meals like that.

When the librarian handed her back the books, Lila slipped them into the bag on top of the paper, and Reuben reached to take the bag from her. For a moment she hesitated, fearing to have the e-mail from Zane out of her possession. She hadn't done anything wrong, had she? When another puzzled expression spread over Reuben's face, she gave in, realizing how ridiculous she was being. He wasn't going to search her bag.

As she followed him out to the buggy a wave of guilt swept over her. Reuben was so trusting. So kind. So good to her. He'd made it possible for her to take care of her grandmother.

And here she was hiding an e-mail from another man. But Zane was her friend. That was all. *"Please e-mail me back when you can."*

It wasn't wrong to receive an e-mail. And it wasn't as if she'd e-mailed him back.

When they arrived at the farm, Beth was headed up the back stairs with a cardboard box in her hands. She smiled and called out, "Welcome home!"

Lila waved, pleased to see her.

"Do you want to come in?" Lila asked Reuben.

"I'll carry your things," he said. "But then I'll

236

go help your Dat with the milking so Rose doesn't have to."

By the time Lila and Reuben came through the back door, Beth had her box unpacked and was slipping a casserole into the oven. A loaf of bread, a salad, and a sheet cake sat on the counter. After Reuben told Beth hello, he turned to Lila and said, "I'll pick you up for the singing tomorrow."

"Won't you stay for supper?" Beth asked.

He shook his head. "After the milking I need to finish cutting an order at the lumberyard."

"Denki," Lila said. She wanted to tell him to go on home and leave the milking to Rose, but she was afraid she'd sound bossy in front of Beth.

Reuben told both women good-bye, and then Lila carried her suitcase, book bag, fabric, and sewing basket to her bedroom. Rose was sprawled out on the double bed she shared with Trudy, staring at the ceiling.

"What are you doing?" Lila asked.

Rose turned her head slightly and said, "Oh, you're back."

"Where's Trudy?"

"Playing with Adam. Shani came and got her." Rose still didn't move.

"Are you all right?" Lila asked her sister.

"Jah, why do you ask?"

"Because Dat's getting ready to do the milking, and you're on your bed."

Rose sat up on the edge of her bed. "I didn't

realize it was that time already. Can't you do it? You haven't for so long."

Lila frowned and shook her head. "You're off the hook anyway. Reuben is helping."

"Oh," Rose said, her face brightening. "He's here?"

"He brought me home." Lila swung her suitcase onto her bed. "Beth's here too."

"Jah." Rose yawned. "I knew she was coming."

"Why did she bring supper?"

"She wanted to," Rose answered.

"Because you were complaining about all the work you have to do?" Lila took the e-mail from her book bag and slipped it into her apron pocket.

"Stop," Rose said. "You didn't even say hello. You just rushed in here and started criticizing me when you've spent the past month resting with Mammi at her house."

Lila shook her head. "I don't understand what's going on."

Rose sighed. "I'm not made for this."

"For what?"

"Work."

Lila rolled her eyes.

"Not work in general," Rose continued. "But all the milking and cooking and taking care of Trudy. I don't even have time to think!" Rose bounced on the edge of the bed. "What am I going to do when you marry Reuben and move away? He won't come anymore to help after that."

"You'll figure it out."

"No," Rose said. "At least not how to make it all work here. I'm going to look for a mother's helper job. Anything to get away from here."

Lila bit her tongue from saying that a mother's helper's job wouldn't be any easier than what Rose had been doing, and besides, Trudy needed one of them here as long as possible. Instead she said, "It's not as if Reuben and I are getting married right away."

She couldn't imagine they'd get married before next fall, not even if she joined the church by June. Summer was such a busy time for Dat.

"You're crazy for stringing him along," Rose said. "If Reuben was interested in me, I'd join the church and get married as soon as I could. And I'd never have to milk another cow in my life."

"Do I need to remind you that you're sixteen?" Lila said. "You're too young to marry." Let alone Reuben.

"I happen to be mature for my age," Rose responded.

Lila almost burst out laughing but then realized her sister was serious. She smiled instead.

"What?"

"Nothing," Lila said. Obviously Rose had no idea of just how immature she was. It made Lila wonder what she was oblivious to in herself. She remembered a quote by Richard Wright from *Native Son*, that Zane read in his junior English class, saying that people could ". . . starve from a lack of self-realization as much as they can from a lack of bread."

Rose flounced to her feet and then said, dramatically, "Guess I'll go see if I can help Beth."

"Has she been coming over much?"

Rose shrugged. "About once a week. Sometimes Dat goes over to her place."

That was more than Lila had anticipated. "When is Trudy coming home?"

"How about if I go get her and you help Beth?"

"Sure," Lila responded, sighing as she put her nightgown into her bureau. Sometimes she could understand what Rose was saying. She wasn't entirely certain she was cut out for this either.

An hour later Reuben came back into the house. Rose hadn't returned with Trudy yet.

"Your Dat is finishing up." He smiled. "I just wanted to tell you good-bye again."

Lila smiled back. "Denki for everything you've done today," she said. "And for doing the milking so I could be with Mammi."

Reuben nodded. "See you tomorrow."

After he left, Beth stopped setting the table for a moment to look straight at Lila. "He seems like such a nice young man."

"Jah," Lila answered. "He is."

"Your father certainly respects him," Beth said.

"Jah . . ."

"Your Dat says the two of you will marry soon."

Lila felt her face grow warm. She didn't know Beth well enough to talk about personal matters. "Jah . . ." Lila said again.

"You don't sound very sure," Beth commented as she put the last fork in place. She turned her gaze back on Lila, her hazel eyes full of concern.

"I'm tired, that's all," Lila answered.

"Well," Beth said, "I remember being your age and courting a young man that everyone thought I should marry."

Lila smiled a little. Beth seemed to have a story for every occasion. "What happened?"

"We married."

Lila met Beth's gaze. No one had said anything about Beth being a widow. "How did he die?"

"He didn't. He left me."

Lila gasped. That was unheard of among the Amish.

Beth nodded. "We'd only been married a couple of months. At first I had no idea where he went, but finally word came through a cousin of mine that he'd moved to the Chicago area and was living Englisch. After about five years he filed for divorce so he could remarry."

"Did you give it to him?"

Beth wrinkled her nose. "I didn't have a choice."

Lila lowered her voice. "Does Dat know?"

Beth smiled as she stepped to the fridge and took out a jar of pickles. "Jah. I told him soon after we met."

Lila's face grew even warmer. She couldn't imagine the conversation Beth had with Dat—but obviously it had gone differently than Lila would have predicted.

After a long pause, Lila asked, "Is your ex-husband still alive?"

Beth nodded.

"Oh," Lila responded, thinking it wasn't like Dat to do something as unconventional as striking up a relationship with a divorced woman. Lila certainly didn't know of anyone who was divorced in their district, and certainly not anyone who was divorced and who had remarried. It wasn't allowed.

Then again, maybe that was what Dat wanted—companionship but not marriage.

Lila wasn't sure why Beth had shared her story. Surely it wasn't because she thought Reuben might leave Lila. She couldn't think of a more ludicrous situation than that. "Did you love your husband?" Lila asked.

Beth placed the jar on the table and then faced Lila again, her arms crossed. "I thought I would come to love him. That's what my parents told me. And I'm guessing that's what his family told him—if he even asked. We were taught to make a commitment. To respect each other. All of that."

Lila nodded.

"I never would have left him," Beth said. "Ever. Even if I never felt an ounce of love along with all that commitment. But he had a different level of tolerance than I did. In retrospect, I wish our parents would have advised us to wait another year. Until we were a little older. Until we'd spent more time together. We never really connected, not in an emotional way."

Lila's face grew warm. "Reuben and I have known each other since we were children," Lila said. And then she added, wanting to change the subject, "I'm surprised your district allowed you to teach."

"Well, they didn't. But several years later I moved to an aunt and uncle's district, with a more sympathetic bishop." She hesitated a moment and then said, "I had a few bad years—I can tell you that. But after a time I was thankful for what happened to me. It taught me compassion."

Lila pursed her lips together, wondering if Beth realized that Dat was short on that particular virtue. As she turned to the stove to pull her thoughts together, Trudy burst through the door. "I got to see Zane!"

Lila's hand flew to her throat, but when she realized Beth was watching her she reached for Trudy's hand. "On Skype?"

Trudy nodded. "He was wearing his uniform. The camouflage one."

Rose stepped into the kitchen. "He has a beard," she said and then grinned. "He looks great. All tanned. His hair has these gold tints. So does his beard." She laughed. "It's so funny. He doesn't have a mustache though. It looks like an Amish beard."

"Why does he have a beard at all?" Lila asked. It didn't seem right for a soldier.

"Joel said it's because he's on a special assignment. They want them to have beards because the Afghan men do."

Bewildered, Lila continued with her questions. "Did Shani know they were going to Skype?" Lila couldn't imagine Shani setting it up while Trudy was visiting.

"No," Trudy said. "Zane called on his phone as he was trying to get through on the computer. Shani opened up her laptop, clicked on something, and there he was."

"He was only on base for a few hours," Rose explained. "He was headed back to the mountains."

"How did he seem?"

"*Gut*. Excited about what he's doing."

Lila was glad he was satisfied with his work, but for someone who had once considered pacifism it seemed to be a strange shift for him to be enjoying his time in the Army. She sighed.

But maybe that had all changed. She patted the e-mail in her pocket. Maybe he changed even since he'd written to her.

"It's not like they're shooting people," Rose said. "Joel said they're helping families, whole tribes. Getting them clean water and safer cookstoves. Working with the women so they can take better care of their families."

Relief rushed through Lila. No wonder Zane was excited about his work. It was perfect for him.

Lila had forgotten all about Beth being in the kitchen, but now she glanced at the woman, self-conscious. Beth was watching her. "Zane is our Englisch neighbors' son," Lila explained. "We grew up together."

Beth nodded, a little too knowingly. "Your father mentioned him." The woman turned to the refrigerator and took out a pitcher of rhubarb punch.

"Go wash up," Lila said to Trudy. "Dat should be in soon."

Rose followed her sister down the hall.

"Zane must be a good friend," Beth said as she stirred the punch.

Lila shook her head. "He *was* a good friend."

Beth smiled. "You can't end a *friendshoft*—not if you still care."

Lila didn't answer. She did still care. But one had to communicate to have a friendship. She patted her pocket again. Zane had reached out to her. But what purpose would it serve to return his e-mail? Knowing he was doing well—and in relatively little danger—helped her resolve not to communicate with him. Maybe she wasn't in love with Reuben per se, but they did respect each other. And they were committed to each other. They were nothing like Beth and her husband. Although Beth's comment about not connecting emotionally did nag at Lila. . . .

She shifted her thoughts. Zane was all right. Maybe he was lonely and needed a friend, but he was fine.

And she would be too, with time.

Two weeks later Lila worked in the shop while Shani and Eve stitched Zane's quilt in the back room. Mammi was doing well enough to help a little. Lila listened to their murmurs between waiting on customers. Today she'd work all day, and tomorrow she had church and then her membership class. She yawned, tired from working the night before at the Plain Buffet and then getting up early to help with the milking. As she covered her mouth, the front bell rang. Lila turned toward the door.

Beth appeared, taking off her black bonnet. "Hallo," she said and then smiled. "Your Dat said you'd be working today."

"Hi," Lila said, surprised to see her. "What brings you this way?"

"I'm working on a quilt and needed more batting."

Lila pointed at the far wall and started toward it. "I'll show you what we have."

"I also wanted to speak with you," Beth said.

"Oh?" That was the last thing Lila wanted. More serious talk with a woman she didn't even know, especially when three women she knew very well were in the next room.

"I'm afraid I shared too much when we spoke about my brief marriage."

"It was fine," Lila said.

"I certainly didn't mean to insinuate that there are any similarities between our lives."

"No, I didn't gather that at all," Lila answered.

"And your father said again, later that night"— the two of them had visited in the living room while the girls retreated to their room—"how pleased he is that you and Reuben are courting."

Lila nodded.

"I didn't tell your father this, but I couldn't help but notice the expression on your face when your sisters mentioned the neighbor boy."

Lila inhaled sharply. "His mother is here today. Along with my grandmother and Aenti." She took Beth's arm, determined to stop the conversation about Zane. "I'd like to introduce you to them."

As they entered the room she made eye contact with her grandmother. "Mammi, I'd like you to meet Trudy's teacher."

"Oh, goodness," Mammi said, standing. "The famous Beth."

The woman laughed. "Perhaps infamous."

"Trudy has told me so much about you," Mammi said, shaking her hand. "It's a privilege to get to meet you. What a wonderful surprise."

"And this is my Aenti." Lila pointed toward Eve. "And Shani, our neighbor."

"I'm so pleased to meet everyone," Beth said. "Trudy has told me about all of you—not to make you uncomfortable or anything."

Eve laughed. "I'm a teacher too. I know how this works."

"Right," Beth responded. "I tell parents I won't believe everything their student says about home as long as they—"

Eve interrupted her. "Don't believe everything the student says about school."

They both laughed.

Beth smiled again. "But honestly, Trudy's said wonderful things about all of you. I can tell she's a well-loved child."

Everyone agreed that Trudy was well supported, and silently Lila confirmed that everything Trudy said about home was probably true. As much as Beth had been around their home in the past month, she must have seen the dysfunction of their family firsthand. Although there wasn't as much drama now with Simon gone.

"What are you working on?" Beth asked,

stepping toward Zane's red, white, and blue quilt.

"It's for my son," Shani said.

"The one in Afghanistan?"

Shani nodded.

"How wonderful," Beth said, touching the topper. "Trudy's told me about him too." She glanced toward Lila but didn't say anything. "I have some extra time today. May I help?"

"Sure," Shani answered, nodding toward a folding chair leaning against the wall.

The door chimed and Lila hurried back out to the shop, thankful to have evaded Beth's questions. The woman was nosy, but besides that she liked her. She seemed to have a keen sense of intuition—except for maybe when it came to Dat. Perhaps she was blind, once again, to a bad relationship.

Beth's story about her marriage made Lila think about her parents and their first years together. She knew her parents didn't always agree—but she also knew her father adored her mother and loved her deeply. Her death had wounded him to his core.

Lila continued to work as the other women quilted. Between customers she'd pop into the quilting room. One time Shani was talking about Zane. Another time Eve spoke about her classroom and how much joy the children brought her. Lila was certain her aunt wanted children but hadn't been able to have them yet. Dat would say

God was punishing her for having an Englisch boyfriend during her Rumschpringe and then leaving the church for good and marrying Charlie. But Lila was sure God didn't work that way. Instead, she was certain he had other plans for Eve and Charlie.

The last time Lila stepped into the quilting room, Beth was gathering up her things. "This has been delightful," she said. "Do you quilt every Saturday morning?"

"Jah," Mammi said. "Please join us again. We'd all like that."

Aenti Eve and Shani nodded in agreement.

Lila walked Beth through the shop.

"Zane's mother seems like a good woman," Beth said as they reached the door.

"She is," Lila answered. "His father is a good man too."

"How about the son?"

Lila grimaced.

"It's none of my business, but . . ." Beth peered at Lila, her hazel eyes full of concern. "Life can be complicated, jah?"

"Not so much," Lila said. "We all have our places. I've always known that." But she hadn't always believed it. She used to think there would somehow be hope for her and Zane. That by some miracle she'd spend her life with him. That had been when she was a child. She'd grown up since then.

Beth took a long time to say anything. When she finally did, she simply said, "I suppose you're right."

Lila waited at the door as the woman left, hoping she wouldn't say anything to Dat about what she suspected. If she did, her father would encourage her to marry Reuben as soon as possible, probably right after she joined the church.

15

Zane hoisted his duffel bag onto his back as he made his way through the crowd of people at the Philadelphia airport. He'd texted from Atlanta that his flight was delayed by a couple of hours, and that he would call and meet them at the curb once he had his luggage. Hopefully his parents had received the text before they left for Philly.

"Thank you for your sacrifice," an older man said as Zane strode by him.

Zane slowed and told the man he was welcome. He appreciated the gratitude, but it always left him feeling a little awkward too. He hadn't sacrificed that much.

He inhaled deeply as he walked toward baggage claim. So many people. And the smells of the food seemed overpowering. He missed the mountains and fresh air. He missed the thin bread and chutney and Aliah's gosh-e fil. He missed Jaalal and even Benham, although he certainly didn't have a relationship with the young man like he did with the grandparents.

In an effort to connect with Jaalal on a deeper level, Zane had shown him some photos of his family and their farm. The higher-ups encouraged it to dispel the misconceptions that all Americans lived fast, self-centered lives. As he went through the photos on his phone, he zipped past the ones of Lila. Jaalal had asked him to go back to those and Zane complied. Jaalal was curious about her, and Zane explained she was Plain. Then he tried to explain the Amish to Jaalal, who couldn't believe there were Americans like that. Several times he repeated the word *Amish*, as if intrigued by the word. Zane explained their religious and nonresistant beliefs and that they educated their children in parochial one-room schools and pretty much operated like a village, even though they lived on farms spread across the countryside.

Jaalal listened closely and then said, "You like the girl, no?" Zane had answered she was a friend, but Jaalal laughed and said he didn't believe him.

Yes, he missed Jaalal and his insights and wisdom, but Zane also missed his team—most of them. Sarge. Casey. Wade, who little by little was becoming more of his own man. Not Grant, though. The more Zane connected with the

Afghan people the more resentful Grant became. He was as far from civil as possible. He continually made derogatory comments about the Afghan people.

At least Wade was backing off from supporting Grant. There were a few times when he seemed downright uncomfortable with what Grant was saying—not enough to call him on it, but at least enough not to back him up.

Zane swiped his hand across his chin. He'd shaved his beard off once he'd reached Bagram, but he was having a hard time getting used to his bare face. Grant never did stop harassing him about his lack of a mustache, but each time Zane weathered the man's barbs, he thought of the Amish resilience and prayed for some measure of hope for the Afghan people, that someday they would know peace.

He knew it was unlikely though. Centuries of fighting hadn't resolved anything for the tribal people, or the ones living in cities throughout the country.

Zane quickened his pace and lifted his head as he heard someone call his name on the other side of security. Adam jumped up and down ahead, a giant balloon in his hand that said *Welcome Home*. His parents both waved, huge grins on their faces.

He waved back and inhaled again. He was glad to be home, he really was. Seeing his family made his heart flutter. He increased his stride, practically running to the waiting area. In no time he had his arms wrapped around his parents and Adam all at the same time. He wasn't surprised that his mother was crying, but when he finally pulled away he realized that they all were. Even him.

Zane spent the first couple of days of his furlough relaxing. Adam wasn't out of school yet, but both Mom and Dad had taken time off. They asked him several times if he wanted to go into Philly or New York or for a hike in the Poconos, saying they'd take Adam out of school. He declined. He hadn't realized how tired he was. He wanted to sleep and rest and read. He'd been reading through the Psalms, soaking it in. He'd felt God's presence in Afghanistan in a way he'd never felt it before. He thought of the cliché "There are no atheists in foxholes." He certainly hadn't been in a foxhole. And there were atheists around— although there were lots of believers too. What he'd felt was a peace that God would take care of him no matter what.

He appreciated the Psalms now more than ever. David had been a soldier and a poet. He'd felt things deeply. His words were honest.

His thoughts often went to Lila. Maybe she hadn't gotten his e-mail. Wouldn't she have at least had the decency to respond if she had? He swallowed hard. Maybe her silence was for the best. He'd sent it in a moment of weakness.

On Zane's third day home, he was sitting on the porch when Tim came down to say hello. He told him that Simon was coming home from Virginia, where he'd recently been stationed, for a few days of leave.

"Will he be staying at the house?" Zane thought maybe he'd stay with his grandparents.

"Jah," Tim answered. "Of course."

Zane was a little surprised.

"It will give the girls a break from the milking."

After Tim left, Zane went into the house and found Mom in the kitchen, setting the table. He told her Tim had stopped by and was quite friendly.

She explained that Tim had a "friend" who seemed to be having a positive influence on him.

"What kind of friend?" Zane asked, confused.

"Trudy's teacher. She's in her early forties, and it seems she and Tim have been seeing quite a bit of each other."

"You're kidding." He couldn't fathom Tim Lehman courting.

"She quilts with us." Mom put the knives and forks in place. "She's the Beth who signed the back of your quilt."

Just before Zane left for furlough, a red-white-and-blue quilt had arrived that had been signed by Mom, Lila's grandmother, Eve, and this Beth. But not Lila. He'd put it in his footlocker back at the base, not intending to take it into the field. He knew how much work went into it—and prayers. It meant a lot. He planned to send a thank-you to the ladies when he returned. It would probably mean more sent from Afghanistan.

"Lila was supposed to sign the quilt too, but she was working at the restaurant the Saturday we finished it."

"Oh" was all Zane managed to say. She hadn't come over, even though she knew he was home. Rose had come over with Trudy a couple of times already.

The next day, he had a text from Simon, asking Zane to pick him up at the train station in Lancaster, with the explanation that Daniel wasn't driving his truck anymore.

Zane hadn't seen Daniel yet, but he still hoped to. It sounded as if he were planning to join the church, which probably meant he and Jenny would soon marry. Zane couldn't help but feel a little jealous. Except for the Amish youth, no one he knew admitted to wanting to settle down. Even Casey talked about the freedom she had by not being married. It wasn't as if Zane had told any-one he longed to be married either though. Why would he when the girl he wanted was off-limits?

He'd probably be finishing up his tour in Afghanistan when Daniel and Jenny married.

That was fine with him. The last thing he wanted to see was Lila and Reuben together at an Amish wedding. Then again, the two of them would probably be marrying around then too, if not sooner.

Zane waited inside the train station, wearing his civilian clothes—jeans and a T-shirt. He spotted Simon in his uniform first and nearly laughed. The Amish boy wearing fatigues while the Englisch soldier wore jeans. It could have been worse—Zane could have borrowed a pair of Simon's old pants, suspenders, and shirt. He wished he'd thought of it.

"Bro!" Simon called out from across the train station and started running. Zane strolled forward, his arms extended.

Simon hugged him hard, whacking him on the back. Two women stopped to stare and then thanked Simon for his service.

Simon stepped back and pointed to Zane. "Thank him. He's home from Afghanistan on furlough."

The women gushed a little and then thanked Zane.

He nodded an acknowledgment. He wasn't serving any more than Simon. He'd just been sent to a more dangerous place.

He grabbed Simon's backpack from him, but his friend held on tight. "No way," he said. "You're my superior."

"Knock it off," Zane said. "I'm your friend."

"You're my brother."

Zane nodded, grabbed the backpack, slung it over his shoulder, and swung his other arm over Simon's shoulder.

"Daniel has the day off," Simon said. "I told him we'd pick him up."

"All right," Zane said.

A half hour later they were with Daniel at his place. Simon changed into civilian clothes and then suggested they go get something to eat.

"Anywhere you want to go," Zane said. It was late on a Saturday afternoon in the middle of May, which meant the entire county was crawling with tourists.

"The buffet on the highway. I'm ready for some home cooking, or at least close to it."

Zane nodded, trying to keep his expression even. That was where Lila worked. He could only hope it was her day off.

On the way, Simon entertained them with stories about boot camp. "I knew I was naive," he said. "But I had no idea how badly. We had all sorts of people trying to prove themselves. Some days I thought everyone was going to kill one another before the Army could."

"How were things by the end?"

"Good," Simon said. "Not totally conflict free but a whole lot better."

"Did anyone go down . . ." Zane stopped, realizing how stupid his question was.

"For my boot camp graduation?"

Zane nodded. "Sorry. I wasn't thinking."

"Your dad offered to."

"Really?" Zane loosened his grip on the steering wheel. He wasn't surprised.

"But I told him not to. Insisted, in fact. I've enjoyed my independence. It's been the best thing for me."

When they reached the Plain Buffet, Simon was the first one out of Zane's truck. He practically ran into the restaurant. Zane could understand he'd be excited to see Lila but was surprised at his enthusiasm. He glanced at Daniel, who shrugged and said, "Obviously he has it bad."

Zane shook his head. "For?"

"Mandy."

"Who's Mandy?"

"A girl Simon was seeing, sort of, before he left."

"Ah," Zane said. That explained it. By the time he and Zane stepped inside, Simon had his arms around a girl wearing a Mennonite Kapp. Zane recognized her from the time he'd come into the restaurant with his parents, when Lila was working. Mandy had a twinkle in her eyes as she unwrapped Simon's arms from around her.

"I'm on duty. Are you trying to get me fired?" she joked, pointing toward a table. "That's my section." She was obviously happy to see him. He grinned and led the way.

Zane glanced around as he followed.

"Don't worry," Daniel said. "Lila's not working. She's at Mammi's shop today."

Zane ignored Daniel's comment and slid into the booth across from Simon. Daniel slid next to Zane. Obviously, they were going to be Simon's audience.

And they were. Simon continued on about how great the Army was and how well he'd done on his marksmanship tests. "Not to brag or anything," he said, "but I got a perfect score."

Daniel kicked Simon under the table.

"Careful or you'll end up being a sniper," Zane said.

"Exactly," Simon said. "I can't wait."

Zane shook his head. "You're kidding—right?"

"No. What better job could I have than protecting other soldiers? It's the most important job in the Army."

Zane shook his head. "A medic is the most important job." And next to that civil affairs, but he wasn't going to say that. Taking care of people was far more important than shooting them.

"Yeah, well, if the sniper does his job there's no need for a medic."

Daniel shifted in his seat as Mandy arrived to take their drink order and then said, "Go fill your plates."

When they returned with their food, Zane asked Daniel about Jenny. He blushed as he pressed his fork tines against his mashed potatoes. "She's good. We both finished our class to join the church." He paused and then added, "So did Lila."

Zane didn't react, at least he hoped he didn't.

"That's why I sold my truck and gave up my cell phone," Daniel said. "We're all joining next week."

"Gideon's going to douse you, huh?" Zane smiled. Lila had explained how the bishop poured water over the heads of those he baptized.

"Yep." Daniel seemed happy as could be about it.

"What about work?"

"I'm still doing construction. For Jenny's uncle, though—not the guy from before."

Zane nodded. Jenny's paternal uncle had taken over her father's construction firm. That was a good place for Daniel. Perhaps he could work into being a partner. The money would be much better than working for anyone else. Monika had probably arranged all of it.

"So are you going to move in with Dat once you're married?" Simon teased.

Daniel didn't take the bait. "Monika and Gideon are building a Dawdi Haus for when they're older. Jenny and I'll live there for the time being." He blushed again.

Simon turned his attention to Zane. "How about you? Have you found anyone in the Army who suits your fancy?"

Zane shook his head.

"You will, in time," Simon said.

Zane shook his head again. "I'm out of there as soon as possible. After I come home from Afghanistan, I'll only have five months left."

"You're kidding," Simon said. "Why would you leave so soon?"

"Don't get me wrong. I feel good about what I'm doing right now—but in general, I still don't think these two wars are right."

A look of disgust passed over Simon's face. "It's your country—love it or leave it."

Zane could just imagine Simon hearing that from some gung-ho military man. "That's not how it works," Zane said. "That's actually what we fight for—so people can have differing opinions. So people like the Amish can live out their beliefs."

"Yeah," Simon said. "But you're not Amish." He shoved a fork loaded with green beans into his mouth.

Zane exhaled, not wanting to get into an argument with Simon. "But I still have a right to my beliefs," he said as calmly as he could.

"Not really," Simon answered. "You sold your soul to Uncle Sam." Then he broke out in a grin, but Zane knew he wasn't joking.

He hadn't sold his soul, but it sounded as if Simon had. Zane didn't fault his friend for his beliefs—he just hated that simplistic thinking.

All of it was complex, whether one was in Afghanistan or back home. Simon had no idea just how complex it could be.

Zane just wanted to make it through without having to do anything he'd regret for the rest of his life. Simon, on the other hand, seemed to think he'd have no regrets. No matter what.

The next Friday, several days after Simon had returned to Virginia, Zane went into town to Dad's work. He wore his dress uniform, at his father's request. They were having a gathering for a group of veterans, and Dad wanted Zane to share about his experience in Afghanistan, saying it was good for them to hear about the positive work going on and that it was helping citizens.

Zane appreciated the meeting more than he thought he would. The vets had all served in Afghanistan and Iraq. Some had pretty severe injuries—from lost limbs to obvious brain trauma. What impacted Zane most was that their physical injuries weren't their biggest hurts. What happened to others—or what they inflicted on others—was what haunted them. One man talked about horrible nightmares after an accidental attack on civilians. Another talked about a car filled with children that exploded at a checkpoint he manned. A third talked about a shootout that left a little boy dead.

He couldn't help but question his involvement

in war, once again, after listening to their stories.

On the way home, after he turned onto June-berry Lane, he slowed even more than usual when he reached the Lehmans' drive. He peered down it, as always. Dresses hung on the line, blowing in the breeze. Burgundy, green, and blue. And black aprons. But no one was in sight. His heart ached at the thought of not even catching a glimpse of Lila while he was home.

Home. That was what he longed for—and it wasn't the house his parents lived in. He wanted a wife to love. A family to care for. A safe place of his own.

It was milking time. Lila was probably helping her Dat.

After he parked his truck, he sat in it for a long while and then headed toward the field, stopping when he reached the halfway point. He stared at the gate. The first time he saw Lila he'd been standing at that gate.

He thought of the gate a lot. Of him on one side and her on the other. He imagined her there again. He continued on but stopped when he heard a voice.

"Go set the table." It was Lila.

Zane stepped toward the edge of the poplars, hiding in the shadows, as Trudy skipped from the barn. He stayed put, afraid Lila might follow. Just as he'd decided to turn around and go back home, he saw her walking toward the house. And then she stopped and looked toward the weathered boards of the fence, her gaze soft. Her expression had a sweetness to it that he remembered from when they were young.

For a moment he thought she'd seen him, but then she kept on going. He waited a moment to make sure Tim wouldn't follow and then headed back home, feeling like a coward. He couldn't help but note the irony of him in his uniform. Yes, he was a soldier, but he was more afraid of a certain girl than anything else in the world.

That night, as he thought about the veterans he'd met, Zane did some research on pacifism. He felt good about his work in Afghanistan, but there was still the possibility that he could get into a firefight. How would he handle that?

Sitting at his parents' computer, he came across information about a group of American deserters from the Vietnam War to the present who resided in Canada. The older ones were doing their best to support the younger ones. It turned out the Canadian people were mostly welcoming to the deserters, but the government wasn't that hospitable.

Most of the ex-soldiers claimed to be apolitical. One said he was disgusted by the prevalent racism of the soldiers he served with in Iraq and couldn't bear to be a part of it anymore. The majority of the people Zane served with weren't racist, but the ones who were definitely impacted morale. Other deserters wrote that their personal philosophy about war had changed after they'd actually experienced it. "I couldn't stomach the thought of killing any more people," one deserter wrote. "I had no idea the emotional toll it would take on me. I've killed sons, fathers, brothers, husbands. I just couldn't do it anymore."

Zane closed down the site and pushed back the chair. He wasn't thinking of deserting. He felt good about the work he was doing. But what if he'd ended up in the infantry instead of civil affairs? What if he'd had to kill someone? Or even lots of people.

He'd been denying the possibilities of what could happen to him, but what could he do about it? There was no use dwelling on it.

His father was right. He had been indecisive before, but now he had a plan. He'd finish out his time in the Army and then go to college on the GI Bill. His time working in the civil affairs unit made him want to study social work. Maybe he could work with Afghan immigrants in the U.S. Or maybe veterans like his dad. There were lots of possibilities.

Going to college, getting a degree, and then finding a job were what he needed to do to get that *home* he so desperately wanted someday, God willing.

On his last day of furlough, Zane went with Mom to the store to pick up shaving cream, blades, toothpaste, and soap. All things that the PX on base in Afghanistan sometimes didn't have. After they were done, Shani said she needed to stop by the quilt shop.

Zane groaned.

"You could come in and tell the women thank you for the work they did on your quilt."

"I could," he responded. But he wouldn't. Mom parked on the side of the building, and Zane could see Lila's buggy parked in front of the little shed. Her horse was probably inside, sheltered from the sun. The weather had turned hot, nearly ninety degrees.

Mom put the van in Park and opened her door. "Aren't you coming?"

Zane shook his head. The less he said the better.

"But you said you would."

He shook his head. "I said I could."

"Don't be ridiculous," Mom said.

Zane stared straight ahead. "Would you let it go?" She'd done a better job not meddling in his life the last two weeks—the best ever in fact. Until now.

Mom made a funny squeak and then climbed down and shut the door. He watched her hurry into the shop. He could tell she was upset by the way her shoulders slumped, just a little. He didn't mean to disappoint her, but if Lila had wanted to see him she would have e-mailed him back or, better yet, walked down the lane to say hello.

A minute after Mom disappeared inside the door it swung open again. A girl in a Kapp appeared. Zane looked away quickly, not wanting Lila to catch him staring.

A moment later, she was gone—he assumed back into the shop.

Mom had taken the key, probably on purpose, so he couldn't run the air. He opened the door to cool off, but even so, within a few minutes sweat trickled down the side of his face. He felt bad about not thanking Lila's grandmother and Eve. And Trudy's teacher. They'd all put a lot of work into his quilt—and here he was, hiding in a hot van because he was too afraid to say hello to the person who had been his best friend from the time he was thirteen until his senior year of high school. He'd gone into unknown villages in Afghanistan with Jaalal, having no idea who they'd meet. It wasn't that he wasn't unafraid in Afghanistan, but he'd never hesitated. He did what he was supposed to.

Three Englisch women stopped in front of the quilt store and then went in. They looked as if they might spend some time shopping. He could slip into the shop and then into the back room without having to say more than a hello to Lila.

He pushed the van door all the way open and stepped down, slamming it behind him. When he reached the door of the shop, it swung open and two of the women stepped out. The third was saying, "Thank you for the directions!"

Zane moved aside, and the third woman exited, holding the door for him. He thanked her and stayed put for a moment until he realized the door chime hadn't stopped singing.

"Zane?" Lila stepped toward him.

"Hello," he said.

"Can I help you with something?"

His face grew even warmer. "I wanted to tell the quilters thank you."

"Oh," Lila said. Her face was full of color, and she seemed more confident than the last time he'd seen her. "It's that way." She pointed to the back of the shop.

"Denki." His heart began to pound, and he started through the shop. But then stopped. He would stop being cowardly. He turned back toward her. "Did you get my e-mail?"

For a moment her eyes glazed over, and he thought she was going to give him that flat affect that she managed so well when she didn't want to discuss something. But then a flash of life flew through her eyes and she said, "I did. It was good to hear from you."

That caught him off guard. Finally he managed to say, "But you didn't answer."

"I didn't have time the day I read it, and I haven't been back to the library since."

He cocked his head. It was a feeble excuse.

And she knew it. He locked his eyes on hers. She remained silent. He turned to go.

"I was afraid to," she said.

Without turning around he asked, "Why?"

"It's probably best that I don't answer that," she responded.

He shouldn't have bothered asking her. He kept on walking toward the voices in the next room. When he entered Mom stopped whatever she was saying and said, "I'm so glad you came in!" She introduced him to Beth, and he shook her hand. Then he hugged Leona and Eve.

"Thank you for the quilt," he said to all the women. "It means a lot to me."

"It was our pleasure," Beth answered.

Zane felt as if he might choke up. All of the women, besides his mother, believed in nonresistance. But they'd made a quilt for a soldier.

Beth smiled at him. "Tell us what it's like over there," she said.

Zane told them about the geography—the high mountains, the deep valleys, and the storms that rolled in without warning. He told them about the lizards the size of small dogs and the camel spiders.

All of the women listened attentively, including his mom.

"What about the people?" It was Lila's voice, coming from the doorway.

Without turning, Zane told the women about Jaalal, Aliah, and Benham, and the work to get a new well dug in one village. He told them about a two-year-old girl who'd fallen into a fire and how badly she'd been burned, and the drive to get safe cookstoves for all of the families they came in contact with. He told them about the work his unit was doing to get schoolbooks for girls in another village and the hygiene skills Casey and her team were teaching. He told them about the different tribes and the villages and the threat of the Taliban. "Usually a village forms an allegiance with whoever will protect them the most. Often it's about survival, not principles."

"Of course," Leona murmured. "They want safety for their children, just as we do."

Zane nodded. "That's what I've thought about over and over. We all want the same thing. A safe place to live. Viable work. Hope for the future."

"What about religion?"

"We don't talk about that much," Zane said. "Although Jaalal did ask about my faith, and I told him I was a Christian. He's positive about our faith—he said he knows Christians have donated money and other supplies to help the Afghan people and others around the world too."

Beth said, "Could we make some quilts for the children?"

"And receiving blankets," Leona added.

"That would be great," Zane answered.

271

"In fact," Leona said, standing, "I have a couple of baby quilts and blankets I could send with you. Do you have room?"

"I can make room," Zane said.

"I'll get them," Lila said, hurrying to the cupboard under the windows and retrieving a stack of blankets and then two quilts.

"Who were those for?" Zane asked.

"They're just samples we keep around," Leona said. "We'll make more."

"I'll go wrap them," Lila said, heading back into the shop.

The other three women started talking about what leftover material they had and what patterns they could use. Zane turned and headed back into the shop after Lila. She stood at the counter with a sheet of brown wrapping paper.

"This is really cool," he said. "I know the mothers who receive these will be thrilled."

Lila nodded but didn't lift her head. He couldn't see her eyes, but her cheeks were red. Perhaps it was the heat.

He stopped in front of the counter. He'd regained his courage. He had to try, one more time.

But before he could speak she raised her head. "I'm sorry I told you to go away, the farther the better, that day." Her voice caught.

He winced. "I went as far away as possible."

She met his eyes. "I didn't mean Afghanistan."

Zane swallowed hard, nodding in response. He knew she didn't. "Would you respond to a letter?"

"Not if you sent it to the house."

"What if I sent it here?" He took a business card from the holder on the counter as he spoke and held it up.

She lifted her head and met his eyes. "Probably. But only until I get married."

He nodded, reading between the lines again. She would marry soon. It didn't matter. If only she'd answer his letters for a couple of months even. He'd take whatever he could get. He exhaled. "Okay," he said. "I'll send the letters here."

Without responding, Lila flipped the brown package over and taped the bottom and then the sides. Then she handed it to Zane. "I'll be praying for the babies who receive these."

He nodded as he tucked the package under his arm.

"And for you."

He held out his hand to her, and she took it. As they shook, he said, "Friends?"

She nodded and then quickly pulled her hand away.

He felt a lump rising in his throat and couldn't speak. A moment later Mom entered from the back room. "Shall we get going?"

After he followed his mother to the door, he

turned and waved to Lila. She waved back and smiled, not like he remembered from when they were children, but at least it was kind. And it appeared to be genuine. That was a start.

16

The next day, Gideon baptized Lila, Daniel, and Jenny during the Sunday morning church service in his and Monika's shed. As Gideon poured the water over Lila's head and it cascaded over her face and sent a shiver down her spine, she was overcome with a sense of peace and a sense of God's presence. Joining the church was the right thing for her. She could sense how pleased Dat was, and she knew her mother would have been as well.

It was the only thing she was certain about, actually. Well, that and that she hadn't been fair to Reuben when she told Zane he could write.

On Monday she left after breakfast to work in the quilt shop. After parking her buggy, unhitching her horse, and feeding and watering her in the shed, she unlocked the shop, raised the blinds, and tucked her lunch and thermos away in the back room in the cupboard.

The doorbell rang, and she hurried back into the shop.

It was the postman.

"You're early," she said.

"A little," he answered as he handed her a stack of envelopes. The one on top immediately caught her eye. It was from Zane. His handwriting. His name. An APO return address.

"Thank you," she said, placing the envelopes on the counter, shocked a letter from Zane had arrived so soon. She checked the postmark. He must have written the same day he saw her in the shop.

As soon as the postman left, she folded Zane's envelope in half, slipped it into her apron pocket, and put the rest in Dawdi's box in the office. He'd be in soon to open the mail and go through the books. Mammi had her chemo treatments on Friday, and Mondays were always her worst day. She wouldn't be in.

Once the blinds were pulled, the Open sign showing, and the knickknacks rearranged on the counter, Lila patted the letter in her pocket. She didn't want to be reading it when Dawdi came in—that was for sure. Or if anyone else she knew came in. She took out the piece she was working on for her crazy quilt. She'd chosen blues, purples, and greens for it, using the prints Mammi had given her, and added solid scraps from the dresses and shirts she'd made at home.

Mammi had been right—designing the crazy quilt had given her something more creative to do, and she appreciated the challenge. Not only did she enjoy the piecing of the quilt, but the stitching too, especially the fancier ones like the feather, fern leaf, and fly stitches. Dat had seen her working on it a couple of times but hadn't asked about it.

That was fine. Otherwise he might have deemed it prideful for her to be putting so much effort into a quilt for herself.

Working on the crazy quilt gave her the same satisfied feeling as memorizing a poem with Zane had. She could feel the emotion welling up inside as she pieced and stitched, just as she could feel the emotion of the poet come through the words. It gave her a sense of harmony.

Soon she had a steady stream of customers— both tourists and locals. Dawdi didn't come in until after noon. He said Mammi was resting. "Stop by on your way home," he said.

Lila shook her head. "I wish I could, but I work at the restaurant at five, remember? You said you'd close up."

"That's right," Dawdi said. Two of their employees were out of town for family reunions. Dawdi headed back to the office. Lila patted the letter again. Even though he usually took at least an hour, she'd wait.

Midafternoon, an hour before it was time for her to leave for the restaurant, Lila heard a wagon outside and the heavy trotting of workhorses. She stepped to the window. It was Reuben with a load of lumber. He parked across the street, hitched the horses, and then came bounding toward her, his hand on top of his straw hat.

She put the crazy quilt piece on the counter and headed to the door, swinging it open for him. "What are you doing out this way?"

He took his hat off. "Making a delivery. I have something I need to say."

"How about some lemonade first?" She'd packed a thermos full and had only had a cup with her lunch. She pondered over his choice of words. It wasn't that he wanted to talk—he had something he needed to say.

Lila led him into the quilting room, retrieved her thermos, and an extra cup from the collection Mammi kept on hand. While Reuben drank, the front bell chimed again and Lila helped a woman looking for material to make a quilt for her grand-baby. Lila hoped the woman would take her time, but she made up her mind quickly. Reuben stood in the doorway to the quilt shop and watched Lila as she cut the fabric, folded it, slipped it into a bag, and then finished the transaction.

When the woman left, he said he needed to get going but first he needed to say his piece.

"Jah?"

"I've been thinking about us," he said. "We've known each other as long as we can remember. Now that you've joined the church, there's no reason to wait past fall to marry."

She liked the idea of marrying Reuben, but the reality of it made her nervous. "What about Daniel and Jenny? I think they're planning to marry this fall."

"That doesn't matter. You won't need to help them. Monika will see to the details."

"But Jenny and Monika won't be able to help us."

"We don't need a large wedding, do we?" he asked.

Lila shook her head. Dat wouldn't have the money for a big wedding anyway. She'd saved some, and she knew Reuben had too. But they'd need help with the food preparation, setup, and cleanup. Simon wouldn't be around. Daniel would be busy with his own responsibilities. She knew Beth would cook and Eve too, if Dat would allow it. . . .

"Let's talk about it Sunday night," Lila said.

Reuben nodded. "I already talked with my Dat some. He said that he and my brothers will do what they can."

That would help.

Reuben bumped against her, and the envelope in her pocket crinkled. Her face grew warm, and guilt stabbed at her heart.

"I've waited a long time, Lila."

She nodded. "I know. We'll talk." After three years of courting, she couldn't put it off any longer.

The door to the office opened, and Dawdi

stepped out with a few envelopes in his hand. "Reuben," he said, his voice welcoming.

"I just stopped in to see Lila."

"*Gut*," Dawdi said. "We always like to see you here."

Reuben told them both good-bye and left. Then Dawdi told Lila to go ahead, that he'd take over so she could leave.

Reuben wanting to say his piece but not being willing to put the effort into talking reminded her of Dat. It was that disengagement that frustrated her. That unwillingness to put out the effort to listen, to talk, and to share one's feelings. But then again maybe Dat did engage with Beth. Lila couldn't imagine the woman investing in another relationship where she didn't have that.

On the way to the restaurant, once her horse had turned onto the highway, Lila took the letter out of her pocket and opened it.

Zane hadn't written much. Just that it was good to see her and he hadn't meant to put pressure on her.

You've been pretty clear that you didn't want to communicate, and maybe I should have left it at that—but I felt compelled to ask one more time. If you decide not to write back, I understand. Truly. I value all of my memories of our childhood above all else. I'm grateful to God for giving you and your siblings to me as neighbors and friends. But your Dat is right. We're grown now.

I can't keep clinging to the past. I'll always treasure it—but I know God will take care of all of us, as he sees fit, in the future. The verse "Be still, and know that I am God" keeps going through my head. Even though it's a war zone, there is a lot of stillness in Afghanistan. I know God is here as much as he is on Juneberry Lane.

I appreciate your prayers for those times that aren't so still.

He signed it, *Your friend, Zane.*

That was all. But it filled her heart to have him share so honestly with her.

The horse came to a stop at the crossroads, and Lila glanced up. To her right was Reuben in his empty wagon, waving at her. She waved back and wondered if he could tell she had been reading something. She continued to wave as he turned right and headed back toward the lumberyard and she continued on to the Plain Buffet, feeling guilty for her deception.

On the other hand the letter from Zane filled her with relief. He seemed so much more settled than when he joined the Army. Maybe they really could just be friends. Perhaps there would be no harm in writing him back.

Once she had her horse taken care of, she

headed to the break room. Mandy came rushing in behind her. "I'm so glad you're working tonight. I just had a text from Simon."

"Is everything okay?"

"He's doing great."

Lila shook her head. Mandy and Simon were like two peas in a pod. Both overly optimistic—that was for sure.

"How's your soldier doing?" Mandy asked.

"He's not *my* soldier."

The girl grinned.

"But it sounds as if Simon is yours."

"Yeah, well, don't spread it around. I haven't figured out how to tell my parents. But I really like your brother—a lot. I think I might even love him."

Lila tried to smile. "I doubt you know what you're getting into—but I'm sure you can handle yourself, and him."

"Your time will come," Mandy said. "Long before mine does. Unless I end up leaving the church sooner rather than later."

Lila nodded. She couldn't imagine Simon ever coming back home now. It would be a big transition for Mandy, but she had the spunk to leave the Plain way of life. Besides, she already knew how to drive a car and use technology.

Lila would never leave. And it wasn't just that she was baptized now. She'd never wanted to leave.

The peace from her baptism still held her. It was the right thing to do. *"Be still, and know that I am God."* Now the verse was running through her head too.

Still she couldn't help but envy Mandy—that she could love someone so effortlessly, without worrying about the future.

And that Simon clearly loved her too.

Reuben showed her that he loved her—but he'd never actually said it. She felt it shouldn't bother her, but it did. Words mattered to her, but not to Reuben.

Lila didn't intercept the next letter. It came two weeks later, and Dawdi delivered it to her. Thinking fast, she said, "It's probably a thank-you for the quilts Mammi sent with him."

She'd written a short reply to Zane's first note, simply saying that it had been good to see him too, asking how his transition back had gone, and how the weather was. She'd said nothing of importance, nothing about him writing again.

Dawdi hesitated a moment, as if he expected her to unseal it in front of him. Instead she folded the envelope and slipped it into her pocket. This time she couldn't wait to open it, and on her break she slipped out the back door to water her horse. Thankfully there was a note to Mammi, Eve, and Beth, thanking them for the quilts and blankets and describing how happy the mothers were to receive them for their babies. Lila exhaled as she read, grateful that the women had made more blankets—mostly receiving ones with the edges serged because that was faster. She'd sent them the week before.

Next was a letter to Lila. He had received her letter. *It came out to the field with a package from my mom,* he wrote. *Thank you for writing. It means a lot.* He didn't mention how shallow the letter had been—and she appreciated that, remembering their many conversations from when they were younger that were anything but shallow.

We're at base for two days—enough to shower, wash our clothes, and get a few good meals, or as good as they get. I know you're still feeling standoffish with me, and I get that. Both Simon and Daniel told me you'll marry soon. Reuben's a good man. You'll do well together. I know you don't feel as if you can be transparent with me now, and I understand that too.

What I want to make clear is how much I appreciated your honesty in the past. I'm not saying you're not being honest now—you are, within the boundaries you're comfortable with. I respect that. But I wanted you to know that your honesty when we were growing up and into our teen years showed me that's what I want in life. To be honest. And to have those I love be honest with me.

I don't know why I'm writing this. I guess just to let you know I appreciate the influence you've had on my life. No matter what happens, know that I loved you.

Lila swallowed hard, fighting back tears.

I didn't know how to show you, and I'm sorry about that. It was probably better, anyway. For all we have in common, I know there's more that separates us. I see the fathers here so desperate to care for their children, and I think of your Dat. I know we didn't always see it, but he loves you—all of you. I can see that in the villagers here. A harshness fueled by love and the desire to do what is right. The Afghan people have taught me nearly as much as the Amish.

It ended abruptly. He'd simply signed it: *Zane.* She tucked the letter back into her pocket. ". . . *know that I loved you.*" She swallowed hard again and headed back into the shop, swiping at her eyes as she walked. Dawdi was at the counter. "Are you all right?" he asked.

Lila smiled. "Just a bit of dust in my eye," she said, pulling the thank-you note out of her pocket. "Zane sent this for the ladies." She handed Dawdi the note.

He read it and smiled. "Nice. For a minute I thought he was corresponding with you."

Lila shrugged. "He wanted Mammi and the rest of the women to know how much the quilts and blankets were appreciated."

Dawdi didn't say anything more. He didn't like conflict. If anything more needed to be said, he'd leave it to Mammi.

Lila felt melancholy the rest of the day. That evening, after the supper dishes were put away, she went for a walk, slipping through the gate and then along the poplar trees. Had her Mamm felt this way about the Englisch boy she'd dated? Before she broke things off. Had it felt to her as if she were being yanked in two?

Her heart felt—again—as if it were breaking. She slid down the bank to their old fort. The frame of it was still solid, and although the sheets of plywood had weathered, they'd stayed in place. The rope they used to swing on when they played Tarzan had frayed, but the stump Zane had rolled down the bank where they used to sit side-by-side while she taught him Pennsylvania Dutch hadn't changed at all. The sound of the water streaming over the rocks soothed her as she reread the letter again in the dusky light. "... *know that I loved you.*" Why had he written that? Even if it meant he loved her as a friend, it only made it harder for her. She folded the letter and tucked it back into her pocket.

On the way back to the house, fireflies flickered in and out of the poplar trees. Lila stopped to watch. She couldn't help but smile at the beauty of them. *"Be still, and know that I am God."*

That night, after Rose and Trudy had fallen asleep, Lila lit the lamp in their room, turned the wick down low, and wrote back to Zane. She told him about how work was going, at both jobs, and about how taken Mandy was with Simon. She wrote him that Daniel and Jenny planned to marry in November, but she didn't write anything about Reuben wanting to marry her then too.

She continued on, writing about walking down to the fort and seeing the fireflies on the way back and what an enchanting moment it had been. She didn't write that the verse, "Be still, and know that I am God," was now playing over and over in her head.

Finally she closed the letter by writing:

I, too, treasure our time as children. I will always value the friendship we had. I learned so much from you. Your enthusiasm for life was contagious and brightened my child-hood. I'm very grateful for that.

She knew she'd be a better wife and mother because of her friendship with Zane. Even though she wanted to close with *your friend,* she didn't.

She simply signed it *Lila*. And she didn't say anything about loving him—not in the past or now. Or ever.

Lila was in the shop when Zane's next letter came. She answered it right away too. But when his fourth letter came, the end of July, one of the other clerks was working in the shop and she gave the letter to Dawdi, who gave it to Lila two days later when she came in to work. "Are you corresponding with him now?" he asked.

"I wrote him back," Lila answered, taking the letter from her grandfather. "How is Mammi feeling?"

"Better," Dawdi answered. "One more treatment and then she'll have another CAT scan."

Lila nodded.

"She's going to come in to the shop later this afternoon."

"*Gut*," Lila answered. She hadn't seen her grandmother for the last week. She'd been working five evenings a week at the Plain Buffet Dat had been making Rose help with the morning and afternoon milking on the days Lila worked at both places. Trudy was helping some now too and a few times Adam helped also.

Dawdi drove Mammi to the shop midafternoon, right before it was time for Lila to leave. Dawdi headed back to the office, but Mammi stayed up front. The day had grown overcast and humid, and her grandmother had a bottle of water with her that she kept sipping. "I had a message from Trudy that she and your Dat and Beth planned to stop by."

"Oh?" No one had said anything to Lila earlier in the day.

"Your Dat had to stop by the feed store, and Beth suggested an outing—to the creamery," Mammi explained.

Lila gathered up her things, patted her unread letter in her pocket, and then started to the door of the shop just as Dat, Beth, and Trudy stepped through it. After saying hello to everyone, Lila placed her hand on the top of Trudy's head. "How fun that you get to go to the creamery."

"Can you come with us?" Trudy asked.

Lila shook her head. "I'm off to work." She gave her little sister a hug. "I'll see you in the morning."

She called back to Dawdi in the office, telling him good-bye.

"Do you have your letter?" Dawdi called back.

"Jah," she answered, knowing her grandfather didn't realize others were in the shop.

"What letter?" Dat asked.

Lila hesitated and then said, "Zane sent a thank you for the quilts and blankets from Mammi and the other ladies. I wrote him back."

"And you encouraged him to respond?"

She nodded. She had, by writing.

Dat stretched his hand out. "Let me see."

"I'll give it to you tonight," Lila answered. "I'm about to be late." She'd never defied her father before.

He started to speak, but then Beth gave him a look and he stopped. Lila hurried out the door.

She didn't read the letter until she reached the restaurant parking lot, where she pulled around the back to the barn. She unhitched her horse, watered and fed her, and then leaned against the weathered barn boards. Zane wrote about their latest village visits and said it had been really hot, with a lot going on. He wrote that he felt he was finally making progress winning Benham's trust, and that the work with the women and children was going well.

I admire these people. I appreciate the simple lifestyle, the focus on family, and the desire to care independently for the clan. The more I see of the world though, the more I appreciate what I've learned from the Amish. I know no group is perfect—just as no person is—but I've seen nothing to change my mind about Plain living. Be thankful for what you have.

At the end of the letter he wrote again how grateful he was that she'd agreed to write.

You writing about the fireflies made me so happy. Your letters give me something more to look forward to. And hope for.

Her stomach flopped. She had no right to give him any kind of hope.

And as I've said before, I appreciate your honesty. I don't expect anything more from you than friendship—but I know you will be truthful. I appreciate that. And know, regardless of how you feel about me, I will always care about you. I will always remember you. I will always think about you. I will never forget you.

Lila folded the letter and crammed it back into her pocket. She was the least truthful person she knew. She hadn't been honest with Zane about her feelings for him. She hadn't been honest with Reuben about her correspondence with Zane. And she hadn't been honest with her Dat either.

She hurried into the restaurant. She did her best to keep smiling and get through her shift, but she wanted nothing more than to climb into her buggy and drive away—far away.

Of course she didn't.

When she got home, Dat was still awake, sitting at the table. He held out his hand. "Give me the letter," he said.

She did. Silently. She knew the less she said the better.

He read the letter once and then a second time. His face didn't give away any of his emotions. Finally he said, "Does Reuben know Zane writes to you?"

Her face grew warm. "No," she answered.

"Reuben thinks you plan to marry him in the fall."

She nodded.

Dat put the letter back in the envelope and left it on the table. "I never expected this from you, Lila."

She didn't respond.

He stood. "I thought you were smarter than your mother and aunt."

"This has nothing to do with Mamm or Aenti," Lila said.

"This has to do with all of you being deceptive."

"Mama and Aenti Eve weren't deceptive. From everything I've heard they were more than honest."

Dat shook his head. "You were too young. What would you know?"

"Probably more than I let on." She sighed. "I do know that what I've done is wrong. I'll take care of things with both Zane and Reuben." She stepped toward her Dat. "I'm sorry for deceiving you too. It wasn't honoring you—I should have been honest."

He stared at her for a long moment and then said, "I appreciate that." Without saying good-night, he stood and headed to the hall.

Lila collapsed into a chair. Worst of all she hadn't been honest with God. She was the biggest liar she knew. *Please forgive me,* she prayed. She needed the community of her church, but she needed Christ's salvation more. She'd always been a good girl, jah, but she was still a sinner. Maybe she hadn't gone wild and run around, but she'd let fear control her.

She'd been afraid to give up Reuben and the security he offered. She'd been afraid of Dat's disappointment. And she'd been afraid of the consequences of accepting—and returning—Zane's love.

She'd been aware of Zane's fears from the beginning, but she'd deluded herself by naming her fears "commitment." And being responsible. And doing the right thing.

She didn't want to marry Reuben. She didn't love him. She couldn't talk to him. He didn't listen to her when she tried. She loved words and communicating. Sure, Reuben's actions showed he was a good person, but she couldn't live without having her soul fed. Without ideas and conversation. Without sharpening one another.

And even if she could talk to him, she doubted he'd truly ever hear her because she didn't think he loved her either. He'd make someone a wonderful husband. But not her. Just like she wouldn't make a good wife for him.

She loved Zane. Over three years had passed since he had joined the Army, since he'd left. Not a day had gone by that she didn't think about him, that she didn't long for him.

Zane made her feel more ferhoodled than anyone—but he made her *feel*. She had to have that in a marriage. He listened to her, he heard her. And he cared enough to go far away when she asked him to.

But she couldn't marry Zane either, not without leaving the church. And she wouldn't do that. She couldn't do that to her Dat, to her family. She'd rather not marry at all.

Nothing had changed—except for her realizing the damage she'd done to all of them.

A few minutes later, she finished her short letter to Zane, saying she wasn't who he thought she was. She would no longer be able to write to him, and she hoped he could forgive her for not being a better friend.

She put it in an envelope, put a stamp on it, grabbed a flashlight from the mud porch, and then took the letter out to the mailbox and raised the flag.

Next she walked to the barn and left a message on the phone at the lumberyard, telling Reuben she needed to speak to him as soon as possible. "I have tomorrow off," she said. "Leave a

293

message and tell me when I can meet you."

As she walked back toward the house, a firefly flittered above the gate. Then another, until dozens congregated for just a moment and then darted back toward the creek. *"Be still, and know that I am God."*

I will, she answered. That was all she could do.

She ended up going to the lumberyard during Reuben's lunch break, even though Dat was working. She sat beside Reuben on his porch, in a plastic chair, while he ate his sandwich.

She explained that she had been writing to Zane, and after asking his forgiveness, she said, "I can't keep courting you."

He kept on chewing.

"I haven't been fair to you, at all. I kept thinking love is a commitment—which it is. And I do care about you, but I don't think in the way a wife loves her husband."

He swallowed and finally said, "What do you mean?"

She shifted toward him. "I can't marry you," she said. "I'm sorry."

He took the last bite of his sandwich and after he'd swallowed asked, "Does this have anything to do with Zane?"

She shaded her eyes and turned her face toward him. "In a way it does. He told me he always appreciated my honesty, which made me realize just what a liar I've been. To you."

He stood then, brushed his hands together, and exhaled as he looked down at her with a pained expression on his face. "So this is it?"

Lila nodded. Without saying anything more, he headed toward the lumberyard. For once she appreciated that he hadn't tried to talk things through. It proved they weren't a good fit. He didn't really want to hear what she was thinking—only how it impacted him. She'd rather be single and make a good life for herself like Beth had than spend her life knowing she'd kept Reuben from spending his life with a woman who loved him. And kept herself from being loved.

She stayed put. She'd rather talk to Dat here than back home with Rose and Trudy around.

It didn't take long for him to march toward her. "What did you tell Reuben?" he demanded as he approached the porch.

She took a deep breath. "I said I couldn't court him anymore."

Dat shook his head. "So you're leaving the church, then? For Zane."

"I'm not leaving the church," she insisted. "I sent Zane a note and said I won't be writing him any longer." She stood. "I won't be courting anyone."

17

Even in the mountains the summer days were blistering hot, but at least the nights were cool. Sarge, Grant, Wade, and Zane stood at the gate of a village, waiting for Jaalal to meet them. Casey and the rest of the FET had stayed back at base. Two of the women were ill, and Sarge wanted all of them to rest. Zane had a duffel bag full of baby blankets slung over his left shoulder. Lila had sent more from the ladies back at Thread by Thread, to give to the mothers in the village.

His team had a tip that one of the local men from this village had information about a group of insurgents over the next mountain pass. Wade had been keeping track of the relationships between different informants and thought it could be legitimate. Zane convinced Sarge to make a visit, saying they could count on Jaalal to help them.

Grant toed the dirt. "I have a bad feeling about this."

Jaalal was usually on time, and that was a concern, but Grant seemed to have a bad feeling about everything these days. It was their fifth visit to this particular village, and they hadn't had any problems before.

Zane was counting down the days—three—

until Grant left for his furlough. His baby girl had been born two weeks before, a little early but Grant said she was doing fine. He'd hoped for another boy though, saying he had no idea what to do with a girl.

Zane told him he'd figure it out, but he wasn't sure he would.

"Just keep alert," Sarge said.

Grant didn't answer Sarge. Instead he turned toward Zane. "Where is he?" Grant glared. "Maybe your buddy isn't as reliable as you think."

"He'll be here," Zane said. Jaalal hadn't let them down yet.

Grant shook his head. "And maybe Mr. Pacifist here"—Grant had seen Zane reading an article on the topic last time they were on base—"is in cahoots with the enemy."

Zane didn't bother to respond. It was one of Grant's new topics.

"Knock it off," Wade said.

Sarge added, "And keep your head up."

"This guy is bad for morale," Grant shot back, nodding toward Zane.

Sarge glared at Grant. "You're bad for morale."

Grant groaned. "I'm tired, is all."

"You'll be home soon," Wade said, his voice low.

Grant gave him a dirty look. "Yeah. Where I'll get even less sleep. You can bet Donna will expect me to get up in the middle of the night with the little princess."

"Yeah, no rest for the weary." Zane couldn't help himself. Poor Donna. Zane turned toward the mountains. He'd known from the beginning that Grant was annoying—he just hadn't guessed how bad it could get. At least Wade was showing, more and more, how tired he was of Grant's negativity too.

"I bet you got lots of sleep while you were home," Grant said to Zane. "Unless your Amish girlfriend was around."

Zane didn't even bother to respond. The guy was relentless. They were headed back to base in two days. Grant would fly to Bagram from there and then on to Texas. Zane was looking forward to two weeks plus four days, counting Grant's travel both ways, of peace.

Although peace was relative. The fighting had heated up in the area—as it did every summer, according to Jaalal.

Sarge pulled a packet from the pocket of his pants. "I almost forgot—we got a mail delivery." He handed an envelope to Grant and one to Zane. "You two are the lucky winners."

Grant opened his, pulled out a couple of photos, and held them up. A shot of the newborn with Donna and Alex. One of just the baby.

He flashed them around.

"Cool," Zane said, downplaying his response.

He wanted to tell Grant he had a beautiful family and to appreciate them. But that wouldn't have gone over well.

"Yeah, well, you do like babies," Grant said. "So what does the Amish chick say? It doesn't look like much of a letter."

Grant was right about that. It couldn't be more than a single page. Her last letter had been four.

"Aren't you going to read it?" Grant asked.

"Later," Zane answered, tucking it into his pocket. Grant lunged as if he were going to try to snatch it, but Sarge told him to focus on fighting the enemy, not one another.

They continued to wait, the sun growing hotter and hotter. Jaalal had never been this late before. Finally Grant, Wade, and Sarge moved to the shade of the wall, while Zane stayed at the gate.

Grant tipped his head back and closed his eyes. Wade leaned against the wall. The conifers across the road swayed in the hot breeze. Zane turned toward the gate, took Lila's envelope from his pocket, and pulled out the letter. It was only a short paragraph.

Dear Zane, I will no longer be able to write to you. I am not the honest person you think I am, and I'm sorry for that. Please forgive me for not being a better friend to you. Lila

That was all. A sick feeling swept over him as

he slipped the letter back into the envelope and secured it in his pocket, wondering what had happened. Most likely something to do with her Dat pressuring her to marry Reuben as soon as possible. She'd probably be wed and pregnant by the time he got home. Maybe they'd already married.

His stomach sank as he glanced back at Grant. He was jealous of the guy—out and out jealous. Grant still had his eyes closed, but Sarge was looking down the road and so was Wade.

Zane heard the truck just as it came around the corner. He stepped out, expecting Jaalal. It was Jaalal's truck, but the older man wasn't in the cab. Benham was driving, and a man Zane didn't recognize sat in the passenger seat.

Sarge hopped to his feet, and Zane waved, stepping out into the road. The pickup slowed and then stopped.

"Easy," Sarge said, just loud enough for Zane to hear. Grant was on his feet now, moving toward the gate, wide-eyed.

Zane stepped toward the pickup, and Benham jumped out. "Where's your grandfather?" Zane asked in Pashto.

"He'll be here in a minute," Benham answered.

"Who's with you?" Zane asked.

"A friend."

Zane hadn't seen the man before, but he tried to look welcoming as he called out, "Salaam."

300

The man didn't respond.

A boy, who appeared to be Adam's age, pushed open the village gate, peered out, and then stepped back.

"What should we do?" Sarge asked, his voice low.

"Try to stall," Zane answered softly.

Grant kept sliding along the wall. "Bet he's not coming. I knew we couldn't trust him."

"Take it easy," Zane said, keeping his voice low. A rustling drew Zane's attention to the gate. The boy stepped out again. Zane motioned for him to go back, but the boy froze.

Benham's friend was a big guy, thicker through the middle than most Afghan men.

Zane smiled. "I'm Specialist Beck." He nodded toward Sarge. "Sergeant Powers, Specialist Turner, and Private Carlson." Wade nodded, but Sarge didn't respond. Grant eased his way along the wall toward the gate.

The man frowned. Zane hoped he would introduce himself, but he didn't.

The roar of another vehicle distracted Zane. Surely it was Jaalal. He'd take charge and vouch for Benham's friend. But as another pickup neared them, Zane could see the pickup bed was full of armed men.

"Take cover!" Sarge yelled.

Zane dashed to the wall, staying away from the gate, not wanting a fight to move inside the village. Benham lifted an AK-47 and was aiming it toward the wall—not toward Zane, but farther up. Toward Grant. And the boy.

Zane swung his rifle into position with one hand and backed up, scooping up the boy with his free hand, lifting him alongside the duffel bag slung over his arm. Benham fired, and Zane shot back before he realized that he'd chosen to. He'd reacted on instinct—it was as simple as that. Benham fell behind the truck.

Zane turned toward the wall, shielding the boy with the duffel bag. Over his shoulder he could see Benham's friend turn and aim. Zane twisted slightly, getting another shot off, as the man fired at Zane. *Pop, pop, pop.* The force knocked him against the wall. He knew he'd been hit, but he didn't know where. He staggered, still holding the boy, lowering him to the ground as gently as he could.

"*Wadrega! Marasta!*"

Zane recognized the words, easy ones. *Stop! Help!* And the voice. It was Jaalal. His friend. But maybe not anymore.

The boy fell the few inches to the ground from Zane's arm. Zane crouched over him.

The boy looked up at him wide-eyed, blood across his face. Zane leaned against the wall, pulling the boy along with him. He expected another shot.

He called out to Sarge, who was coming toward

him in slow motion, "Don't shoot Jaalal." They couldn't afford to lose him.

Zane scooted the boy flush against the wall and then attempted to stand, trying to hold up his rifle with his right hand. His arm didn't work. He collapsed, jerking away from the boy, his head slamming against the hard-packed ground.

He came to, staring up into Jaalal's worried face.

"The little boy?"

"He's right here," Jaalal answered.

"He's bleeding."

Jaalal shook his head. "It's your blood. He's all right."

Relief swept through him. "How about Benham?" Zane asked.

Jaalal shook his head. "He's a stupid boy."

"But alive?"

Jaalal nodded. Thank God he wasn't that great of a marksman. Jaalal scooped up the little boy, pulling him out from between Zane and the wall. The boy stayed quiet in Jaalal's arms, looking over his shoulder, as Jaalal hurried him away toward the gate, yelling at the other Afghan men as he did. Thank God the little one was all right.

Sarge yelled for everyone to climb down. Zane could hear a clamoring and a few shouts. Again he expected a firefight, but nothing happened. A minute later Jaalal returned.

"Is everything all right?" Zane asked.

"The men are with me," Jaalal said. "To stop Benham. If only we'd gotten here sooner."

"Are you sure the boy's all right?" Zane couldn't stop thinking about him.

Jaalal nodded. "Shaken up, but that's all." He picked up the duffel bag that had fallen to Zane's side. "This helped." Bullet holes had torn through the canvas and blankets and out the side. The bag had changed the trajectory of the bullets.

Zane shuddered. He would have taken more bullets—and the boy would have been hit too. "How about Grant? Was he hit?"

"Benham missed," Jaalal answered.

That was when Zane noticed Grant hovering to the side. Had Zane spoken to Jaalal in Pashto or English? He wasn't sure. "Manana," he said.

Jaalal shook his head. "Don't thank me. I nearly got you killed."

"Step aside," Sarge said to Jaalal with his back to Zane, his gun still pointed toward the pickup.

Jaalal obeyed the command and moved a couple of feet away. Zane guessed Wade was standing guard over the others.

Zane couldn't feel anything, so maybe the wound wasn't that bad—or maybe he was in shock. But his right shoulder was warm, and he thought that was where the bullet had hit. He touched it with his other hand and it came away bloody. That's when he realized his helmet was off and his head hurt. He moved his hand up to his neck and the back of his head. More blood. He felt faint again and concentrated on his breathing.

"Radio for a chopper," Sarge ordered Grant. "Tell them we have a soldier down—and two enemy combatants too. Ask for reinforcements. Tell them we have an undetermined situation."

Zane must have hit Benham's friend too. Zane could hear Grant on the radio, his voice quavering a few times. When he'd finished, Sarge ordered him to check on Zane's wounds.

"The others can be trusted," Jaalal said. "I don't know what set Benham off, but it's not a conspiracy, I can assure you."

Sarge didn't answer for a long minute but finally said, "We'll see."

Grant stood above Zane. "Look what you got us into," he muttered.

"Shut up," Sarge hissed. "He saved your life."

Grant knelt but didn't seem inclined to help. "It's probably bad enough to get you out of here for a while, but not out of the deployment altogether." He frowned as he pulled Zane's jacket open. "Tough luck for you, Mr. Pacifist."

"I mean it, Turner." Sarge stayed rigid. "Another word and I'll write you up for insubordination."

Jaalal towered over Zane, both his hands up. "Sarge, may I see to my friend's wounds?"

Zane met Sarge's gaze, nodded, and mouthed, *Please.*

Sarge took his first-aid kit from his pants pocket, tossed it at Jaalal, and stepped back against the wall, where he could keep his gun on Benham and his friend. Grant hopped to his feet and pulled away.

Jaalal squatted beside Zane, pulling the scissors from the first-aid kit. Next he undid the Velcro on Zane's jacket, eased it aside, and began cutting Zane's T-shirt.

"Denki," Zane said, relaxing a little.

Jaalal met Zane's eyes for a second and shook his head.

"Thank you," Zane translated, smiling just a little that he'd reverted to Pennsylvania Dutch, but a stab of pain stopped him from explaining.

Jaalal tore open the quick-clot packet and pressed it against Zane's shoulder. Wade appeared, his face ashen. He pointed to Zane. "He's bleeding from his head too."

"Give me your first-aid kit," Jaalal said to Grant. "I need another packet."

"Get Zane's," he answered. "I might still need mine before the day is done."

"It's in my pants pocket," Zane said. With Lila's letter. Was she still praying for him? Or had she stopped?

Jaalal opened the pocket.

"Be careful with the letter," Zane said. He didn't want blood all over it.

"I'll do my best," Jaalal answered, tucking it

back inside. He pulled out the packet, ripped open the package, and pressed the quick clot against the back of Zane's head. Then he scooted closer to Zane and pressed his other hand against his shoulder. The man's brown eyes were watery, and the whites of his eyes a little yellow. "You're going to be just fine," Jaalal said. "You'll be home before you know it, and that's where you should stay."

"Speak in English," Grant said. "We need to know what you're saying."

Again, Zane hadn't registered the Pashto. "Let your God bless you," Jaalal said, still in Pashto. And then in a whisper he added, "And don't come back here."

Zane closed his eyes, aware of Jaalal's hands pressing against him and his breath on his face. If he never came back he'd never see Jaalal again. But he'd never forget him either.

By the time the helicopter arrived, his wounds felt as if they were on fire. Jaalal kept pressing until the medics took over. Then he stepped back. Zane lifted his good arm in farewell to his friend.

"God keep you," Jaalal said, the wind of the chopper blasting against his face.

"And you," Zane whispered.

Grant stood by Sarge now, his weapon pulled too. Sarge turned to Zane quickly. "We'll be down to base as soon as we can. Hopefully before they fly you out."

One of the medics ran back to the chopper. As Zane waited, he watched the branches of the trees above his head dip in the wind. *"Yea, though I walk through the valley of the shadow of death, I will fear no evil. . . ."*

He was as near to death as he'd ever been, yet very much alive, as alive as he'd been as a child, running through the field at dusk, the fireflies dancing among the poplar trees. God was with him, just as he had been then. *I will do my best to be still and know that you are God,* he prayed.

The medic returned, and two of them moved Zane onto a gurney and then lifted him. For a split second he could see the other Afghans still standing around the pickup. Clearly they were under Jaalal's control. The medics loaded Zane into the chopper first and then Benham and the other injured man.

"Why didn't you wait for my signal?" the second one asked Benham in Pashto.

"I was tired of waiting," Benham answered. "Don't talk now. That man you shot—he's a translator. And a friend of Grandfather's."

"Figures," the other man said. The medics secured them to the gurneys and blindfolded them both. Benham cursed but then stayed quiet. There was quite a bit of activity around him for a while, and when Zane asked the medic how Benham was doing, he answered that everything was fine.

• • •

Sarge must have alerted Casey to what was going on, because when the medics hauled Zane off the helicopter at the base camp, she was waiting.

She stepped to the side of the gurney.

"I'm okay," he said before she could say anything.

"Barely," she answered, trying to smile. At least she wasn't crying.

When they reached the door to the clinic, Casey stopped. "I'll be with you as soon as I can," she said.

"Thanks," he answered.

Soon nurses and a doc surrounded him. "Looks like you're going to make it," the doc said in a southern drawl.

"Unless you screw it up," Zane said.

The doc laughed and then said, "Mind if I pray for you? And for myself?"

"Are you a chaplain?"

The doc's eyes danced. "No, son, but I double as a Baptist preacher back home."

"Then by all means," Zane responded, "please pray. And for my family too. This is probably going to be harder on them than me."

The doc grabbed Zane's good hand and prayed, asking God for healing and comfort for the family. Then the doc got to work.

It wasn't a big deal, not really. He was going to be okay. The bullet just grazed the back of his head. And his shoulder would heal. It could have been so much worse.

"Blood pressure's dropping," one of the nurses said.

He didn't hear anything else. He was back in the field where the fireflies darted in and out among the poplar trees.

Zane groaned as he came to. A voice asked, "How's the pain?"

"Not so good," Zane answered.

"We'll do something about that."

Zane opened his eyes, expecting a nurse, but it was the ER doc again. "Your blood pressure tanked—you had a bleeder in your shoulder. We had a few rough minutes there, but we got you into the OR and got it fixed."

"Wow" was all Zane could say in response.

"Hold on, I'll get the nurse."

Fifteen minutes later, after more medicine, Zane started to relax a little. After twenty minutes the pain was manageable.

"Are you up to having a visitor?" the nurse asked. "There's a soldier worried about you."

"Which soldier?"

"Casey Johnson."

"Yeah, that would be great." Zane tried to sit up a little. "But wait—"

The nurse stopped.

"What do you need?"

310

"The stuff that was in my pockets." He had his phone and a little Bible his mom had given him and the pieces of jasper rock from the creek down by the fort and, of course, Lila's letter.

"Everything's safe. In a plastic bag, waiting for you."

"Thanks," Zane said. "Tell Casey to come on in."

The nurse started for the curtain again.

"Hey, did anyone call my folks?"

The nurse shook her head. "We were waiting for you to wake up. You can if you want or your sergeant can."

"He's here too?"

The nurse nodded.

"Please send them both in."

This time Casey had tears in her eyes, and Sarge looked like the battle-weary soldier he was.

"I'm okay," Zane said.

"Now," Casey responded. "As if what happened out there in the field wasn't enough—tanking in here was a cruel thing to do."

"Sorry," Zane said sheepishly and then turned his head toward Sarge. "How did everything turn out once the reinforcements arrived?"

"All right," Sarge said. "Jaalal said Benham was set on ambushing us. It wasn't Jaalal's intention or that of the guys in the second truck—at least we don't think so. Jaalal said he wanted them as backup against Benham and the other guy."

"He was going to shoot his own grandson?"

"If he had to."

"Yikes," Zane said.

"Yeah." Sarge frowned. "He said he was glad you did it for him—and he's glad you're not a better shot. But that was before—"

Zane tried to sit up straighter. "Before?"

Sarge cleared his throat. "Benham didn't make it."

"But he was talking. He seemed fine."

"The bullet nicked his lung. It collapsed by the time they reached the base."

Zane's head fell back against the pillow. He'd killed a man. Jaalal's grandson. *God . . . this wasn't supposed to happen.*

"Sorry," Sarge said.

He wouldn't cry, not now. *Why?*

Sarge must have been nervous because he said, "I was about to kill Turner by the time we got out of there."

Casey elbowed him.

Sarge's face grew red. "Sorry."

Zane tried to shake his head but it hurt. "Don't worry about it."

"At least Turner's leaving on furlough. Hopefully I can pull it together while he's gone. On the other hand, Carlson said to tell you he's pulling for you. He was pretty shook up—in a normal way, as opposed to Turner—about you being wounded."

"Tell Wade thanks," Zane said.

Sarge sighed. "I don't know what I'm going to do without you."

"They'll send another translator," Zane said.

"I don't want another one," Sarge said. "I want you to get yourself better ASAP, so you can stick with our unit."

He might not be too bad off, but he wasn't going out in the field anytime soon. He looked at Sarge. "What did the doc say to you?"

"As long as you're stable, they'll fly you to Bagram in the morning and do a CT scan. Then maybe on to Landstuhl."

Germany. That was where his dad had gone when he'd been injured, where his mom flew when Zane was twelve.

"How long would I be there?"

"They don't think too long. Depending on how things look they'll either send you back here or on to the States for rehab."

Zane sighed. "That sounds like it might take a while."

Sarge shrugged. "You never know. I'm going to be optimistic. I'm hoping they send you straight back here from Bagram."

"Speaking of the States," Casey said. "Do you want to call your folks? Or I could call your mom if you want. I can phrase it so I don't freak her out."

Tears filled Zane's eyes, and he blinked quickly. "Maybe. . . . What time is it?"

"Seven p.m. here," Casey said.

"So still morning back home?"

Casey nodded.

Mom wasn't working as much this summer while Bub was home from school. Just a day a week. Chances were she'd be home. He toyed with calling his Dad first but decided it would be better to call Mom. Who knew what the news might trigger in his dad? Then again, who knew what it might trigger in his mom?

Sarge said he was going to go get a shower and some sleep before he gave the mission any more thought. Casey asked the nurse for Zane's phone, and then stood at the edge of his bed. "Where do I find her number?"

"Let me see it," Zane said, reaching out with his good hand. He took the phone and clicked his photos icon. Up popped the photo of Lila.

"Want me to call?" Casey asked.

Zane shook his head. "I can do it," he answered.

He closed the pictures app and then clicked into his phone.

Favorites.

Mom.

He pressed her number.

18

Shani placed the last of the ripe tomatoes into the basket and then moved on to the cucumbers. Adam yelled something to Trudy in the field, although Shani couldn't make out what. She put three cucumbers into the basket as her phone buzzed in the pocket of her shorts. She carried it everywhere these days, hoping Zane had a chance to call. He was headed back to Bagram this week, so the chances were good he would. She retrieved it quickly. Sure enough, it was Zane. It was evening in Afghanistan.

She pushed accept and gushed, "Hi, sweetie, how are you?"

"Mom?" His voice didn't sound right.

"You okay?" she asked.

"Yeah, I'm fine. I'm on base, in the hospital."

Shani's heart began to race. "What happened?"

"A couple of bullets—"

Her legs weakened. She stepped from the garden, to the grass. "Where?"

"In my shoulder." His voice grew faint. "And the back of my head."

"Baby," Shani managed to say.

"I'm okay, really."

Shani took a deep breath, willing herself to remain calm. "How long will you be in the hospital?"

There was a long pause.

"Zane?"

There was a muffled sound, and then a woman's voice said, "Shani? This is Casey."

"Is he all right?"

"Yeah. He had a bleed in his shoulder so they had to rush him to OR, but he's okay now."

Shani's hand began to shake. "What about his head?"

"The bullet grazed his skull, so a lot of blood, but not any lasting damage."

"Thank God," Shani said. "What's next?"

"Bagram and then possibly Landstuhl."

"I can meet him in Germany if he goes. I can be there in a day or two." She'd done it before—she could easily do it again.

"I'll ask him," Casey said.

More muffled voices, and then Casey came back on. "He says for you to stay put. He'll call if he ends up there."

"All right. Tell him I can do whatever he needs."

"He'll have a better idea once he knows what's going on," Casey said. Then she added, "Hold on."

She came back on. "He said he's sorry he can't talk—he's pretty wiped out. He says to make sure to tell Adam and his dad that he really is all right. He doesn't want any of you to worry." Then Casey's voice choked up a little. "But he wants you to pray—not just for him but also for Jaalal and his family."

"Was Jaalal hit too?"

"No," Casey said. Shani was pretty sure there was more to the story. Casey continued, "He wants you to ask everyone else to pray too."

He meant the Lehmans, Shani was sure. "Of course," Shani said. "Tell him I'll ask everyone right away."

"I'll make sure his phone is charged," Casey said. "For the trip. And that his charger gets packed."

"Thank you," Shani said. "For everything." She liked the girl—a lot. "How are you doing?" Shani asked.

"Okay, now. He gave us a scare . . ."

Shani's heart sank, wishing someone had called her earlier. "When did it happen?"

"This morning," Casey said. "They were out in the field. I was on base . . ." More muffled voices, then Casey came back on. "He said he'll give you the details soon," Casey said, her voice low.

"Can you give the phone back to Zane?" Shani asked.

"Sure," Casey said.

"Mom?"

"I'm so thankful you're okay. Know how much we love you. We're praying for you. I'll call Daddy right now."

"Thanks, Mom," Zane said. "I'm sorry I can't talk more right now. I'll call soon."

Casey came back on the connection. Shani asked her to call if anything changed.

"Of course," Casey said. "Just remember no news is good news. And that he's on a lot of pain meds so it's hard for him to communicate." After the girl said good-bye, Shani couldn't move.

Her worst fear had happened—Zane had been shot. But . . . he was alive. She stopped a moment and thanked God for that. Finally she headed toward the house to collect herself and call Joel. But her phone rang again. A number she didn't recognize. She answered it anyway. It was Casey, calling from her own phone.

"Sorry," she said. "I didn't want to give too many details in front of Zane. I'm outside now."

"Sure," Shani said.

"So . . . this is what happened. Zane shot Jaalal's grandson."

Shani gasped.

"Yeah, because the grandson shot at Grant but missed. There was a little boy right by Grant, but Zane scooped him up. That's what Sarge said. Then Benham's friend shot Zane—but Zane got him too."

"Goodness," Shani said, trying to process it all.

"Then Jaalal arrived with backup. It was Jaalal who attended to Zane. He said he wasn't in on the shooting. Sarge hopes he can be believed,

318

but our entire mission is at risk now. If Jaalal isn't trustworthy, we need to find someone else who is."

"Of course," Shani said, her legs shaking as she walked up the steps to the house. "Is the little boy all right?"

"Yeah," Casey said. "Those blankets Zane had probably saved his life. A couple of bullets hit the duffel bag, and it changed their trajectory. Away from the boy."

Shani gasped again and stopped on the porch.

"Are you okay?" Casey asked.

"I'm fine. I'm going to call Joel now," she said, realizing she was speaking slowly, a syllable at time. "Thank you so much for giving me the details. I can see it would be hard for Zane to tell me all that."

"Yeah," Casey said. "It gets worse though."

Shani gasped a third time.

"Benham—Jaalal's grandson—died. I think that is harder on Zane than his own injuries."

"Of course it is," Shani said, tears welling up in her eyes. He'd always empathized deeply with people who were in pain, no matter what they had done to deserve it. *Poor Zane.* They'd all prayed he wouldn't have to kill anyone.

"Benham's buddy is going to make it. He's in the field hospital too. They'll ship him out to Bagram, and once he's well enough he'll go to the jail there."

She thanked Casey again, desperate to get off the phone and call Joel.

"Call anytime—I'll answer," she said, and then said good-bye.

As soon as she pushed End, Shani tapped on Joel's number. He picked up right away.

"He's going to be all right," Shani said, "but Zane's been shot. He's at the field hospital." Her legs gave way as she spoke, and she sank onto the rough boards of the porch.

"I'm on my way," Joel said.

Shani told Joel all she could remember and then hung up when he reached his pickup. As she waited on the porch, she prayed for him as he drove home, asking God to keep him calm. He'd made so much progress in the years since his own injury. She hoped this wouldn't bring him down again.

Adam kept playing with Trudy in their pretend house as Shani sat on the top step waiting for Joel. She didn't want to call Eve or walk down the lane and tell Lila—to ask her to pray, to ask all of them to pray—until Joel arrived. She needed to see him first. Then she'd be strong enough to tell Adam and everyone else.

The children's voices brought her comfort. A horsefly buzzed by, and Shani swatted at it. Then a blue jay flew out toward the first maple tree along the lane. She stood and headed down the steps, stopping at their driveway. She waited, hearing the children now and then, until Joel's pickup finally appeared. He lowered his window and stopped as he neared her.

"Any more news?"

She shook her head.

He parked and then climbed out, leaning against his cane and wrapping one arm around her. "He's going to be okay, right?"

She nodded. It wasn't like it had been with Joel. He'd been unconscious for three days. They hadn't known, for sure, until he woke up how bad his head injury was. And then it was iffy for a couple of more weeks until the swelling went down. And his leg had been badly damaged. Hopefully Zane's shoulder would heal quickly. Thank God his head was okay.

"I told him I'd go to Germany if he ends up there, but he said not to make plans yet."

"Yeah, we need to follow his lead. He's not our little boy anymore."

"I know," Shani said. "I just hate to think of him all alone."

"He won't be alone."

She nodded.

"We should tell Adam—but Trudy's here."

"We'll just tell Adam that Zane was injured— then we'll give him more details after we walk Trudy home." They approached the children and told Adam, whose eyes grew huge. But he didn't ask any questions.

Shani put her arm around Adam. "Right now it's time for Trudy to go, so we're going to walk her home."

"Can't she stay?" Adam asked.

"Not now, but maybe she can come back later," Shani said.

The children ran ahead in the field, staying away from the cows that were huddled along the poplars, trying to crowd under the shade.

Joel took Shani's hand. As they stepped through the gate to the Lehmans' farm, Tim came out of the barn. He called out a hello. Joel waved.

"Did you take the day off from work?" Tim asked.

"Zane got hurt," Adam answered. "Daddy came home to tell me."

Tim took off his hat and shaded his eyes. "What happened?"

Trudy took Adam's hand and started toward the house. "Lila was going to make banana muffins this morning. Let's see if she did."

Adam glanced at Shani, and she nodded in encouragement.

Tim squinted. "Does Adam not know?"

"Not all the details," Joel answered. "Not yet. We didn't want to tell him in front of Trudy." Then Joel told Tim what happened to Zane. Even in the bright sun, Tim grew pale, probably thinking of what Simon could experience.

"Zane's going to be all right," Shani said. It

helped to keep saying that. "But he asked us to pray, and to ask all of you too. And for the Afghan family he knows . . ." She could hardly bear to tell Tim the details, but she managed to. That Zane had shot Jaalal's grandson to keep him from shooting one of the soldiers in the unit, and that the young Afghan man had died.

Tim shook his head. "What a tragedy, jah?"

Joel nodded.

Tim shook his head again. Then he hesitated for a moment and finally he said, "Go on and tell Lila. I don't want to get the details wrong. I'll keep the children busy."

When they reached the house, Tim opened the door and called out, "Trudy and Adam, come with me out to the barn. I have something to show you."

He sent the children on ahead and then shook Joel's hand. "All of you will be in my prayers."

Lila stepped onto the mud porch, wiping her hands on her apron. Her usually stoic expression had turned to panic. "Zane was injured?"

"He'll be all right," Joel said.

Lila motioned them in and then to sit at the table. Rose stepped from the living room to the kitchen. By the time Shani finished telling about the conversations with Zane and Casey, and Joel explained what he surmised about the situation, Lila had tears streaming down her cheeks. She

323

stood, grabbed a clean dish towel, and wiped her face with it.

"We really do think he'll be okay," Shani said.

Lila whispered, "Excuse me," and headed toward the hallway.

Shani stood, thinking she'd follow Lila, but Rose stopped her. "She's all out of sorts lately."

"What's going on?" Shani asked. Usually it was Rose who was out of sorts. Not Lila.

"She broke up with Reuben. Dat's afraid she'll leave the church. She's been really moody." Rose leaned closer and spoke softly. "Simon thinks she's in love with Zane."

Shani's head began to swim. "Rose . . ."

"I think Simon's right. She and Zane were writing back and forth, but Dat found out and made her quit. She wrote Zane one last time, over two weeks ago, and said she couldn't write any-more."

Shani wondered if he'd received it—maybe not yet. Rose smiled just a little, clearly happy to have the scoop on something. "She broke up with Reuben right after that."

"Goodness," Shani said.

"This is none of our business," Joel said, standing.

Shani stood, too, but then stepped to the hallway and knocked on the door to the girls' room. "Lila?" She turned the doorknob and pushed just a little. "May I come in?"

When she didn't answer, Shani stepped to the bed and sat down beside her, putting her arm around her shoulder. "Rose said that you'd been writing Zane."

Lila took a deep breath. "We were but I told him we had to stop."

"That's what Rose said."

She turned her face to Shani. "Do you think he got my letter already?"

"I have no idea. He didn't say anything about it."

"It was harsh—even though I didn't mean it to be." Lila leaned against Shani's shoulder. "I've always cared for him."

Shani drew the girl close. "And he cares for you too. You've been friends for such a long time."

Shani knew there was more to this than Lila was willing to say. She knew it from the way Zane had acted the last three years too. Her son loved Lila, and it looked as if she loved him back.

Shani sat there until she heard Joel's voice in the hallway saying, "We should go on home and let Tim get his dinner."

She squeezed Lila again.

"I'm sorry," Lila said. "I should have been the one comforting you."

"No," Shani said. "I'll let you know when we hear from Zane again."

"Denki," Lila answered.

Shani forced herself to look Tim in the eye as she told him good-bye. She didn't want any more conflict with their neighbor. All this time she thought Lila genuinely loved Reuben. But she'd been wrong.

She couldn't see any way Lila would leave the Amish—and how could a soldier in the U.S. Army become Plain?

A week later, on a Friday, Shani spoke with Zane on the phone after he arrived at Walter Reed Medical Center. The CT scan, before Zane left Bagram, had shown the shoulder bone was broken but not shattered. He had been sent on to Landstuhl, where an army surgeon operated on and set his shoulder, but instead of a cast Zane only needed a sling. He'd need to do physical therapy though, which was a relief to Shani. It meant he wouldn't be going back to Afghanistan anytime soon.

As soon as she hung up the phone she told Joel, who was working from home that day, trying to catch up without interruptions, and then headed over to the Lehmans' to tell Lila.

Rose answered the door and said that Lila was working at the Plain Buffet. Ten minutes later, Shani stepped through the door of the restaurant, inhaling the comforting scent of roast and ham and gravy and stuffing. Lila was holding drinks in each hand when she saw Shani.

She froze.

"Everything's okay," Shani said as she approached.

Lila exhaled and then said, "Let me deliver these."

When she returned, Shani said, "Zane's at Walter Reed. We're going to go see him tomorrow. Can you come with us?"

Lila froze and then stuttered, "I don't know—I doubt he'd want me to."

"No, I think he would," Shani answered.

"Did you ask him?"

Shani shook her head.

"Would you?"

"I'll call him right now." Shani pulled her phone from her purse.

Lila looked over her shoulder. "I'll be right back."

Zane didn't answer the first time, so Shani left a quick message and then tried again. He picked up on the fifth ring, the second time.

"Hey," Shani said, "do you mind if Lila comes tomorrow?"

Zane didn't answer.

"Are you there?" Shani asked.

"Yeah. Did you ask her?"

"Uh-huh. She said to ask you."

"Sounds as if she doesn't want to."

"No," Shani said, watching Lila clear a table. "I don't think so."

"Yeah, well, I'd have to hear it from her." His voice sounded flat.

"What's the matter, sweetie?"

He didn't answer.

"Zane?"

"Look, the doc is coming by any minute. I'll see you tomorrow, okay?"

Now Lila was headed toward her again. "Bye," Shani managed to say, but the call cut off before she could tell him that she loved him. Every time they talked he seemed more and more unsettled. It was to be expected, she was sure. He had to be in a lot of pain. Plus there was all the uncertainty of what was next for him. And the guilt of taking a life. Plus he was on heavy pain meds too.

"How is he?" Lila asked.

"All right," Shani answered.

"Does he want me to come?"

"I'm not sure. He couldn't talk."

"Thank you for asking," Lila said, "but I'm supposed to work tomorrow, and it would be really hard to find someone else to take my place at this point. Talk with him and see what he wants. Maybe I can go next time."

Shani nodded. It had been foolish of her to interfere. She wanted more than anything for Zane to have all the support he could, and she suspected that out of everyone he'd prefer to see Lila the most. If he'd only admit it.

She reached for Lila's hand. "I'm sorry," Shani said.

"For what?" Lila asked.

"For meddling."

Lila leaned toward her, tears filling her eyes. "Don't worry about it. I don't think any of us knows what to do—not really."

"Did you get back together with Reuben?"

Lila shook her head.

Shani wanted to ask more, but Lila pulled away from her. "I've got to get back to work. Let me know how Zane is, once you get back."

"I will," Shani answered and told Lila good-bye. She stopped by the store before she went home and bought everything she could think of that Zane might need—a toothbrush, toothpaste, shaving cream, aftershave, snacks, writing paper, and pens. She picked up a couple pairs of shorts and sweatpants, several T-shirts, and two zip sweatshirts. She'd asked him what he needed and he'd said nothing.

She'd also asked him how his pain was, and he'd just grunted. Honestly, she thought having Lila around might have encouraged him to be a little bit more communicative.

Shani was surprised at the turmoil she felt about going to see Zane. He'd been injured, but they had so much to be thankful for. Still there were so many uncertainties. Something more had happened between him and Lila. Would that make him less likely to come home after he was discharged from the hospital?

And would he have to go back to Afghanistan? The answer to that question was the one she feared the most.

They arrived at Walter Reed Medical Center in Maryland at noon, exactly when Zane said they should. The old Walter Reed had been closed down several years before and combined with the National Naval Medical Center. Joel had never gone to the old Walter Reed, not when he was injured or recovering. And they hadn't been to the new one either—not until today.

A sign out front that read *Where the nation heals its heroes* stood sentry. Shani hoped it was true. The place was huge, but Zane had given them good directions. When they reached his room he was waiting, sitting up in the bed, his right arm in a sling. Adam hung back a little until Zane said, "Come close, Bub, so I can hug you. Over to my left side."

Adam followed Zane's instructions and got the first half hug. Next Shani hugged him. Zane patted her back once, but that was all. Then Joel hugged him. Shani opened the bag she'd brought his things in and started pulling them out, placing them on the end of the bed.

"You didn't need to do that," he said. "They have toothbrushes and stuff here."

"I know," Shani said, "but it's what moms do."

"Thank you," Zane said. Then he turned his attention to Adam and they talked about when school was starting and how Trudy was. Zane didn't seem as flat as he had on the phone.

"Have you talked to Casey lately?" Shani finally asked.

Zane nodded. "She called this morning."

"How are things over there?"

"Fine, I think," he answered.

"How is Casey?"

"Good." He shifted in the bed, appearing annoyed. "We're still just friends," Zane added. "That's all it's ever going to be."

Shani nodded. She understood that now. "What did she say about Jaalal and his family? We've been praying, like you asked."

Zane's expression darkened. "As far as I know everything's the same." Clearly he didn't want to talk about any of that either.

After a while Shani suggested that she and Adam go find a snack to bring back to the room. She hoped maybe Joel could get Zane to talk.

When they came back with a tray of individual milk cartons and cookies from the cafeteria, Zane's eyes were closed and Joel was sitting in a chair staring at the wall.

"Is he asleep?" Shani whispered.

Joel shook his head.

"Just resting," Zane replied.

Shani put the tray on the table. Zane opened his eyes and said he wasn't hungry, but he patted the bed for Adam to sit beside him. After a while, Zane said they should probably all go. "I'm tired," he said.

"Have you been up?" Shani asked. "Walking around?"

He nodded. "Lots, Mom."

"What does the doctor say?"

"That I'm doing fine."

"Can you come home? And do physical therapy as an outpatient?"

"No. I'll stay here."

She wanted to ask if he wished to come home at all. Instead she started to say, "Lila was—"

Joel cleared his throat. Zane sighed.

"—wondering . . ." Shani's voice trailed off. It was best if she didn't say anything at all.

After a long silence, she asked, "When can we come again?"

Zane shrugged. Joel cleared his throat again.

"We'll talk later," Shani said. "You can let us know what works best." If only she knew what Lila had said in her letter. Obviously Zane had gotten it. He was much colder than he'd been when he was home on furlough. *Home.* He seemed to have no desire to come back.

Shani and Joel didn't have a chance to speak in private until they'd returned home and walked out to look over the garden together. It needed to be weeded, and the tomatoes needed to be picked. So did the zucchini. She'd abandoned it as soon as Zane had been injured, when everything had shifted.

"Did he talk with you after we left the room?" she asked as she turned toward the field.

"Not really," Joel said.

"What did he say about getting shot?"

"Nothing."

"Did he say anything else?"

Joel exhaled and then said, "Just that he doesn't think he could ever shoot another person again."

"Then he can't go back," Shani said. "Right?"

Joel frowned. "I think a lot of soldiers probably feel that way after they kill someone."

Shani knew Joel had never had to shoot anyone in Iraq. Neither had Charlie. Joel put his arm around Shani. "I know you mean well but you need to take it easy. Zane will talk when he's ready."

"What if he's never ready?"

"Then we keep waiting."

Shani turned back toward the house. Zane had shut them out for three years, pretty much, except when he was home on furlough. But she never would have expected that he'd shut them out even more after being wounded. Was it Lila? Or because of Jaalal and his family? What was bothering Zane the most? And why did he have to take it out on her and Joel?

No matter what his reasons, Shani knew Joel was right. They'd keep waiting. And trusting. God would comfort Zane in ways she never could.

19

The next Sunday Zane stared at the vase of mums on the coffee table in the lobby as he waited for Simon. He'd been seeing an occupational therapist and doing a few yoga moves, ones he could do with his arm in a sling, to learn to reduce stress. A chaplain had visited quite a few times, but Zane hadn't really told him anything.

The chaplain stressed how important it was for Zane to talk to someone. "Look for a new buddy," the guy had said. "Someone who's been through something similar." Zane doubted he would. He was growing weary of the banter between soldiers, sure the majority of their stories were exaggerated to match how they *felt* about what happened—not what actually *did* happen.

Except for the times when it really was bad— when someone had died or when the soldiers in question had been hurt enough to land them back stateside. No one talked about *those* times. Zane hadn't said a word about killing Benham to the chaplain or anyone else here. And he wouldn't.

He'd been having nightmares nearly every night. He'd wake up agitated and in a cold sweat, unable to remember his dreams. He didn't plan to talk with anyone about those either.

Dustin, a guy he'd met on the ward, rolled along the sidewalk outside of the sliding doors with his mom. She'd come out from Arizona as soon as he'd arrived and had barely left his side. He was much worse off than Zane. He'd lost both legs in an explosion. Pretty much everyone in the hospital was worse off than Zane. He'd been incredibly lucky—except for having killed Benham.

He knew it could have been so much worse. The innocent boy that reminded him of Adam could have been killed too.

He couldn't help but think of the John McCrae poem. The beginning two lines bounced through his head, over and over. *In Flanders fields the poppies blow; Between the crosses, row on row . . .* " He thought of all the soldiers who never made it home through the last hundred years. And then the ones who did, like Dustin, whose lives would never be the same.

The true cost of war was beyond his comprehension. Soldiers and families and civilians all paid for it their entire lives.

Simon was late, which wasn't surprising. He

was stationed at Fort Belvoir in Virginia and said he was going to borrow a friend's car to drive up. Last Zane knew, Simon didn't have his license, but maybe that had changed.

Zane stood, stretched, and ran his good hand along his sling. No one would give him a straight answer about going back to Afghanistan, probably because no one knew for sure. Rehab would be three or four weeks. That would put him into mid-September. Would they send him back for three months?

As much as he wanted to see Jaalal, he didn't think he could pull a trigger again to save himself or anyone else. But he wasn't sure how to communicate that to Sarge. He wasn't sure what he would do if given orders to return to Afghanistan. He thought about the deserters he'd read about in Canada. Maybe he should get his truck from home and drive north.

He knew when he joined he'd have a hard time shooting someone, let alone killing another human being. But he didn't fathom it would be this hard. The reality of it felt like a poison seeping through his body, through his soul.

The sliding doors opened before anyone appeared, but then Simon literally jumped through the door. "I'm here!" he shouted, spreading his arms wide. "Better late than never."

Zane couldn't help but laugh.

Simon wore a plain black T-shirt, jeans, and

old tennis shoes. It still didn't seem right to see him out of trousers, suspenders, and a shirt.

The two hugged, as best they could around the sling.

"Hungry?" Simon asked.

"Not really," Zane answered.

"Well, I'm starving. What's there to eat around here?"

"Are we driving or walking?"

"How do you think I got here?"

Zane shook his head. "I'm not sure how legal it was."

Simon lit up like a Christmas tree. "I got my license."

"When?"

"Two days ago."

Zane groaned.

"So, seriously," Simon said, "what's to eat around here?"

"Well . . ." Zane pointed to his sling. "I'm not going far in this thing."

"And how exactly does a sling inhibit your ability to use your legs?" Simon laughed. "You're just afraid to ride with me, right?"

"Exactly. There's a cafeteria down the hall."

Simon groaned. "No way. We're going somewhere."

Simon started for the door. When Zane didn't follow, he turned back and said, "Are you coming or not?"

Zane shrugged and followed his friend.

Thanks to driving Tim's tractor, Simon had the shifting down on the Toyota Camry he'd borrowed. The signaling, steering, and braking were another matter.

As Simon took a turn too sharply, Zane gasped. Simon laughed as he straightened out the wheel. "Shot in Afghanistan, but done in by a former Amish kid's driving." He grinned. "I figured you've been bored and needed a little excitement."

Zane exhaled. "Bored. Right."

Simon turned sharply into the parking lot of a pizza place. "How's this?"

"Great," he said. "As long as I don't have to ride another minute with you."

"Better watch out. I just might make you go all the way back to Virginia with me."

As they walked toward the front door, Simon pulled out his phone and started a text. Zane patted his pocket. He'd left his phone in his room. Not that he had anyone to text anyway.

He increased his stride as Simon slowed down. "Who to?" Zane asked.

Simon grinned again. "Mandy."

"You two pretty serious?"

Simon shrugged. "As serious as a soldier and a Mennonite girl with a dad can be."

Zane's stomach fell. It held more promise than a soldier and an Amish girl with a dad.

Simon ordered a medium pizza, all for himself, while Zane ordered a single piece. "How're you gonna get your strength back? That wouldn't even make a chicken full," Simon said as they filled their cups at the fountain.

"I had a big breakfast," Zane lied.

When they'd settled into a booth, Simon leaned across the table and said, "So tell me what happened."

Zane gave him the short story.

Simon whistled. "You shot two dudes? No one told me that."

Zane frowned. "One died."

"Yeah, but you saved a little boy. And the soldier, your brother, right?"

Zane didn't really consider Grant a brother, but yeah, Zane might have saved his life. And Simon was right about the boy.

"The bad guys shot first, right?"

Zane nodded.

Simon's eyes shone. "So it was purely self-defense."

"I was there to build relationships with the Afghan people. Not kill them."

"You're in the U.S. Army, dude," Simon said.

"Lots of people make it through without having to kill anyone."

"But it was kill or be killed."

"Yeah," Zane said. "But I still feel rotten."

Simon shook his head. "I don't get it. You had

339

to keep your brothers safe. That's your number one priority, right?"

Zane sighed. "I'm just glad I won't have to go back—at least I doubt I will."

"How can you live with yourself, not wanting to go back?"

"How can I live with myself, having taken a life? What if I have to take another?"

"You'll be fine," Simon said, "because you're saving the lives of the good guys. I wouldn't hesitate to take someone down if they were shooting at me or my brothers."

"I know you wouldn't," Zane replied. He hadn't hesitated either, but he'd never shared Simon's bravado.

"So how's the family?" Zane asked, trying to change the topic.

"Fine, I think. Daniel won't say it, but I'm guessing he and Jenny will get married in November."

"Any other upcoming weddings?" Zane asked.

Simon shook his head. "Nah, I don't think so."

Zane forced himself to continue. "What about Lila?"

Simon pursed his lips together and said, "What makes you ask?"

"I got a letter from her. While I was still in Afghanistan. She said she couldn't write to me anymore, and I figured that meant she was getting married."

"Nope. In fact she and Reuben aren't courting anymore."

Zane involuntarily jerked back against the booth, bumping his shoulder. He squelched a cry of pain and instead sputtered, "What?"

A smile crept across Simon's face. "Yeah, I don't know what happened exactly. Daniel just said that Dat was upset."

"When did it happen?"

"Maybe a week or two before you got shot. Something like that."

The server called their number, and Simon went to get the food. Zane leaned back in the booth. Had she and Reuben broken up before she wrote the letter? But if so, why did she write it?

Simon returned and slid Zane's plate toward him. "Eat up."

Zane still didn't have the hang of eating with his left hand, but he was getting better. He took a bite.

In no time Simon finished his first slice of pizza and picked up a second. He'd filled out even more in the last few months. He was definitely going to be a big man.

Simon held the pizza in midair. "You should call Lila," he said.

"Why?"

Simon narrowed his eyes. "Why do you think?"

"I have no idea," Zane answered.

He grimaced. "Because you two care about

each other. And you are both too cowardly to do anything about it."

Zane's eyes began to burn, and for a second he was afraid a tear might escape, but he swallowed hard. Simon was wrong. Lila didn't love him. "It doesn't matter how we feel about each other. There's no future for us, even if she really did break up with Reuben. She's joined the church. It's hopeless." Zane swallowed again. "So just knock it off, would you?"

Simon stood and leaned across the table and cuffed Zane on his good arm, jarring his whole body. Pain shot through his bad shoulder again, but he didn't let on that it hurt.

"No, Zane Beck," Simon said, still standing. "You knock it off. You've been a whiny mess for the last three years because of my sister. It's been pathetic to watch. If you love her, why don't you tell her?"

"I did."

Simon dropped back down onto the bench with a thud. "Three years ago? When she was seventeen?"

Zane stared Simon down, not responding.

Finally Simon said, "Maybe it's time you tell her again."

Zane bristled. "I told her in my letters that I cared about her, and that I had loved her."

Simon raised his eyebrows. "So . . . past tense?"

Zane nodded.

"You're pathetic."

Zane swallowed. "You think I should just call her? Leave a message on the barn phone for your Dat to hear? That would go over big."

Simon picked up another piece of pizza. "Daniel said he plans to come see you next weekend. Maybe she'd come with him."

"She didn't want to come with my folks."

"After you begged her to come?" Simon's nostrils flared. "Because I heard that you told her to stay home."

Obviously the Amish grapevine was still working, even though Simon wasn't Amish, even though he didn't have the details quite right. But in a way it still comforted him. Lila was talking, to someone, about him.

"Did she call you?"

"Yeah, she did. After your mom and dad saw you." He shook his head. "You've got to have some faith," Simon said. "Take it a step at a time. Pray about it. Talk to her. See what happens."

"Did you get all this newfound wisdom from Uncle Sam?"

"Nah." He grinned again, back to his happy-go-lucky self. "It's what Mandy and I are doing. We have no idea how everything is going to work out—just this feeling that it might."

Zane was sick to death of feelings. He wanted something tangible. Something real.

●●●

A week later, Zane breathed out as he tried to relax in the yoga class, listening carefully to the instructor, trying his best to balance his Warrior II pose—which looked nothing like the real warriors he'd seen—with one arm in a sling. The Army was doing its best to provide alternatives to pain meds. Zane remembered his dad being on opiates for a really long time after he returned from Iraq and was thankful he wouldn't have to be. They were already weaning him off.

He yawned. He'd woken up in a cold sweat the night before and couldn't get back to sleep. He'd been beside the wall of the village, scrambling to get to the little boy. But he couldn't. The boy kept moving. The bullets kept coming.

He yawned again.

"That's all for today," the instructor said to him and the fifteen other soldiers. "We'll start back up on Monday."

He'd start physical therapy on Monday too. Three weeks of it, and then he'd have some time off—at home, he guessed. Then he'd see what his future held.

He'd started down the hallway back to his room when he heard Daniel call out his name. They were early. He turned around, nodding at Daniel and then looking past him. Jenny was a few feet behind him. At first he didn't see anyone else, but then Lila stepped around the corner. His heart raced.

There was an awkward moment when Daniel stuck out his hand and then realized Zane couldn't shake it—not with his right hand, anyway. Zane did with his left though, and Daniel relaxed a little.

"Hi, Zane," Jenny said. Her smile was kind and caring.

He returned the greeting and then, his voice a little shaky, said, "Hello, Lila."

"Hi," she answered, her voice soft. Her blue eyes were as clear as ever. She wore a sapphire sweater over her dress and apron. For a moment their eyes locked. She didn't smile or give anything away. Nothing at all. Perhaps she'd only come because she felt sorry for him. Then Daniel cleared his throat and Zane said, "We could sit in the lobby." It was only 11 a.m. Not time for lunch. "Or go for a walk."

"Stretching my legs sounds good," Daniel said, glancing at the girls. They both nodded. As they headed toward the exit, Daniel said they'd hired a driver to come to Maryland. "It was super hard giving up my pickup," he said, quietly. "And worse to have to ride with someone else—who was all freaked out by the traffic around here."

"I can imagine." Zane lowered his voice. "I'm also guessing it will be worth it—giving up your truck, I mean."

Daniel's face reddened a little, and then he smiled and said, "I suspect so."

Zane's heart skipped a beat, aware of Lila walking behind him, of the swish of her skirt as they headed down the corridor to the front door. His heart began to ache, but then Daniel asked him how his shoulder was doing and the girls stepped up so they could hear.

Lila still walked next to him as they triggered the front door to open, but then his left hand brushed against hers, and she stepped away. He slowed down, allowing her to exit the building first.

Zane guided them toward the peace garden, but as they neared it Daniel spotted a coffee kiosk and said he wanted to grab a cup. "Anyone else want one?" he asked.

"I'll go with you," Jenny said.

Zane pointed down the pathway. "We'll be this way."

Neither he nor Lila said a thing as they walked. When they reached a small garden, Zane pointed to a bench and hoped Lila couldn't tell his good hand was shaking.

After they both sat, she said, "I'm sorry."

"For what?" he asked, keeping his head down, thinking maybe she was going to apologize for the letter.

"For your injury." She paused. "How are your wounds, really?"

"The back of my head is fine." He turned a little so she could see the scab where the bullet grazed it. "And they say my shoulder should heal up. I might have some lasting tissue damage, maybe some messed-up nerves, but I'll make it."

"How about on the inside?"

He swallowed hard and peered behind her, to see if Daniel and Jenny were coming toward them. They weren't. Chances were they planned to give him and Lila some time alone.

"I shouldn't have asked," she said.

"No," he managed to say. "I'm glad you did." He wanted to take her hand. More than that he wanted her to take his. "I killed someone," he said.

She nodded. "I know."

"I didn't want to."

"I'm sorry," she said. "I prayed you wouldn't have to, the whole time you were over there."

"Thanks," he said. "I don't know why God didn't answer that prayer."

"But the man might have killed you. Or another soldier. Or the little boy." She sounded like Simon, minus the bravado.

"Yeah," Zane said. "Maybe. But I'll never know for sure."

"You did what you had to do."

He nodded. It helped to hear her say it.

"But I'm still sorry, Zane." It had been so long since he'd heard her say his name. "I know the wound on the inside is worse than the one in your shoulder." She inched a little closer to him but didn't touch him. "I'd like to hear what happened, if you want to tell me, from you."

He started with waiting by the wall—after he read her letter. He wasn't ready to tell her that part yet. After he'd gone through the whole story, including the part the quilts and blankets played, clear to when he woke up and found he'd been rushed into surgery because of a bleed, tears filled Lila's eyes.

"That's when I found out that Benham had died. He was talking in the helicopter, and then I thought he was going to be all right. Casey—" He paused. "She's a woman in my unit."

Lila nodded.

"She said the bullet nicked his lung and it collapsed before they knew what had happened." Zane looked down at the ground. "They tried to save him, but it was too late."

Lila put her hand on his good shoulder and left it there. It felt warm and comforting.

He raised his head. "Why did you come?"

"Simon told Daniel you wanted to see me." She met his eyes. "And I wanted to see you. I wanted to come with your parents. . . . I just wasn't sure."

He inhaled sharply, grateful for her brothers and their meddling. "Simon told me you broke up with Reuben."

She nodded. "I did."

"Why?"

"That's what I meant when I wrote about being dishonest." She paused for a moment, her eyes holding his gaze. "Did you get that letter?"

He nodded. "Right before . . ."

She grimaced. "I hadn't been honest with Reuben. I kept telling myself love was a commitment, because I was trying to please everyone who wanted us to marry—but in the end I realized I needed more than that. That it wasn't fair to him or to me. He deserves someone who truly loves him."

Zane felt as if he'd just had his first drink of water after being in a desert for three years. Lila was talking to him. Telling him how she felt. He started to reach for her hand but stopped. He didn't want to scare her away.

She glanced away, toward the children's playground. "I couldn't marry someone I couldn't talk to. Someone I didn't love. Especially when I love someone else."

For a moment he hoped he was the *someone else,* but then his heart fell. Simon had been wrong. Lila would never leave the church for him. She didn't love Reuben—she loved someone else who was Amish. Nothing had changed, not really.

"Who is it?" he asked.

She returned her gaze to him again. "What?"

"Whom do you love?" He didn't like the harsh tone that had seeped into his voice, but there it was. And as much as he tried not to, he was afraid he sounded bitter. Why couldn't he just be her friend? Just treasure the time he had with her instead of always feeling as if it weren't enough.

She stared at him, her eyes boring into his. Finally she said, "Who do you think?"

"I have no idea."

"Don't be a jerk," she said. Then she looked past him and said, "There's Daniel and Jenny."

Zane exhaled as she stood. He wasn't sure how he'd done it. But he'd definitely messed things up, once again.

20

Lila marched away from Zane, not sure if he was following or not. She'd forgotten how intense he was. Worse now than ever.

But she hadn't meant to call him a jerk. It came out of her mouth before she could stop it.

Keeping her focus on her twin, she continued forward until Daniel and Jenny, disposable coffee cups in their hands, ducked into a building as if they were trying to evade her. She stopped, flustered. She didn't want to go back and face Zane.

Mandy had shown her his Facebook page just

last night. Casey had tagged Zane in more photos of her and him together, and then she'd posted that he'd been injured. *Prayers appreciated,* she'd written. *He's the best friend a girl could ever have, and the best soldier I know.*

Zane was probably asking whom she loved so he could break it to her that he and Casey were together. Why had he written to her? Why had she agreed to write him back? Why had he told Simon he wanted to see her?

Zane stopped behind her and cleared his throat.

He'd almost been killed. He was still wounded, both in body and in spirit, and she had just called him a jerk and then stomped off as if she were thirteen again.

Lila turned around. Zane was three feet away from her. "I'm sorry," she said.

He frowned a little. "I probably deserved it."

"No, you didn't." She nodded back toward the park. "Can we try again?"

They didn't return to the bench but instead walked on toward a circle of pathways made of bricks.

"What's this?" Lila asked.

"A labyrinth. The idea is that you pray as you walk around in it."

That's what she did walking through the field, down to the creek.

"So," she said. "Could you tell me one thing?"

He nodded.

"Are you dating Casey?"

"What do you know about Casey?" he asked.

Her face grew warm, even in the cool air. "Mandy showed me her picture."

"On Facebook?"

"Jah . . ."

"I see," he said. "So you've been stalking me." He stepped off the bricks and back onto the sidewalk.

Lila smiled, relieved to hear the teasing in his voice. "No, but Mandy has. Then again, I didn't refuse to look when she thrust her phone in my face."

"So you're pleading innocent?"

"Guilty by association," she countered.

"Well, now that you've admitted guilt, I'll answer the question. In that last post, if I remember right, Casey wrote something about me being a friend, right?"

" 'The best friend,' to be exact," Lila answered.

"There you have it." He stopped walking. So did Lila. "I've been a better friend to Casey than I was to you," he said.

Lila tried to ignore a twinge of jealousy. "How come?"

"I learned my lesson more than three years ago," he said. "I *was* a jerk, that night before I joined the Army. Making a decision like that just shows how stupid I was."

Or how much she'd hurt him. She'd been the

one who told him to go as far away as possible.

"Is that the only reason you've been a good friend to Casey?" Lila asked, aware of the teasing in her voice now, partly fueled by him admitting how stupidly he'd acted.

He cocked his head. "Actually, no. The truth is, I was never interested in being more than a friend to Casey." He gazed down at her. "But you're right. Only wanting to be a friend does make it easier to be one."

He motioned over to a low cement wall. "Mind if we sit again?"

"Of course not." She led the way.

Once they were settled, he said, "Can I ask you again?"

She knew but she asked anyway. "What?"

"Whom do you love, Lila Lehman?"

Her heart contracted. She was tempted to be honest this time, but she couldn't. "I can't tell you. I can't say it out loud." Her leg accidentally bumped against his, and she moved it away quickly. But then he scooted closer and, although she wanted to put her head on his good shoulder, she didn't. They sat quietly.

"I think you know," she finally whispered.

Their eyes locked, and his filled with tears. He understood. "I tried not to," she said. "And I'm still trying because no good can come of it."

He took her hand then and leaned closer to her. He swallowed, his Adam's apple bobbing along his neck. His voice broke a little as he asked, "What's to become of us?"

"What *can* become of us?" she answered.

"So you think it's hopeless?"

She shrugged, but she did think it was hopeless. Her being honest didn't change their circumstances.

"Fifty percent hopeless?" he tried to tease. "Eighty per cent?"

"Don't ask me," she answered. "Ask God."

"I have, believe me. Relentlessly. He's tired of me, I'm sure."

"No," Lila responded. "Never."

Zane shook his head. "Simon said we just need to take it step-by-step."

"Ah, Simon the wise one. Offering relationship advice now, is he?" Lila tried to smile.

"Seems that way," Zane said. "Who would have ever thought?" He grinned, but then it quickly faded. "But he's wrong. You deserve a nice Amish boy. Reuben would have been perfect."

"Stop it," she said, glaring at him. "I'm finally honest with you and that's how you react."

He exhaled as he squeezed her hand. "I'll try not to overthink things right now. I'll try to take each day as it is. As long as you're willing to at least be my friend."

She nodded. "I'll do the same." Sensing someone nearby, she turned her head. Behind them, on a bench, were Daniel and Jenny. "Look who's watching us." She let go of Zane's hand. He slid off the wall and helped her stand. "They won't tell," she said.

"Sibling confidentiality and all of that?" he asked. It used to be a joke between all of them. But they always held to it. Although in his case it had been neighbor confidentiality.

She nodded as she straightened her apron. "Simon told me I was a fool if I didn't come to talk to you. He's on our side."

"What about Daniel?" Zane asked.

"He doesn't want me to leave the church—but . . . Let's just say he's ambivalent," Lila answered as she started toward Daniel and Jenny, still looking at Zane. "Step-by-step, it is."

Zane grinned. It was good to see him smile again.

The mid-September day had grown warm, and Lila wiped her brow with her forearm. Then she pulled the two roasters seasoned with rosemary from the hot oven. She set them on top of the stove to stay warm while she mashed the potatoes. Jenny and Daniel were coming to dinner, along with Monika and Gideon. Thank goodness Beth was coming too. Lila hadn't spent any time around Gideon and Monika, outside of church, since she'd stopped courting Reuben.

Lila wasn't worried about Monika. She'd get over it. But she didn't want Gideon to get involved, to feel as if he needed to guide her back to marrying his son.

Rose came in from helping with the milking, mud splattered on her work dress.

"What are you doing?" she asked.

"Cooking . . ." Lila answered. The rolls were ready to put in the oven. Two blueberry pies sat on the counter.

"You were humming," Rose said.

"I was?"

"I haven't heard you hum in . . . years."

"Oh." Lila slid the rolls into the oven. "What was I humming?"

" 'I'm in the Lord's Army.' "

Lila suppressed a laugh and grabbed the potholders. She hadn't thought of that song in years. "Be still, and know that I am God" and "I'm in the Lord's Army" had a similar theme. Both demanded a day-by-day trust in him. "Go get changed so you can help get dinner on the table. Everyone should be here soon."

Rose dipped her finger in the whipped cream that Lila hadn't put in the fridge yet. "I hope your hands are cleaned," Lila said.

"Just washed them," Rose retorted as she stuck her finger in her mouth and headed for the hall.

Lila shook her head, drained the potatoes, put the pan back on the stove, and then put the whipped cream in the fridge.

She dumped butter in the potatoes, added milk,

and began to mash them as Trudy came in through the back door. "Wash up and set the table," Lila instructed.

Her little sister skipped on down the hall, and Lila realized she was humming again. It struck her that she was happy—and that she hadn't been for a long time. And she also knew why. Her nightly phone calls.

Dat didn't know it, but Zane called her every night at ten p.m.

A knock fell on the open back door, and then Beth called out, "I'm here."

"Come on in." Lila still didn't understand what Beth gained in her friendship with Dat, but it was comforting to have her around. Dat interacted more with all of them when she visited, plus he was better behaved. Not that he was horrible when she wasn't around. He just wasn't always responsive. And when he was it was usually a harsh response, unless it was to Trudy.

Beth set the salad she'd brought on the counter. "Smells delicious," she said, lifting the foil to peek at the chickens as Trudy came into the room. Beth gave the girl a hug, asking as she did, "What can I do to help?"

"Set the table with Trudy," Lila said.

Monika and Gideon arrived next, and Daniel and Jenny were the last to arrive. "I keep miscalculating how long it takes in the buggy," Daniel joked.

"You'll get used to it again, soon enough," Gideon answered. Lila couldn't imagine Gideon with a car. But then again, he certainly might have owned one once. In a few years Daniel could be a deacon or even a bishop.

The conversation revolved around the wedding as they ate. Daniel and Jenny's wedding would be announced at church in a month, but the planning needed to start before then. The wedding would be held at Monika and Gideon's. It would easily accommodate everyone. "We'll rent one of the kitchen wagons," Monika said. "To give us more stoves to work on."

Jenny asked Lila to be one of her witnesses at the wedding. "I'd like that," Lila said. For a moment she felt a pang of sadness. Simon wouldn't be able to sit with Daniel. She wasn't sure if he'd come to the wedding at all.

Then Jenny asked Rose to sit with her too. Rose was ecstatic. "Who will sit with you?" Rose asked Daniel.

"Reuben, for sure," he answered, keeping his eyes on Rose. Lila had only seen Reuben at a distance, at church. She knew he was avoiding her, and she didn't blame him. But she was sure they could get along for Jenny and Daniel's sake.

The conversation continued. As Lila cleared the table, Beth grabbed a pen and paper to take notes. Monika walked to the mud porch and came back with a binder. "This is what I used for the older girls," she said. "I kept lots of notes."

They discussed who would be asked to be the cooks and the servers. Who would care for the horses. What the menu would be for dinner and then for supper.

Lila served the pies while everyone else went over the details. Inside her head she started humming again. She was happy, but she wasn't entirely sure why. Nothing was settled between her and Zane. She couldn't ask him to join the church. It would be so much easier for her to leave, yet she would never do it. She had committed herself to her church and community. It would break Dat's heart for her to go against her vow.

She served Monika first, then Beth. It did no good to think about Zane and her future. It made her think of her crazy quilt, which was now halfway done. She had no idea how all of the pieces would stitch together—she just had to trust they would.

By the time they'd completed the items on Monika's list, everyone was finished with their dessert. Jenny and Daniel left first. Beth settled on the couch with Trudy to read her a bedtime story, and Dat sat in his chair. Lila could tell he was listening to the story even though he didn't say anything.

"Help me with the dishes," Lila said to Rose.

"I'll help," Monika said.

Gideon cleared his throat and said to Lila, "Could I talk with you a moment?" He nodded toward the back door. She followed him through the mud porch and down the steps, afraid maybe she'd misjudged him. Maybe he was going to scold her after all.

He put his hat on his head and then stopped in the driveway and turned toward her. "How are you doing?" He tugged on his beard, flecked with gray, as he spoke.

Her face grew warm. "*Gut*. I have no complaints."

He smiled a little. "I don't expect you to share your heart with me, but I just wanted to let you know that although I'm sad for Reuben I believe you've done the right thing. There's no blame or shame. Reuben will find the right person, and you will find the right person too. There's no reason for despair."

"Denki," she said.

He crossed his arms. "Is it hard for you to be around Jenny and Daniel, as they're planning their wedding?"

"No," she answered. "I couldn't be happier for them."

"That's *gut* to hear," Gideon said. "In fact, that helps to confirm that you did, indeed, do the right thing." He nodded at her then, as if to release her. "Denki," he said. "For answering my questions."

Relieved that he hadn't asked any more, Lila

360

headed back up the steps. It was nearly seven thirty. In less than three hours she'd be talking to Zane.

Lila checked one more time to make sure Rose and Trudy were both asleep before she grabbed the flashlight off the mud-porch shelf and snuck out the back door. Dat seldom stayed up later than nine anymore. At forty-six, getting up at four every morning was catching up with him.

She kept the flashlight off. The sky was clear, the moon nearly full, and the stars super bright. The temperature had dropped when the sun set, and the crisp air was filled with woodsmoke. When she reached the barn, she flicked the flashlight on and made her way to Dat's office. She only waited a minute until the phone rang.

"Hallo, Zane," she answered.

"Gotcha." Her heart raced until she realized who it was.

"Simon! What are you doing?"

"Messing with you." He laughed.

"Good-bye," she said, her hand on the receiver.

"No, wait. I know you're expecting a call." He laughed again. "But I just wanted to say hello and see how everyone is doing."

"Fine."

"How are you and you-know-who doing?"

Lila turned toward the wall. "Obviously you've talked to him."

"Yep. But I wanted your perspective."

"Why would I share it with you?"

"Come on, Lila. Give me a break."

She put her free hand on her hip. "We've been talking . . ."

"I know that."

"And if you don't hang up, I'm going to hang up on you."

"That desperate to talk to your sweetheart, huh?"

She didn't reply.

"Okay," he said. "I'm going. Give me a call sometime when you're not busy. I really do want to know how everyone is."

"Bye," she said and hit the receiver. Surely Zane would call back if he'd gotten a busy signal.

She sat down in the desk chair and only waited another minute until the phone rang again. This time it was Zane. After talking about their days, Zane told her he'd had an e-mail from Casey and that the new translator was working out really well.

"What a relief," Lila said.

"Jah," Zane answered. "Casey said Sarge thinks I'll be reassigned to an office job."

"Back in Texas?" Her heart fell.

"That's right. But it will just be until next June."

"Will you come home first?"

"Of course," he said. "I should have two

weeks of leave before I report back to the unit."

"Can you come back for Daniel's wedding?"

"I hope so," he answered. "I'll do my best."

"Getting Casey's e-mail changes everything," he said. "I was actually considering filing for conscientious objector status if I had to go back to Afghanistan."

She drew in a sharp breath. She didn't know what all that would entail, but she could imagine how Joel might react. It sounded as if it would be a complicated situation.

"I honestly don't think I can shoot a weapon again, not at a person. Not even to defend myself. And if I couldn't, I'd have no business going back. If I froze I could get my whole team killed."

"Then, thank God that won't happen." He'd get himself killed too.

The topic shifted to Mammi and Dawdi. "Rose, Trudy, and I are going to go see them tomorrow." She hadn't been working at the quilt shop as often because Mammi was done with chemo and able to take a few shifts a week now. Her prognosis looked good.

Finally, close to midnight, Lila said she should let him go. "We both need to get some sleep," she said. The next day was Saturday, but that didn't matter with her schedule. She was always up early. Hopefully Zane would be able to sleep in.

"Oh, man," he said. "I didn't realize it was so late. I'm sorry."

"I'm not." She rested her head on her free hand. "I'd rather talk than sleep."

"Me too," he said.

"But you need your rest, to heal."

"I need you," he said, "to heal."

Her heart stopped for a moment, and she wasn't sure how to respond so she didn't say anything.

He groaned. "I shouldn't have said that."

"No. Don't apologize."

"I'm always saying the wrong thing to you," he said.

Neither of them seemed to know the right things to say.

After they said their good-nights, Lila slipped back into the house, put the flashlight away, and then headed to the pitch-black hallway, her heart pounding. She stopped at the bedroom door. Zane needed her, but in a different way than everyone else needed her. He didn't need her to cook or do laundry. Not that she minded, but anyone could do those jobs.

Zane needed her because he loved her. And she needed him for the same reason.

The door creaked open in the darkness and Lila slammed her hand over her mouth to keep from screaming until someone said, "What are you doing?"

Lila managed to hiss, "Rose! What are *you* doing?"

"Going to the bathroom." Her sleepy sister

slipped past her. Hopefully she wouldn't remember in the morning that Lila hadn't gone to bed until after midnight.

After they'd cleaned up after breakfast the three girls headed toward Mammi's and Dawdi's house. Lila still hadn't told them that she stopped courting Reuben. She didn't want to face her grandparents' disappointment too—but she would today.

When they arrived, Aenti Eve was just pulling up.

"Are you quilting today?" Lila asked as she stepped down from the buggy.

"No," Eve said, closing her car door. "I just brought your grandmother a spinach and black bean salad."

"Goodness," Lila said. "Thanks for helping to keep her healthy."

Eve grinned. "I'll give you some recipes for your Dat."

Lila laughed. "Right." Dat would never eat anything like that.

After they all hugged Mammi and had settled down in the living room, the conversation flitted from one thing to another. "How is Zane doing?" Mammi asked Eve.

"I think all right. Shani talks to him every couple of days. She said he seems to be doing better emotionally."

Lila shifted in her chair, tried to breath evenly, and avoided looking at Rose.

"Have they been to see him?" Mammi asked.

"A couple of times," Eve answered. "He hasn't wanted them to visit much."

"How odd," Mammi said.

"Lila can tell you all about Zane. She went to see him with Daniel and Jenny." The volume of Rose's voice rose with each word. "And I don't know the details, but she was up late last night, I'm guessing talking to *someone*."

"To Reuben, right?" Mammi asked.

Lila grimaced. She hadn't meant to keep it from Mammi but she certainly hadn't gone out of her way to tell her.

Rose jumped in again. "They aren't courting anymore."

"Oh." Mammi turned toward Lila. "What happened?"

Lila didn't want to say anything—not in front of Trudy, but especially not in front of Rose. "How about if I make some tea?"

Rose snorted.

"Stop," Lila hissed at her sister as she walked by. She filled the teakettle and put it on the stove, turning on the burner. A minute later Mammi came into the kitchen. Lila expected Rose or Trudy to follow her, but neither did.

"What happened?" Mammi asked as she

stepped beside Lila. "I thought you and Reuben were perfect together."

Lila shook her head. She shouldn't have avoided telling her grandmother. It just made it harder now. "We looked perfect together, but I didn't love him. There wasn't any spark." She thought of the way she felt being around Zane when she saw him at the hospital, of how she felt every time she talked to him on the phone. Warm and cold at the same time. Free yet connected.

"Ach," Mammi said. "Sparks eventually burn away. Sometimes love comes later. After marriage."

Lila hesitated and then said, "Reuben's a *gut* man. He'll make someone a wonderful husband. Just not me."

"Maybe it's a little hiccup," Mammi said. "Perhaps you'll change your mind."

Lila shook her head.

"Well, you were talking to someone last night. Is another young man wanting to court you?"

Lila shrugged. Not in the way Mammi hoped at least. The kettle began to whistle. Lila grabbed the potholder and then the kettle, rinsed out the teapot, and then put the bags of the tea in the bottom and filled it with hot water, all while Mammi scrutinized her.

"Go sit back down," Lila finally said to her grandmother. "Have Trudy recite her multiplication table. She's getting really good."

"Ach," Mammi said. "I guess you're not going to tell me any more than that, are you."

Lila shook her head.

Mammi left, but a minute later Eve came into the kitchen. "I've got to get going," she said. "But I wanted to say good-bye."

As they hugged, Eve whispered, "What's going on?"

"Nothing," Lila lied, pulling away.

Eve peered into Lila's eyes. "Shani said when she talks to Zane on the phone not only does he seem to be doing better emotionally, but he actually sounds happy."

"That's *gut*, right?" Lila turned away and put a towel over the teapot to keep the heat in.

Eve put her hand on Lila's shoulder. "So who were you talking to last night?"

"Whom do you think?" she whispered.

Eve winced. "Does your Dat know?"

"Of course not."

"Don't hurt Zane, Lila. He's too vulnerable right now."

Lila faced her aunt.

Eve shook her head. "I can't imagine you leaving the church."

"I don't plan to."

"Do you talk to him because you feel sorry for him?"

"Of course not," Lila said.

"What's going on, then?"

"I care about him. I've always cared about him."

"But he loves you." Eve touched Lila's shoulder. "You'll break his heart again if you're not careful."

Lila blinked, fighting back the tears.

Eve shook her head.

"Don't tell Shani, please," Lila whispered. "Zane wouldn't want that."

"I won't," Eve answered. "Just be careful."

Lila nodded, overwhelmed with what a crazy quilt her life had become. Maybe she would spend her entire life being Zane's friend, longing for more but never having it. Her life would be one long zigzag stitch of emotions.

"Sorry," Eve said. "I didn't mean to scold you."

"No," Lila said. "You're right." She swiped at a tear. "I just don't know what to do."

Eve wrapped her arms around her. "I know how you feel. But I also know you're not me."

For the first time Lila wondered if it had been easier for Eve to leave the church because both her parents were already deceased. But Eve had told her once she hadn't been totally sold on joining the church in the first place.

Lila had cherished the day she joined. It felt right. Completely right.

But so did Zane.

21

Zane sat in one of the middle-row captain's seats of his mom's van, and Lila sat in the seat beside him. She'd asked if it would be okay to come with his family to spring him out of Walter Reed. Of course he'd said yes.

Bub sat in the back seat, prattling away. But it was a good prattle. School had been in session for a few weeks and he liked his teacher and they were studying photosynthesis and he'd written his first short story.

By the time they were off the Beltway and headed north, Bub had grown tired, and soon his prattling stopped and his head rested against the window.

"Does your shoulder hurt?" Mom asked Zane, shifting in her seat as Dad turned onto the highway, heading west.

"Not much," Zane answered, moving his arm. The physical therapist was pleased with the progress he'd made and had released him, saying he'd be fine to drive to Texas. "You're good to do anything," the woman said. "Well, maybe not dig a ditch yet or lift a hundred pounds, but you're fine to shoot a gun."

He hadn't reacted. He might have to qualify another time on the shooting range, but he'd never have to shoot at another person. That was all that mattered. And he didn't have to worry about trying to become a conscientious objector to get out of it either. God had worked everything out.

"Zane," Mom said, shifting her gaze. "Your footlocker arrived. Casey sent it. Wasn't that nice of her?"

Zane nodded. Better Casey than anyone else. She wouldn't have been as freaked out by the pacifist literature he had at the bottom of it, under the quilt his mom and the other ladies had made. Hopefully she didn't dig that far though—they were tucked in with the letters from Lila.

Mom straightened around in her seat and talked with Dad as they neared Baltimore.

Zane patted the side of his jacket. In the inside pocket was the letter from Lila, the one she'd written after breaking up with Reuben. He thought of how devastated he'd been to receive it, but it hadn't turned out to be what he thought, not at all. So many things were turning out to be different than he'd expected. He and Lila had talked about everything over the phone—everything but their future. Hopefully they'd have time for that while he was home.

Surely Lila would meet him down by the creek. And bring Trudy over to play with Adam after school. He hoped the Indian summer weather held so he and Lila could take walks in the field.

After the two weeks were up he'd drive down to Texas for a month, fly home for Daniel and Jenny's wedding, go back to Texas, and then fly home for Christmas. By then his entire unit would be back from Afghanistan and any chance of deployment before he discharged from the Army would be over. He'd be home free, literally, in June.

He had no idea what he'd do then. Maybe still go to college on the GI Bill. Maybe get a job with a social services agency. Try to figure out what was next for him and Lila—by talking it through with her. But he didn't want to rush her or crowd her or try to control her, not like he'd tried when he was eighteen.

Step-by-step, is what Simon said. Don't look too far ahead. Zane peered out the window. That was easy for Simon to say—he'd never been a planner. But that was what Zane needed to learn to do, to be happy in the moment.

Lila took a large piece of fabric out of her bag.

"What are you working on?" he asked.

"A crazy quilt."

He noticed then that the squares weren't uniform. "Is that the blue fabric from my quilt?" he asked.

She nodded and pointed at a green print. "And this is from Simon's."

The fabrics were blues, greens, and purples, and the thread was gold. She'd embroidered a gate and a flower on the square. Zane pointed to the gate. She nodded.

It was their gate, just as he'd suspected. He wondered what she'd embroidered on the other pieces.

He smiled at her, and she ducked her head, probably embarrassed at the attention over the quilt. But he was pretty sure she was telling her story through her stitching—maybe even their story.

Adam bumped Zane's arm. "What do you need, Bub?" he asked without turning around.

"What's up with you two?"

"What do you mean?"

"You're all googly-eyed."

Zane turned in his seat, accidentally bumping against Lila's leg. She scooted it away from him. "Sorry," he mumbled, and then turned his attention to Adam.

"You told me you and Lila grew up—that you weren't friends anymore."

"Shani," Lila said, leaning forward.

Zane bristled. He didn't want his mom's attention directed to the back of the van.

"How is your new quilt coming along?"

Mom started talking about how hard the pattern was, much more difficult than she'd thought when she chose it. "I think maybe it's too hard for me."

Lila knew what she was doing. Mom wouldn't

hear a thing in the back as long as they were talking.

"Are you and Trudy friends?" Zane asked Adam.

He nodded.

"So are we. Except we've been friends longer than the two of you have."

"You guys can't be anything more than friends, right? Because she's Amish and you're a soldier."

"That's right," Zane said. "That's how it works."

Lila gave him a quick glance and then turned her attention back to his mom.

"That's good," Adam said. "Because that's all I want to be too—Trudy's friend."

Zane turned back around, bumping Lila's leg again. This time she didn't move it, but he moved his in front of his seat and then stared back out the window, half hearing the talk about his mom's quilt.

He'd always wanted to be more than just Lila's friend—for as long as he'd known her. He swallowed hard, trying to quell the sense of dread rising in his throat. He didn't want to take things step-by-step. But what other choice did he have?

Saturday afternoon, Zane looped the hammer into his tool belt and repositioned the board on the outside of the chicken coop. He was afraid it would fall down on Adam and Trudy one of these days as they played house along the back of it. He called out to Adam. "Come help me, Bub."

When his brother didn't respond, Zane called out his name again.

"I can help." Tim stood on the other side of the hedge.

"Thanks," Zane said as their neighbor approached. "I don't know where Trudy took off to. Probably back in the house with Adam."

"I'll find her after I hold this for you." Tim pressed against the boards, and Zane hammered the nails into place. Once it was secure, Tim let go.

"Is your shoulder doing all right, then?"

Zane nodded. "I don't have full mobility but enough to do what I need to."

"To go back?" Tim asked.

"Into the Army, but not to Afghanistan. They already replaced me."

"*Gut.*" For once, Tim's eyes reflected compassion.

Zane didn't want to admit just how *gut* it was. "I'll be done, altogether, in June."

"Will you come home for good then?"

"I'd like to," Zane said.

"Trudy said you'll be home now for another ten days or so."

Zane nodded.

"I could use some help with the milking this afternoon. Rose is off working as a mother's helper

375

today for Monika's oldest girl, and Lila's going into the restaurant for a few hours."

"Of course," Zane said. "I can come over right now." He enjoyed the milking. He enjoyed everything that had to do with farmwork. "I'll go tell Mom where I'm going and find Trudy too."

By the time Zane had the kids rounded up, Tim had already headed to the barn.

"Can I help too?" Adam asked.

"Probably," Zane answered. "We'll ask Tim."

Zane breathed in the cool air. The afternoon had grown crisp, a perfect autumn day.

By the time they reached the barn, Tim had the first group of cows hooked up to the vacuum milkers. He was fine with Trudy and Adam helping, as long as they stayed out of his way. Zane directed Adam to feed the cows, the first job he'd ever done way back when he helped the Lehman boys with the milking.

Trudy and Adam chatted a little, but mostly everyone kept quiet. That was fine with Zane. But then Lila came in the barn.

"What are you doing?" she asked.

"Helping your Dat."

She stuffed her hands into her pockets. "Why?"

Tim poked his head out from the milking room where the big vat was kept. "I asked him to help."

"Oh," she answered, giving Zane a confused

look and then turning toward her Dat. "I'm off to work. Dinner is in the oven. Rose will be home by seven, and I should be home by ten."

Tim acknowledged what she said and stepped back into the milk room.

Zane put his hand to his ear as if he were holding a phone.

She shook her head. He gave her a questioning look. "Don't do that," she mouthed.

He nodded and put his hand down. He shrugged and smiled. She shook her head again, just a little. "Bye," she mouthed and waved without smiling. Then she called out a good-bye to Trudy and Adam, who had run after a couple of kittens.

Adam headed home a little while later, but Zane kept helping until the work was done. Tim shook his hand and told him he appreciated it.

"I'd be happy to help tomorrow," Zane said.

"How about in the morning? Lila seems a little tired lately."

Zane swallowed hard. Probably from all of her late-night phone calls with him. "Sure," he said. "I'd be happy to help. Do you still get started at five?"

"Jah," Tim said. "So make sure and get to bed early."

"Will do," Zane said, turning to go.

"Zane?"

He stopped and turned, afraid for a moment about what Tim might say.

"Denki," he said. "I appreciate your help."

Zane nodded and said, "See you tomorrow." He stretched his arm and shoulder as he walked back through the field, trying to shake the soreness out. As the last *Licht* of the day skirted above the trees, he wondered what had come over Tim. His kindness made Zane feel as if he should tell the man he was in love with his daughter. Zane hated to be deceptive about his feelings and the nightly phone calls, but he didn't want to betray Lila either.

After dinner, Zane checked his Army e-mail account on his parents' computer. There were a couple of generic ones, one from his physical therapist with a copy of his release and one from Casey.

Things have been pretty busy around here— the fighting keeps going even though the weather has cooled. More bad guys are getting through the passes, compromising our work. The other team got shot at on Monday up in the mountains and took a couple of minor injuries. Another unit from base landed on an IED and lost two. Sad times.

The new translator has had a lot of lower back pain. Could be kidney stones. We're down at base and he's in the clinic. I'll keep you posted.

Zane groaned. Hopefully the guy had just pulled a muscle.

We saw Jaalal day before yesterday. Sarge is still leery of trusting him. Of course Grant thinks we're crazy to. I honestly don't have any bad vibes though. We miss you, but I'm glad you're home. Have a good trip back to Texas, and we'll all see you there soon.

He really couldn't have asked for a better friend than Casey. She had his back.

At ten p.m., Zane put on his father's heavy coat, turned off the porch light, went outside, and sat down on the top porch step. Thankfully his parents had gone to bed. He dialed the number of the phone in the Lehmans' barn and then waited as it rang. After the ninth ring, right before the answering machine would have come on, he hung up. After another five minutes, spent gazing at the stars overhead, he called again.

This time she answered.

"How was work?" he asked.

"*Gut*," she answered, but she sounded a little stilted.

"Sorry about making the phone gesture," he said.

"Jah," she answered. "I don't want Dat to get suspicious."

"We should talk to him, then," Zane said.

"Not yet."

Zane gazed up at the stars again as he spoke. "I'm helping with the milking in the morning."

"No, I'll do it."

The tip of his nose was growing icy in the cold. "Your Dat asked me."

She didn't answer.

"Everything all right?"

"Beth is coming over for breakfast before church. I don't think Dat will ask you to stay, but if he does tell him you can't."

Zane stood. "Lila . . ."

"Dat might be obtuse, but Beth will guess how we feel for each other if she sees us together."

He walked to the bottom of the steps. "Maybe that's best."

"What would we say to him? That we have no plan? No idea how or if we can be together?"

"We'll be together, Lila," Zane said, keeping his voice as calm as he could as he walked toward the field.

"Do you plan to join the Amish? Because I don't plan to leave."

"I know you don't," he said, rubbing his forehead with his free hand. "I can't say what I plan to do. I need to get out of the Army first."

When he was home working on the chicken coop or helping Tim with the milking, he honestly thought he could join the Amish. But it seemed ridiculous to say that now, as a U.S.

soldier. Perhaps both he and Lila could become Mennonite after he was discharged. He could hope anyway.

"I should let you get some sleep," he said, gazing down the inky black field toward where he knew the gate was. "Will I see you in the morning?"

"No," Lila answered. "I'll be making breakfast. And please, no matter how compelled you are, don't say anything to Dat. Him asking you to help with the milking means he's not suspicious that we care for each other. Things are better with him than they ever have been, thanks to Beth. He's changing—but not enough to cope with our uncertainty. I promise you, as soon as we have a plan we'll talk to him. But not yet."

"All right." He wished he could see all the way to the gate and then beyond to the barn. If only he could see her when they talked each night. "I hate that we're so close . . ."

"Jah," she said.

"You could meet me in the field. Or down at the creek."

There was a long pause, but she finally said, "Not tonight."

"What about tomorrow night?"

"I told Dat I'd go with Rose to her first singing —at Monika and Gideon's. He wants me to keep an eye on her."

Zane could understand that. If he were Tim,

381

he'd want someone to keep an eye on Rose too.

"Call me tomorrow evening," she said. "Same time. I'll be here."

After they said good-night and hung up, Zane gazed up at the stars for a few minutes longer and then turned and trudged up the steps back into the house.

When Tim invited Zane in to breakfast the next morning, he thanked him but said he had plans. He didn't add that those plans were to go home and pine after Lila. Actually he planned to go to church with his parents, which he hoped would keep his mind off things. It didn't. Instead he spent the entire service thinking about Lila, although he did manage to pray for her in between thoughts.

He finished the work on the chicken coop after lunch and then headed down to the fort and repaired it as best he could, pulling off rotten boards and nailing the rest back into place. In the later afternoon, he dozed on the couch while Dad watched football. Although he wasn't having nightmares every night, he'd had one the night before and had been awake for a few hours. He was back at the wall again, his rifle aimed at Benham, the boy too far away to grab.

After supper, he logged on to his parents' computer, doubting he had any additional Army e-mails but thinking he might as well check.

There were none from Casey, but there was one from Sarge, sent just a few minutes before.

New translator has kidney stones. Going home. How soon can you get back here?

Zane's stomach fell. He tried to keep his cool, to keep from panicking as he typed:

I'm headed to Texas next week.

He didn't expect an answer back from Sarge, not for a day at least. But one zipped into his inbox.

Negative on Texas. Ready to request orders for your return here, ASAP. Hope you're up to it.

Emotionally and spiritually? No. Physically? The answer was probably no again, but did he really have a choice? He'd been cleared.

Can you give me a day to figure out if I am?

He waited and waited but Sarge didn't reply. Either he was ignoring Zane or he'd logged off.

Finally he pushed back from the desk and stood, running his hand through his hair. He couldn't return to Afghanistan. He wished Lila was home. He needed to talk with someone who would understand.

As he started down the hall he could hear laughter from the living room. His parents and Adam must be watching TV. He didn't bother to see what. He just grabbed his coat, feeling for his truck keys in the pocket. Right now he needed some fresh air.

"What's the matter?" Mom asked from the living room.

"Nothing," he answered.

She must have clicked the TV off or least muted it, because it went silent. "Something's wrong," she said.

"What is it, son?" Dad asked. "Bad news?"

They knew he had been checking his e-mail. He stepped into the living room.

"Uncertain news," he said, pulling his keys from the pocket of his coat. "The new translator has kidney stones, and he's going home."

"Oh, no," Mom said, as she landed on her feet. "They don't expect you to go back, do they?"

"If he can repair a chicken coop and help Tim milk, he's well enough to," Dad said.

"Yeah, well, Sarge doesn't know about either of those things."

"Maybe the doctor can overrule the orders," Mom said.

Dad shook his head. "It's your duty to return."

Adam scooted down from his chair and ran

toward Zane, grabbing him around the waist. "I don't want you to go back."

"Jah, Bub," Zane said. "I know how you feel."

"When do you report?" Dad asked.

Zane shrugged. "I asked Sarge for another day before he puts in the orders."

Mom stepped across the room and put her arm around Zane while Dad continued to sit in his chair.

He of all people should understand. How would he have felt if they'd sent him back to Iraq after his injury? They wouldn't have, of course. His injury was much worse than Zane's.

Dad was right. He had to go back.

"It's just for a couple of months," Dad said.

Three. And all it would take was a few seconds for him to kill someone else.

Dad continued. "Don't you want to complete your mission? See Jaalal? Be there for Casey?"

Zane didn't bother to reply. "I'm going for a drive," he said, tousling Adam's hair.

"Can I come with you?" Adam asked, releasing him.

"Not this time, Bub," he answered. "I need an hour or two to think." He hurried out the door into the dark night before Adam's disappointment and his mom's concern could pull him back.

He turned his truck around quickly and headed up the lane, slowing as he passed the Lehmans', just in case Lila hadn't gone to the singing. When he didn't see anyone, he kept on going, turning left on the highway. He shivered in the cold and flipped on the heater.

He didn't have time to file for conscientious-objector status. It was too late for that.

He didn't think about where he was going. Instead he thought about the soldiers who had gone AWOL and ended up in Canada. What would it be like to live up there? He knew it wasn't ideal. They weren't able to come back to visit their families.

He kept driving until he reached the lane to Monika and Gideon's. Monika hosted him and Mom after Bub was born, when Dad had fled back to Philly. That's what bugged him about his father. Didn't he remember what he went through after his injury? Now he was all about duty and loyalty and glossing over the past, but things weren't so great back when Zane was a kid. Dad was angry, and everything seemed muddled.

Canada wasn't that far from Lancaster County. He couldn't imagine going, but if he did, at least Mom and Adam would come see him—he wasn't so sure about his dad.

He'd read about different Plain communities in Canada, in Ontario. Maybe one of them would take him in. Would Lila visit?

As he backed his truck in next to the shed, on the other side of the buggies, he wondered if he should have gone to Charlie and Eve's instead.

Then in his headlight beam he saw Gideon coming toward him. He'd most likely heard the truck and headed out, expecting some Amish kid on his Rumschpringe.

Zane turned off his lights and engine, hopped down and waved. Gideon squinted.

"It's me." He could hear the singing from the shed.

"Ach, Zane," Gideon said. "What brings you here?"

For a moment he didn't know what to say. *Pain? Fear? Lila?* "I've had some troubling news," he finally said.

"Would you like to talk about it?" Gideon asked, directing him toward the house. "We have a while until the singing ends."

Zane hesitated a minute. What would he tell Gideon, a bishop in a nonresistant church? That he was terrified of having to shoot someone again? Or that he loved Lila, his son's ex-sweetheart? Or both. "Sure," Zane said and followed the man into Monika's dark kitchen. Gideon lit a propane lamp hanging over the table, casting shadows against the walls.

Gideon sat down at the head of the table and nodded at the place next to him. "What's going on?"

He'd start with his Army problems. "I just got an e-mail from my sergeant in Afghanistan. He needs me to return."

"You didn't expect that?"

"No. They'd replaced me over there. They were sending me back to Texas."

"I see," he said. "And you don't want to go back?"

Zane explained how he felt about the possibility of having to shoot someone again. "I took a life, the grandson of someone I care about," he said. "I prayed I wouldn't have to, but God didn't answer that prayer. I injured another man too."

Gideon nodded. "I heard you saved the life of a soldier and probably your own. And a little boy. Maybe some other Afghans too."

"Who told you that?"

Gideon shrugged. "Tim. Your father talked with him."

Zane hadn't thought it through that far. Would Benham and the other man have ended up shooting Jaalal and the other men? Surely Benham wouldn't have done that, but if Jaalal challenged him, who knew what might have happened.

"I don't know if there's any way we can make a lasting difference over there. There are too many variables. Too much corruption." He stopped for a moment.

"Go on," Gideon said.

"I felt good about our mission, about helping the women and children. I made a good connection with an Afghan translator. I liked talking with him about his family, about his clan—and sharing about my family." Including showing him the photos of Lila. "Even if there wouldn't be a lasting change, I felt as if good would come from our work. But now I'm afraid it was all for nothing."

Gideon sighed.

"I don't want to live a life that's for nothing," Zane said.

"What kind of life do you want?"

"I've been researching pacifism for the last couple of years." Zane met Gideon's gaze. "I admire the Amish, I really do. And the Mennonites. Both of you have the life I want. Family. Community. Peace."

Gideon grimaced. "You know enough about us to know it's not all roses. Peace is hard to attain in any culture."

Zane smiled a little. "No one's shooting at each other. Everyone has food and water. The children are well cared for and don't have to worry about stepping on a mine."

"That's true," Gideon said. "But the majority of Englisch children have that too, here in America."

"To some extent, but there's a violence throughout our culture that isn't in yours. Think of the school shootings."

Gideon grimaced again. "We had one of those."

"But it wasn't an Amish shooter. It was an Englisch one."

"True."

Zane placed his palms on the oak table. "Jesus said blessed are the peacemakers."

"Some people would say you were a peacemaker . . ."

"Until I killed another human being." Zane met Gideon's eyes.

"You did what your country asked you to."

"No," Zane said. "I volunteered. Out of absolute foolishness."

Gideon cocked his head. "And does that past motivation—foolishness—have any part in how you're feeling now?"

Zane took a deep breath and dragged his hand over his mouth.

Gideon spoke softly. "Forget that I'm Reuben's father."

"She didn't break up with Reuben because of me."

"I wondered," Gideon said.

"We were corresponding some, for a short time. But she wrote and said she couldn't write anymore, but she didn't tell me that she'd stopped courting Reuben."

Gideon placed a hand on Zane's arm as if anchoring him to the table. Zane was appreciative. He needed something to keep him from fleeing.

"What's going on now?" Gideon asked.

"I'm being honest when I say I'm not the reason

she broke up with Reuben, but the other truth is that I love Lila," Zane said. "I always have. I fear I always will. If she'd become Mennonite, I would too after I get out of the Army, in June."

"What if she won't?"

Zane shook his head. "I don't know what we'll do."

"Would you consider becoming Amish?" Gideon asked.

"I've thought about it. I never told Lila, but the night before I joined the Army I wanted to talk with her about that possibility, but then Reuben interrupted us." Zane sighed. "But how could I, really?"

"You know the language."

But he couldn't make a living off his parents' farm. Besides, Tim needed to lease the land to help him make a living. "What would I do to feed a family?"

"Trust," Gideon said, his voice deeper in that single word than Zane had ever heard it. Funny, Simon had said almost the same thing.

Zane took a deep breath. He had to get through the next seven months before he could consider such a thing. But maybe Gideon was right. Maybe joining the Amish was his best option.

And sooner rather than later.

They heard voices outside.

"Is Reuben here?" Zane asked.

Gideon shook his head.

Zane exhaled. "I don't want to be disrespectful to him."

"He's okay." Gideon stood. "He'll find the right wife."

Zane stood too, hoping to catch Lila before she left.

Gideon shook his hand. "We would welcome you into our community, Zane."

He nodded. "Denki, you've been a good help." He hurried toward the door. He'd speak to Lila. Then he'd get on home. He had a lot of planning to do before tomorrow.

22

Lila turned the buggy onto the highway as Rose pouted on the other side of the seat. She'd wanted to stay longer and see which boy would offer to give her a ride home first, but Lila wasn't in favor of that. Dat had made it clear he expected Lila to be responsible for Rose. She wasn't going to let her ride home with a boy after her very first singing. Dat would have thrown a fit.

"Why wasn't Reuben there tonight?" Rose asked.

"Maybe because he's too old for singings."

"He's not that old."

"He's twenty-five," Lila said.

"Like I said, not so old."

Lila glanced over at her. "Too old for you."

"I don't think so. Dat was at least that much older than Mamm."

Ten years, to be exact, but Lila wasn't going to point that out to Rose. It wasn't the age difference between her sister and Reuben—it was the difference in maturity.

"I think he's avoiding you," Rose said. "So please don't come to the next singing."

Lila sighed. If only Dat wouldn't force her to. Escorting Rose was just one more task added to her already busy schedule. At least she didn't work the next day. And Rose wasn't working as a mother's helper—she could do the laundry. Lila gripped the reins a little tighter.

If only she could leave her family for a life with Zane. She'd peeked into the barn that morning while he helped with the milking. He'd always been a natural with the chores. And the other day when she'd walked Trudy up the lane to play with Adam, she'd heard Zane humming as he fixed the fence along the field. He enjoyed farmwork, more than he realized probably. He was a hard worker. She was sure he could succeed at whatever he put his mind to.

Headlights came up behind them and then slowed. Lila pulled the buggy farther to the side to let the vehicle pass. But then a horn honked.

Lila peered into the rearview mirror, her heart racing.

Rose craned her neck to look behind them. "It's Zane," she said.

Something must have happened. She drew back on the reins, pulling the horse as far to the right as she could. Zane stopped his pickup behind the buggy.

The pickup door slammed shut, and Zane started jogging.

"What's wrong?" she asked as he approached.

"I need to talk with you," he said. "It's important."

"I can go home alone," Rose said. "You can go with Zane."

"No," Lila answered, afraid Rose might return to the singing. She turned toward Zane. "Follow us home. Rose can take care of the horse while you and I talk."

Zane nodded and hurried back to his truck. Lila snapped the reins, and the horse continued on. Zane pulled in behind her, his hazard lights on. She knew he worried about her driving the buggy on the highway, especially at night.

"What do you think he wants?" Rose asked.

"I don't know," Lila answered.

"You're not fooling anyone," Rose said. "Everyone knows what's going on between you and Zane."

"Really? Because I have no idea what's going on between us."

"Love is what's going on," Rose said. "It's as

obvious as the noses on both of your faces."

Lila pursed her lips together. The less she said to her sister the better.

"Don't you think it's a little hypocritical that you're set on getting me home safely from the Amish young men—and then you plan to sneak out with your Englisch boyfriend?"

"He's not my boyfriend."

"Right." Rose crossed her arms. "Well, he's definitely Englisch. And a soldier to boot. Dat's getting soft in his old age to ask Zane to step foot on our property at all, let alone to help with the milking. His behavior only encourages you to—"

"Stop," Lila said. "You have no idea what you're talking about."

"Don't be so self-righteous. You've always loved Zane. You'll leave, just like Aenti Eve did. It's just a matter of time."

Lila didn't respond.

"I'll never leave," Rose said. "Ever. I'm going to get married as soon as I can and start a family. I'll make Dat proud."

Lila took a deep breath to keep from shaking her head. No doubt Rose would make Dat proud, but it wasn't as if it were a competition. Except it was. To Rose. Dat had always favored Simon and Rose, his first-born biological son and daughter. Now Rose was clearly the favorite. No wonder Dat wanted Lila to keep an eye on her.

Dat wanted at least one child to be a success in the eyes of the church, especially after Lila had broken up with Reuben. Dat had done his duty as far as Lila and Daniel, and she would be eternally grateful and indebted to him, but he'd never been loving toward them.

She turned down the lane, the hazard lights following right behind her, casting a red flashing glow in the buggy. She glanced at Rose, who had a pout on her face. Her sister *would* be married in no time. With her dark hair, brown eyes, and dimples, she was the prettiest girl in the district. And she was fun in a way Lila had never been and never would be. True, Rose could be lazy and annoying, but she stepped up to work when she had to. And she could also be the life of the party, joking with others and pulling the quietest of people into a conversation.

As they turned down their driveway, Lila said, "Put the horse away. If Dat's still up and asks where I am, tell the truth. Say that Zane wanted to talk with me. I'll deal with Dat in the morning."

Rose made a disgusted face. "You didn't expect me to lie for you, did you?"

"Of course not. I just told you . . ."

"Because I'm not going to rescue you from your own bad choices."

Lila bit her tongue as she turned the horse into the shed. Jah, the life of the party, and the most dramatic sixteen-year-old around.

• • •

Ten minutes later she sat in Zane's pickup under the willow tree, off the highway. He'd left the engine running and by the light of the dashboard he spilled his heart, telling her about the e-mails from his sergeant. Then he said he couldn't go back to Afghanistan.

As he finished, he checked his phone. "I have another e-mail from Sarge. He already booked a ticket for me. Wednesday evening, out of Philly. I have four days to figure this out."

Lila shivered. "What are you going to do?"

He turned in the seat toward her and took her hand. She leaned toward him. "I've been thinking about the Amish settlements in Canada."

"In Ontario?"

Zane nodded.

That was just over the border from New York.

"Will you marry me, Lila?" He tightened his grip on her hand.

"I can't leave the church."

"I'm not asking you to," he said.

"You would become Amish?"

He nodded again. "Once we reach an Amish community in Ontario we can make a life together."

Her voice caught in her throat. "When would we leave?"

"Tomorrow."

"Zane," she whispered. Tomorrow? She'd need to decide tonight.

"Otherwise I have to report back to duty. I'll be going AWOL, but I should be safe in Canada, especially if we're part of a Plain community." He inhaled. "What kind of ID do you have?"

"I got a passport card a few years ago," Lila said. "Instead of an ID card." Gideon had recommended it to the youth, saying it would be all they'd ever need for identification. She met his gaze. "Will you ever be able to come back home?"

"Not for a while but Mom would come visit, with Adam at least." His eyes watered. "And you would be able to see your family whenever you want. I'd make it a priority."

Lila's heart raced.

"I know it's a lot to ask," he said. "And it's sooner than we planned." A wry smile passed over his face. "Or didn't plan. But I want to be your husband, Lila, more than anything."

"Jah." She nodded. She believed that with her whole heart. "But I didn't think you wanted to be Amish."

"I do," he answered. "I've been thinking about pacifism and nonresistance for years now. I even considered it three years ago, before I joined the Army."

Lila's heart began to ache.

"I don't want to raise children in the Englisch

world. I did think Mennonite would be best, but I'm willing to be Amish. Now more than ever."

"What about—" She couldn't manage to say "our children." "What about the issue of education?" That had always been Zane's biggest criticism of her church, that one's formal education ended in the eighth grade.

"We could homeschool after the eighth grade, don't you think? Or encourage correspondence courses? And I'll do the same, for myself—and you can too if you want."

Lila's heart raced faster. Could she really leave home and her community, just like that?

"We can't say anything to anyone though," Zane said. "I don't want my dad coming after me. That would be awful. We can call once we're in Canada and let our parents know."

Lila couldn't imagine that. Dat listening to her voice on the answering machine, saying she'd fled to Canada with Zane. That they were getting married. It was nearly as heartbreaking as the thought of Joel listening to a message from Zane saying he'd deserted.

Lila shivered. She knew the Army wasn't a good fit for Zane, but she never guessed he'd desert. She couldn't imagine the fear he must be feeling. "I don't know what to say, Zane. I have to think about it."

"Of course."

"What time would we leave in the morning?"

"Are you helping with the milking?"

She nodded.

"How about if I come over and spell you? I'll just show up and offer my help. Let me know then—give me a thumbs-up when your Dat isn't looking. If that's the case, then I'll drive down the lane at nine a.m. Meet me at the end of your drive. Just bring a small bag."

"And what if I decide not to go?"

He paused. "I don't know."

"Will you go on your own?"

He started to smile but then stopped. "Then I'd be in Canada and you'd be down here."

"But if you don't go, then you'll be farther away, in Afghanistan."

"Either there or a military prison," Zane answered.

"You can't go to prison." She squeezed his hand.

Zane leaned closer. "I love you, Lila Lehman."

She turned her face toward his. She loved him too—she just couldn't say it. Not yet.

For a moment she thought he might kiss her, but then he said, "I'd better get you home."

The next morning was cold and frosty. Even in the barn Lila could see her breath. She shoveled grain into the trough, and soon the bodies and breath of the cows warmed the air. It wasn't long until Zane called out a hello, to her relief.

Dat smiled and motioned him into the barn.

"I woke up early," Zane said. "Need some help?"

"Lila's here," Dat said, glancing her way.

"But she probably has enough work in the house to keep her busy." Dat turned toward her. "Do you want Zane to help this morning?"

"Sure," she answered, making her way around the trough. She leaned the shovel against the grain chute. Dat headed down the line of cows to the first one, and as Lila passed Zane he held his thumb up.

She returned the gesture.

He smiled and whispered, "Mission's on."

Three hours later, after returning from delivering Trudy to school, Lila headed down to the basement to check on Rose.

She was pulling a towel through the wringer. "You can pin the first load on the line."

Lila almost answered that Rose would need to do it, but if her sister dawdled she'd be outside when Zane came by. Lila had told Rose she had a driver coming to run some errands, and she needed to buy some time. At least Dat had gone to the lumberyard to work so she didn't need to worry about him, but she didn't want Rose to see her leave with Zane and call Dat. Lila grabbed the basket and headed up the stairs. She'd packed a small bag last night after Rose and Trudy were asleep and slipped it under her bed. She'd stuffed her nearly finished crazy quilt topper in too— she still had some stitching left to do, and then she'd need to quilt it.

Tears stung her eyes as she pulled her heavy coat from the hook and headed out the back door. Jah, the day was cold, but that wasn't what was making her cry. She'd walked Trudy to the door of the school and gave her an extra hug, but she'd avoided seeing Beth, afraid of her sensing something was wrong.

She quickly pinned the towels on the line and then hurried back into the house. She only had a few minutes until Zane arrived. She returned the basket to the basement, where Rose was wringing the next load. Guilt and sadness swept over Lila. "You're doing a good job," she said to her sister.

Rose didn't seem surprised by the compliment but simply nodded in agreement.

Lila hurried upstairs, afraid she might cry again, and grabbed her bag. Although her sister annoyed her, she would still miss her.

By the time she made it to the end of the driveway, Zane was waiting. She climbed into his truck and buckled her seat belt.

"Are you okay?" he asked as he accelerated.

She nodded, but she wasn't. "How about you?"

He glanced at her. "I guess as well as can be expected."

"Jah," she said.

Zane turned right onto the highway. "This is harder than I thought it would be."

"Does your mom work today?"

Zane shook his head.

"Was she home when you left?"

"No. She's running errands."

"Won't she wonder where you are when she gets home?"

"I told her I was hanging out with a friend today."

They rode along in silence. She suspected they were both troubled. She knew she was. None of this felt right. Staying wouldn't have. Leaving didn't. But Zane going back to Afghanistan or prison certainly didn't either.

Yet she couldn't help but wonder what he might regret later. And what she might regret too.

Zane turned left on Highway 30 toward Lancaster. As the sunlight grew stronger, the red and orange leaves on the trees glowed against the blue sky. Lila settled back against the seat. The warm air from the heater swirled around her legs. He'd have to sell his truck once they were in Canada. She didn't know much about the settlements in Ontario except that they drove buggies without tops, which probably meant they were more conservative in other ways too. She might be seen as a spoiled Pennsylvania Amish girl, and Zane might be considered suspicious. Might? Of course he would. He'd be seen as suspicious in any Amish community, except her own, and that was because Gideon had known Zane since he was a boy.

They chatted some about what they saw along the way. Zane detoured through Harrisburg so she could see the Capitol building, along the Susquehanna River. On any other day, she would have been taken by the architecture and full of questions about when it was built and the history of the building. But today she couldn't concentrate on anything but the journey ahead of them.

When would Rose and then Dat realize she wasn't coming home? What would they say to Trudy? She'd leave a message on the machine in the barn once she and Zane were in Canada, but she hated to think of them worrying before then.

They stopped for lunch in Williamsport and then continued on, crossing into New York.

"What's it like for deserters in Canada?" Lila asked.

"Most are caught in an appeal process to return them to the States," Zane said. "I'm hoping as part of an Amish community, I'll fly under the radar. We won't have to sign up for national health care or any of that, so maybe it won't be that big of a deal."

"You'll have to take classes before you can join the church," Lila said. "It could take a while."

He nodded. "Hopefully they'll accept us though,

help us find individual places to live and jobs until we can marry."

She hadn't had time to think this through like she should have. They would arrive as an unmarried Amish woman and an Englisch man. A deserter from the U.S. Army. She couldn't see any way they could marry before Zane joined the church. And after, they might never be in good standing with an Amish community unfamiliar with them, one in which they were strangers.

"As far as the government of Canada, if they go after me, it could be a problem," Zane said. "I came across an article last night about a Marine who fled to Canada a couple of years ago who is now at risk of being deported. I've read before that the prime minister isn't sympathetic to U.S. soldiers who go AWOL."

"Does that worry you?" she asked.

"Some. But if I got deported, it's not like I'd be shot. They haven't done that since World War II."

"But you would still go to prison."

"It's worth the risk," Zane said. He glanced toward her, his eyes heavy. "Going back to Afghanistan would be easier than leaving our families—if I knew I wouldn't have to shoot someone again."

She nodded. "But there's no guarantee."

"I think this is the moral thing to do. But so

would be keeping my commitment to the Army." He sighed.

She could see he was conflicted. He'd slowed down. She glanced at the speedometer. He was going fifty. A semi behind them honked and then passed. Zane slowed even more as they drove past a sign with information about the border crossing—even though they were still a couple hours away.

After a long pause, he asked, "How do we know the right thing to do?"

"I'm not sure," she answered. Breaking up with Reuben certainly had been full of conflicting feelings, but in the end she'd known it was right.

Zane shook his head. "I feel paralyzed," he said.

She understood. She felt the same way. The comfort of "Be still, and know that I am God" running through her head seemed so long ago. Her heart didn't feel still. And she was certain Zane's didn't either.

As he kept driving, she started praying, silently. She had just over two hours to figure out what God would have her do.

When they neared Niagara Falls, Zane pulled into the Visitor Center parking lot and they climbed out. The view was as magnificent as the photos Lila had seen. The cold mist from the spray blew up into her face. Zane stood behind her, wrapping his arms around her and pulling her close, tucking her head against his chest and under his chin. It felt so right to be with him—but she still felt unsettled. They belonged on Juneberry Lane.

Three years ago, she had convinced him to leave her. Maybe this time she could convince him to go back.

"I'm sorry for getting you into this," he said, competing with the roar of the falls. It sounded like a whisper, but she knew it wasn't.

"It's not your fault," she said.

"I never should have joined the Army."

"I never should have told you to leave." There was no undoing what they'd both done. "It won't do any good for us to be sorry now."

She'd been too young then to think about allowing herself to love someone who wasn't Amish, and he'd been too rash. They'd both learned a lot—and she guessed the learning wasn't done yet. "I believe it will all work out," she said. "But I don't know that going to Canada is what we should do."

"I was afraid you'd change your mind." He let go of her, and she turned toward him.

"I haven't changed my mind about loving you or wanting to be your wife. I just don't think running away is the right thing to do." She touched his face. "I think there are things you need to deal with. Like your commitment to the Army. And your relationship with your dad."

He swallowed hard but didn't respond.

"And I think there are things I need to take care of too. Like my issues with my own father. And why I was so eager to come with you, to help you, without thinking it all through."

"Lila, don't."

"No. Whether we marry or not, I need to stand up for what I believe in. I want to be with you, but I don't want you to get deported from Canada to a military prison. You could lose years of your life when you only have eight months until you're done with your duty."

"Three of them in Afghanistan."

"We should trust God with this. We both have to find our own peace."

"The Amish girl is telling me to go back to war to find my peace?"

"I'm not going to tell you what to do, Zane. You get to decide. I'll support you either way."

He took a step away from her. "I can't go back to Afghanistan. I'm going to Ontario."

"All right," she said.

"What are you going to do?"

She took a deep breath and let it out slowly. "I'll go with you." She couldn't bear the thought of him going alone, despite her angst. As they turned back toward the parking lot she said, "You might as well call your parents from here."

He dug his phone from his pocket, and once they reached the pickup, he placed the call.

Zane said hello and then, "I'm with Lila. We're at Niagara Falls, headed to Ontario."

There was a long pause. Then Zane shook his head and said to Lila, "Mom went to get Dad."

When his dad came on the phone, Zane said hello but that was all. Finally Zane put his phone on speaker.

Joel's voice was calm, but he was talking a mile a minute. ". . . think all war is wrong? World War II?"

"No," Zane answered.

"You're not a pacifist, then. Or a conscientious objector. Soldiers don't have the luxury of choosing which wars they fight in. You signed up for this on your own. No one forced you."

"I know, but I can't go back."

"Did you talk to your sergeant about a desk job in Afghanistan? About not going into the field."

"I don't have a choice. The translator is being sent home, and they need me."

"Chances are you won't have to shoot someone again."

"But there's the possibility—and there's more fighting going on even than when I left. I'd be a danger to my team." And to himself.

Lila put her face in her hands.

Joel kept talking. "I don't think you could ever be nonresistant. Not really."

"I could try."

"What if Lila was attacked? Wouldn't you

defend her? What about a child someday? How could you not defend them?" Joel asked. "That's what a husband and father does."

Zane didn't respond. Of course he'd defend his family.

Shani came back on. "Are you sure this is what you want to do?"

"Yes," Zane said.

Shani was silent for a long moment and then said, "Lila, do you want me to call your Dat?"

"No," she answered. "I'll leave him a message." The thought of it made her ill. She was going to disappoint him horribly.

"Zane?" Joel had come back on the line. "I'm hoping you'll change your mind."

"I won't," Zane said. After he said good-bye, he hit End.

He handed the phone to Lila and she called the phone in the barn, leaving a quick message that she was with Zane, headed to Canada, and she would call soon.

When she hung up, Zane gave her a sly look and said, "Chicken."

"I know," she answered. "I just couldn't spell it all out yet."

Lila scooted across the bench seat, close to Zane. He put his arm around her, and they sat and watched the water crash down the cliff. "I don't blame you," he said. "I know what it's like to be afraid."

She rested her head on his shoulder.

"Jaalal told me not to go back to Afghanistan."

"That was a strange thing for him to say," Lila said.

Zane shook his head. "He knows it's a dangerous place to be."

She leaned her head against his chest and wished she could hear his heartbeat, but all she could hear was the roar of the water and her own blood racing in her ears.

"We should get going," Zane said. "And get across the border." He started up the engine and made his way through the parking lot. Once they reached the road, Lila pulled out her crazy quilt, hoping to distract herself. She had enough daylight to work on it as he drove. She began stitching a stump. She was telling their story. But she had no idea how it would end.

Zane started quoting "Splendour in the Grass" as he drove.

"What through the radiance
which was once so bright
Be now for ever taken from my sight,
Though nothing can bring back the hour
Of splendour in the grass,
Of glory in the flower."

Lila joined in, and they said the rest together, slowing down more and more toward the end.

"We will grieve not, rather find
Strength in what remains behind;
In the primal sympathy
Which having been must ever be;
In the soothing thoughts that spring
Out of human suffering;
In the faith that looks through death,
In years that bring the philosophic mind."

Lila swiped at a tear. "It's so much more depressing than it was four years ago."

"That won't be us," Zane said. "Things will work out."

" 'The faith that looks through death . . .' What do you think that means?" Lila asked.

"That faith survives loss," Zane said as he stopped at the back of the line at the border crossing. "It has to. Otherwise what hope do we have?"

She pointed to the flower on the quilt, next to the gate. "It's the flower from the poem," she said. "That's what it represents to me anyway."

"The quilt is beautiful," he said. "I've never seen anything like it."

They inched along in the line. Lila retrieved her passport card. The uneasy feeling in the pit of her stomach grew stronger. Shouldn't she feel excited about what was ahead of her? Zane was going to join the Amish. She was going to marry him. It was her dream come true.

And yet . . . it wasn't.

23

After they crossed the border, for the next two hours as Zane drove through farmland toward the nearest Amish settlement, he silently rehearsed what he would say. Nothing he attempted sounded right.

"We should stop to eat," Lila finally said.

She was right. They didn't want to arrive expecting to be fed. He'd wanted to get to the Amish settlement before dark but soon after would have to do. They stopped at a restaurant in Hamilton, ate quickly, and then kept on going.

Once they neared the settlement, Zane pulled into the first Amish-looking farm they saw. The smell of a dairy greeted them. In the dim light, the siding on the house and barn both appeared worn and not nearly as spruced up as what they were used to in Lancaster County.

"I'll go knock on the door and ask where the bishop lives," Lila said, slipping into her coat.

"Denki," Zane answered, lowering his window and watching as she climbed the front steps. Woodsmoke and the spicy scent of autumn filled the cold air.

A few minutes later she headed out of the house, followed by a middle-aged man who could have been Tim's brother.

Zane hopped down from his truck, realizing he should have accompanied Lila to the door. None of this probably looked good to the Amish man.

The man extended his hand and Zane shook it, introducing himself.

"I'm John Miller," the man said. "So you traveled up from Pennsylvania?"

"Yes, sir," Zane said. "We're looking for a community to become part of here."

"But you're not Amish."

"That's right. I plan to join."

The man looked him up and down and then back at Lila. "How about if I ride over with the two of you to the bishop's place?"

"Denki," Zane said. "We appreciate that."

Even if John Miller had given them detailed directions, Zane doubted they would have found the bishop's farm. He lived on a dirt lane several roads off the highway. By the time they reached his house, it was completely dark. Thankfully a lamp shone in the window.

John led the way, and Lila and Zane followed.

Another middle-aged man opened the door. "John. What are you doing here so late?"

"I have some strangers with me," John answered. He introduced the bishop as Matthew Miller. "My cousin," he said with a smile. Then he introduced Lila and Zane.

The bishop invited them into a small living room furnished with straight-back chairs and a bench. A clock sat on the mantel but that was the only kind of decoration. The room was much plainer than any Amish home Zane had seen in Pennsylvania.

John explained why Zane and Lila had come.

"I see," the man said, looking at Zane. "What are you running from?"

Zane winced at the bishop's insight. He thought of his father fleeing back to Philadelphia after Bub had been born, abandoning those he loved most. But that's not what Zane had done—he'd brought Lila with him.

Zane hadn't told John about being in the U.S. Army. He took a deep breath and launched into his story, telling about what happened in Afghanistan, being sure he wouldn't have to return, and then getting orders to fly back.

The bishop didn't seem sympathetic. Nor did he ask any clarifying questions about Zane being a soldier. Instead he asked, "Were you willing to join the church to marry this young lady earlier?"

"I was considering it," Zane answered, aware of how hard the chair was. His shoulder began to ache. "After I was discharged from the Army."

"But you've decided to do it now—to save your bacon, so to speak."

Zane's face grew warm, even though the temperature of the house was cool.

The bishop continued. "Are you wanting to use us to get out of a commitment you made?"

Zane began to feel sick to his stomach. What if that was how Lila felt too—as if he were using her?

"I'll have to think about that more," Zane said.

The bishop turned to Lila. "Had you considered marrying him before this?"

"Jah," she answered.

"Have you been baptized?" he asked.

She nodded.

"So you were willing to leave the church?"

She shook her head. "I hoped he'd join. That's why I agreed to come with him."

"I see," the bishop said, glancing at John. "Why don't we all sleep on this tonight? I'll make a few phone calls in the morning."

Zane guessed he'd probably get in touch with Gideon. Zane didn't know if that would be a good thing or a bad thing.

"John, can Zane stay at your house tonight? Lila can stay here."

Zane was about to protest when a middle-aged woman and teenage girl stepped into the room from the kitchen. "I'll show you the spare bed," the girl said.

"I'll grab my bag," Lila answered. Zane followed, but he didn't catch up with her until she was at the truck.

When she opened the passenger door and the interior light came on, he could see tears in her eyes. "Nothing about this feels right," she said.

He nodded. Being with her felt right—but that was all. This wasn't their community. They weren't wanting to join for the right reasons.

"I'm sorry," he said.

"I know," she answered. "So am I. I feel so unsettled. . . ."

"I know you were troubled on the way here. But I continued on anyway." He gazed down at her until she shut the truck door and it was too dark to see her eyes.

"We'll figure it out tomorrow," she said.

He walked her back to the front porch where the two men were talking and then told her a quick good-bye. He'd been so determined not to pressure her or control her—and here he'd done it anyway. Dragging her along had been worse than leaving on his own.

Zane tossed and turned, fighting nightmare after nightmare. The next morning as the rooster crowed he finally checked his e-mail—surprised he had service. He had three from Sarge and two from Casey, all asking him to confirm he was flying out that night.

Zane groaned and closed his e-mail app. Then he dressed in the icy cold room and headed downstairs to help John with the milking. It was the least he could do after the man let him spend the night.

Two hours later he was on his way back over to the bishop's house.

When he knocked on the door, Lila opened it holding her bag with her crazy quilt folded on top. "The bishop was right—none of this is for the right reasons," she said to him, speaking in her softest voice. "Take me home, or I'll call your mom to come get me."

"What's going on?" he asked.

The bishop stepped into view. "I went over to the neighbors and called Gideon Byler this morning. Lila gave me the number at his lumberyard. He said Lila's father is upset."

Zane exhaled. That was to be expected.

"And Gideon was surprised you'd do something so foolish."

That wasn't exactly what Zane had expected. He'd hoped Gideon might support him.

"Gideon hopes you'll come home. Talk things through." The bishop's gray eyes were intense. Zane glanced at Lila. Her eyes brimmed with tears.

"We'll leave right now." Zane reached for Lila's bag. "We'll go straight home," he said to the bishop. "And thank you for your good advice last night. It was helpful."

Once they were in the truck and buckled in, Lila said, "I don't think we should go home."

Zane backed the truck onto the highway and headed south. "Where do you think we should go?"

"To Philly—to the airport."

He cringed inside. He wasn't truly nonresistant. He'd tried to use this Amish group. He'd never want to join it otherwise, not the way he did the district in Lancaster County.

"I know you're afraid," she said. "Afraid you'll have to shoot someone again. But what if God has someone for you to save? Another child? Or a soldier?"

"He doesn't need to use me," Zane said. "He could use anyone."

"Don't say that," Lila responded. "You were the one who scooped up the little boy. You have to trust God with this. You can't keep running." She met his eyes. "We should go to Philly."

Lila was right. It was the airport or the brig. His dad was right too—he wasn't nonresistant. He wasn't even a pacifist, not truly.

"I don't have my stuff," he said. There was no way he could make it home and then back to catch his flight on time. It was at least eight hours to Philly, and he'd need to be at the airport by six p.m.

"Call your parents. Have them meet us there."

He knew she was right. He continued on in silence.

"I'll call your mom," Lila said.

Zane pulled over to the side of the road, fumbling his phone from his pocket as he did.

They'd agreed to meet at a restaurant near the airport and have dinner before Zane needed to check in for his flight. Zane and Lila arrived earlier than they expected, and Zane turned off the engine and put his arm around Lila. "You're right about me needing to figure things out. I'll find my peace, and somehow, some day, we'll be together."

She nodded but she wasn't warm to him the way she'd been the day before.

"I'm sorry I put you in that predicament," he said. "I wasn't using you . . ." But maybe he had been. Maybe he still had a lot of changing to do before he was ready to be Lila's husband.

He pulled the pieces of rock from his pocket and held his hand up to the light. "They're jasper," he said. "From down by the creek." He handed the bigger one to her. "Keep this one for me, would you?"

She nodded and slipped it into her apron pocket.

He put his arm back around her and tightened his hold until his phone buzzed. It was a text from Mom. *We're almost there. Tim and Beth are with us. So is Adam.*

He showed the text to Lila.

"One big happy family," she said, but she wasn't laughing.

"Your Dat won't fly off the handle, not in front of Beth and my parents."

"I know," she answered. "I just can't fathom why he'd come."

He texted back. *Okay.*

Zane had gone from planning to become Amish to returning to Afghanistan all in the last eight hours. Zane figured he had a couple of more minutes and clicked on his e-mail app and then on Sarge's last message, typing *On my way* and then hitting Send. He did the same with Casey's last message too and then slipped his phone back into his pocket. "You should have married Reuben," he said. "Your life would be far less complicated."

"Hush," she said.

"I'd like to think I'm your best friend, but all I've brought you is uncertainty."

"You are my best friend," she said.

Mom's van came around the corner and then parked beside them. Everyone started tumbling out at once.

"Ready?" Zane asked.

"No," Lila said. She took his hand. "I'll be praying for you. And for us. Know that."

"Denki," he answered. There was more he wanted to say, but after all that had happened he figured his words would sound hollow. He didn't deserve her. But he guessed that was what love was all about.

24

Greeting everyone felt awkward, so Lila held back, letting Zane do the talking. He handled it well.

"I made a big mistake," he said to the group. "Thank you for understanding."

"Let's go eat so we can get you on your way," Joel said, leading the way to the front door of the restaurant, the rubber tip of his cane thudding along the pavement of the parking lot.

When they were all seated and holding their menus Zane, who sat down by his parents and Adam, asked Dat who was doing the milking.

"Reuben and Rose, with Trudy's help," Dat answered.

Beth smiled at Lila and then said from across the table, "We were all so worried."

Lila fought back her tears. "I'm so sorry. I didn't really think it through."

Beth reached out and covered Lila's hand with hers. "I just wanted you to know how much we all care."

Lila stole a look at her Dat, who sat next to Beth. He was listening to Zane talk about going back to Afghanistan.

"You're right," Zane was saying to his father.

"I'm not really a pacifist. And I'm certainly not nonresistant."

Dat leaned forward a little. "What do you mean?"

"I think some wars are justified," Zane said. "And I think we often don't know until long after the fact if some are or not."

Dat pushed back in his chair. "Jah, that's a problem."

Zane nodded. "And I don't see how I could stand back and not protect someone I love—or even a stranger—from getting hurt."

Dat tilted his head. "That's a more complicated issue. If that was truly the criteria for belonging in the church, most Amish men I know wouldn't meet it."

Lila wanted to ask what he meant, but Zane beat her to it. "What are you saying?"

"There are decisions made with the brain and decisions made with the heart. Those heart ones are hard to control sometimes. I think God expects us to protect those who are vulnerable."

Lila put her menu down. "What about Jacob Hochstetler?" They'd learned about him in school. Way back in the 1700s, he was an Anabaptist man who hadn't fought back during an attack by Native Americans and his wife and daughter were killed, while he and two sons were captured. There were many nonresistant stories from back in Europe too, long before the Amish fled to America.

Dat shook his head. "Frankly I've never fully understood how a man could watch someone kill his family without putting up a fight."

Puzzled, Lila drew a deep breath. Her Dat was full of surprises.

Zane cleared his throat and then said, "I'd like to write to Lila if that's all right with you."

Dat spread his hands flat on the table. "Are you asking my permission?"

Zane nodded.

"What are your intentions?" Dat's eyes practically bore through Zane.

He didn't flinch. "I'd like to marry her, sir. But I'm not sure how everything will work out."

Dat leaned forward again, his eyes still on Zane. "Any chance you intend to join us once you get back? It seems you were willing to join the Amish in Ontario. If an Englischman could become Amish, it would be you."

Zane hesitated, caught Lila's eye, and then said, "I need to see how things go in Afghanistan first."

Dat nodded. "I understand. And I think you'll understand this. Wait to write Lila until you get back to the U.S. Both of you need a few months to clear your heads after running off like this. I appreciate that you did the right thing by coming back, but your emotions are too high. You need more than feelings to fuel a good marriage. You need a love that is steadfast, faithful, and strong."

Lila had never heard such eloquent talk from her Dat. She couldn't help but wonder if he was parroting Beth's ideas, but it seemed as if he'd taken the words to heart. And it was good advice.

"That's fair," Zane said, catching Lila's eyes. She realized she'd been holding her breath, exhaled, and then nodded. Dat had been far more reasonable than she'd expected. The time of not being in touch would probably help both her and Zane figure out what they wanted, what they needed.

As the waitress approached the table, Lila slipped her hand into her apron pocket and clasped the piece of jasper. His intention behind giving it to her was the sort of thing she loved about Zane. He made life rich and full of meaning. He also made her heart break in two. But he did make her feel, that was for certain.

After they'd finished eating, Dat rode with Joel and Adam in Zane's truck, while Lila and Beth rode in Shani's van to drop Zane off at the airport. Lila managed to tell him she'd pray for him as she squeezed his hand and said good-bye. Shani had to pull away from the curb before Zane reached the door. He turned and waved, his duffel bag slung over his shoulder. But then Shani moved over a lane, and a car moved in front of Zane, and when Lila caught sight of the door again he was gone.

Lila fell asleep to the soft murmur of Shani

talking to Beth about trusting God with Zane. "I don't have any other choice. . . ."

When Lila woke, Shani had stopped in front of the little cottage Beth rented from a family in the district. When Lila woke again, they'd reached Juneberry Lane and were turning up the driveway. Dat waited for them by the steps, and as soon as Shani stopped the van, he swung the side door open and extended his hand to Lila. She thanked Shani and followed her father into the kitchen.

The lamp was lit and sitting in the middle of the table.

Dat put his hand on top of the back of his chair and said, "I'm proud of you."

"What?" He'd never said anything like that before, not even close. And why would he now, after all she had put him through?

"I thought I wanted conformity more than anything in my children," he said. "All these years that seemed to be what mattered most. I wanted you to marry Reuben. To stay close. I thought that was how I would be successful as a father."

"I'm not leaving, Dat."

"That's not what I'm getting at," he said. "Jah, I was disappointed in your decision not to marry Reuben, but I can see now it was the right one. I know you don't have things figured out, but I'm proud of you for not doing what so many of us wanted you to."

Lila didn't know how to respond. She never would have expected such a statement from her Dat. She guessed having Simon run off to join the Army had humbled him some. Or maybe Beth had helped him see things from a different perspective. She supposed that's what it meant to be a friend—to be willing to see things from another point of view.

Finally she said, "I want to do what God wants me to do."

"He will lead you," Dat said. "Just give him time."

25

Zane flew from Philly to Dublin, on to Kazakhstan, then to Bagram, and finally to their base, arriving fifty-six hours after he'd left. As they landed, the sun set behind him over the Hindu Kush. Sarge and Casey met him at the airfield, on the runway he left from three months before on a stretcher.

"Glad you could join us," Sarge said.

Zane just nodded as he slung his duffel bag over his left shoulder.

"Are you healed?"

"Pretty much."

"Can you shoot?"

"I'm guessing so." He hadn't actually tried, but

427

Dad was right—if he could repair the chicken coop he was sure he could shoot a gun. Although there was the possibility his aim would be worse than ever. He sighed. Or that he would freeze.

"Get some sleep," Sarge said. "We're leaving in the morning." He took off toward the mess hall.

"You're in with Grant," Casey said.

Zane suppressed a groan.

"Fair warning, he's worse than ever. Wade won't even room with him anymore." Casey reached for his duffel bag. "Let me help."

"Are you kidding?" Zane pulled away from her. "You're not carrying my gear." He stopped. "Listen," he said. "I want to tell you something before we're around the others. Thank you for having my back all this time. And for being good to my mom too." His mother had been a saint through his shenanigans. He couldn't imagine why he'd been so annoyed with her before.

Casey looked up at him. In the dim light she smiled just a little. "You're welcome." Then she shook her head. "So why did you take so long to e-mail us back?"

"You don't want to know."

"I do, honestly."

"I took a little trip to Canada."

"By yourself?"

He didn't answer.

"I won't tell anyone else," she said. "Not even Sarge."

"I know." Next to Lila and his parents, he trusted Casey more than anyone. "I was with Lila."

"Zane . . . What were you thinking?"

"That we'd make a life together up there."

"What happened?"

"She changed her mind. And then she told me to keep my commitment and come back here."

"Really?" Casey asked. "Why'd she do that?"

Zane sighed. "She said I'd regret it."

"And you agreed?"

Zane frowned. "Time will tell."

Casey smiled, her dimples flashing. "Happy to be back, then?"

"Well, happier than I expected. It's good to see you, and I'm looking forward to seeing Jaalal."

"Yeah, about that, you'll have to convince Sarge. Grant's been feeding him a boatload of you know what. We haven't seen Jaalal in weeks."

"What have you been doing since the last translator left?"

"Sticking around here, except for a few day-trips to nearby villages." She leaned forward a little. "Which is exactly what Grant wants. He's full of it—as long as we're on base. If you think getting shot shook you up, you should see what getting shot *at* did to him." She grimaced.

"Is that what everyone thinks? That getting shot shook me up?"

She nodded.

He shook his head, weighing his emotions again. "It wasn't getting shot that sent me to Canada."

"What was it then?"

"Having to shoot back." He hesitated. "And killing Benham."

"He was a bad guy."

"I know. But he was a human being. Doing something he thought he needed to do too."

Casey kicked at the dirt. "I can see that would bother you." She glanced up at him and smiled. "And getting shot."

"Yeah, well, it's probably better if that's what everyone thinks."

Casey's face grew serious again. "So what's the status as far as you and Lila now? Broken up for good?"

Zane shook his head. "We're taking a break. Again. We're not going to make any decisions yet."

"So she might leave the Amish?"

"We'll see," Zane said. He trusted Casey with his life—but not enough to tell her he was considering becoming Plain.

Grant grunted when Zane stepped into the room and said, "I was hoping you'd gone AWOL." Then he returned to the movie playing on his laptop.

Swinging his duffel bag onto his bunk, Zane decided to ignore him. But after a few minutes he asked Grant what he was watching.

"*The Longest Day.*"

"That's a World War II movie, right?"

"Yeah."

With John Wayne. Big, strong, and brave. Zane pulled his extra uniforms out of his duffel bag. The good soldiers in the movies were always tall and handsome, while the cowards were scrawny and homely. The heroes never questioned anyone's authority, but the cowards whined and sniveled.

In the real Army some of the best soldiers were short. Some were downright small. Some were as homely as could be. In the real Army, the handsome ones were sometimes the ones that whined and dodged their duty. And the ones who seemed fearless were really afraid, although Zane doubted he appeared fearless to anyone.

"How's your baby doing?" Zane asked, turning toward Grant.

"Shhh," he said. "I'm at the good part. They're about ready to cross the bridge."

Zane turned back to his unpacking. Three months and they'd be back in the States. That's all he had to get through.

Zane's unit stuck around base for a week, day-tripping to local villages, finishing up business that had been left undone once the translator fell ill. The nightmares continued, and a couple of times Zane woke up to the screech of his own voice, surprised he hadn't woken Grant too. But it seemed the man could sleep through anything.

The next week they headed up the windy road safely strapped in an MRAP and finally into the mountains, where some new intelligence was waiting at the farthest village, or so the speculation was. No one talked much until they reached the first village. Casey and her crew gathered a few of the women around and showed them one of the new stoves. Zane translated how it worked while Casey demonstrated. The plan was to keep children, especially toddlers, from falling in the cooking fires and burning themselves.

If people in the states believed the Amish lived primitively, Zane thought they'd be flabbergasted by an Afghan village. But even in the midst of war, the people were relatively happy, as long as their children had enough to eat. The smaller ones played with sticks and rocks, while the mothers cooked in a group. The fathers were off in their fields and the older kids were herding the goats and sheep.

Zane stumbled a few times over words, but overall he was grateful for how the language came back to him. That evening after supper, he sat around with some of the Afghan men and visited and drank tea. The air was cool and crisp, and the temperature would likely drop below freezing that night. Hopefully the colder weather would mean less fighting.

One of the men asked if he'd seen Jaalal yet.

Zane shook his head.

"Go see him," the man said. "He'd like that."

"I hope I can," Zane answered.

The next day he asked Sarge about detouring to Jaalal's village, but he refused. "I'm not going there," he said. "That's why we brought you back."

"I can't do what Jaalal can. He's an elder. He can rally the people, not to mention uncover intelligence I never could. Can't you give him a chance?"

Sarge shook his head.

They moved on to the next village that morning and went through the same lesson with the stoves, but this time only two Afghan women joined in, and all the men in the village stood around in a semicircle, observing.

Zane spoke loudly so they could hear, and when they'd finished asked if they could give the children a treat. The men shook their heads. They'd hoped to stay at that village for a night, but instead traveled on, skipping Jaalal's village and going toward the fourth, where the man with new intelligence was rumored to be, nearing it late in the day.

A pickup blocked the road before they arrived. It seemed to be empty, but there were no guarantees that someone might not be hiding in the brush. It had started to rain, and dusk was falling, adding to the poor visibility.

"Taliban," Grant said.

"Maybe," Sarge answered. He unbuckled his seat belt and began moving up toward their driver, Private Anderson, saying, "We should turn around."

Wade paled.

"Where to now?" Zane asked Casey.

"Probably back to base. That's been our MO lately. That's why we've hardly gotten anything done."

Zane leaned back against his seat. He was supposed to be the coward, but they were all as punchy as could be. He'd come back reluctantly, at Lila's urging, but now that he was here he wanted to be able to complete their work. And the only way they could get it done was to bring Jaalal back on board.

The rain grew heavier and Private Anderson slowed as he turned the wheel.

"I have a bad feeling about this," Grant said.

"Give it up," Casey hissed.

"It's Taliban. I can feel it."

"You're like a broken record," Casey said to him.

Zane couldn't help but sympathize with Grant, thinking of the last patrol the two of them had been on to gather intelligence.

Grant crossed his arms and scowled at Casey,

but then the MRAP jumped, followed by the sound of an explosion. Then a scream. Zane was pretty sure it wasn't his, but he couldn't be certain. Smoke began to flow into the front of the vehicle's interior.

"Everyone okay?" Zane asked, feeling oddly calm.

"Yeah," Casey responded.

"We'd better get out." Zane unbuckled.

"It's not safe," Grant answered. "It's a trap."

"It's not safe to stay in a burning vehicle either." It could have been that the IED was freshly set, or perhaps it was an old one. But considering the pickup blocking the road, it had likely been a trap. They'd probably been lured to the village by the promise of information, but they'd arrived sooner than anticipated. Maybe that had saved them—no one seemed to be in the immediate area, but they wouldn't know for sure until they exited the MRAP.

Zane turned toward the front and called out, "Sarge!"

When he didn't answer, Zane started crawling forward on his hands and knees, yelling back to Casey and Wade, "Go out the back door—but watch for any insurgents. Let me know if you see anything."

He felt Sarge before seeing him. His helmet was off and he was unconscious, but he had a pulse. Zane crawled over Sarge to Anderson, who was slumped over the steering wheel. He appeared dazed but hadn't lost consciousness.

Smoke was now pouring into the cab from the engine.

He crawled back over Sarge and now saw that there was significant blood coming from a head wound. He pulled out his first-aid kit, pressed the quick clot packet over the wound, and strapped his helmet back on. He then grabbed Sarge by the feet and pulled him toward the back. Grant still sat in his seat.

"Come on," Zane ordered. "We've got to get Sarge to safety." Maybe it was the appeal to help someone else, maybe it was the smoke, but something finally compelled Grant to move. "Call for help," Zane ordered him.

Grant just stared at him.

Wade said, "I'll do it." As Grant and Zane stumbled out the door with Sarge, who had regained consciousness, Wade spoke into his radio.

Casey stood sentry with her gun pointed toward the brush. "I haven't seen a thing."

"Head to the stand of trees off to the right," Zane ordered and then followed with Sarge between him and Grant. Wade fell in behind.

They lowered Sarge to the ground, and Zane went back to the MRAP for Private Anderson. He pulled his T-shirt up over his mouth as he entered. Anderson was fairly alert and appeared to be shutting down the MRAP systems. By the time they were out of the rig and in the stand of trees, both Zane and the driver were coughing.

After examining Sarge, who was unconscious again, Zane knew he'd hit his head pretty hard. His left arm and leg were both bleeding and his uniform was torn up. Zane packed those wounds and then checked his pulse again. It was steady. He revived and after a few more minutes seemed to be doing better.

"What now?" Casey asked.

"We should go back to Jaalal's village for help," Zane replied, saying a silent prayer that it was the right thing to do. He wasn't certain it was—but he couldn't come up with a better plan.

He turned toward Grant. "Go back and destroy any sensitive items we can't carry." The last thing they wanted was for radios and electronic equipment to get in the wrong hands.

Grant frowned but followed Zane's instructions.

Anderson had dropped to the ground once they reached cover, and now he groaned.

Zane knelt beside him. "We're going to walk to Jaalal's village. Do you think you can make it?"

The driver nodded. Zane helped him to his feet as he motioned to Casey to come support him.

Then he instructed Wade to make a "chair" with Zane, linking their hands together to carry Sarge. It would be slow going, and they'd need to trade off with Grant, but hopefully it would work.

"We'll lead the way," Zane said. He called out to Grant, as he came back across the road, "You take up the rear."

"Great," Grant said. "I'll be the target."

"Would you rather be in front?"

"Yeah. Actually, I would."

"Go for it." Zane and Wade fell back.

As darkness descended, they stopped and put on their night-vision goggles. Sounds startled them now and then, and Zane kept expecting whoever owned the pickup to follow, but after thirty minutes of walking, he started to feel more confident.

They had to stop over and over to rest, and an hour later they were taking a break in the middle of the road when Grant bellowed, "Truck!"

Sure enough headlights were coming their way.

"Hide," Zane commanded. He and Wade lifted Sarge, who continued to move in and out of consciousness, again.

Grant reached the trees first, followed by Casey and Anderson, and then Wade, Zane, and Sarge. They'd just made it into the trees when the truck drove by. It was an old Toyota, white and beat up. It looked a lot like Jaalal's.

As the pickup went by, Zane stepped out into the road—hoping to appear as if he were alone in case it wasn't Jaalal—and started waving his arms.

"You're going to get us all killed!" Grant hissed.

The pickup stopped and started coming back, in reverse.

Zane stopped waving. Even if it was Jaalal, it didn't mean he'd come to help. Zane didn't budge though until the pickup stopped. Then he walked up to the driver's side.

The door swung open. "It is you," Jaalal said. "I had a call. I've come to help. Hurry though, the insurgents are headed this way."

Zane ran back to the others.

"I don't know about this," Sarge said, groggy but talking for the first time, which encouraged Zane.

"What other choice do we have?" Zane said. "We can't spend the night out here." He and Wade lifted Sarge again and started to stumble, but Jaalal was there to help them. Together they got Sarge spread out in the back of the pickup and as comfortable as they could.

"You sit up front," Zane said to Anderson. "You too, Casey."

She shook her head. "Go ahead, Grant."

Zane climbed into the bed of the truck, after Casey and Wade were seated. Once they'd all hunkered down, Casey said to Zane, "Thanks for taking charge."

"You could have done it," Zane said.

Wade shook his head. "Grant won't listen to Casey. If you hadn't been here, he'd still be in the MRAP, dying from smoke inhalation. And the rest of us would be across the road in the trees."

If he hadn't been here, they'd all have probably been back at base.

They slept in the front room of Jaalal's home, and the next morning a helicopter landed in the clearing outside of the village and took Sarge and Anderson back to base.

"I'll drive the rest of you down," Jaalal said.

Grant was against it, saying they should wait for transport. "Someone has to come recover the MRAP," he said.

"It could be a couple of days, and we don't have much as far as supplies," Casey said. "I think we should take the ride."

"Wade and I'll ride gunner in the back," Zane said. "Grant, you and Casey ride up front."

Zane silently recited the Twenty-third Psalm on the bumpy ride down the mountain and prayed he wouldn't have to shoot anyone, prayed they'd get there safely. Prayed Jaalal would get back home.

When they finally reached the base, it took some talking to get the MPs to allow Jaalal through the gate. "I can vouch for him," Zane said. "I promise. He won't leave my side. I'm just going to gas up his truck and then send him back up the mountain."

By the time they reached the hospital, Sarge was already on his way to Bagram. "Will he be coming back?" Casey asked the doc, a new one from when Zane had been through the ER.

The doc shook his head. "I wouldn't count on it."

Zane turned toward Jaalal. "I'll get you back to the gate. You should go home."

Jaalal nodded.

"I'll meet up with you at the mess hall," Zane said to Casey.

Zane climbed into the cab of the pickup. Before he could ask Jaalal anything, the old man said, "I told you not to come back."

"I didn't have a choice," Zane said. "So what's going on? Sarge was afraid you'd joined up with the Taliban."

Jaalal shook his head. "Never. But the pressure is getting worse and worse."

"I can try to get you out," Zane said. "You and Aliah."

He shook his head. "We're too old to start over. I would have asked for Benham . . ."

"I'm sorry," Zane said.

"I know you are," Jaalal answered, starting his pickup. "But he brought it on himself. There was nothing else you could do."

Zane swallowed hard. "Still, I'm so sorry."

"I know," Jaalal said again, looking straight ahead.

"For all of it. For what war has done to your country. For the decisions ahead for you. For your son's death and Benham's."

"We have never known peace, not in my lifetime," Jaalal said. "First the Russians. Then the Taliban. Now this. For a time I hoped, but I'm afraid we are doomed to violence."

Zane didn't respond.

"Go back home as soon as you can. Marry that girl, that . . . What do you call them?"

"Amish."

"Yes, marry that beautiful Amish girl. Have a houseful of children." Jaalal looked at him for a moment. His eyes were rimmed with red. Then he turned onto the road and headed to the gate. "Remember me and Aliah, of all the things we wanted, of the things we had, of what we lost. But know we had each other, and that kept us going. We'll be all right, in the end."

"I'll always remember you," Zane said, digging in his pocket for his pen and little notebook. He took them out and scribbled his e-mail address on a scrap of paper and then his parents' address. "Get a phone with access to the Internet," he said. "And e-mail me. Or write a letter. If you need anything . . . I'll do everything I can to help you."

Jaalal stuck out his hand, and after Zane put the paper on his palm, he made a fist. When they reached the gate, Zane climbed out of the cab and jogged around to Jaalal's door. The man stood, and they hugged and Zane snapped a photo in his mind of the old Afghan man, his white tunic flowing.

"God go with you," Jaalal said.

"And with you," Zane answered.

He watched as the man climbed back in his pickup and drove away toward the cloud-covered mountains.

A week of hanging around base in the rain made everyone restless and cranky. Casey avoided Grant, and Zane tried his best, but it was hard when he roomed with him. A few times he worked out with Wade. The guy didn't talk much, but he was easy to be around.

The other team stayed at base too. The rain and mud were making it hard for anyone to travel.

Grant was the first to see the new orders come through on his e-mail. He didn't say anything, just started packing.

Zane finally got it out of him. "We're going back to Texas," he said, throwing a pair of socks into his bag.

Zane headed to the service center to check his e-mail and ran into the commander of their unit on the way.

"Come on," the commander said. "I need to talk with you."

Zane followed him across the compound. When they reached his office, Casey was already there, waiting for them. Zane nodded at her, and she returned the gesture.

"The teams are going back to Texas next week," the commander said. "We can't secure the area, and travel is nearly impossible. With the downsizing that's going on, our work won't be continued after we leave. It doesn't make any sense to bring in new troops to replace those who have been injured for only six weeks."

Casey's face fell. Obviously she hadn't heard.

"But you two aren't going to Texas," he added. "The USAID needs a Pashto translator and a project manager at the State Department in Maryland. I think it's obvious who will be in each position. You'll both report there."

"Thank you, sir," they said in unison.

As they walked in the rain to the mess hall, picking their way through the mud, Casey groaned. "We were the worst civil affairs team ever."

"That's not true."

She shook her head. "We didn't make a difference."

"We can't know, in the long run," Zane said. "Besides, we did lots of good. Fewer kids burned in cooking fires. More girls in schools. More women with ideas to start a business. Better medical treatment. We can't know what impact we made in the long run."

She smiled a little. "Thanks," she said.

"On the bright side, we'll be home for Thanksgiving," Zane said. It was only a month away.

"You will be," Casey said.

"You can come with me," Zane replied.

"What about Lila? Will she be all right with that?"

Zane nodded, sure she would once she knew the circumstances.

"What did Jaalal say to you?" Casey asked.

Zane raised his head. "That I should go home and marry that Amish girl."

"It's a shame, because you're such a great soldier," Casey said. "But that's actually what I think you should do too."

Had he figured out his peace, like Lila told him he needed to? He didn't feel frantic the way he had for the last three years. *"Be still, and know that I am God."* He'd see Lila at Thanksgiving. A little more time apart would do them both good, give them more time to sort things out and trust God with their future.

26

O n the fourth Tuesday of November, Lila shivered as she drove the buggy back from Monika and Gideon's as the sun set. A cold front was moving in, just in time for Daniel and Jenny's wedding.

They'd finished the last of the cleaning and cooking. Lila would return early in the morning to help with breakfast and the final details before the morning wedding.

Monika, of course, had every detail seen to, but it would still take an army of workers to pull it off. It was the biggest wedding in the district that Lila could remember.

She hoped Shani, Joel, and Adam would attend. She'd had a short note, via Dat, from Zane two weeks ago telling her that he'd been transferred to Maryland, where he was doing translation work for a government organization, and that he'd contact her soon so they could talk.

Her prayers had been answered. He was all right and he'd returned from Afghanistan weeks earlier than expected. She hoped he'd come for the wedding too, but she hadn't heard from him again. Shani said he would visit soon to collect his truck, she just didn't know when.

If he wasn't coming for Thanksgiving, then he

surely wasn't coming for Daniel's wedding either. It made her wonder, for all of his talk about how important she and her siblings were to him, if he really meant it.

And then there was his love for her. Two months ago he was ready to marry. She wondered what he was feeling now. Perhaps he'd been frozen by fear again.

Several times she'd gone out to the barn at ten at night, hoping he'd call, but he hadn't.

Zane may have changed his mind about her, but she still loved him.

She was trying to find her peace, but the last couple of weeks—not knowing, not hearing from Zane—had been hard.

Simon was coming home for the wedding and staying for Thanksgiving. But then he had to get back to Virginia. He was going somewhere in December, although he couldn't say where, which sounded especially scary to Lila.

The first snowflake flew just as she turned off the highway down Juneberry Lane. She hoped the snowfall would be light and not keep guests away from the wedding. Lila sighed. God was in charge. They had to trust him with the details.

Ahead, Rose pulled clothes off the line. The snow was coming down harder now, and Trudy ran toward the barn. By the time Lila had the horse unhitched, Trudy approached, a kitten in her hand. "You have a message," she said, her eyes sparkling. "Dat listened to it, and so did I."

"Who from?" Lila asked, guessing it was some-one from the Plain Buffet. Her manager probably forgot she couldn't work the next day.

"Guess," Trudy said, a hint of teasing in her voice.

Could it possibly be Zane? Lila hurried the horse along as Trudy ducked into the tack room. After Lila had the mare in her stall, rubbed, brushed, and fed, she headed toward the milk-ing room. Dat worked alone. "Trudy said I have a message."

"Could you help me?" Dat asked. "Rose said she had too much to do with finishing up the laundry and the cooking."

"Sure . . ." Lila answered.

"Go ahead and listen to your message first, though," Dat said without looking up.

She grabbed an apron off a hook as she headed for the office, pulling it over her head as she did, thankful she had a work dress on. She hit the button on the message machine as she leaned against Dat's desk, anxious to hear Zane's voice.

"Hi, Tim," Zane said. "I hope this finds all of you well. I'd like to come for Daniel's wedding, if that's all right with you." His voice sounded strong and untroubled. "I'd also like to bring a friend—one from the Army whose folks live in Hawaii, which means it's too far to go for the holiday. If bringing a guest would be a problem, let me know." Then he said, "Looking forward to seeing all of you tomorrow and Simon too. Bye for now."

That was it.

The message hadn't been for her at all. And he was bringing Casey to the wedding. Dat couldn't have known the friend was a girl, not from what Zane said. But Lila was sure that's who it was. No wonder he hadn't called her. He used to refer to Lila as his "friend" too. Perhaps Zane was confused about friendship.

She inhaled deeply, composed herself, and then headed into the milking room, marching around to shovel feed into the troughs as Dat brought in the next cow.

"Well, then," Dat said. "It sounds as if Zane will be here tomorrow too."

She nodded but didn't answer.

"Have you talked with him since he's been back?"

She shook her head. "He just sent that one note."

Dat gave her a sad look.

She shrugged.

"Ach," Dat said. "That last night we saw him I felt he might consider joining us."

Lila had thought so too. They'd said they'd talk everything through once he was back, but it seemed something had happened in the short time he was in Afghanistan.

A wave of loneliness swept over her and then

settled as an ache in her chest. If only she could make herself *stop* loving Zane.

"Well, keep your chin up," Dat said. "Life will work out one way or the other."

"Dat," Lila said, "how is that helpful?"

He frowned. "I overheard Beth say that to Rose."

"Not about her future, surely," Lila muttered. It was more likely about some household task.

Dat shrugged. "Sorry."

Lila kept on shoveling feed. The cow snorted. At least it was warmer in the barn. And with the wedding, for the time being, she had something to distract her thoughts.

Snow had fallen all night long, but it was light and fluffy, and even though it was still dark, the plows were out well before Lila, Rose, Trudy, and Dat headed over to Monika's. Dat held the reins, and Rose sat up front with him, while Lila and Trudy sat in the back seat.

Simon hadn't arrived the night before, as planned, but he had left a message on the machine that he'd make it for the wedding. Lila thought it would be nice if he made it in time to help set up for the wedding, but she wouldn't count on it. He'd probably spent the evening before with Mandy and then crashed somewhere.

When they arrived at Monika's, the girls piled out of the buggy and Dat kept going to the barn. A lantern hung on the front porch and from under the edges of the dim light, Daniel waved and then got back to shoveling the snow from the front steps. Someone else shoveled the front walk. It wasn't Reuben. Lila squinted and then called out, "Simon! Is that you?"

"Jah!" he called back and started toward them, raising the shovel in his hand in greeting.

Trudy squealed and ran toward him, followed by Rose. A shiver shot down Lila's spine and tears filled her eyes. They'd all be together one last time. She followed her sisters and when it was her turn, she gave Simon a hug.

"Still mad at me?" he whispered into her ear.

"Always," she said.

"I figured," he teased.

She pulled away from him. "Did you see Mandy last night?"

He shook his head and glanced at Trudy. She was bounding toward Daniel, followed by Rose.

"What's going on?" Lila asked.

"We broke up." Simon shrugged. "She had second thoughts about leaving the Mennonites. . . . I don't know what's ahead for me. It was all too much for both of us."

"Can you say now where they're sending you?" Lila asked.

He shrugged and then grinned. "Zane's coming," he said.

"So I heard," Lila answered.

"You don't sound like you're happy about it."

It was her turn to shrug. "He's bringing his friend."

Simon stepped back to the sidewalk. "Casey, right?"

"Jah," Lila answered and quickly changed the subject. "So where did you stay last night?"

He nodded to the right, toward the Dawdi Haus. "With Daniel."

Lila's heart melted a little. Daniel had moved in the week before to prepare it for him and Jenny. It was sweet that Simon had wanted to hang out with Daniel the night before the wedding.

She gave Simon a pat on the shoulder and followed her sisters into the house. Monika already had breakfast made, thanks to the help of her older daughters. They and their families had all spent the night, making for a full house. Children in their nightclothes scurried around while their mothers chased them. Lila guessed the men were out finishing up the chores or putting the last-minute touches on the shed where the service would be held.

Beth soon arrived, much to Lila's relief, and together the women worked to serve breakfast and then finish all that needed to be done to host the wedding.

By eight thirty, everything and everyone was in order. Lila and Jenny waited together in the front room, glancing out the curtains from time 7to time. Mammi and Dawdi arrived in their car,

452

and Lila watched as they made their way to the shed. Mammi appeared strong.

Lila didn't see the Becks' van arrive. Perhaps Zane and Casey had been delayed, preventing the whole family from coming.

Gideon and Daniel entered the living room, along with the ministers. The older men would instruct the bride and groom while the congregation sang the first songs during the service. Lila excused herself, grabbed her coat by the back door, and headed down to the shed. She'd sit by Jenny once she arrived, but she'd wait to walk down with her. She slipped in the door, on the women's side, and scanned the crowd. Dawdi sat close to the front, in a row with a group of older men that he'd known since he was a boy. About midway sat Joel, Charlie, Adam, and Zane.

Lila's heart began to race. He'd come. And he looked so confident and content, as if he belonged.

She scanned the women's side. Mammi sat in the row in front of Eve, Shani, and Casey. Lila's stomach clenched. She was jealous. Casey had experienced a part of life with Zane that Lila couldn't even comprehend. And here she was sitting beside Shani, wearing a black sweater and white blouse. Her dark hair was pulled back in a bun. From her profile, Casey looked far more beautiful than Lila had imagined.

Not long after the first song ended, Gideon, Reuben, Daniel, and Jenny slipped in beside her.

When the second song ended, they all walked down to the front of the church and sat along with the other witnesses on the benches designated for them.

No Amish service went quickly, especially not one with a wedding in it. First was a sermon, then a Bible reading, then a prayer. Then a second sermon. Finally, Jenny and Daniel were called up front and were married. That part of the service was short and to the point. Gideon officiated, mentioning both Jenny's father and the Lehman children's mother. Lila felt a tear in her eye but quickly brushed it away. Mamm would be proud of Daniel. He loved Jenny with all of his heart, and he was good and kind to her.

Lila wasn't sure whether Mamm would be proud of her or not. Would she have wanted her to marry Reuben? Would she have been hurt by Lila's love for Zane? One thing was sure, her Mamm wouldn't want Lila to leave the church for Zane, even if that was what he wanted. Her mother hadn't left, not even when she was pregnant with an Englischer's babies. She'd stuck by her commitment.

After the wedding, Lila headed toward the side of the shed, away from the men's side. She wanted to talk with Zane—but not in front of Simon or Casey. Eve stepped away from the other women, who were talking with Monika, and hurried toward Lila. When she reached her, Eve wrapped her arms around her niece. Lila hugged her back and teared up, again, at her Aenti's warmth. "Mamm would be proud of Daniel," Lila said.

"Of course she would," Eve said. "But not more than any of the rest of you."

Lila wrinkled her nose. "She wouldn't be proud of Simon, and I doubt she'd be proud of me."

Eve smiled. "Your Mamm wouldn't exactly understand Simon, but she would love him no matter what. As far as you, why in the world would she not be proud of you?"

"I didn't marry Reuben. I didn't do the right thing, like she did."

"Whatever do you mean?"

"She could have married the Englisch man, jah? And left. But she stayed."

"Oh, dear," Eve said. "I guess we weren't very clear about all of that. She never considered leaving."

Lila nodded in agreement.

Eve took Lila's hand. "Sweetie, your birth father never knew about you and Daniel. He left before your mother realized she was pregnant, and then she never tried to find him."

"He never knew?" All this time Lila had thought her mother hadn't wanted to marry him and leave the church, but maybe she didn't have a choice. "Why didn't she tell him?"

"He returned to Virginia before your mother

455

knew she was expecting. Patrick—my . . ." She stopped, glanced around, and then said, "My boyfriend knew him but not well. It wasn't the way it is now with social media and everything. And no one had a cell phone. I suppose he might have had an e-mail address, but none of us knew it. It was like he just disappeared."

"No one tried to track him down?"

"Well, I think your grandmother thought it would be the right thing to do, but your Mamm didn't want to. I think she was afraid—of outside influences."

"So she really didn't love him?"

A pained expression crossed Eve's face. "I'm afraid I'm not saying this very gracefully, but she didn't know him very well . . ."

"They didn't court for a long time?"

Eve shook her head. "They really didn't even date."

"If she had loved him, do you think she would have left the Amish?"

Eve hesitated. "Why do you ask?"

Lila shrugged.

Eve sighed. "She wasn't opposed to someone leaving because of love. I considered it back then, and she never tried to discourage me. I think she would have been in favor of what I did when I left to marry Charlie."

Lila nodded. "Denki," she said to Eve. "That gives me something to think about."

Eve held on to her hand. "Is there more you can tell me?"

Lila shook her head. "But I have a question. What's my biological father's name?"

Eve tilted her head, paused, and then said, "Everyone called him Butch. At the time I thought it was his name, but it could have been a nickname."

"What about his last name?"

"Wilson."

Lila exhaled. It was probably a pretty common name.

"What did he look like?"

"He was fair skinned. Gray eyes, I think." Lila had definitely gotten her blue eyes from her mother. "Light brown hair. Medium height."

"Like Daniel?"

"Some," Eve said. "But both of you favor your Mamm more, especially you."

"There you are!" Shani headed toward them, the young woman at her side. "I want you to meet Casey."

Lila stuck out her hand and stood tall.

Casey's eyes lit up as Shani said, "This is Lila."

"I'm so pleased to finally meet you," Casey said. Her hand was warm and firm and her dark eyes sparkled. She seemed sincere. "Zane has told me so much about you." She didn't say it in a condescending way or in a victorious way either.

"It's good to meet you too," Lila said. Zane had told her some about Casey, but most of what she knew was from Mandy stalking her on Facebook. But she wasn't going to admit that.

"Have you talked with Zane yet?" Casey asked.

Lila shook her head.

"You and your brothers were all he talked about the whole way here last night," Casey said. "It about drove me crazy."

Lila couldn't help but smile.

"You all had an amazing childhood."

"We did," Lila said. Despite all the hardships in both families, they had. She smiled at Casey again and said, "I'll see you during the meal. I need to get over to the house and help."

She slipped away as Shani, Eve, and Casey continued talking. She didn't want to leave the Amish—not ever—but if she'd thought her mother would have sanctioned it, would she have responded differently way back when? Would she have considered becoming Mennonite?

But what had she known when she was seventeen?

It wasn't long until the meal was ready and Lila joined the bride and groom at their table, along with Reuben. They sat on either side of the couple, until after Daniel and Jenny finished eating and started going around to greet their guests. Lila stood and reached for Reuben's plate to take it to the kitchen.

"Would you like a piece of pie? Banana cream?" she asked, as a goodwill gesture.

He nodded, but a pained expression passed over his face when their eyes met.

She realized he still hadn't recovered from their breakup and said softly, "I'm sorry."

He smiled and shook his head.

When she returned with the pie, he patted the chair beside his. "Can you sit for a moment?" he asked.

She could—for just a minute.

"So what's going on with Zane?" Reuben asked and then took a bite of pie.

Lila shrugged.

"Who's the girl?"

"Casey. She's working with him in Maryland."

"Oh." Reuben took a few more bites and then said, "I thought you wanted to quit courting because of Zane, but now it looks as if he's with someone else."

Her face grew warm. "I didn't stop courting you because of Zane. I stopped because I needed to be honest."

Rose must have been watching the two of them, because she walked over then and leaned over Reuben's shoulder. "Can I get you another piece?"

Lila stood and said, "Here, take my place. I'll bring you both some more pie."

• • •

It wasn't until the second group was seated that Lila was finally within talking distance of Zane, but he was deep in conversation with Gideon. The next time she spied him, he was sitting at a table with her Dat.

Later, just before he left with his parents, he sought her out as she helped dish up the last of the pie.

"Could we talk soon?" he asked quietly.

"Jah," she said, meeting his gaze. "Just the two of us?"

He nodded.

"I'd like that. How about at the fort?"

He glanced at his watch. "At seven p.m."

She smiled.

"Hey, Zane, are you about ready?" Simon asked.

Lila turned toward her brother. "Why are you leaving so soon?"

"I'm going to go borrow Zane's truck for a while."

Lila shook her head. "I thought you'd stick around and help."

He grinned and then said, "We're going to go do the milking for Dat." He grabbed Zane's arm and pulled him away. "Come on. Your folks are waiting for us."

Casey waved as she followed Simon.

Lila stepped to the window and watched them go, her heart racing. The afternoon shadows had crept over the snowy yard. Casey walked beside Simon, with Zane trailing behind. Adam played out in the grove of trees with Trudy and her friends from school. Zane stepped their way and scooped his little brother up with his left arm and flung him over his shoulder.

All of them walked toward the end of the driveway, where Joel had most likely parked the van.

Rose laughed behind her and Lila turned. Her sister still sat at the table with Reuben. He seemed to be enjoying himself. Lila smiled and headed to the kitchen to help Mammi with the dishes. Maybe Rose was more mature than she'd given her credit for.

Two hours later, as the women finished serving the evening meal for the relatives and young people that remained, Simon and Casey returned. Lila guessed Simon had driven Zane's truck over. Dat and Beth were sitting with Monika and Gideon at the table.

"I thought you were doing the milking," Lila said.

"Zane's finishing it. He actually likes it." Simon grinned. "Go figure."

"All by himself?"

Simon shook his head. "Joel and Adam are helping. It's like a field trip for them or something."

Lila rolled her eyes as Simon asked Casey

if she wanted a piece of pie and a cup of coffee.

"Sure," she said and sat down next to Dat. "I'm Casey Johnson," she said, sticking out her hand.

Dat shook it. "So you're Zane's friend."

She nodded.

"When he left his message, I was expecting a soldier."

She smiled, just a little. "I am a soldier."

Dat smiled back. "Well, I gathered that now, but at the time I was thinking a man."

Casey nodded her head. "I can see why you'd expect that." Lila liked the girl. She seemed comfortable or at least tolerant of being in a totally new environment. And it seemed that she and Zane truly were just friends—Lila hadn't seen a spark between them all day.

Lila leaned against the wall and closed her eyes. She'd need to leave soon to meet Zane, but she didn't want to go before her duties were done.

"Are you feeling all right?" It was Beth, putting a hand on her shoulder.

"Jah," Lila answered, opening her eyes. "I'm just tired."

"You should go home," Beth said. "Tomorrow's another big day."

Lila nodded.

"Your Dat said the Becks invited us all to their place for Thanksgiving dinner."

"Really?" Relief flowed through her. "That's so nice of Shani."

"Actually," Beth said, "I think it was Zane's idea, but Shani seemed to welcome it. Your Dat said you'd bring the side dishes and the pies."

"Of course," Lila said. She still had quite a bit of work to do, but not having to oversee everything and host it was a huge blessing.

"Eve and Charlie will be there too," Beth said.

"Dat's okay with that?"

Beth nodded. "In fact, he suggested it."

She leaned closer to Lila, her voice low. "Go on home. I'll give your Dat and the girls a ride after all the cleanup is finished. I'll tell them you needed to get started on preparing for tomorrow."

"Denki," Lila said, sad that Dat and Beth could never marry. But maybe they were content being friends. The woman was a gift from God, an absolute blessing. What would Dat have been like all these years if Mamm had lived, if he'd had a partner to help him navigate life?

When she reached her buggy, the boys assigned to take care of the horses hitched hers quickly while she lit her lantern. After she thanked the boys, she climbed up into the cab, pulling the woolen blankets over her legs, and soon turned onto the highway.

She wanted to be with Zane. He'd been right all along. Just because her Mamm hadn't left the church didn't mean Lila shouldn't. And Beth would help Dat cope. Becoming Mennonite was the compromise Lila needed to make for Zane.

The lights of a semitruck shone through the back window. She waited until she'd rounded a curve to pull as far over to the side of the road as possible so the driver could get safely around her.

As she did, bright headlights from the other direction momentarily blinded her. It took her a moment to realize that a pickup was passing a car. She jerked the reins to the right—better to go in the ditch than be hit—but the wheel stayed on solid ground and she realized she'd pulled into a wide driveway. She yanked on the reins, stopping the horse, as the pickup made it around the car and then the truck, its horn blaring, passed her on the left.

She exhaled, her heart racing and her hands shaking. She hopped down to check on her horse. She was spooked, that was certain.

Lila comforted her, stroking her head. *Thank you, Lord,* she prayed as she did, relieved their time on earth wasn't up.

All she could think of was Zane. She needed him. Wanted him. She ached for him.

After the horse calmed down, she climbed back in the buggy and urged the mare on, heading home to Juneberry Lane.

27

Zane threw one last pebble into the creek and then stood. The snow had started again. Big flakes floated down from the dark sky. He zipped his coat up to his chin. He'd wanted to call Lila every night since he'd returned to the U.S., but he hadn't wanted to say too much too soon.

He had an appointment in two weeks to talk with an Army psychologist about his nightmares and hoped that would help. Seeing Jaalal again had settled him, but he knew he had more work to do. He felt hopeful about dealing with his internal wounds, though.

The biggest reason he hadn't contacted Lila though was that he'd needed to speak with Gideon first and then Tim. He hoped she'd understand.

He checked the time on his phone. She was late. Waiting for her physically hurt.

A rustling in the field interrupted his thoughts, and he scampered up the bank. He opened the flashlight app on his phone and turned it on.

The rustling stopped. A soft voice called out, "Zane?" It was Lila.

"Here I am." He held the light toward her voice.

She wore her heavy coat and her black bonnet, and held a flashlight—pointed at him—in her hand.

"I was afraid you might not come," he said.

"I almost got sandwiched between a semi and a truck."

He stopped and took her hand. "You're shaking."

She nodded. "I'm fine. But it scared me."

"I'm so glad you're all right." He squeezed her hand and then nodded toward the fort. "We'd be out of the snow."

"Okay," she answered, still holding his hand as she followed him down the bank and into their fort.

"Who fixed it up?" she asked.

"I did. When I was home . . . before."

He motioned to the stump, and she sat, scooting to the edge, leaving enough room for him. He sat beside her, still holding her hand. He wanted to wrap his arm around her, but he was still afraid.

He squeezed her hand. "Did you finish your crazy quilt?"

She shook her head.

"I've thought about it a lot," he said. "About our story."

She nodded. She hadn't told him that was what she was doing—but he had known.

His eyes glistened, and she rested her head against his arm. "Tell me what happened when you went back," she said.

He told her about the MRAP hitting the IED and about Jaalal rescuing them and then spending the night in his home. "He was a true friend to me," Zane said. "A true neighbor even though we live half a world away geographically and a world away as far as religion and culture."

He went on to tell her about the mission being called off because of the downsizing that was going on. "Once Sarge was injured, they decided it wasn't worth it to bring in someone new when we only had two months remaining—not when the mission wouldn't be continued once we left."

"Was it sad to leave?"

"It was. Especially leaving Jaalal." Zane stopped for a moment, not sure what more to say, but then he took a deep breath and continued. "When he told me good-bye he said to go home and marry that beautiful Amish girl. Have a houseful of children. And then he said, 'God go with you.' "

Lila shifted toward him and met his eyes. "How did he know about me?"

"He saw the photo on my phone, the one Simon took. Way back before I was injured."

Lila shook her head. "You had a photo of me?"

"Two," Zane said. "I'm sorry."

She smiled. "No, I'm glad you had them."

"I want what Jaalal said." He leaned closer. "To marry you. To live here." He smiled at the thought of living in their fort. "If we could."

She nodded.

He grew serious. "And have a family."

"That's what I want too," she whispered. "I'll leave."

"What?"

"I'll become Mennonite. That's what's best for us."

He shook his head. "No."

"What do you mean?"

"I want to join."

She tilted her head in that questioning way of hers.

He continued. "I think me joining the Amish makes more sense than you leaving."

She shook her head. "Why's that?"

"Because if I join we'll have your Dat's support—"

"Are you sure we would?"

He nodded. "I asked him this afternoon."

"And he gave us his blessing?"

"Yes—as long as that was what you wanted. And as long as I was willing to join your church." Zane let go of her hand and put his arm around her, pulling her close, reminding himself not to do all the talking but to listen. "What made you decide you'd be willing to become Mennonite?"

"Eve told me my birth father never knew about Daniel and me. All this time I thought my Mamm had chosen not to leave, but it turns out she didn't know him very well, and she never even considered leaving."

"And that made you want to join the Mennonites?"

She smiled and shook her head. "No. It made me realize my Mamm wouldn't want me to stay Amish for her and miss spending the rest of my life with you."

He tightened his grip on her shoulder.

"But, Zane, honestly, if you try to become Amish and it just doesn't work, we can leave. I can live with being Mennonite. Truly."

He leaned his head against her forehead. "Denki," he said, and then, *Ich liebe Dich.*"

"I love you too," she said, turning her face up toward his. He leaned down and kissed her then, first lightly and then, as she responded, more passionately. All those years he'd waited, and finally, the time was right.

28

Lila followed Dat and Beth up the steps to the Becks' home, while Rose and Trudy ran and knocked on the door. Each carried a dish in their hands—cranberry sauce, broccoli salad, stuffing, and green beans. Lila had sent the pies and the rolls over ten minutes before with Simon in Zane's truck. Dat hadn't said anything to Lila about Zane during breakfast. He'd cleared his throat a couple of times but then had stayed quiet.

The door swung open, and Zane stepped out onto the porch, motioning the girls in and then taking the pot of stuffing from Beth. He greeted her warmly, then Dat, and then nodded to Lila, his eyes dancing.

Her heart fluttered, and she stopped for just a moment at the top of the stairs while the others continued on.

"Come on," he said, nodding toward the door. "Come in out of the cold."

She brushed against his arm as she passed by, remembering their kiss. A jolt of electricity shot up her spine. Eve swept in and took the green beans from her, following Zane into the kitchen, while Lila hung her coat.

Simon and Casey stood by the wood stove, along with Adam and Trudy. Rose stood along the wall, probably wishing she was over at Monika's with Daniel and Jenny—and Reuben.

The kitchen table had been pulled out into the living room, just before the hallway, and another long folding table had been added. All of them would sit together. Charlie was filling water glasses, and Dat joined him, picking up the second pitcher on the table. Lila followed Beth into the kitchen and Shani greeted both of them, giving Lila an extra-long hug.

When Lila stepped away, Shani had tears in her eyes. Zane must have said something.

Eve gave them both a funny look but didn't

say anything until Lila stepped past the refrigerator. Eve followed her and whispered, "Are you becoming a Mennonite?"

Lila shook her head and whispered back, "I'll tell you later." She and Zane didn't want to make any sort of announcement today. He didn't want to come off as prideful, as if he thought he could make it as an Amish man. Not very many Englischers tried and not many who did stayed. Then again, none of them were fluent in Pennsylvania Dutch either. Or had grown up on Juneberry Lane.

More importantly Zane had seven more months in the Army. He'd move home in June and get a job doing construction or working in a dairy or something else. Gideon had told him he could live with them or another family in the district. He'd sell his truck and buy a horse and buggy. He'd take classes to join the church. He'd see if it was a way of life he could embrace.

"All of this can go out to the table," Shani said, motioning toward the platters heaped with food on the counter.

Zane grabbed the stuffing again, and Lila grabbed the rolls. Soon they were ready to eat.

After everyone was seated, Joel led them in a silent prayer and then prayed, "Lord, our hearts are overflowing with gratitude for everything you've done for us. You've kept us safe and well. You give us all we need—our families, our neighbors, and our friends. Thank you for bringing Zane home to us. Please protect Simon. Use this food to strengthen us to love each other more. We are thankful beyond all measure. Amen."

When Lila opened her eyes and looked up, Joel had his eyes on her. He smiled, and she smiled back before she realized Simon was watching. He grinned in a knowing way. She quickly picked up the fruit salad, dished up her portion, and then passed it on to Zane.

By the time they'd finished eating, it was snowing again.

"Why don't all of you kids go out?" Shani said.

Zane glanced around the table. "Kids?"

"Well, you're all still kids to us," Shani said. "All of us old folks can clean up."

Rose said, "I don't want to get cold. I'll stay and help too."

The rest of them put on their coats, boots, and gloves and traipsed outside.

"Shall we play Romans? Or Tarzan?" Simon joked.

Casey turned toward him. "What?"

"Yeah, your buddy here used to lead us in all sorts of different maneuvers."

"That explains him leading us on our trek through the mountains," Casey said. "You just didn't know he was in training as a kid."

They headed into the field, and then Zane veered off toward the fort with Simon and Casey. Trudy and Adam stopped and started building a snowman. Lila followed Zane down the bank.

Once they reached the fort, Simon sat on the stump and pulled Casey down beside him.

"So what's going on with you and Zane?" Simon asked Lila, loudly.

Lila cleared her throat and said, "What's going on with *you* two?"

Simon laughed. "Who, us? We just met."

Casey nudged him. "And someone's being deployed."

"Yeah, well," Simon said, patting his pocket, "at least I've got FaceTime figured out. We can stay in touch."

"At least I'll have an idea of what you're going through."

They were all silent for a moment, and then Simon looked up at Lila and said, "I never thought you'd leave the church."

"She's not," Zane answered.

"What?" Simon shifted his weight on the stump. "Don't tell me you're going to have a bowl cut and be wearing barn pants soon."

Zane shrugged. "I guess we'll have a good idea about that by the time you get back."

Casey broke out into a laugh. "I won't say anything, I promise."

"I don't care if you do," Zane answered.

"Especially to Grant. It would probably push him completely over the edge."

Casey grimaced. "He'll end up over the edge all on his own, I'm sure. Without any help from you."

Snow fell from a branch above them. Simon stood and grabbed the rope that had hung there all those years.

"Don't do it," Lila hissed, just as he grabbed up higher on to it and swung out across, landing on the other side, a huge grin on his face.

Lila grabbed the rope as it came back and held on to it. Simon scooped up a snowball and threw it at her. Zane threw one back at him. Soon snowballs flew back and forth until, finally, Lila sent the rope back across the creek and ran up the bank. Casey followed her.

Up in the field, Trudy and Adam had the bottom half of a snowman made and were now making snow angels. Lila fell to the ground beside her little sister. Big, fluffy flakes were falling now, and Casey scooped up handful after handful, forming them into snowballs. When the guys came up the bank she started lobbing them at Simon.

Zane snuck on through and collapsed beside Lila, throwing his arm over her middle. She took off her glove and pulled the jasper stone from her coat pocket. "Do you want this back?" she whispered.

"Of course not," he said. "Keep it."

She slid it back into her pocket. "I'm going to stitch two stones to my crazy quilt," she said. "And finish it."

He rolled closer to her, their heads side by side, her eyes on the sky above. She wished they could stay in the field forever. But they had seven months to get through and then another spell until they could be sure exactly what their future held.

Knowing her future held Zane was enough though—for now.

ACKNOWLEDGMENTS

M any, many people are involved in every story I write. For this one, my biggest thanks goes to my husband, Peter, who recently retired from the Army Reserve after a thirty-year career. In many ways he inspired this story, and he was my go-to person for all things military and medical (any mistakes are mine), along with supporting me through the writing process. Our four children—Kaleb, Taylor, Hana, and Thao— also encouraged me.

There are many other soldiers and military family members who have inspired me through the last thirty years, including Larrie Noble (Col., retired); Joyce Clarkson-Veilleux (LTC, retired); Diane and Chuck Cumiskey (Col.); Marilyn and Jim Weisenburg; and Dr. John McGraw (Col., retired) and his sweet wife, Ann, who is a reader and thinker extraordinaire. My sincere gratitude goes to all of you.

My sincere thanks goes to Marietta Couch for her friendship, insights, and encouragement, and for sharing her Amish experiences with me. I'm also grateful to Laurie Snyder for generously giving me feedback in the early stages of this story, to Melanie Dobson for helping later in the process, and to my agent, Chip MacGregor, for taking a chance on me thirteen years ago and continuing through the years to believe in my ability to tell a story.

Last, but certainly not least, all of the good people at Bethany House Publishers have my gratitude for all they do on behalf of my books, from helping to shape the story to the cover design to marketing to sales. This is the sixth book my editor, Karen Schurrer, has guided me through, and each time we come to "the end" it feels like a miracle. Thank you!

ABOUT THE AUTHOR

Leslie Gould is the coauthor, with Mindy Starns Clark, of the #1 CBA bestseller *The Amish Midwife*, a 2012 Christy Award winner; CBA bestseller *Courting Cate*, first in the COURTSHIPS OF LANCASTER COUNTY series; and *Beyond the Blue*, winner of the Romantic Times Reviewers' Choice for Best Inspirational Novel, 2006. She holds an MFA in creative writing and lives in Portland, Oregon, with her husband and four children.

Learn more about Leslie at
www.lesliegould.com.

Center Point Large Print
600 Brooks Road / PO Box 1
Thorndike, ME 04986-0001 USA

(207) 568-3717

US & Canada:
1 800 929-9108
www.centerpointlargeprint.com